FINDING THE WAY BACK

A STEALTH OPS NOVEL

BRITTNEY SAHIN

D0006568

EMKO MEDIA, LLC

Finding The Way Back

By: Brittney Sahin

Published by: EmKo Media, LLC

Copyright © 2019 EmKo Media, LLC

This book is an original publication of Brittney Sahin.

Editor: Deb Markanton

Editor: Lawrence Editing

Proofreader: Judy Zweifel, Judy's Proofreading

Cover Design: LJ, Mayhem Cover Creations

Ebook ISBN: 9781947717190

Paperback ISBN: 9781087236032

❁ Created with Vellum

For my parents.

Thank you for always believing in me. Love you!

PREQUEL

THEIR BEGINNING - ATLANTA (2000)

ADRIANA

"You don't have to drop me off around the corner."

"Showing up to a party in a police cruiser doesn't seem that cool to me. I know I'm not down with what's hip, but I—"

"Mom." I rolled my eyes and unbuckled. "You're like the coolest mom on the planet." I eyed the passenger window, seeking the mansion off in the hills around the block—a world away from where we lived.

We had a decent home, a great life, don't get me wrong—but the people I went to school with were the kind of rich you only saw in the movies. So rich you just didn't think it could be real.

And I was now going to their school. It didn't take long for them to realize I was the "scholarship kid." The girl without the expensive clothes or car—the girl who didn't belong.

I was at the school because my dad wanted me to be. He was a college professor and had begged and begged until he was blue in the face for me to apply for the scholarship— promises of a brighter future if I graduated from the academy. I mean, if we were talking Hogwarts, I'd be game. Or maybe if it was Sunnydale, and I got to be Buffy and fight vampires —sure, count me in. But this?

There was literally only one perk to Riverness Academy of the Arts and Sciences—and it was Charlie Bennett.

The idea of him being inside the house up the street had my heart beating as if Angel, the vampire with a soul, was about to steal my virginity and then turn evil moments after. Charlie would be my Angel, the star of my show.

Charlie was everything all rolled up into one amazingly beautiful man—but he was a senior. Also, the richest kid at the school. And did I mention son of a senator?

I could do without all the money and glam. Strip that away, and I'd take the guy he was this day and any other day of the week.

I'd even give him my fifteen-year-old virginity. I'd give him my first kiss. My first everything.

Sigh. Sigh. F***ing-I don't-usually-swear-sigh.

"Honey?"

Mom was probably talking. Some sort of speech about how I needed to make friends yada yada yada.

I had my books and my favorite shows to keep me company. And I had a few friends left from my old school who hadn't abandoned me—not yet, at least. I could feel it coming, though.

I glanced at my palm, which now held a red Nokia. "What's this?"

"I got you a phone."

"You—what?" I gasped.

I'd been asking for months for a phone, and now . . . okay, so if I had to suck it up and mingle with some rich kids, well, I'd do it if it meant getting the phone.

Sure, I'd even—maybe—approach Charlie and say hi. Okay, so I'd be like ten feet away and not look his way when the word floated from my mouth like a breath. But I'd do it. Maybe.

"You're so miserable, and I hate seeing you like this. I'll even turn the cheek if you have a beer tonight." She squeezed my arm. "I want you to have fun. Live a little."

I know what you're thinking—my mom is a cop. And my mom just told me to drink.

She's a cool mom. But she's also a smart one.

I mean, most of the things we do as teens are just to piss our parents off. If they actually gave us carte blanche to do it —would we?

Also, my mom may have been a touch of a hippy in the seventies before she reformed to her more buttoned-up, badge-wearing self.

"I'm gonna stock up on all the peanut buttery chocolate candy goodness I can find before I pick you up. Promise."

I kept my eyes glued to the phone, still in shock that I, Adriana Foster, had a phone. And no, I don't have a middle name. My mom said middle names were to be used whenever someone got into trouble. No middle name and maybe no one would ever get into trouble. Apparently, she'd been three-named a lot by her father growing up.

My mom—yeah, she was awesome. I was so lucky to have her.

"Why don't we just go to the movies? You're meeting a friend tonight since dad has to grade papers, right?"

"I'll only be a phone call away if you need me."

"And on the other side of town, probably. *Our* side of town." This was not our side. No, it was where the one-tenth of the one percent lived.

"Have fun. Maybe even kiss a boy." She winked and shooed me away. "Now get out of my car."

I kissed her on the cheek goodbye, tucked my coveted phone into my back pocket, and started down the street.

She stayed a good distance behind with her lights dimmed to make sure I made it to the party.

I wasn't sure if this was some cruel prank—invite the new girl and embarrass her or not, so I had no idea what I was walking into, but honestly—what ended up happening . . . I never would've believed.

***

CHARLIE

"Just do it. Go and bang her and her friend." My buddy was eyeballing the two best friends across the room. "They want you at the same time, bro. What are you waiting for?"

I lowered the beer from my lips, followed his focus to the girls in matching red mini-skirts and halter tops. I mean, hell, I could pretty much see the outline of their nipples through their shirts from across the room.

"Not interested," I grumbled and peered at the table off to my right where a tower of beers was on the verge of collapsing.

"How do you not want to tap that? Double the pleasure, double the fun," he said with a laugh.

"I'm not that guy."

My reputation was total bullshit. Fabricated by tall tales from the locker room by my buddies who liked to spin them.

"Okay, then—how about her? The new girl? She's got a tight little body that I'd like to—"

"Would you shut the fuck up?" I didn't mean to snap at him. But damn it, ever since I saw Adriana Foster walk the halls at school, I'd been unable to think of another girl since.

Fifteen.

A sophomore.

Too.

Too.

Young.

But yeah, she was all I could think about even when I told myself not to. Damn that smile of hers.

I even went out of my way to see her at her locker whenever I got the chance.

I'd stride past her close enough just to breathe in her perfume. But that's all I'd allow. I couldn't talk to her because not only was she too young, I didn't want to drag her into my world.

My world was tight and cramped. I was suffocating here. Hands around my neck—it was so damn hard to breathe at times.

I had to get out of this place. College would be better, right? It had to be. But maybe I needed to go even farther.

"What's your problem, man?"

I hid a scowl and kept my eyes on her. *Why are you here?*

Fridays and Saturdays. Two parties every weekend. The parties rotated locations. And I was growing bored.

But her at the party—this was new.

I brought the beer to my lips and sucked it dry as I followed Adriana's movements around the house.

Tentative and nervous steps.

A shyness all over her heated cheeks.

I wanted her. Hell, I more than wanted her.

But damn the guy who just set his sights on her.

Seth Shane, a twenty-one-year-old lowlife who supplied alcohol for our parties. His eyes were pinned to her. His gaze tracked her entire body. From her kicks up to the hole in the knee of her jeans all the way to the too-innocent-for-this-party pink T-shirt.

Adriana didn't flaunt her looks like the double-the-trouble-girls. No, she didn't need to, either.

Her hair was down. Soft dark waves over her shoulders. Her C cup breasts that Seth Shane couldn't stop ogling. I only knew boob sizes because my ex always forced me to go bra shopping with her—and maybe that sounded hot, but it wasn't my idea of a good time at all.

I tossed my beer, anger licking up my back at the sight of Seth now standing in front of her. He wrapped a hand tightly around her bicep, and he leaned in, bringing his mouth close to hers. She jerked her neck back in surprise.

I started to cross the room to get to her—to save her from the flick of his tongue that darted from his mouth like a serpent, but . . .

She smacked him hard across the jaw and swept her leg behind his and brought him to the ground.

The music died at that moment.

My heart may have taken a brief pause as well.

She turned and fled out the back doors at the realization everyone was staring at her, and also, Seth was cursing as he rose.

I resisted the urge to kick him on my way to get to her—not sure why I felt the need to check on a girl who could hold her own—but I couldn't stop my feet from moving, from going to her.

"Wait up," I called once I was outside on the back patio.

She was inside the gazebo off to the side of the covered pool. Her hands slid up and down her arms, and when I got to her, she was panting. A fierce anger still in the jerky movements of her touch.

"Hey."

She popped her hands in the air defensively between us but then relaxed at the sight of me as if she knew I wasn't a threat.

"You okay?" I didn't want to come too close because I liked my balls and preferred them to remain intact in case she changed her mind about me. "That was"—I scratched the back of my head, at a loss for words—"I've never seen anything like it."

"My mom taught me a few moves in case any creeps ever bothered me."

"Smart mom." I tucked my hands into the pockets of my jeans and studied her.

Christmas-style lights wrapped the white wooden beams of the gazebo, casting a sort of glow on her face. She was breathtaking. This was also the closest I'd been face-to-face with her.

I wanted to reach out and tuck her hair behind her ears just in case any strands fell into her face, obstructing the view of her eyes I craved.

I needed her to look up—to see me. I had to know if whatever intense effect she had on me was reciprocated.

Age at the moment took a back seat to everything else as I stood in front of her, one step away.

I even forgot my last name. My Porsche. The seventy-five-million-dollar trust fund I'd get at twenty-five. Absolutely everything vanished from my mind. I was just Charlie.

Her eyes FINALLY journeyed to my face, and her lip caught between her teeth. She extended a hand, and I stared at it, not sure what in the hell to do.

The only times I'd been greeted by a handshake—well, those hands had belonged to my parent's friends at political parties.

I kept my eyes on her slender fingers. On the one freckle off to the side of her pinky.

She started to pull her hand away, and I grumbled something—I can't remember what—and rushed for her hand as if the offer to touch her may never come my way again.

Yeah, that was how everything started for us. And I also had no idea how it'd end. And full disclosure—maybe I didn't want it to ever end.

***

ADRIANA

Books. Movies. TV. Everything I read or watched was so much more exciting than my life. More romantic. Just *more*, in general.

But this moment was heaven, and I wanted to live in it forever.

We talked. He laughed at my lame jokes. He even rested his hand atop my knee. Then he pulled back as if guilty of touching me without my permission, and I grabbed his hand and placed it right where it belonged.

And when I told him about my crush on Patrick Swayze, along with every prince in all versions of Cinderella, as well as my devoted love of sexy vampires with souls—he'd stared at me as if I were the most beautiful woman on the planet instead of some recluse teenager with a diary full of hearts and no life.

And when he smiled—like one of those I-want-you-but-I'm-holding-back smiles . . . I think I may have died just a little bit at that moment.

How was the most popular boy in school staring at me like he wanted to kiss me?

And when he literally said it—said the words—but followed them with *"You're too young"* I about fell off the bench inside the gazebo we'd been sharing for two hours.

I'd stood. Given him my back. And then I'd channeled every ounce of strength inside of me and finally faced him, only for the quick movement to cause a collision of his muscular frame with my body.

"Why me?" I had asked, the question a whispered breath in the air that took a few seconds to reach him.

Then his brows had pulled together as if surprised by my question, and I'd wondered if I read him wrong, until he'd replied, "I guess I have a thing for Cinderella-vampire-Swayze-loving girls with the most gorgeous green eyes I've ever seen."

He did kiss me after that. But what happened next, I never would've predicted.

What started as a handshake led to a night I'd never forget.

But it also didn't turn into a fairy tale.

Not even close.

No, it ended in death.

***

ATLANTA (2005)

CHARLIE

"Hey," I said, a bit breathless from speeding to her dad's house. I probably would've gotten a ticket had everyone in the city not been gorging themselves on Thanksgiving dinner to notice my Porsche racing down the streets.

Adriana pulled me inside and locked up behind us. "Sorry we didn't make it to dinner. I meant to text you but I just got Dad to bed."

My stomach dropped. Her dad must've fallen off the wagon. Holidays were always more difficult for him, which meant Addy had to pick up the pieces and help sober him up.

"He okay?" I leaned my back against the door, nearly forgetting why I'd hauled ass over there to begin with. Her unhappiness would become mine. I'd own it, too, and do everything in my power to make things right.

"Maybe I should move back home? Find a campus closer so I can take better care of him."

I shoved away from the door and gathered her into my arms. She cried into my chest, and I rubbed my hands up and down her back in an attempt to soothe her. "I'm so sorry." I kissed her forehead. "But you leaving school to take care of him—he'd never want that. He'd hate himself more for that."

She swiped away the last of her tears and motioned for me to enter her living room.

Her dad probably should've downsized at the loss of his wife, but he couldn't handle leaving the only home they'd ever shared—too many memories.

An anonymous donor from the police force paid off their mortgage and set aside money for college tuition and taxes on the home for the next twenty years. Adriana only just found out last year—by accident—that I had asked my father to be that anonymous donor.

And now, I was about to reject the money and everything that came with being a Bennett.

But could I leave Adriana? We already lived in two different states because of college, but if I joined the Navy, we could end up in two countries.

My shoulders sagged, and I faced the wall, worried she'd see the torn look on my face, and I knew her—she would never let me sacrifice my wants out of concern for her.

"You rushed here to tell me something, what is it?" Her hand touched my back. "Did you finally decide? Are you dropping out of med school?"

I nodded but didn't turn.

"You did it?" A near squeal surprised me enough to finally spin around. "Ah! I'm so proud of you!" She hooked her arms around my neck. "You're going to make one hell of a sailor, Charlie Bennett."

I kept her in place, unable to move with my hands on her waist and her arms around my neck. I could barely think a straight thought with her gaze pinned to mine. Pride shimmering in her eyes despite the reality of what my decision meant.

I swallowed, the sudden desire to press my mouth to hers overwhelming, but I chalked it up to excitement. She'd become my best friend the night her mom died, and I couldn't lose her friendship—meeting her had become the most incredible thing that'd ever happened to me.

"But I'll . . . we may not see each other as much as I'd like. And who will keep an eye on you?"

She stepped back only so she could lightly swat my chest.

"This is serious." I'd stepped in for her dad. I'd kept an

eye on her when he couldn't. I'd made sure she called me after every date to ensure she was back at her dorm safe, and then I was the one who'd flown in to interrogate any guys who she'd decided to date long-term.

"I want you to join."

I considered her words and fought back. "If I do, you can't leave school."

She frowned.

But I was right.

She couldn't give up her dreams.

"Fine."

"Handshake?" I stepped back to extend my palm.

"You hate handshakes." A smile touched her lips, and my chest tightened at the sight. Her smile still got to me. No amount of her dating, or me dating, would change the effect this woman had on me.

There were more reasons than ever as to why I couldn't turn the clock back and try and recapture what we almost had the night we met.

The brush of her lips would forever remain on my mind, though.

But maybe someday we could try again.

She perked a brow, her eyes on my lips as if the memory of our kiss was on her mind this very minute.

Her gaze dragged to my eyes, and my heart almost busted out of my chest.

Maybe someday should be now. I wished it could be, at least.

But I was joining the Navy, and she had college to finish —so no, someday would have to wait.

PROLOGUE: RECRUITMENT

VIRGINIA BEACH (2013)

"I'm coming!" He tightened the towel around his waist, water dripping onto the hardwoods with each step as he hurried down the hall to answer the door.

Not bothering to check who was on the other side, he braced his left hand on the wall and quickly yanked open the door with his right. Momentarily startled, he froze.

"Well, well, well." Adriana popped her dark brows up and down a few times and flashed him a smile. "What a way to greet a lady."

Knox huffed out a laugh and secured the towel that was dangerously close to slipping off his hips.

"What the hell are you doing here, girl?" He gathered her into his arms for a tight hug before stepping back to take in the sight of her.

Her shoulder-length brown hair was in a loose ponytail with a few messy strands around her face. Her long legs were hidden beneath faded denim. Glow-in-the-dark bright orange Nikes for kicks. And a fitted black long-sleeved top that hugged the woman in places a friend shouldn't be thinking about. And now he was, so . . .

"What?" Her cheeks pinked as a smile touched her lips, the kind of smile she wore in her green eyes as well.

"Just looking at you." He was one not-so-subtle throat clear and towel-tenting moment away from letting her know exactly what was on his mind.

"Checking for damage?" She reached for a familiar-looking black-labeled bottle sitting on the ground next to her shoes.

"Can you blame me? You showing up unexpectedly has me a bit worried." And that was true, but it didn't change the fact he was still a single man, and she was a gorgeous woman. "Are you okay?" he asked when concern zipped up his spine at the realization it was late at night, and she'd driven to his house without a heads-up first.

"I'm more than okay," she said, and his body relaxed at her answer. "But is this a bad time?" She pressed up on her toes to try and get a look over his shoulder.

"No one else is here," he told her, knowing what she was thinking. "I just got out of the shower."

"You do deploy in two days. I wouldn't blame you for having a few pre-deployment hookups."

Talking about his sex life with her was a hard limit for him and always had been. "Why the hell are you still standing there?" He stepped aside so she could enter, then closed the door behind her and accepted the bottle she offered. "You came straight here from D.C.?"

"Yeah, I got some news, and I don't know, I hopped into my car and drove here." Adriana's light green eyes whipped from his six-pack to his face. "It's not fair you get better with age."

"This takes a lot of work." He smoothed his free hand

over his abs.

"Sure." She dragged out the word, her lips twitching, then she pointed to his bedroom. "Clothes and then Jack."

"You invite another brother over?" It was his turn to tease now.

"And share my best friend?"

He squeezed one eye closed and held the bottle up. "Oh, you mean my buddy here." He pointed to the bottle with a smile. "Yeah, he and I go way back."

Her shoulders trembled as she fought a laugh. "Maybe Jack was a bad idea. The last time we got drunk on it—"

"We nearly got arrested during Mardi Gras." New Orleans had been one hell of a trip. Maybe they needed to take another vacation after he rotated back home.

"Not my fault."

"Yeah, sure, blame Jack."

"More like you! You almost popped that guy in the face who hit on me, a guy who happened to be an off-duty cop." She waved her hand in the air. "Will you get dressed already? I can't handle staring at all that rugged gorgeousness and maintain a straight face."

"Yes, ma'am." He handed the bottle back to her and went into his bedroom.

His two-story townhouse wasn't much. A living room, a galley kitchen, and two bedrooms comprised the actual living space on the first floor. The entire second floor was dedicated as a game room. A ping-pong table that doubled as a pool table. Two old-school pinball machines. And a drop-down movie screen he and his buddies played Xbox on.

He may have earned his nickname, Knox, after Fort Knox Depository because of his rich father, but once he'd joined the Navy, he'd never taken a dime of his old man's money. Pretty much forgot all about his trust fund, too.

After throwing on a white tee and black sweatpants, he headed back to join Adriana in the living room. "So, you gonna spill the news, or what?"

She kept her eyes on the floor. "I did something, and I don't want you to freak out."

And there went his heart. It was about to fly out of his chest. When she started a sentence warning him to remain calm—yeah, he now knew why she brought the whiskey.

Last time he'd suffered heart failure from one of her announcements was two summers ago when she'd alerted him via email she was going to Barbados to swim with sharks.

"And, uh, what exactly did you do?" He took a moment to ground himself. To ensure his feet were planted firm, so he didn't hit the floor when she leveled him with whatever she was about to say.

"I'm joining the Secret Service." Her don't-kill-me smile worked its way to her mouth. "Training starts in Georgia in two weeks." She held two fists in front of her mouth when her eyes lifted to his.

He took a breath. A long, long breath.

He'd yet to harness the power of speech. He was stuck somewhere between a *Hell, no* and *Congrats!*

As much as he hated sharks—even though swimming in the ocean was a requisite for his profession—he'd take them and Barbados over the news she'd be in danger on a regular damn basis.

Knox held one finger between them. "Last time I checked it wasn't April first. You're not playing me right now?"

"No." Her hands crashed to her sides as the disappointment of his reaction tossed a shadow over her face.

"This is unexpected." He pressed both palms to his face and pulled them down. "Why?" A three-letter word he knew

4

she wouldn't want to hear, but how could he not ask the question? She'd never mentioned the Secret Service before tonight.

Cop? Yes.

After finishing undergrad at Georgetown, she had an offer to attend grad school at GW. She had come to him torn. Her desire to join the police academy, despite her father's protests, had yet to disappear.

She'd wanted Knox's advice, but he'd known he wouldn't be the best person to give it because he'd choose grad school to keep her safe. He'd side with her father out of fear.

So, he'd told her it was her decision to make, and when she chose George Washington, he remembered how to breathe again.

Apparently, the need to serve and protect had only grown stronger over the years.

But she knew what politicians, people like his father, were made of—nothing good as far as he was concerned. She'd seen the results of their hypocrisy. Why, then, would she willingly put her life on the line to protect them?

Her shoulders slumped. "You don't look happy."

"Shit, it's not that." He had to sit. Time had slowed to the point he was sure he could actually feel the rotation of the earth. "But why? You haven't—"

"Charlie." She was deploying her soft tone, hitting him where it'd hurt.

She was also the only one who called him by his given name. A reminder he was still the son of a senator. Charlie was the name of the man he'd left behind. A man he'd prefer not to be anymore.

Once on the leather couch, his gaze pinned to his hands—hands that, as far as his family had been concerned, were supposed to belong to a doctor.

"I didn't expect you to take it so badly." Her voice was soft, gentle as she eased herself down to sit next to him. He veered his focus to her face and swallowed a groan. She was using her damn puppy dog eyes.

He'd be putty in her hands now.

"I get why you're not a fan. You hate politicians. But maybe I'll get assigned to the investigations division."

He grunted. "You didn't join to sit behind a desk and find money launderers. No, you'll want to be on the front lines of the action." He swiped his hand over his closely shaved head but kept his gaze steady on her beautiful lighter-than-light emerald green eyes.

She was still dodging the hell out of his question, and there had to be a reason for it.

"Be happy for me, please."

"I already worry about you. If anything happened to you, I'd never survive that." He attempted to hide the break in his voice.

He was going to J-Bad in two days. How would he focus knowing she was joining the Secret Service?

"Uh, need I remind you what your own job entails? Don't be a hypocrite, okay?"

"You teach criminal justice. It's—"

"Safer, I know."

She'd landed a professor job at George Washington after getting her doctorate there only two years ago. None of this made sense.

But trying to convince her not to put herself in the line of fire when he lived and breathed that life every day? Kettle calling the pot black. Or whatever the hell that saying was.

He needed that Jack. He rose and went to the bar and poured two glasses. Before he considered facing her, he drained his glass and refilled it.

"I was going through some boxes in the attic at my dad's place a few months back, and I found a journal of my mom's."

He knew what was coming, and maybe he should've known sooner.

"Mom applied to be in the Secret Service before I was born." Her words were light. Like she was worried her voice would break if she spoke in a normal tone. "She got accepted but then found out she was pregnant, and so she stayed on the police force."

His stomach plummeted to the depths of the deepest ocean.

His mind catapulted him back to October of 2000. The night he met the most amazing girl in the world. The night that girl's mother died.

At the feel of her hand on his back, his muscles snapped together.

He slowly faced her with both drinks in hand, and every painful emotion layered atop him brick by brick as he stared at the incredible woman that girl had become.

Her lashes lowered, and a touch of crimson flowed up her graceful neck and tinted her cheeks.

"Dad never told me. *She* never told me." Adriana took the drink. "She gave up her dreams because of me."

He remained unmoving. Like he was trapped in time and watching her fall to her knees in despair all over again at the news of her mother's death.

"Are you doing this because you think you owe it to her?"

"I want you to be happy for me. I was so excited to share the news with you."

"You were nervous." Knox gulped down his second drink and set the glass on the bar. "Did you come here so I'd talk you out of it?"

"No." She downed her glass in one long swig before shaking off a wince.

She was drinking away her nerves, which meant he was right. But he also knew she was stubborn and trying to get her to back down would be pointless. She had to come to the realization on her own.

He faced the bar again and bowed his head, struggling with what the hell to say or do.

It could've been a minute, or an hour, that he'd remained frozen without speaking—he wasn't sure, but he finally whispered, "Addy."

"Charlie Jackson Bennett, don't you Addy me. You turn around and give me a proper hug and congratulations." Her Southern drawl sank deep into each word as if she were biting down on her back teeth, trying not to cry, and he hated himself for making her feel that way.

"Pulling out all three names on me, huh?" He tried to soften the blow, to ease the touch of discomfort he'd inflicted when he hadn't thrown her the full weight of his support.

"Well, it worked," she announced as he turned, feeling like he moved both heaven and hell to face her. "You're looking at me, at least."

She pouted. Damn her.

He forced a smile, hoping to sever the ropes of concern that tethered his body to the ocean's shore while wave after wave relentlessly attempted to swallow him. If anything ever happened to this woman, he'd drown.

A smirk matched his as she set her glass aside. Happiness had returned.

As terrified as he was at the idea of her joining the Secret Service, he'd be the friend she needed even if it pained him. Always.

"You got some fly shades to wear, at least?" he joked. "I hear it's a requirement."

She slapped his chest, but thank God, her smile had broadened. "That's all Hollywood."

"It could get sunny out." He kept up with the charade, hoping another shot of Jack would tamp down the flame of worry that threatened to turn into a full-blown fire.

"Well"—she waved a finger between them—"are you going to hug me or what?"

"Didn't we already hug when you first got here?" She reached out to playfully swat him again, but he caught her wrist this time. "I'm going to miss you when I leave." He palmed her cheek with his free hand, not ready to lose hold of her.

"I'm glad I got to see you before you deploy." A quick pout followed. "Deployment sucks."

He loved his work. His squadron. The only downfall— leaving her. Not being there to protect Addy. "I know," he whispered, fighting to maintain a tight thread of control in his tone.

"I'm doing the right thing." She lightly nodded. "I promise."

It was then that he finally hugged her. Her cherry blossom shampoo found his nose, and he committed the scent to memory. And for the first time, the fear of not making it home from his next rotation struck him.

Who'd protect her if he died?

Her dad was only in the picture on the random days he decided to sober up.

Shit.

But no, she needed him to be strong. To be happy for her.

He didn't want to screw this up a second time tonight even if he was right about her joining for the wrong reasons.

Then again, hadn't he done the same when he joined the Navy, and it turned out better than okay?

"I need another drink." She sidestepped him to pour herself a Jack, then sucked it down like a champ.

"I'm sorry for the way I reacted," he said on a sigh as she set down her empty glass. "Congratulations. If you're happy, I'm happy."

She eyed him cautiously, almost as if she didn't believe his words. "You have to promise me you won't do the thing." She flicked her ponytail to her back. "And don't you dare use those dimples against me right now. You know what they do to me."

"Same as the puppy dog eyes you give me," he countered and deepened his smile. "I'll use my ammunition all day long."

"Charlie," she scolded. "Promise."

He rolled his eyes and crossed his fingers behind his back. "I won't do the thing."

"You go overboard when it comes to keeping me safe, and I—"

"I'm not that bad." Maybe he was, but he couldn't help himself when it came to her.

"You had an entire SEAL Team show up on my date the last time you were overseas."

"Because you were going out with that douchebag MMA guy who has been known to hit his girlfriends, and he needed to know if he laid a hand on you, he'd die."

"I've never seen a professional fighter piss himself before." A smile pulled at her lips.

"And you'll never see it again if I have anything to do with it. You shouldn't give guys like that your time."

"You're jealous." Adriana had one dimple. One beautiful dimple in her right cheek that popped whenever she got embarrassed. "Not of dating me, I mean," she said with a nervous laugh. "Of his profession." She waved her hand through the air. "He gets to beat people up for a living."

"And I shoot people." He was trying to come across as some badass, but she knew him too damn well.

"You hate killing, don't give me that."

"Anyway. You've got to stop dating assholes, babe." *Or hell, stop dating period.* He'd suggest a monastery, but then his dirty thoughts about her might secure him a spot in hell, and he'd prefer his soul make a beeline toward the Big Man in the sky when it was his time.

"They aren't all assholes." She tightened her ponytail and tucked the loose strands behind her diamond-studded ears. She was wearing the half-carat diamonds he'd given her last Christmas. Bought with his hard-earned money, not his pop's dough. "And you've gone and distracted me. How can I trust you won't go into protective-guy mode on me in my new job?"

"I promised I'll be good." The lift of her perfectly sculpted brows meant she didn't believe him, but he knew her well enough to know she didn't mind his protection as much as she let on.

"And I know you had your fingers crossed behind your back when you made that promise."

His gaze whipped to her backside as she poured their drinks. Her low-slung jeans were snug, and that particular pair always managed to catch his eye.

She was his best friend, damn it. He shouldn't be checking out her ass. But in his defense, the woman had an ass like no other. And maybe he needed the distraction right now.

But . . .

He cupped the back of his head and shifted toward the

plain white wall that at some point probably needed a picture on it.

Grandma. Grandma. Grandma.

He had to stop the blood flow shooting through his dick at breakneck speed.

Wrong time. It'd always be the wrong time for anything other than friendship between them, though, even if he wanted more.

A few breaths later, he faced her. "If you fall for one of those shade-wearing-Secret—"

"I have training. Georgia then D.C. I'll be too busy to date." She handed him his glass.

"Good."

"Well, I plan on continuing to drink. Can I crash here?" She plopped on the couch and kicked off her Nikes.

"When have you ever had to ask?" He joined her and stretched his legs out.

"I didn't want to interrupt some sort of pre-deployment shag fest you might have planned."

"No 'shag fest' on the schedule. And what, are you British now?" He fought a smile.

"I wish." She fanned her face. "Love the accent."

"So, that's why you dated that MMA douche? Because of his accent?" He'd really hated that guy. Well, he hated every guy she went out with.

"Oh, no. It was for his body." She tipped back more of her drink, then a light moan left her mouth when she mirrored his position, extending her long legs. "Driving four hours nonstop—I'm sore." She squeezed her right thigh, her hand brushing his leg in the process. "I need to get out of these jeans, too. You still have some of my stuff here?"

"Nah, I chucked it."

"I'm gonna kick your sarcastic ass in about two point

five."

He held up his arm as if checking the time on a watch that wasn't there. "How many threats has that been since you've been here?"

She flicked a finger in the air between them and squinted in an effort to be threatening, which on her only looked cute.

"Your stuff is in the guest room closet where it always is."

"But you know what I really want, right?" She purred her question in a far too sexy voice for his comfort.

They'd been nothing more than friends for years. You'd think his dick would've learned a thing or two about boundaries. Guess not.

"I'll be right back." He dropped his feet to the floor and went to his bedroom.

When he came back, he halted outside the living room at the sight of Adriana peeling her shirt over her head. The music channel on his TV playing now, too.

She faced him with her give-me arms. "My favorite shirt."

He didn't move. He was too sidetracked by her black lacy bra and the fact it barely held her breasts in place. "You and I are close, but maybe change in the other room?" He'd done his best to loosen the words free without sounding like a pubescent teenage boy.

"What?" She tossed her shirt aside. "I mean, you've even seen me buck naked before."

"That was years ago, and it was your fault. You were drunk and strutting around naked singing an Ace of Base song."

He tossed her the basketball jersey he'd had since his college ball days. She pulled it over her head—*thank God*—but then started shimmying out of her jeans, kicking them in the air once she'd managed to get them off. *Damn it.* The liquor was speeding through her veins and steering her into the danger zone. The zone where she lost all inhibition and good sense. The zone where she had a tendency to flirt with him.

"Come on, you're my best friend." She removed her bra from the sleeve of the jersey like a magician.

She had underwear on, right? God, he hoped so. Of course, now he was wondering if they matched her bra.

"Can't handle a little skin?" She puckered her lips and kissed the air, then closed the gap between them and rested her hand over his heart.

She had his back to the hall wall. Nowhere to go. But hell, was there any place he'd rather be?

"What's wrong?" she asked, and the beat of his heart intensified under her palm. "You still not a fan of country music? This guy is pretty good, you have to admit."

Damned if he knew who the hell was singing right now. He could barely hear anything over the thundering of his pulse.

It was much easier to resist temptation when they were separated by an ocean. And *that* was the only perk to leaving her.

Her lips parted as she stared up at him. He'd seen this look before.

She let her defenses down whenever she drank the hard stuff. She also became vulnerable. But hell, so did he, or he wouldn't be contemplating making a move right now—a move from which there'd be no turning back.

"Why haven't you kissed me since that night?" she whispered.

This wasn't her first time asking about the kiss, but she only uttered the question when she'd been drinking. Nothing like liquid courage.

And he'd always issued the same response. "You know why." He eyed her long neck, noticing the flutter of her pulse there.

"There's a list as long as my arm," she murmured, her voice sultry. Seductive.

Part of him wanted to throw the list to hell and let it burn.

Maybe he did want to grab hold of her shoulders and press his mouth to hers. See how she tasted. To have her lips part for him in invitation.

But this was Addy.

He couldn't lose her friendship. It was a friendship he'd die to protect.

But he also couldn't stop himself from allowing his gaze to lower to her breasts, which were hidden by the jersey. And to the rise and fall of her chest.

"Charlie." The soft sound of his name from her lips forced his eyes back to hers.

We can't. But he refused to verbalize it because for a moment he wanted to live in a world of *can.* A world where her mom hadn't been taking her last breath while he'd kissed her the night they'd met at a high school party.

She flinched at the sound of a sudden knock at the door.

A hard, heavy . . . military knock.

He'd removed the bell because he hated when it sent the neighbor's poodle into a barking frenzy.

Three more knocks from someone who sounded like they could easily breach a door.

"Your Jeep is outside, so I'm hoping you're home." He recognized the deep voice calling out on the other side of the door. Luke Scott.

What the hell was Luke doing there?

"I have to answer that." He forced himself to move, but

when she caught hold of his arm, he halted and peered back at her.

"It was the alcohol. And the long drive." She blinked a few times. "The excitement. I'm sorry."

She was apologizing for something that didn't happen. Maybe in her mind, the moment had been as real as it had been in his head.

"I should—"

"Get that." She released his arm.

"I'm here," he called out, so Luke didn't leave. "You mind not being half-naked in front of a SEAL buddy of mine?" he asked with a smile, causing her one dimple to appear.

"Be in the guest room." She snatched her clothes and hurried from the room.

"Did I interrupt something?" Luke asked when Knox opened the door.

Only something that probably needed interrupting. "I have a friend over," he answered and gave him a quick one-armed hug. "Come in."

"This isn't a personal call," he said. "Mind if we talk in my car?"

"Of course." He slipped on his loafers and followed Luke to the black four-door RAM parallel-parked out front. "What's up?" he asked once inside as rain began pelting the street in thick and heavy sheets.

Luke turned in the driver's seat and draped his wrist over the wheel. "I put off this visit because I didn't know if I should even be here, to be honest."

His pulse pricked at his words. "Everyone okay?"

"Everyone's fine." He heaved out a deep breath. The man almost looked nervous.

He'd been with Luke at BUD/S. And so, Knox knew

Luke well enough to know the man didn't get nervous.

"Yo, brother, you've got me worried here."

"I'm gonna ask something of you that's not going to be easy, for you in particular. My sister normally travels with me on these visits, but I wanted to meet with you on my own."

"Sister?" What the hell was he talking about? And now his heart was ramping up to the highest of possible beats. "So, drop the bomb on me. What is it?"

"I heard rumors you're thinking about heading to Green Team to possibly be a Tier One guy. So, asking a man who's broken almost every record in Navy history to quit isn't an easy thing to do."

Knox sat up taller. "Quit? You wanna run that by me again?"

Luke's shoulders slouched. Again, not something he'd witnessed before. "I want you to quit so you can join a different team. Everyone will be made to think you left the SEALs. You'd still technically be one, but no one would know."

"What the hell are you talking about?" He scratched at the back of his head, a growing discomfort stretching across his chest.

Not even ten minutes ago, he'd nearly kissed Adriana, one foot poised and ready to step across the friendship line. And now, here he was sitting with a legend, a legend who was asking him to quit?

"My sister, Jessica, left the CIA and pitched an idea to the president about forming a black ops group to run covert ops without the knowledge of Congress."

"Aren't Tier One guys pretty much running off-the-books ops already?"

"Only with government approval. We'd bypass all the red tape and get the shit done that needs getting done without waiting for some dickhead behind a desk to approve it. Er, no offense," he said, probably referring to one particular dickhead—Knox's senator father.

"And the president approved this?"

"Yeah, only a few high-ups will know about us, and to avoid notice, we'll mostly be self-funded."

Knox almost laughed. "Self-funded black ops missions?"

Luke held a hand in the air between them as if to say, *I know, I know.*

"This sounds like some Hollywood stuff."

"No one—absolutely no one outside the team—can know what we really do. You'd have to keep this from everyone and sign some NDAs. POTUS gave approval for ten guys. I had hoped for twelve, so we could have two teams of six, but ten will work. Five on Bravo and five on Echo."

"And you want me?" He leaned back in his seat and looked out the front window, the tap-tap-tap of rain fading into the background as he grappled with what Luke was asking of him.

"I gotta be honest, as much as I wanted to recruit you . . . your father being a senator gave me some reservations. It could put you in a shit spot with the press wondering why you dropped out of the SEALs to go into private security."

He didn't give a flying fuck about the press, or what his father thought. "My dad and I still aren't on the best of terms. But uh, private security?"

"It's how we'll get most of our funding, plus, it provides us with a handy alias," he answered. "My sister is a bit of a cyber genius, so she already has ideas about how to score some major cyber protection contracts with corporations under our alias. Plus, we can do some bodyguard gigs in between ops to make money and keep up with appearances. We couldn't think of anything badass, so my sister named us

Scott and Scott Securities." He grumbled. "I'd prefer something else, but I guess it doesn't matter."

"And everyone we work with will be Teamguys?"

"Yeah, and then we'll hire some retired SEALs to run the day-to-day stuff for the alias when we're not around, but they can't know about our ops for POTUS."

"Shit, man."

"No more deployments," he added.

Well, at least he could keep a better eye on Adriana if he wasn't overseas all the time.

"We can tell the media you suffered an injury, and you were forced into medical leave, maybe. POTUS can come up with something. But I know it's a lot to ask of you, and if you say *no*, I won't hate you for it." He lifted a shoulder. "I won't exactly love you, either, but . . ." He chuckled.

"You really think we can make this work?" he asked, already accepting the idea in his head.

Luke nodded. "It'll carry about the same risk as a Tier One guy, only if we're ever caught, Uncle Sam will claim we acted alone, so there won't be any QRF bailing us out." He was quiet for a minute, letting his words simmer. "So, what do you say? Can I count you in as Bravo Five? With your abilities and medical training, we could really use you on the team."

Knox glimpsed his townhouse out of the corner of his eye, his thoughts wandering to Adriana, to the fact he'd have to lie to her. And this new job had the potential to carry more risks than his current position with the Navy. Meaning . . . he'd truly have to kiss any ideas of *more* between them goodbye.

Maybe it was for the better? He wanted her to be happy, and he'd be there for her as long as he had breath in him.

He looked back at Luke. "I'm in."

He wrapped up the conversation with Luke and went inside. He swiped the rainwater from his head and shook out his soaked T-shirt.

"You alone?" Adriana called out.

"Yeah," he answered, relieved she didn't come out in his jersey with Luke present.

Maybe she was right, and he was too protective of her. But this was the only way he knew how to be with Adriana even if it didn't always make sense.

"So, who was that?" She folded her arms and leaned against the wall. The same wall he'd had his back to when he'd nearly kissed her. And now that blank wall was never going to be the same again—because it'd always remind him of the moment he almost said *To hell with it* and told her how he really felt.

But that moment was gone, and maybe he'd never be able to find his way back to it. He resisted the urge to grip his chest as it tightened.

"It was Luke," he finally said.

Her spine straightened at the mention of the name. Of course, Adriana would remember. She'd been on the phone with him nearly every day during BUD/S. She knew Luke had been the reason why he didn't give in and ring the bell early on.

"What'd Luke want?" The curve of her cupid's bow-shaped mouth flattened into a straight line, a look of worry in her eyes.

He couldn't lie to this woman.

But . . . what choice did he have?

"He offered me a job." Knox grabbed his tumbler and gulped down the rest of the drink.

"What kind of job?"

"Private security. No more deployments. Still helping

people, though."

Adriana stood in front of him and reached out for his arm. "You're thinking about leaving the Navy? Is that even possible?"

"He's got an in with the president, so it's doable." He really hated himself for lying.

"You're not considering doing this because of me, are you? Because of my new job?"

"No," he rushed out. "Now, let's have some more Jack and get back to celebrating your Secret Service gig."

God, this night had been all sorts of crazy.

He needed to shut everyone and everything else out and pretend for a few minutes they were alone in the world.

He turned up the volume to the music and handed her the remote. "Your microphone, my lady."

She smiled and accepted it, then clutched it between her palms, a look of suspicion on her beautiful face. "Are you deflecting?"

Absolutely. "Nope." He tipped his chin and pointed to the remote. "Now sing."

He hoped his nerves would calm down the second her lips moved and she began to belt out a song in her so-bad-it-was-actually-good voice.

He refilled their drinks and handed her the glass. "Cheers to our new jobs."

"So, you're saying *yes*?"

I am, right?

Her green eyes thinned, and he couldn't tell if she was worried or excited about the prospect he was leaving the Navy.

He stared into her eyes and surrendered to a deep breath. "Yeah," he said while clinking his glass to hers. "I'm saying *yes*."

21

CHAPTER ONE

THE SITUATION ROOM. IT WAS THE TEAM'S FIRST TIME THERE. And it scared the hell out of Knox it could also be their last.

Knox sat at the long, oval table and studied the room, which was in the basement of the West Wing. Some of the most important moments in modern history had taken place in that very room, as evidenced by the snapshots occupying prime real estate on Google.

POTUS had summoned the team to D.C. without telling them why, and since it hadn't been a *Get here now* kind of summon, that meant it wasn't op-related. But hell, no one needed the president to tell them why they were there. They knew.

The election was in November, and Rydell was finishing his second term. There were two main candidates in the race, and to make things more complicated, one was Knox's dad. Isaiah Bennett, the man who'd inherited a small fortune after leaving the military and turned his money into the kind of wealth even rich people dream of.

"Your hand, babe, it's trembling." Jessica's words carried everyone's attention her way as she clasped Asher's palm between hers.

"No, it's not." Asher pulled his hand to his lap, and his throat moved with the mother of all swallows.

"Shit." Harper let out a breath like a whistle. "You're worried." She leaned back in her seat, sitting off to Asher's left. "If the Big Guy is nervous, we're screwed."

Harper was the newest addition to the team. She'd joined in May of last year, and wow, time had flown by since then. And now Jessica, who co-led the teams with her brother, Luke, was pregnant with Asher's child.

"We'll be fine." There was an eerie hollowness in Luke's tone that hit Knox in the chest. "You okay?" He focused his attention on Owen off to this right.

"Sam's about to go into labor, so yeah, my plate is a bit maxed out on what I can digest right now," Owen answered pretty damn honestly. "If her water breaks while we're in here—"

"You'll get a police escort to the hospital," Liam said to him. "Or fly out of here in POTUS's chopper."

"Funny." Owen gripped the chair arms.

The man was about to become a father. First Luke, then Liam. And hell, now Jessica and Asher. Babies were popping up everywhere on Bravo Team.

"Can we talk about something else?" There was a plea to Owen's voice. "I need a distraction."

"How about Knox's friend, a friend he's kept a secret from all of us," Wyatt spoke up.

Knox's heart raced. The about-to-swim-with-sharks kind of beats. A SEAL who hated oceans—there was a word for that, right?

He had no idea what to say because he honestly had no

answer to give them. He'd created a list of reasons in his mind to keep his work-life separate from Adriana, but he was afraid if he actually verbalized the list, he'd sound like a fool.

"No clue who you're talking about," Knox joked to buy himself some time.

"Yeah, sure. Elaina thinks she looks like Wonder Woman." Liam's smile stretched.

The man beamed whenever he talked about his daughter. He was happy. So damn happy. And part of Knox wished he could have what Liam had, but was that possible?

"Gotta give me more than that, brother. When Elaina dragged me up to see her poster collection last weekend, I was a bit overwhelmed. I can't believe you let her plaster her bedroom walls with photos of guys."

Was this pathetic? His attempt at deflection? But really, what could he possibly say to a room full of his buddies, guys who'd lay their lives on the line for him, that'd make any sense?

"Elaina thinks we're secretly superheroes in real life, right?" A.J. took the bait. "Liam's Thor. Then Chris over there is—"

"You're just jealous she doesn't think you look like a superhero." Chris stroked his dirty blond beard, his light green eyes creasing as his lips pulled into a grin.

"Hell no. A cowboy in tights?" A.J. smoothed a hand over his white dress shirt, the sleeves rolled to the elbows.

"Boys." Jessica opened her arms wide, interrupting what could quickly become a laughable pissing match.

"At least Wonder Woman is on her bedspread," Liam announced after a beat. "Although she said she's thinking about swapping Wonder Woman for Captain Marvel soon. She's been schooling me on all the characters."

Knox drew up a picture of Wonder Woman in his head. Yeah, she reminded him of Adriana.

Slightly wavy dark brown hair. Sculpted dark brows. High cheekbones and a killer smile that traveled to her gorgeous green eyes. There were similarities, but there was only one Adriana.

Adriana could probably do the actress's stunts in a movie, though. He'd talked her into learning Krav Maga back during his deployment days, and that training had come in handy when she'd become Secret Service.

"*So*, how is that friend of yours?" Wyatt peered at Knox.

And shit, he'd have to answer now.

"And does she really have a boyfriend?" A.J. asked.

Finally, a question he could answer. "She's married to her job." So, maybe he'd given Adriana a fake boyfriend when he'd introduced her at the barbecue last weekend. But, on principle, he hated everyone she dated, and he'd prefer not to have to hate his friends. Or kill them.

"Who are you guys talking about?" Luke asked. "I'm lost."

Right. Luke and Eva had been in Hollywood during the barbecue, so he hadn't met Adriana. His wife was Hollywood royalty. Her background, all the cameras and attention, were a no-no for Special Forces guys, but Luke had fallen in love. Hit the ground face-first.

"We're talking about the friend Knox brought to Liam and Emily's. A friend who was gazing at Knox with stars in her eyes," Harper said in a singsong voice. "At least, that's what Elaina told me. But I agree with her, and I do have a knack for reading people."

"That's in our job description." A.J. angled his head to catch Harper's eyes. "We can all do that."

Harper could joke all she wanted, but if Elaina saw

something . . . well, the kid was the closest thing to a psychic in his eyes.

Goose bumps greeted his skin, and he tugged at his shirt sleeves to hide the evidence. He didn't need to get ridiculed by his buddies.

"Guys." Luke looked toward the now opening door.

President Rydell entered the room alone, his detail waiting in the hall as instructed.

Thinking about Adriana getting assigned as the president's Secret Service detail someday had his stomach protesting the black coffee he'd had earlier.

As was the customary show of respect, and in their case a requirement, the team rose from their seats to greet POTUS.

"Sit, please." Rydell positioned himself at the head of the table and leaned forward, clasping his hands together.

His silver hair was slicked back and parted to the side, and his tan skin creased even more as he surveyed every team member at the table, a grim look crossing his face.

"What's wrong, Mr. President?" Luke spoke up, and thank God because a Colorado-sized boulder had begun to obstruct Knox's airway.

"I'm afraid your mission a few weeks ago might be your last," he said, his tone somber. "I'm coming up on the final months of my presidency, and I'm not sure if the team can continue under another president."

The world should've stopped at that moment. At his words.

But it kept rotating right the fuck around.

Because they'd been anticipating the news.

Luke rose to his feet. "Can't we finish out the year?"

That'd been the part no one had expected. Bravo and Echo to be done now. Like as in to-damn-day.

Rydell leaned back in the leather chair. "We have a few

problems on our hands," he began. "If Jefferson Lyle wins the White House, not only will he dismantle your team in a heartbeat, he'll expose everything we've ever done."

Would they be called murderers for operating without legal authority, even though they'd been protecting their country? End up in prison or on death row?

They'd be kidding themselves to claim ignorance to how Congress, maybe even the American people, could perceive their work.

Vigilantes? War criminals?

The list could go on and on.

"Aside from the fact Lyle's calling for a drastic reduction in military spending if elected—why else do you think he's dangerous to us?" Jessica asked, her voice remaining calm despite the impending storm.

"Lyle served on the Intelligence Committee with me before I became president. A covert off-the-books group had been proposed, and the conversation had been tabled and fast."

"Because of him?" Luke asked.

"Most of the committee was certain an off-the-books group couldn't maintain a life in the shadows, that their exposure would be inevitable. They worried about funding, too." He paused for a moment. "Lyle also mentioned rumors of black ops groups existing under previous administrations during the Cold War days. Groups that'd gone sideways. He believed it imperative that any and all operations go through the proper channels."

So, a Lyle win would destroy us no matter what.

"Lyle's VP nom, Leslie Renaldo, may not be opposed to the teams," Rydell said. "However, we'd be shooting ourselves in the foot if we go straight to her and leave Lyle out of the loop, so . . ."

"Sir, if I may?" Knox stood and bared his knuckles to the table. "Even if my father wins, we'll most likely face another set of challenges."

"You may be right." Rydell nodded. "Your father is former military. An advocate for a strong and healthy American defense. He already has my endorsement for president." He let go of a hard breath. "But I have no idea how he'd react if he discovered the existence of Bravo and Echo, especially since his own son is on the team."

Knox's father hadn't wanted him to join the Navy. He'd changed his mind over the years, but had it changed enough to get him on board with his current line of work? He wasn't so sure.

"We've done a lot of good work in the last seven and a half years," Jessica said, her voice cracking as if she were on the verge of tears. Pregnancy hormones, maybe? "But I was hoping to do even more. And then train others to take our places when we're done."

"You have Scott and Scott," Rydell said as if they'd forgotten. "Your agency has done some admirable work, too. You can still help people."

Four weeks ago, Bravo and Echo Teams had fast-roped into an old communist compound in Panama and taken out a man who'd been responsible for wiping out villages of people in his own country. They *did* make a difference. They wouldn't conduct ops like *that* for Scott & Scott.

"No." Knox pounded the desk, forgetting the room, the audience. "If my dad wins, and I have to leave so you all can stay together and keep working, I'll do it." He wouldn't hesitate. Whatever was best for the teams, for the nation, he'd do in a heartbeat.

"There's no Bravo without you, brother." Liam's Aussie accent thickened. "We stay together."

"Agreed," Chris said right after.

"I'm gone, if you're gone," Roman, one of the quietest guys on Echo, spoke up.

Knox proceeded to move his gaze slowly around the table, falling on Jessica's face last.

"I know you and your father reconnected not too long ago . . . what's your take on how he'd handle the news that you're part of a not-so-legal covert team of operatives?" Rydell asked.

He straightened and unclenched his fists, allowing his arms to fall to his sides, allowing gravity to grab hold of all of him like an anchor so he could stand firm.

He'd only started speaking with his old man again because the team had needed him to for an operation, but things had improved between them since then. He'd even gone to a few family dinners at his mother's request. Of course, he'd forced Adriana to go with him to make it bearable. But would his father authorize the continuation of Bravo and Echo Teams, especially with Knox on Bravo?

He let go of a sigh. "I could feel him out. Join the campaign trail, maybe?"

"I can't imagine you playing dress-up in a shirt and tie and touring with your old man." Owen scratched his trimmed beard, studying him. "No way."

"It'd be for the good of the team," Jessica said in her low don't-cross-me tone. "To keep us together."

And that shut up Bravo Two, but was Owen right?

Could Knox find his way back to that life again? The life of walking on eggshells as the son of a politician, never knowing who was watching or listening?

He'd been off the grid so long he'd hoped the media had forgotten about him.

He'd have to put himself in front of the public eye again. Would the teams get dragged into the limelight, too?

Shit. What choice did he have, though?

"What do we know about the polls?" Harper's question carried his focus to her. "It's almost September. Is Bennett a front-runner?"

He doubted Harper paid attention to the news, same as Knox and the rest of the guys. They didn't serve a political party. They didn't have to play political footsie to get things done. They served the American people, even if the people didn't know about it.

"Isaiah Bennett's got a ten-point lead, but we can't be certain of anything until November," the president responded.

Rydell had been worried enough to assemble them in the Situation Room, so he had to have a pessimistic view of the future for the teams.

"Maybe head home, spend some time with your families. Stay low-key for now, and we'll touch base in a few weeks." Rydell looked at Owen. "You have a baby on the way." He shifted his focus to Jessica and Asher. "And shouldn't you two get married already?"

Asher and Jessica exchanged a quick look. "Maybe we could . . . I mean, we're going to have a baby, so . . ."

"You're pregnant?" Rydell's eyes widened. "Congratulations."

"Thank you, Mr. President." A soft blush crawled up her cheeks, and her hand slipped to her abdomen, even though she wasn't showcasing a bump yet at six weeks.

"We'll figure this out," the president said, unable to hide the uncertainty in his tone. "Enjoy your lives for a bit, and we'll—"

"This *is* our life," Finn interrupted.

31

"He's right." Chris stood. "This is my life. The teams. The missions."

No one on Echo—not Wyatt, A.J., Chris, Roman, or Finn, had girlfriends or wives. They didn't have daughters or sons to go home to when they walked out of this room.

Everyone on Bravo could still look at the glass half full if they had to, even Knox because he had Adriana, but Echo . . . it'd kick the wind out of their pipes to go back to civilian life.

The president opened his mouth to respond, but a series of urgent knocks at the door silenced him. "Come in."

Knox pivoted to find White House Chief of Staff Coleman entering the room.

"Mr. President, we have a situation," he announced straight away.

"This is the Situation Room," Chris said in his lame attempt at a joke.

"What's wrong?" Rydell stood and circled the table.

"There was an assassination attempt on Isaiah Bennett."

Knox's stomach dropped. His skin grew clammy. His entire world shifted. "What?" He'd mouthed the word, his voice refusing to participate.

"Everyone's okay," Coleman rushed out.

"Maybe you should have led with that," Rydell grumbled. "What the hell happened?"

Coleman's eyes widened when he spotted Knox. "You're the senator's son." His gaze returned to the president. "I'm sorry. I didn't know he was in here."

The president waved his hand in the air, telling him to calm down. "Tell us what happened. You can speak in front of them."

The man's Adam's apple bobbed in his throat. Sweat trickled down the sides of his face as if he'd sprinted from the other side of the building to get there. "Bennett was leaving a campaign rally at an arena in Charlotte. Two shots were fired. The first shot is estimated to have been an inch from hitting" —he focused on Knox again—"your mom. She was right next to your dad."

"My mom?" It was one thing for his father to put his life on the line in his efforts to obtain power, but he'd be damned if his mom got hurt because of him. "You said two shots."

"One of your father's bodyguards shielded your parents as the second shot was fired. He was wearing a vest, so the guy's fine," Coleman explained. "I'm so sorry."

"We didn't get the shooter?" Rydell asked, a dark grit underlining his tone.

"Not yet," he answered. "Agents are swarming the area. The shots were fired from the hotel across the street."

"I'm betting the shooter has two first names," A.J. said casually. "They always do."

"Says the guy with two first names," Asher responded.

Jessica shot both men her signature look that threw daggers—a silent, *Shut up.*

"Aren't the two-named guys usually framed? A conspiracy?" Harper noted, clearly missing Jessica's warning shot.

But hell, their back-and-forth had allowed him a second to control his thoughts. His breathing. "I need to go to Charlotte."

"Your parents are being taken to the local FBI field office," Coleman told him. "Your dad declined Secret Service detail after he won the primary. He didn't want to spend government money when he has plenty of his own cash. But maybe if . . ."

"My dad's stubborn."

"I'll go with you to Charlotte," Liam said.

"I should go, too," Wyatt added.

"I'll be in my office soon. Cancel my trip to Camp David," Rydell instructed Coleman, effectively dismissing him. Once the door closed behind his chief of staff, the president faced the team crowded around the table.

"Sir," Wyatt began, "I know you instructed us to stand down as of now, but I'd like to get a look at the scene."

"Liam and Wyatt are the best snipers on the planet," Jessica said while pinning her gaze to Knox, offering a look of condolence in the process. "They could possibly discover details that others might miss."

Rydell shifted his blazer out of the way as he squared his hands on his hips. "We'll have the best people working the case, I promise."

"With all due respect, Mr. President, our team . . . they're the best," Luke said in a low, raspy voice.

"I can't have you all running around a crime scene. Too many eyes on you."

"What if we can convince Bennett to hire us?" Jessica asked. "Scott and Scott Securities? He's used our services before."

It could work.

Hell, it had to work.

"If you do this, you're on your own. I can't officially authorize it," Rydell said on a sigh. "But off the record, go for it."

"Everything we do is already off the record, Mr. President," A.J. pointed out.

True. A few minutes later, they left the room and went upstairs, everyone powering on their cell phones. Knox's began ringing straight away.

Adriana.

"I gotta take this. I'll meet you all outside." He looked up at his team, and Jessica gave a stiff nod, then followed everyone down the hall to a private exit. "Hey," he answered, pressing a palm to the wall for balance, his knees still a bit weak.

"I just heard," she said softly. "You okay?"

He closed his eyes.

Was he okay?

Better now hearing her voice.

"Yeah, are you good?" he asked, knowing the shooting had to be a painful reminder of what had happened to her mother.

"You've got to stop worrying about me."

Easier said than done.

It'd taken him years to accept the fact she was Secret Service. And then another few years to stop allowing his fear of something terrible happening to her, to drive him crazy.

If she ever took a bullet on the job, though, he'd have to go *John Wick* on everyone involved. Maybe he hated killing, but he'd make an exception. He sure as hell hoped he never had to cash in on that exception.

"I'm planning on going to Charlotte."

"Figured you'd say that. I'd come with you, but the PM of Sweden is here for a few more hours. I can fly in after. I don't have any assignments scheduled, and I'm owed some time off."

"Don't you have a date or something tomorrow?" Deflection should've been offered as a college course. He usually had it down pat, but shifting topics to her dating life, and at a moment like this, wasn't the best idea.

"With that fake boyfriend you made up at the barbecue when introducing me to your friends?" An eye roll he couldn't see carried through her tone.

"There is a guy, though. A blind date." He couldn't get

himself to stop. And the words had even rolled so obviously bitter out of his mouth, too.

"I'm canceling. You're way more important."

"I probably won't be in Charlotte long. I'm gonna go on the campaign trail with them for a few weeks."

She was quiet for a moment. Processing his words. "How'd your dad convince you to travel with him?"

This would be a hard sell, especially to her.

"I'm doing it for my mom." Lying to her shredded him. It always messed him up. And maybe that was one of the main reasons he kept her away from his work-life.

He glanced over his shoulder, worried she could possibly be in the building right now, and he'd come up empty as to why the hell he was at the White House.

"Well, I gotta go. And I'll be—"

"Fine," she finished. "You said that. Please let me know the second you get to Charlotte."

"Yes, ma'am." He started for the side door, which exited out to West Executive Avenue.

"You're not driving, are you? You're probably not in the best state of mind."

"Some buddies from the company are coming with."

"Good. And, Knox?" She'd finally given in to his request to call him by his SEAL nickname—well, most days. When he did something to piss her off, she usually whipped out Charlie. "Stay safe. Love ya."

Love ya. The "ya" had a way of toning down the actual statement. It was a safety net. A way to keep her guard up, and he knew it. He hated it. And he wanted to tear it the hell down.

But he was a hypocrite, because he usually only managed a, "You, too."

He ended the call, took a second to pull himself together, then went outside.

He slipped on his shades when the sunlight hit him in the face. It was too bright for a day like this. A day when someone shot at his family.

"Hey, you okay?" Jessica stood next to Luke and Wyatt outside one of their parked Suburbans. "What do you want to do? Tell me, and it's done."

He glimpsed the backseat window as it scrolled down. "We got your back, brother," A.J. said.

"I know." And he'd be forever grateful.

"I'm thinking you, Liam, and Wyatt head to Charlotte first." Jessica shoved her glasses to the top of her blonde head. "You can work your magic to ensure we get invited onto the case. Harper, Finn, Roman, and Chris can fly to New York and work out of our main office. We might need a tech assist from there. The rest of us will join you all tomorrow after we get some stuff prepped."

"I don't think you all need to come. Obviously not Owen," Knox replied. "And you're pregnant."

"I don't do well with idle time," A.J. said. "So, I'm going with y'all today."

"Just promise me you won't walk around the hotel in your bloody—"

"For you, I might," A.J. cut off Wyatt and kissed the air.

A.J. had a penchant for strutting around in his American flag boxers and cowboy boots, and Knox was damn sure he only did it to irritate Wyatt.

Wyatt jerked a thumb toward the door. "He stays here."

"You can't survive without Echo Two, and you know it." Luke smiled.

"You care to make a wager?" Wyatt grabbed his shades hooked at the top of his shirt and put them on.

"You've been batting zero on bets lately," Jessica reminded Wyatt.

The guys loved betting, but Wyatt had lost about every one that year. Beers would be on him for life if he kept it up.

"We should get moving," Luke said after a few moments.

"Right." Knox snapped his attention back to the op . . . he needed to call his parents. It probably should've been the first thing he did after learning about the assassination attempt, but he was still lightyears away from being buddy-buddy with his family despite a few dinners here and there. "My dad has gotten death threats before," he said once they were in the SUV and on the move. "The US Marshalls have had to babysit him on more than one occasion while my dad was a senator."

"But this is the first time someone tried to kill him, right?" Liam asked from behind the wheel.

"Yeah," he said as they drove past the EOB building alongside the White House—Adriana's office. "And hopefully it'll be the last time."

CHAPTER TWO

ADRIANA: *WHY HAVEN'T I HEARD FROM YOU YET?*

A few dots popped onto her screen and then disappeared before popping up again. She set her phone on the kitchen island and removed her blazer.

She was officially off duty, and yet, no word from Knox.

As soon as they'd ended their call earlier that day, she'd immediately pulled up the GPS on her phone to calculate the distance and driving time from D.C. to Charlotte, and he should have arrived by now.

And the friend finder app they used . . . of course, he'd turned it off.

At the sound of the chime she had set for Knox's texts, she snatched the phone off the counter.

Knox: *Traffic. We're ten minutes away. You worried about me?*

Adriana: *Me worry? Nah. That's your job.*

A total lie.

She poured a glass of wine, turned on the news, and muted the TV.

She missed him already. He'd been in town since the

second week in August. She hadn't spent this much time with him since summers during their college days.

Somehow, sharing one of the worst nights in her life had bonded them in a way that couldn't be described in books or depicted in films.

A relationship born out of tragedy that she'd defend until the end of time, even if she wanted more.

But was she scared of losing what they had to even take *more* for a test drive? And Knox, well, he'd nearly fled from her apartment last weekend as if worried *more* might happen, and it'd been a prick to her lungs, deflating her and pulling her back to their stuck-in-the-friend-zone reality.

But Knox's parents were shot at today, so the last thing she should've been thinking about was her relationship with him. No, she needed to worry about how to be his rock. To support him as he'd always supported her.

If Knox's dad had died . . . or his mom killed in the crossfires . . .

As much as Knox griped about his family, she knew he loved them. And she never wanted him to experience a loss like that.

She forced away the emotions stirring inside, fighting back the sting of pain that gathered whenever she thought about the night she lost her mom.

Knox: *Maybe I should've brought you with me. My dad has always had a soft spot for you. He'd do anything you ask.*

It took her four years to discover the Bennetts, at Knox's request, were the reason her father was able to keep their home after her dad turned to the bottle. It'd been the Bennetts' money that kept her family afloat, but it was Knox who kept her head above water.

Adriana: *You're a good son, you know that, right?*
Knox: *Tell that to my dad.*

Adriana: *He loves you in his own way.*

His father had retired from the military years ago, but he walked like a soldier. Squared shoulders. Head held high. Eyes gleaming with respect. Knox was the same in that way. A strong man.

Knox: *Where's that date of yours taking you? What does he do? Social Security number?*

Adriana: *That's a lot of questions.*

Knox: *Pick one and go from there.*

And he was deflecting.

Adriana: *I canceled. And why are we talking about my love life when someone just tried to kill your dad?*

Love life? God. What love life? She hadn't had sex in FOREVER. But after Knox crashed her last attempt at dating back in the spring, and she'd so easily tossed her date aside for a night to hang out with her best friend, she was pretty sure she needed to figure out where her head was at before she dipped a foot back into the dating pool.

Knox: *I have to live vicariously through you since I don't get any action.*

"No action my ass," she grumbled, and a sting of jealousy —no, a full-on assault of jealousy—hit her at the idea of him with another woman. But she had to be the cool girl who could be friends with a hot guy and not get jealous, right?

Adriana: *Lies. Lies. Lies.*

You're H.O.T. and women THROW themselves at you. The few friends Adriana had introduced him to always fell in love instantly. They said he reminded them of that actor who loved to call every fan he met "baby girl" . . . but she'd given her friends one hard and fast rule.

Knox was off-limits.

They were welcome to date any of her exes, coworkers, the president's son for all she cared, but not Knox.

41

She'd never met anyone Knox dated. Of course, Knox refused to talk about other women with her, but she was certain he didn't have girlfriends.

One-night stands were probably his go-to. The man was married to his job, after all.

But Knox was always up in her business about men. None were ever good enough, and he made sure she knew that.

For a while, she'd convinced herself he wanted to keep her to himself. They'd have a fairy-tale happy ending. Not glass-slippers-pumpkin-turned-carriages kind of happy, but their version of happy. Their version, in her mind, would be far superior to Disney's.

Adriana: *You need to stop deflecting. You can't talk about sex and pretend today didn't happen.*

Knox: *We're talking about sex?*

Adriana: *Action = Sex. Does it not?*

And he's distracting me again. Damn him.

Knox: *You have a dirty mind, girl.*

"Yours is way worse," she said at the phone as if he could hear her. She turned off the TV, unable to handle the barrage of footage showcasing the shooting.

Adriana: *Call me when you're at your hotel later and let me know how everything went.*

Knox: *Wish me luck. I'm gonna need it.*

Before she could respond, her work cell began ringing.

"Hello, ma'am," she quickly answered the call.

"You have a new assignment," her boss began. "We need you in Charlotte."

If she hadn't already been sitting, she would've fallen to the floor.

"Isaiah Bennett has finally given in and accepted a Secret Service detail. No doubt today's incident was the deciding factor. We're assigning eight agents. Two or three of you will run point on the investigation with the FBI and DHS, and the rest will handle protection and future threat assessments. You do want the position, right?"

Yes, but . . .

"Is there a problem?" she asked when Adriana hadn't yet found her voice.

Yeah, there was a problem. No way in hell would the Bennetts allow her to protect their family.

"I—"

"Pack your bags. You fly to Charlotte in an hour." Adriana's boss ended the call abruptly, which was her normal MO.

She held her phone out and stared blankly at the last message from Knox, now back on her screen.

Shit. You're going to kill me, aren't you?

CHAPTER THREE

"So . . ." It'd been years since Knox had engaged in small talk. As the son of a politician, he'd learned the subtle art as well as the finesse necessary to talk in circles, making everyone dizzy while impressing them at the same time. After a while, he'd gotten used to it, but those days were long gone. He no longer talked for the sake of talking.

He and the guys—well, they didn't fill space with unnecessary words. But as the Chevy approached the FBI building on the outskirts of Charlotte, he wanted to jam every inch of space possible with words if it meant slowing them down.

"What's up?" Liam asked. "Getting cold feet?"

"No," he said. "But, um, how's Elaina? Anything new?" He attempted to dust off his son-of-a-politician wheels and deflect.

When he turned and glanced back at Liam, he was met with an *Are you kidding?* look. "You mean anything new since you saw her last weekend at the barbecue?"

"Uh, yeah." Okay, so he now sucked at small talk. But he

did genuinely care about Liam's daughter, and he'd much rather talk about her.

"Well, she's got a date. His name is Kenny. Emily's taking them to the movies Friday." He shifted back and tipped his head to the ceiling.

"You should've stayed in D.C. I would've understood," Knox said in all seriousness.

"Emily knows how to shoot, remember?"

True. His wife had taken down an assassin in her apartment last year.

"And since when do nine-year-olds date?" Wyatt asked from behind the wheel.

"Since she informed me that she's almost ten, and since Kenny reminds her of a young Clark Kent. Do I want to know what that means?"

"Emily is letting this happen?" A.J. asked in surprise.

"Elaina has a way of wrapping you both around her pinky," Wyatt said with a laugh.

"Don't get me started." Liam slapped a hand to his heart. "I'm gonna get a bloody ulcer. If I think about this Kenny kid with my Elaina—I might put my fist through a concrete wall."

"And ruin your trigger finger?" At least Knox was distracted now. *Thank God.*

"You run a background check on him?" A.J. spun his American flag ball cap backward.

"He's not in the system," Liam grumbled. "But his dad's a reporter, and his mom's a doctor."

"Reporter? Well, shit." A.J. tsked. "End that and fast."

"Guys. Speaking of the media, we're not getting in that building without walking through a wall of press." Wyatt's voice was grave, a stark contrast from moments ago.

Knox turned to face forward in his seat and peered out the

tinted windows. "Maybe they can let us in through some secret back door?" His stomach roiled at the thought of all the people who'd be clamoring to shove a mic in his face.

"Still gotta go through security, especially since we're here as civilians." Wyatt pulled the Suburban into the parking lot and parked at the back.

"We'll have to plow through them in a hurry," A.J. said before climbing out of the SUV. "We've got your back, though."

Knox put on his black and red Falcons hat before they made their way through the parking lot and toward the entrance.

Liam and A.J. flanked his left and right respectively, and although Wyatt strode in front of Knox to keep him from being seen, someone must've sensed his presence, because a chorus of voices hollered out his name.

Every reporter turned toward them like a pack of dogs at the smell of bacon. Bam!—they were on him and fast.

"Charlie Bennett!" His name was nails on a chalkboard out of one man's mouth.

He hadn't missed this. Not for a damn second.

"Are you here because your father was the target of an assassin? Or are you finally joining his campaign?"

"How do you feel about someone trying to kill your father?"

"Why haven't you been on the campaign trail? Do you not support your father's run for presidency?"

"Rumor has it you had a falling out with your father—is there a reason he shouldn't become the next president? What's the true story?"

"What have you really been up to for the last seven years?"

"Back off!" A.J. roared, and Knox caught sight of the

vein throbbing at the side of his neck.

"And who are you?" A middle-aged reporter shoved a microphone in A.J.'s face, and Knox winced at the very real possibility that A.J. would knock the guy out.

"We're his protection," A.J. seethed, taking a step toward the man. Knox grabbed hold of his arm, urging him to back down.

It wasn't easy being in the spotlight, especially for the teams. In their line of work, it was something they actively avoided, and the last place they should've been.

Eva's Hollywood family had been the main source of Luke's apprehension about marriage, but if Luke could navigate the bright lights of the press without hitting anyone, Knox would do his damned best, too.

"How the hell do you deal with that garbage?" A.J. asked once they were safely inside.

"I don't. I left that life behind," Knox said.

"You leave your family name, or lordship, whatever you Brits call it, for the same reason?" A.J. prodded.

They'd only learned last year Wyatt had ditched his lineage and changed his last name when he'd become a U.S. citizen. He hadn't talked much about it since dropping the truth bomb, and Knox was in no hurry to push. He understood Wyatt's wish to leave his past where it belonged . . . in the past.

"I left for other reasons," Wyatt said when a woman in a black pantsuit approached them, her heels clicking across the floor. Her gaze laser-sharp on them. A touch of anger in her brown eyes. Yeah, she probably worked for Knox's dad.

"Shonte Stevens." She continued to appraise Knox as if deciding why in the hell the son of a presidential candidate would only now make an appearance. Yeah, he was about as low as one could get on approval ratings in her eyes. A possible roadblock to his father's success. An obstacle to deal with. "I'm your father's campaign manager. I've been waiting for you." Her dark brown eyes tightened on Knox's face. "Let's get you through security, and I'll bring you to your parents."

"How's my mom?" he asked once they were in the elevator.

"She's handling it better than anyone expected. But that's Kathleen Bennett for you." She motioned for them to follow her after the doors opened, which revealed an office bustling with uniforms and plain-clothes officers.

He spotted his mom talking to an old friend of hers on the other side of the floor. Five-ten without heels. Dyed blonde hair that offered the appearance of being natural—best hair color money could buy. And her red pantsuit made her stand out all that much more in the sea of dark suits.

"Charlie!" Her hand shot up in the air, and she immediately started for him, her friend forgotten.

"Damn, your mom looks like a hot Kim Basinger," A.J. muttered, elbowing him in the side.

"Is there a non-hot version of Basinger?" Wyatt asked.

"This is my mom, guys," Knox chided, preferring not to know his friends thought of his mother as *any* kind of hot.

He crossed the busy office space with long strides and met his mom halfway, then pulled her in for a tight hug.

She'd never been much of a crier, but there were legit tears in her eyes.

Shonte Stevens had been right about his mom. Kathleen Bennett would collect her composure and command her tears not to fall, but seeing the gloss causing her blue eyes to shimmer rattled him.

"You okay? Dad?" he asked after letting go.

She pulled back her shoulders and straightened her white

48

silk blouse beneath her red blazer. When her eyes cut to him, there was a moment her face betrayed her true concern for what had happened earlier. The moment was a blink in the space of time, though. She'd returned to the wife of a senator in a nanosecond.

"You know him. Unphased. Worried about missing the next event." She glanced at Knox's buddies as they closed in on them. "Thanks for getting him here safely." A tight, toothless smile crossed her face.

"Ah, Knox can handle himself, but we were happy to come with," Liam said.

"You remember Glenn Sterling, right?" She motioned to the tall, distinguished man at her right, who had government carved into every line of his face.

"You haven't been around in quite some time." Glenn reached for Knox's hand. "What's it been? Fifteen years since I've seen you?"

"Yeah, I've been busy." He forced a smile, the kind he'd learned from his father growing up. Toothy and fake, but not too much tooth, so it looked believable. "How's your wife? Daughter?"

"Nancy died a few years back. Lung cancer. I never could get her to quit smoking." His light blue eyes shifted briefly to the floor. "But Sarah's great. She's a world-class surgeon over at the Cleveland Clinic now."

Knox had been in med school with Glenn's daughter. Sarah had obviously finished, unlike him. "Sorry to hear about Nancy."

"Glenn's the Department of Homeland's deputy secretary," his mom quickly said as if trying to squash any sudden awkwardness at the mention of Glenn's late wife. "He came here to make sure the investigation was going okay."

"Your mom and I go way back, and I can promise you,

son, I won't let anything happen to her." He patted him on the shoulder.

Wyatt leaned in and whispered, "This place is way too crowded."

The teams were used to operating solo and off the grid. Being thrown into a room packed to the gills with unfamiliar people made them all twitchy.

"Did you know FBI Director Mendez was going to be here?" A.J. asked, and Knox followed his line of sight.

Mendez was holding a tablet in hand and talking to a team of men Knox guessed to be his dad's private security. Hopefully *former* security after their fuckup today.

"President Rydell placed him in charge of the investigation," Glenn said. "I'm gonna go have a word with him."

"Where's Dad?" Knox looked at his mom.

"Second office on the right." She hooked her arm with his.

"I'll be right back," he said to the guys.

"We'll try and see what we can find out from Mendez." Liam gestured toward the FBI director.

"You look more like my son than a SEAL today," she commented as they walked.

He hadn't had time to change out of the pressed white button-down and black slacks he'd worn to the White House.

He considered challenging her words, though. They rubbed him the wrong way. How was he not her son as a SEAL? He'd always thought the heavy hand of his political upbringing had been more from his dad, but maybe his mom's comments and actions had been more subtle.

He kept his mouth closed since a bullet almost clipped her earlier, and he was thankful to have his mom alive, even if she still had issues with his profession.

"How are you really holding up?" he asked instead.

"You know me. I'm always fine. And I've had about a million people calling to check on me today. I'm tired is what I am." A touch of West Virginia, where she grew up, clung to her words as if still fighting for a place in her life.

"You almost took a bullet, Mom."

"It's not the first time someone has come after our family."

"The other times involved threats and no follow-through." He pulled his arm free of hers. "This was worse. There was no warning beforehand." Not that they were aware of, at least.

"Remember Austria? There was that explosion . . . that attack may have been directed toward us. So—"

"It wasn't." He hadn't meant to snap at her, but he still felt guilty about Austria. The explosion was directly related to an op Knox and the teams had been working. Not that he could tell her that. His mom would probably have slapped the back of her hand to her forehead and fainted.

"Charlie." At the familiar sound of his father's deep voice, now void of his Southern upbringing, Knox turned.

His dad stood there in his three-piece custom suit that stretched over the length of a body that at sixty-five still exuded strength.

He looked . . . presidential, as if this was just another day at the office and not a moment the history books could've captured as the day he died. "Glad you could make it." He ate up the space between them in a few quick strides and pulled him in for a hug.

Knox froze. He hadn't hugged his dad in years. They'd exchanged the "man-hug," that firm handshake where a guy pulled the other in for a quick slap on the back. But this was two arms. Chest to chest. It was real. He didn't know his dad

51

still knew how to do real. Real was an *I love you* that didn't need to be said, but it was said because you wanted to. And damn, when was the last time he'd heard those words from either of his parents?

"Son?" A throat clear followed their hug, as if his dad had become aware that his emotions were on display. "Come into the office. Could you give us a minute, honey?"

"Sure." Her eyes lingered on Knox for a brief moment. And he almost stopped her before she left and asked her what she was thinking, but he didn't. He let her go because he didn't always know how to do real with his folks either.

"Please, sit down." His dad motioned to a brown leather couch on the other side of a large polished desk probably reserved for the bigwigs.

There were family photos and accolades on the wall behind the desk. An American flag on one side. The FBI flag with the motto: *Fidelity, Bravery, and Integrity*, on the other. His dad had probably hijacked a senior FBI agent's office.

"I'd prefer to stand." Knox strode to the window and looked between the blinds. They were running out of daylight, and he was anxious to get to the scene of the shooting to assess the area. First, though, they needed permission from the FBI to join the investigation.

"I'm glad you came," his father rasped.

Surprised, Knox turned to face his father, a man he'd never once heard speak in any manner outside of total strength and confidence. Today had hit a nerve, as it should've.

"How long do I have you?"

"Have me?"

He removed his blazer and rolled the sleeves of his white dress shirt to the elbows. "I didn't mean it like that. I don't expect you to do a song and dance. No questions. No public speaking. I know you wouldn't want that."

Politicians were adept at twisting and contorting everything to their needs. His father may not expect a "song and dance," but he'd convince Knox to walk out on a few stages with him. Say a few words.

For now, Knox would shelve his distaste for politics and focus on the fact the shooter missed.

"I was planning on coming down to visit with you and Mom," he admitted. "The shooting bumped up my schedule. I'm sorry about what happened today."

"I'm so glad your mom is okay, and no one got hurt because of me." He slowly lowered himself on the couch and rested his elbows on his knees, wearily placing his head in his hands. Grief-stricken. Weak posture.

Who the hell was this man? His father had encountered close calls with death when he served in the military. Had he forgotten those days? Forgotten what it was like to feel death breathing down his neck?

No man or woman should know what it feels like to be in the spotlight of death—but utopia didn't exist. People like Knox would always be needed.

"This life isn't easy. I get that." His dad sat up straight but didn't look at him. "I never even asked if you wanted to be the son of a politician. Maybe I should've asked."

"And if I'd said *no*?" He almost smiled. "At thirteen, would you have listened to me?"

"But you would've liked to have been asked, right?" He lifted his chin to view him.

He blinked back to his first semester in med school when he'd told his parents over Thanksgiving dinner his change in plans.

"I'm dropping out. This isn't the life I want."

"You don't want to be a doctor?" his mom had asked, her brows popping up in surprise.

"That was your dream for me. Doctor. Senator. Something fancy, right?" He'd tossed his napkin onto his plate and stood from the table—the entire meal had been catered since his mom didn't know her way around the kitchen to save her life.

"And what is it that you want?" His dad had leaned back in his chair and folded his arms across his chest.

"I'm joining the Navy. Gonna see if I can get a contract with the SEALs after that." He'd never forget how fast his heart had been racing like it might beat right out of his chest.

"You don't belong in the military. You're not cut out for that life."

"I'm sure as hell not cut out for this life!" he'd yelled louder than he'd meant to.

His dad had shaken his head. *"Wow, what a bad life. You want for nothing. You've had the best education money can buy. The—"*

"There's more to life than money and power." He'd turned his back, unable to look his father in the eyes.

"Don't you dare join the Navy to spite me. They deserve a better man than that."

Knox let go of his memories and focused on his dad. "I joined the Navy to piss you off," he admitted. "You were right." And if he hadn't met Luke at BUD/S, who gave him the kick in the ass he needed to get his head on straight, he may not have lasted long in the Navy.

"Well, there are a lot of things I said to you I wish I could take back."

Like? He wondered if his dad would fill in the blanks.

"I used to think every man, in some way, should serve our country—everyone except my son. But what kind of a leader would that make me if I was willing to let other parents put

54

their kids' lives on the line but not my own?" He stood. "I was wrong. And I'm proud of the man you've become. The Navy was good for you."

"I joined for the wrong reasons, but I'm still in for the right ones."

"But you're—"

Shit. "I . . ."

The door swung open before he could backpedal. It was Director Mendez. "The agents are en route. Their plane should arrive soon. We'll take you to your new hotel once it's been secured."

"Are you clearing out his floor, and the ones above and below like you do at hotels for POTUS?" Knox asked.

"Rooms on each side of his suite will have agents posted. Above and below as well." Mendez tipped his head in apology toward Knox's dad. "Best we could do, but we're almost done sweeping the hotel and checking guests. You should be able to head over soon."

"Will we still be able to stick to my schedule?" his dad asked. "I have a fundraiser ball in Atlanta Saturday I can't miss and a debate Tuesday in Cleveland."

"Can your VP nom step in for the ball, at least?" Mendez asked.

"No, Bethany's in California for the week, but I did put in a call to have her security beefed up in case anyone tries to come after her."

"Good idea," Mendez said.

"What made you change your mind about Secret Service?" Knox asked his dad.

"Shonte convinced me to get my head out of my ass." He braced a hand on Knox's shoulder, holding his eyes. "I'm going to let go of some of my security since they dropped the ball today."

"Hire Scott and Scott instead. Well, in addition to the Secret Service, I mean."

"Your company?" His dad lowered his hand. "Why do I get the feeling this is the only way I'll be able to keep you with me?" His eyebrows drew together.

"I'd feel better knowing my people were with us."

"You sure this is what you want?" his dad asked.

"What I want is for you to win this election." Most of the team was getting up there in age in the world of special ops. Chris, at thirty-six, was the youngest. It was only a matter of time before they were replaced, and they wanted every year they could get. And hell, they wanted to know they'd be replaced in the future. New guys to fill their shoes when they were ready to retire. Because bad guys didn't take breaks. They usually didn't have 401Ks to collect from.

So, yeah, his dad had to win. And then he needed to convince him why Bravo and Echo were desperately needed.

"Really?" He flashed him what his mom referred to as his Denzel Washington smile. The physical similarities between the two men were uncanny, though. "Does that mean you're going to vote for me?"

"Yeah, Dad, you've got my vote." Their best chance at survival was his father.

"Mind if I steal your son, Mr. Bennett?"

He'd nearly forgotten Mendez was in the room.

"Sure." His dad nodded. "Thanks again for coming, Son."

Knox followed Mendez to another room two doors down and found Liam, A.J., and Wyatt waiting inside.

"Why do I feel like we're about to get lectured at by the principal?" A.J. asked when catching Knox's eyes.

"Because we probably are," Liam mumbled as Knox took a seat across from them.

Mendez removed his blazer and tossed it over the back of

the nearest chair at the table. He was in his fifties, his hair more silver than black, and the lines on his face a sign of stress rather than age.

"I don't like you all being here." Mendez never was one to sugarcoat things, which was fine by Knox. He preferred it. "It makes me uncomfortable."

"I am his son, though."

"Stop trying to bullshit me. That's not why you're here." Mendez's brows lowered. "I don't know how you managed to rope the president into letting you on to this investigation, but if you get in my way, I won't hesitate to revoke your privileges."

"Say what?" Knox pushed back, the wheels of his chair sliding on the polished floors. "The president authorized us being here?"

POTUS changed his mind. He was risking his legacy for the teams. They owed him one.

"You expect me to believe you didn't know?" Mendez crossed his arms. "We already have a multiagency task force assembled. I've got Homeland breathing down my back." He threw a hand toward the busy office area on the other side of the door. "But the bureau is fully capable of handling this, and the last thing I need is a bunch of SEALs running around playing commando."

A.J. cupped his mouth, hiding a smirk at Mendez's words.

Either Mendez didn't know jack shit about the SEALs, or he did, and he was trying to piss them off.

"Liam and Wyatt are two of the best snipers in the country. If anyone should take a look at that crime scene, it's them. We're assets. Not your competition." Knox's biceps tightened, but he kept his hands in his lap so he wouldn't come across overly defensive. Too much was at stake to get booted. "Let us help you."

"And what do you get out of it?"

"Easy," he returned. "I get to ensure my parents stay alive."

CHAPTER FOUR

"ANYONE ELSE SURPRISED POTUS CALLED IN A FAVOR FOR us with Mendez?" A.J. asked as they drove through Uptown Charlotte, heading toward the arena where Knox's dad had given his speech earlier.

"Guess he had a change of heart. Rydell wants Bennett to win as much as we do." Liam braced the side of Knox's front seat and leaned forward. "Hopefully, your dad will be on board with keeping us if he wins."

After the talk he had with his dad, he was semi-hopeful that he might even approve of Knox staying on board, too. Now he had to keep him alive.

"Well, at least your dad supports us tagging along for a bit," Liam said as Wyatt parallel-parked the Suburban behind Mendez's black sedan. They were down the street from the roped-off crime scene. Police and agents had barricaded the entire area. An active shooter was still on the loose, and the city had been placed on high alert.

"Thanks again for coming with me." He repositioned his Falcons cap and tugged at the brim.

"What else would we do if we weren't here? Sip mojitos at the beach?" Wyatt flashed him a grin.

A.J. reached forward from the back seat and socked Wyatt on the bicep. "When in your life have you ever had a mojito?"

God, the two of them—they never stopped, but he'd sure as hell miss working missions with them if their off-the-books world came to an end.

Once they were out of the SUV, Knox examined the area as they walked a few paces behind Mendez.

The stadium took up the entire block on one side of the street, and the hotel was in perfect position across the way for a sniper to take the shot.

Mendez showed his badge to two officers protecting the entrance to the crime scene and motioned for them to follow.

"I'd like to know what type of wind we were dealing with earlier," Liam commented as they ducked under the yellow caution tape, which swayed in the slight breeze.

"Your father and mother exited the arena at ten o'clock this morning out that entrance," he said while pointing to the doors off in the distance. "There were ten minutes on the schedule to answer questions from a group of reporters assembled out here, and they were walking toward the media when the first shot was fired. The bullet went right between your parents and hit the ground behind them."

Knox crouched, removed his glasses, and studied the ground where the bullet had landed.

"How long between shots?" Wyatt asked as Knox rose and placed his shades back on.

"It was quick—only long enough to realign his target," Mendez said.

Knox thought back to the media footage of the event he'd

watched on his phone over and over again on the drive to Charlotte. It'd been surreal.

"Two bodyguards were positioned in front of your parents and two behind, which would've made the shot pretty difficult," Mendez explained. "After the first bullet, the bodyguards immediately used their bodies as shields."

"And the second bullet hit a vest." Knox cradled the back of his neck, observing the scene.

"Shortly after, the fire alarm at the hotel went off."

"Guaranteeing his escape." Knox frowned.

"Hundreds of people flooding the streets—it was chaos." Mendez pointed to the hotel. "Also, the security cameras were disabled in the hotel lobby and on the tenth floor prior to the shooting."

Wyatt's attention winged across the street to the hotel, his eyes narrowing once he'd locked on to the tenth floor.

"We're issuing warrants for all the private security cams within the vicinity, but it was basically a clusterfuck. I'm not optimistic we'll get much," Mendez said.

"You're questioning everyone on my dad's security staff? Maybe the shooter had help."

"Yeah, we've had our best interrogators talk to them. Nothing looks off, but we'll keep at it," Mendez responded.

"Are all the guests and employees from the hotel accounted for?" Knox asked as Liam stood off to his right with his hands in front of him, calculating angles and distance.

"I'll need to check with Special Agent Quinn. She's been coordinating all the interviews with the guests. She should still be at the hotel now. All guests they tracked down have been relocated to other local hotels during the investigation."

"We're losing daylight, boys. We should get a look from inside the hotel. I'd like to see the vantage point the shooter had." Wyatt darted across the empty street since it was still blocked off by patrol cars at all major access points.

"Where are you at on ballistics?" Liam asked once they were in front of the hotel lobby elevators.

Mendez pulled out his phone. "A three-zero-eight Winchester cartridge. One hundred and eighty grain. Soft nose jacket bullet. Brass case."

"The notches around the jacket mouth produce a massive energy release," Wyatt said as the doors finally opened. "More ideal for a medium to heavier target, but it also gives you a fast kill on a lighter frame."

"Since we're talking less than two hundred meters, our shooter didn't have to worry too much about the bullet dropping fast," Liam added as a few plain-clothes officers stepped out of the elevator.

"This is Special Agent Quinn," Mendez introduced the team to one of the officers. Her red hair was pulled back in a tight ponytail. Minimal makeup. The all-business kind of look Adriana had going for her whenever on the job. "She'll be working point with me as the special agent in charge out of the Charlotte office."

"And you are?" She shook Knox's hand. An impressive grip.

"We're Bennett's new security team. I'm Alexander James," A.J. butted in and reached for her hand before Knox could answer. "But you can call me A.J."

"His mom couldn't decide on a name. Don't mind him. I'm Wyatt. And your *first* name?"

"Special Agent Quinn works." With her shoulders pinned back and her eyes now on Mendez, it was clear she didn't fear the man. Her pant legs covered heels she was probably wearing to give her petite frame a height boost. "Why'd Bennett bring these guys in?"

She was irritated with their presence. It was going around. And the two notorious flirts with him sure as hell weren't going to help win any fans at the straight-edge FBI.

"That's Charlie Bennett." Mendez jerked his chin Knox's way.

"*Knox* works," he bit out, unable to help himself.

"Oh." Her brows slanted. "The son of a presidential candidate is serving as protection?"

"Working the investigation. I have a team who can step in for protection if needed," he replied.

"I don't think that's a good idea. This shouldn't be happening. *How* are we letting this happen?" Her hands went to her hips, and maybe Mendez outranked her, but she stood her ground.

"Call POTUS if you want. They're here because of him." He flicked his wrist for the guys to join him on the elevator. "Where are we at with the guests?"

"Almost everyone's been accounted for. Still tracking down a few people who were probably not at the hotel during the actual shooting."

"And the staff?" Mendez shot his arm out to keep the doors from closing. "Anyone have their badge stolen? Possible accomplice?"

"I would've led with that," she replied dryly.

"Okay, keep me updated on our missing people." He pulled his hand back. "I'm taking them to the tenth."

"You sure you want to do that?" she asked.

"Not really," Mendez said as the doors closed.

"Oh, I like her. And she's a redhead. Damn. She dating anyone?" A.J. flashed Mendez a smile. Jesus, this guy. Did he want to get shot by the 9mm Mendez probably had holstered at his hip?

"Like she'd date you," Wyatt said with a smile.

"Are they always like this?" Mendez looked at Knox.

Sometimes humor was the only way they got through shit. "Usually much worse," he answered, allowing his lips to tilt into a semi-smile, feeling slightly guilty for it given the reason he was at the hotel.

"Is there another way for our shooter to leave this place aside from the stairs or one of these main elevators?" Liam asked once they were on the tenth floor.

"The service elevators at the back don't have cameras, but they require a special card to access them. Since the gunman somehow managed to get a hotel room key, it's possible he also stole an access card to the service elevators, too, and he left that way." Mendez stopped outside room 1010 and unlocked the door.

"I'm betting a lot of people come in and out of this hotel every day," A.J. commented. "I'd check delivery drivers."

"This isn't my first rodeo." Mendez stepped aside so they could enter. "This suite was the only one not checked out at the time with a view of the Bennetts. You can't open the windows in the room, but it's got a small balcony with a sliding door in the bedroom."

"What's he doing?" Mendez asked once they were all inside the master suite. Liam had lowered his body to his elbows in front of the sliding door.

"What's it look like? Recreating the shot." A.J. stood alongside Liam. "Not our first rodeo, either." He couldn't hide the snarky bite to his tone.

"We're assuming he acted alone without the help of a spotter," Mendez noted a moment later.

"Yeah. If he's highly trained, he wouldn't necessarily need one." Knox crossed his arms, observing his teammates as they broke down the scene and calculated possible angles for the shot.

Liam and Wyatt rarely used spotters on ops. They didn't have the luxury, so they'd honed their skills to be more precise than ever before.

And Liam and Wyatt never missed. Well, Liam did last year—but love . . . well, love can do a thing to a man.

Friendship, too, he supposed. He'd do anything for his brothers. Anything for his family—for Adriana.

"I don't like this angle. He'd have to shoot with the door barely open to remain unseen, and with the metal bars on the balcony—it's nearly an impossible shot." Liam stood.

"Well, guess that's why he missed," Mendez said.

Wyatt peered at the ceiling and shut one eye. "Two rooms to the left and one floor up. That might work."

"That's what I'm thinking," Liam agreed.

"Then why disable the cams on floor ten?" Mendez asked as Liam shut and locked the glass door.

"Because where's the Feds' focus right now and where is it not?" A.J. held both palms in the air.

"Disabling the cameras only on this floor was a distraction." It was a strategic move. A smart one, too. "If the gunman had access to the service elevators he probably came and went that way, pulled the fire alarm when he got to the ground level, then waited for the crowd to rush out. He slipped out unnoticed."

Mendez produced a notepad from inside his blazer pocket and flipped through a few pages. "The room you mentioned on the eleventh was checked out. Same with the neighboring rooms. A couple in eleven ten, a single female in eleven twelve, and a couple with a child in eleven-zero-eight."

"I'd like to take a look at the cameras on the eleventh floor," Knox said. "Can we head to security?"

"We have people down there still going through the footage from the day," he replied.

65

"So, they won't mind a break." A.J. winked and slapped Mendez on the back before walking past him toward the door.

"Liam and I can check out the rooms while you view the cams." Wyatt held out his palm.

"Yeah, okay." Mendez handed him an access card.

After a few minutes, they entered the security area on the second level of the hotel. "We're going to take over the cams for a couple minutes," Mendez told the two FBI agents who were sitting in front of the screens.

Knox sat next to Mendez once the agents left, and A.J. remained standing off to his left.

"So." Mendez grabbed the mouse. "I'll start when the fire alarm was pulled and go backward, I guess."

"The cams in this hotel are shit," A.J. said a minute later. "No great angles of any of those rooms, either."

"Wait. Stop it there." Knox scooted to the edge of his seat to get a closer look at the screen when Mendez paused it. "Switch to slow motion."

A man and woman were walking down the hall then moved out of sight of the camera. "Rewind it." He watched another few seconds. "They're heading for the service exit."

"We can't prove that. It's conjecture," Mendez said.

He leaned back in his chair. "Forty seconds after those two are in the hall, the alarm is triggered on the first floor."

Mendez went back over the footage again. "I'll see if I can get a better look at the couple. You think she's his spotter?"

"No, I think she's his hostage," Knox answered.

"Head down. Ball cap. The man knew what he was doing," A.J. said. "He never looks at the cameras. She doesn't try to hide her face, though."

Knox stood. "He could have a gun to her back. Too hard to tell."

"I have a feeling the beautiful Quinn will be calling you back to let you know this woman never made it to her new hotel. I guarantee she's on that missing person list," A.J. said.

"See the bag he's got, too?" Mendez zoomed in on the screen. "Guessing that's the rifle. Something else in there, too. Computer, maybe."

Knox's cell vibrated a second later. "Hey, which room are you thinking?" he answered.

"My money is on eleven twelve," Liam replied.

Knox shifted the phone away from his ear to share the news. "Eleven twelve, that's the woman's room, right?"

"Yeah, let me call Quinn." Mendez grabbed his phone and left.

"Looks like our shooter may have taken a hostage with him," Knox told Liam.

"Not an accomplice?"

"The tech in here isn't exactly top of the line, but nah, from the looks of it, I don't think she's in on it."

"All right, we're heading your way now." Liam ended the call.

Mendez returned a few minutes later. "Her name is Sarah Reardon. And you were right, she's on the list of people our agents have been trying to locate. Agent Quinn's calling her family now."

Knox sat back down. "I'd like to look at more footage and see how the shooter initiated contact. Since there's no vantage point of her room on camera, we'll have to check the other angles in the hall and outside the elevator."

A few minutes later, Wyatt and Liam joined them in the office. "Anything?"

"The gunman must've hacked the security systems remotely. We have the man and woman on camera exiting the elevators and heading to her room before the first shot was fired."

"Maybe she met him at the hotel bar, and he persuaded her to invite him up to her room?" Liam speculated.

"But he has no bag when he heads to her room, so how'd he get his gun inside?" A.J. pointed out.

"We're going to need to scroll through all the hotel footage from the moment she checked in up until the shooting," Knox said.

"I have to meet with your father's Secret Service detail. They should arrive at Bennett's new hotel soon. We can head to the field office afterward, and maybe Quinn will have more for us to go on at that point. I'll have the team over there get started on this now."

The guys weren't used to working this closely with so many official agents, but it did have its advantages—like having an entire office devoted to the case.

"So, the shooter kills the cams in the lobby and on the tenth for a distraction. He exits the hotel after pulling the first-floor fire alarm and takes this woman with him as his stay-out-of-jail card," Knox summed up what they'd learned once they were back in the Suburban ten minutes later and en route to Knox's parents' hotel outside Uptown.

"The gunman bought himself at least nine hours with his tenth-floor camera act," A.J. said from the back seat. "You think this Sarah woman is still alive?"

"No one died this morning from the shooting," Knox answered softly. His parents didn't get hit. The bodyguard survived. "I sure as hell hope that's the way the story remains."

CHAPTER FIVE

"WHY DO YOU LOOK LIKE SOMEONE KILLED YOUR DOG?" Calloway asked Adriana inside the elevator at the hotel in Charlotte.

"I don't have a dog." And Calloway knew that. He was the only one from work she'd ever dated.

"And why do you wear shades inside an elevator?" Chen asked Calloway. "Don't be a movie cliché."

Rodriguez, her friend and the agent in charge, barked out a laugh. "He's right, man."

"Chen's always right." Adriana rolled her shoulders back, trying to loosen up. To free herself of the nerves even Calloway had noticed with his sunglasses on.

"You're from Atlanta, Foster," Rodriguez said. "You know the Bennetts?"

This wasn't really a question. Rodriguez knew her background. He knew her history, which meant he wanted to hear the words from her mouth that her relationship with the Bennetts wouldn't interfere with the job.

"She knows him," Calloway grumbled, clearly still bitter

about how things had ended between them a few months back.

"You ever date the senator's son?" Rodriguez interrupted her thoughts.

If Rodriguez wasn't in charge of their assignment, and his girlfriend didn't cook delicious food for her, she would've probably told him to mind his own damn business.

She had to remind herself he was doing his due diligence. Not overstepping boundaries even if it felt like it.

"You would think they dated." Calloway jammed his hands into his pockets, irritation springing through his words.

"There a problem I need to be made aware of?" Rodriguez shifted to the side to get a good look at both Adriana and grumpy-as-hell Calloway.

"No, sir," she quickly replied.

"Calloway?" Rodriguez asked.

Calloway remained quiet but shook his head as he removed his sunglasses.

"So, it's Hummingbird for the wife and Hawk for Senator Bennett," Rodriguez announced.

"I remember. You checking to make sure I did my homework?" She painted on a smile, trying to suppress the pressure of this moment—the winging around of jets in her stomach.

"This is a big day for you all. Just making sure you're ready." Rodriguez turned back around, and she did her best not to bump into the agents standing behind her.

Seven guys. One woman.

But this was her moment. It was the closest to the White House she had ever come.

Chen and Calloway had the best chance of rotating to protection detail for the next POTUS since they had the most experience, but maybe someday she'd have a shot.

And maybe one day she'd make her mom proud even though she wasn't there to see her. And she'd stop worrying about her dad slipping off the wagon.

And, oh yeah, maybe Knox would kiss her again.

So many maybes . . .

"Stacey told me you canceled your blind date but didn't reschedule," Rodriguez said as the elevator doors opened and they all moved into the hallway.

Calloway shot her a quick look at her boss's words. *Great*. The last thing she needed right now was a jealous Calloway. The second he and Knox were in the same room . . . she shuddered to think about how things might play out between them.

"So, you gonna tell me why you canceled?" Rodriguez asked, toying with the ends of his handlebar mustache.

"We're here, aren't we?"

"But why not reschedule?" He wasn't going to let this go, was he?

"And why are you and Stacey so interested that I date this friend of yours? Is he third in line for the crown of some incredible country I haven't heard of?" she teased. "I mean, if he cooks as good as Stacey, I might marry him now, but—"

"Because I know the kind of men you date, and we'd like you to meet a nice guy."

Nice guy was usually code for boring. Bland. Probably a few more B words she could come up with, too.

Nice guys were also safe. But she didn't need safe. She had Knox to keep her safe. And she'd done a fairly decent job of protecting herself as well.

No, what she needed was someone who gave her that spine-tingling-weak-in-the-knees type of feeling. And she knew who that was, but . . .

"You are thirty-five," Rodriguez went on, his steps

slowing as if to ensure they had time to continue their talk before the job started.

She stopped and faced him, and a touch of red met his cheeks.

The movies always depicted agents as humorless and bland. Not true at all. The men and women who worked for the Secret Service were human. They had to rein in their emotions like everyone else during working hours.

"I'm not that old." She hid a nervous smile.

His hand raced over the top of his perfectly styled black hair. "Stacey wants to see you happy. Me, too. Sorry to pry."

"Thank you, but I'll be fine. I promise." She turned back toward the direction of the presidential suite and regretted it because now she had to focus on what was about to go down —a meeting with the Bennetts.

The second Knox or his father set eyes on her she'd have to stand her ground and demand she remain on the assignment. But her nerves were getting to her at the thought, and her heart rate inched higher.

"You okay?" Rodriguez was near the door, but at the sight of her glued in place, he strode back her way.

Maybe there was a way for her to stay without a one-punch knockout from the Bennetts at her presence. "A few of us are assigned to work the investigation. Can I do it? I have the most experience in that area. It makes sense."

"I thought protection is what you wanted. Didn't you practically beg me for the chance if it ever arose?" Rodriguez cocked his head. "I put in a good word for you, Foster. There are a few bigwigs from Homeland here, and we really can't screw this up."

There's a lot more on the line than looking good at our jobs, but . . . "Yeah, of course." Her gaze lifted as the Bennetts' door opened ten feet away.

Knox was there, and he was blinking as if seeing a mirage.

The man was tall. Six-two. Muscular but lean. Handsome as ever. Even more so with age. The kind of sexy everyone seemed to notice but himself. In her opinion, one of the most appealing traits in a man was a good-looking guy who didn't seem to know it.

He checked off all her boxes, even ones she didn't know she had until him.

Knox stepped aside as another man exited the suite. And now Knox was looking somewhere other than at her.

Shit. He'd spotted Calloway. The two men had met in the spring when Knox had crashed her date. She'd been on date five with him that night. She had an eight dates before sex rule. Well, eight didn't guarantee sex, but she refused to have it any sooner than that.

But when Knox had shown up that night, she'd actually thought he'd finally admit he wanted to be her date instead. A real date. Not a friendly one.

But she'd been dreaming. Living in her head. The part of her that still believed in fairy tales and happily-ever-afters.

Of course, who was she kidding? She still believed in happily-ever-afters, even now with Knox's eyes dead set on her.

"I'm FBI Director Mendez." The man who'd exited the suite a few moments ago pulled her attention his way and back on her job where it needed to be.

But her heart continued its intense climb with Knox so close.

"Good to see you made it," Mendez added. "We're about to head to the office to interview some possible witnesses."

Rodriguez shook the director's hand and then introduced the rest of the team.

"Glad to have you here." Mendez added a phony smile. The director was a lousy liar, and she had the distinct impression he was anything but glad they'd joined the case. "Let's have you meet the Bennetts, and then I assume you'll want to assign some of your people to the investigation? They can come with us."

"Sounds good." Rodriguez followed Mendez, but Adriana remained stuck in place.

Knox wasn't moving either. His eyes were pinned to her. His jaw set in a hard line. A noticeable clench there. On second thought, maybe she should get him and Calloway together and divert Knox's energy away from her.

Because.

He.

Was.

Pissed.

"Can we have a minute?" She peered at Rodriguez with a plea in her eyes. Her puppy dog eyes, as Knox liked to call them.

"*One* minute," he said before heading into the suite.

Knox didn't waste a second once they were alone. He lunged forward, wrapped his arms around her, and pulled her in tight for a hug. Not what she'd been anticipating.

"I thought you'd be mad," she murmured into his chest, hugging him back. Hell, she was clinging for dear life.

"I am." His warm breath tickled her ear. "But I need to hold my best friend for two seconds and hope, when I open my eyes, this shit day will have been a bad dream."

Her shoulders sagged.

This wasn't just a case.

This was Knox. Her go-to on the bad days and the good.

"I'm so sorry," she whispered with regret.

His big hands moved up to grasp her shoulders, and he

held her slightly away from his body, his eyes running over every inch of her. "How are you? Are you okay?"

Of course he'd worry about her, too, even though this day should have been strictly about his parents, his family.

But he knew her well. Each time she'd closed her eyes during the flight from D.C. to Charlotte, the painful image of the coroner covering her mother's lifeless body appeared in her mind.

"I'm fine." And she had to be. "How are *you*?" she asked when he palmed her cheek as if he were relieved to see her alive, and she'd been the one to nearly take a bullet.

"I feel better knowing my people are here and looking into things. But you appearing out of nowhere," he said with a shake of the head, "and finding out you're on the case . . . well, it's like getting hit in the nuts with a baseball."

"You don't play baseball." Okay, so humor probably wasn't appropriate right now, but she needed to take some of the edge off the shock of her presence.

"Okay, a basketball." He shifted farther away and observed her again, allowing his hand to fall to his side. "You don't actually think you're going to stand in front of a bullet for my dad, do you?"

"You know it's a myth. We never actually sign our names in blood and promise to die for POTUS."

"It's an unspoken rule." He crossed his arms, offering her his "don't mess with me, you won't win" look. "Does your boss know your connection to my family?"

She needed to zip up her emotions and store them in one of those mess-free leak-proof containers if she was going to get through this night unscathed.

"Rodriguez knows, and I had nothing to do with my being here."

His brows pulled together. "Oh, mustache-guy. Yeah, I

recognize him now. His girlfriend makes you all that delicious food you're always going on and on about." His smile was equivalent to a dozen pillowy-soft arrows, with heart-shaped tips, plunging into her chest.

But his smile was brief. So brief, she barely had time to enjoy the moment.

"If you get hurt, or worse, because of my dad, what do you think that'll do to me?" There was a crack in his voice. A deep drop where his words descended briefly into the abyss of fear as he'd spoken them.

She tried to hide the unexpected wobble in her bottom lip as her resolve massively failed, exposing her emotions for him to see. "And how do you think I feel every time you go on one of those mysterious jobs of yours?" *And why do you have to keep that part of yourself from me?*

His warm brown eyes remained connected with hers. His pupils constricted. More emotion stirred, a reflection of her own.

"Please support me," she said when he refused to speak. "When I go into that room, I need you to have my back. I already know your dad will object to having a woman protect him, especially when that woman happens to be me."

The door behind her opened, and Rodriguez called out, "Your minute is up, Foster."

"Coming." The word came out like a choked whisper. Her throat scratchy and worn from fighting back a million things she wanted to say to Knox. An epic battle that had seemed to rage with new life over the past few months.

She reached for his arm when the door shut.

He stared at her hand. No eye contact.

And when he didn't respond and pulled his arm free of her grasp, her heart could've fractured into a million pieces, but she refused to let it. Because Knox would be there to pick the pieces up. Because he was always there for her. And the last thing she wanted was to add more to his plate. He didn't deserve it.

He slipped inside his father's suite, and she took a minute before she followed.

"Everything okay?" Rodriguez asked once she was inside, concern in his eyes as both friend and boss.

"Yeah, I'm good. What's the situation?" They moved farther into the suite, and she put her game face back on.

"Making the introductions." Rodriguez motioned her down the hall and into the living area. The place was more like an apartment than a hotel.

Isaiah Bennett's eyes widened, and he rose from the couch in the spacious room and loosened the knot of his tie at the sight of Adriana. He was a little shorter than Knox. A touch stockier, too. But he had the same eyes and killer smile as his son.

"Adriana?" A gasp left Kathleen Bennett as she stood alongside her husband.

Kathleen was blonde and blue-eyed. Tall. Gorgeous. But not in a way that screamed look-at-me. Subtle. Sophisticated. She always had this look in her eyes, too—like she could get a read on a person within seconds.

She'd met both Isaiah and Kathleen the same night she'd met Knox. He'd called his parents after driving her to the crime scene as if he'd hoped his senator father could bring her mom back to life.

"You're assigned to protect us?" Kathleen's gaze raked over the length of Adriana before she crossed the room to get to her.

"Yes." The second the word was out of her mouth, Kathleen hugged her.

It wasn't the warm type of hug her mom had given her as

a kid, but Adriana was sure it was as motherly as Kathleen knew how to be.

"Are you okay?" Adriana asked once Kathleen had let go of her, doing her best to avoid the curious eyes of her coworkers.

"I think I'm still in shock." Kathleen's eyes moved to Knox then back to Adriana as if worried about a potential battle of the sexes over her presence as their Secret Service.

Yeah, me, too. She focused on Isaiah. "Sir."

"You're not stepping in front of a bullet for me, Adriana," he announced right off the bat.

Like father like son.

"After what happened to your mother, I have no clue what possessed you to join the agency." Isaiah's commanding voice captured the room. She felt all eyes ping back and forth between the presidential candidate and herself. And that's how she had to think of him from now on, or she wouldn't be able to separate emotion from the job.

"I'm here because of my mom. She sacrificed her life to protect others, and that's what I'm doing. She's my—"

"I won't let you sacrifice yourself for me," he interrupted, his voice louder now. "Charlie, say something!"

His dad still called him by his given name, and maybe that was why he clung to his nickname so fiercely over the years.

"A woman is fully capable of protecting a man," Kathleen said, to Adriana's surprise. "Don't you dare say otherwise." She peered at Knox next. "Either of you."

Knox frowned and kept quiet.

"I can reassign Foster to work the investigation. We'll be coordinating with DHS and the FBI to find the shooter," Rodriguez noted.

"We're about to head to the office now," Knox said.

Was this a white flag? His way of saying he wouldn't be a roadblock?

"The president authorized him to be part of the investigation," Mendez said as if reading the what-the-F look now on Rodriguez's face.

"Why?" Rodriguez turned toward Knox.

"The 'why' doesn't matter," Knox said. "I'm going to help out. So, if we're done with introductions, we should get a move on it." He slipped his hand into his pocket, grabbed his phone, and left the room without saying another word.

"Are you sure this is what you really want?" Isaiah asked her.

"More than anything."

He braced her shoulders. "Do me a favor then, keep an eye on my son."

If he'll let me. But she smiled and murmured, "Always."

CHAPTER SIX

Adriana leaned against the side of her Tahoe as Knox locked his Suburban. They'd taken separate vehicles to the FBI office. It was already eleven at night, so she wasn't sure how much they'd accomplish, but they couldn't exactly sleep with a shooter out there.

"Why aren't your friends here? Don't you always travel in a pack?" Her lips teased into a grin, and his mouth tipped into a smile at her words.

"We're not wolves." He looked heavenward. "I don't see the moon right now, but I doubt it's a full one." He winked. "Anyway, the boys are back at the hotel for now. More coming tomorrow." He tucked his keys into his pocket and positioned himself in front of her. So close a hint of his cologne mingled with the night air and touched her nose. An aquatic scent. Probably Nautica, his go-to in the summer.

"And why are you waiting for me when the rest of your people are in the building?" He cocked his head, the smile still resting on his face like he could keep it there forever for her.

"You're a slow driver. Someone had to wait for you." She

pushed away from her ride, but he didn't step back at the proximity.

"Funny."

They needed to go inside. To do anything other than stand face-to-face in the parking lot as her thoughts about his so-called "other life" begged to slip free.

She'd managed to keep the questions mostly at bay for years, but if they were going to work together, she was now part of that world he'd kept from her. She needed to know if he'd let her in or try and keep her on the sidelines out of some moral gotta-protect-you code of his. She didn't want it to be business as usual. Not now. Not with his father's life on the line. A shooter on the loose in the Queen City.

"Is this going to be a problem? Us working together?"

"Of course," he rushed out, which wasn't what she wanted to hear.

"I don't mean because of your crazy need to keep me safe." She had to stand her ground. "Because your friends are here, and you finally brought us together, and I'm worried about how this whole us-working-together thing might go. I still don't even know why the hell you've kept them from me, but—"

"We're scattered all over the place, and it was the first time we were all together for a non-work-related purpose." He reached over her shoulder and propped a hand on the Tahoe, which forced her to shift a step back, so her body was flush with the SUV once again.

"Don't lie." It hurt too much. Maybe that's why she'd never asked him. She didn't want to force him to lie to her, and for some reason, she knew he'd have to. "Parties. Weddings. You guys have all hung out socially before." She'd heard about it from some of the guys' wives at the barbecue last weekend when she'd met everyone.

"Only Teamguys and their families have ever gone to any of those events."

"I'm not family?" Maybe she'd rather him lie. Those words were like a cold bucket of water over her head on an already freezing day.

"I didn't mean it like that. You're everything to me, and you know that."

Everything as long as they remained in the tight world they'd created. Their safe haven. But were they playing make-believe all that time by ignoring the very real fact he had a whole other life he kept from her?

"Before there became an Emily and Liam, she was still included." She had ammunition to use in her defense now that she'd met some of the wives. Using it didn't make her feel any better, though. Worse, maybe.

He shoved away from the vehicle. "Why'd they tell you this?"

"They didn't," she admitted. "I overheard them talking. They were wondering why I hadn't ever come to a get-together before."

"Jesus. I'm sorry." There was more he wanted to say. She could see it. Feel it. Even read between the lines. But would he say it?

"I'm not upset about that." It had more to do with the fact she'd felt left out from whatever truth the spouses all seemed to know. "They were curious, and they couldn't exactly ask me." She wet her lips. "I should've brought this up right after the barbecue and not now of all times." God, she was going to tell him what was on her mind tonight of all nights, wasn't she? "You've been keeping this whole other life from me, and I . . ."

He stepped closer and seized her face with both palms as

if he were going to whisper sweet words of love and affection. But he simply stared at her.

"What is it?" she whispered.

"Addy." His eyes closed when he said, "Maybe I kept you away from them because I wanted you all to myself." He took a breath, and his lids lifted. "When I'm with you, there's *this* me. And when I'm with them, there's *that* me. And I—"

"There only has to be one you," she protested, wishing he understood he had nothing to hide from her. "You don't have to be someone else when you're with me. How can you not get that?"

She understood he compartmentalized when he was in the Navy, but he was a civilian now. His job at Scott & Scott wasn't as dangerous. It didn't make sense. It never did. And yet, she'd refused to try and understand out of some ridiculous fear she'd somehow lose him.

He lost his hold of her to turn his back.

Shoulders sloped down. Defeat she rarely saw in the lines of his body.

"We don't need to talk about this now. I'm sorry. As long as we're on the same page about the case—"

"We are," he responded.

"So, are you and the president friends? How'd you even get assigned to the case?" She'd meant it as a joke, but when he faced her, there was something in the tight draw of his lips, the narrowing of his gaze, that told her it was true.

She jogged through her memories, pausing at the night he'd announced he was leaving the Navy. He'd said Luke had an in with the president and could help get him out of the SEALs early.

"My office has access to some technology even the bureau doesn't have, and we'll be able to help," he explained, his voice even-toned, but it was as if he were fighting to keep it that way.

"What kind of tech could you have that the Secret Service doesn't?" she asked, knowing she was taking the bait to guide her away from whatever truth he couldn't seem to share with her.

Calloway's head poked out the front door, and he waved them in. "You two coming or what?"

Great.

"Do I really need to work with him?" Knox seized the opportunity to shift the conversation. The man had skills when it came to the art of deflection.

She held a finger up Calloway's way. "One sec!" She faced Knox once Calloway shut the door. "He's not that bad."

"He only wanted to date you to get into your pants. You and I both know it."

"At least he tried."

"What?"

Damn it. "Nothing."

She flipped her eyes to the sky in search of her star. The star Knox had pointed to the night her mother had died and said, *"She's there. Already watching over you."*

"Maybe I can't work with you. You might be a distraction," she admitted when her eyes returned to his. *You already are, and I just got here.*

"Since when am I a distraction for you?"

"Since when are you not?" She turned and started for the building, regretting she'd even waited for him.

When she pulled open the door, she realized Knox hadn't followed her.

His phone was pressed to his ear, and he was leaning against the side of her SUV.

"She's taken," he'd said, almost immediately when

introducing her to his work buddies at the barbecue last weekend. He didn't want her, but he didn't seem to want her with anyone else, either.

"Don't say a word," she said to Calloway once she was inside the building. He'd been the only one who'd stayed back and waited for her, and he'd probably observed her exchange with Knox through the window. *Lovely.* "We're only friends," she said after they'd gone through security.

"Sure, and I'm a priest."

"You'd look good in the robes," she teased as they waited for the elevator doors to open.

"Priesthood would never work for me."

She didn't need to hear more to read between the lines of what he was trying to say. She kept her mouth shut on the ride up, replaying her conversation with Knox.

His parents had almost taken a bullet today, and she needed to focus on catching the shooter.

Rodriguez spotted them after they exited the elevator, and he flicked his wrist, beckoning them.

They navigated through the maze of desks and agents still working. From what she could tell, most of the so-called bigwigs Rodriguez had been worried about weren't there, though. Probably already asleep.

"This is Special Agent Quinn," Rodriguez made the introduction when she reached him. About the same age as Adriana. Same pantsuit and tight ponytail as well.

"Hi." Adriana shook her hand. It was nice to see another woman on the case.

"Thanks for coming," Quinn said. "If you two could take a look at all of the latest threats the Bennetts have received that'd help us out."

"Didn't his bodyguards check those out before the rally today?" Calloway asked.

"Yeah, but maybe they missed something," Quinn answered and motioned for them to follow her into a conference room.

"Any leads on Sarah Reardon?" Knox's deep, husky voice from behind had the hairs on the back of her neck rising.

"Ah, you again," Quinn said, facing him, a smile in her eyes. "Where are your friends? Hopefully not getting into any trouble."

"They wouldn't dream of it." Knox flashed his dazzling smile, his white teeth showing. Dimples popping. His mood now different from the parking lot. Probably an act.

"And who is Sarah?" She hated that Knox knew more about the case than she did.

Quinn grabbed a remote off the conference table where a few other agents sat, working on laptops. She pointed at the image on the screen on the far side wall. "Sarah Reardon. Twenty-six. From Kansas City, Missouri. She arrived into Charlotte Douglas at three in the afternoon yesterday. She flew business class. No one matching our shooter's height or build anywhere around her seat on the plane. And according to her Uber driver, she rode to the hotel alone. She was here for a work conference."

Director Mendez filled everyone in on what had been learned about the gunman, the eleventh floor, and how the agency now believed Sarah's life was in danger.

"We've uploaded Sarah's image into our facial recognition program to identify where she may have visited recently. With any luck, we'll get a hit on where she is now, too," Quinn said.

But based on the grim tone of her voice, it was clear Quinn assumed Sarah was most likely dead.

"Any hits on her credit cards?" Adriana asked.

"Dinner at the hotel bar last night," Quinn responded. "That's it. Nothing since."

"What about those other two rooms on either side? When you spoke to the couples—what'd they say?" Knox asked. "They hear anything abnormal coming from Sarah's room?"

"They didn't hear anything other than the screams from outside after the first and second shots. And then the alarm went off and they panicked," Quinn answered. "We showed them a picture of Sarah. The daughter from the neighboring room remembered seeing Sarah outside her door with a man last night, though. But she said he was only saying goodbye, and he didn't go inside. But she's also ten, and she couldn't give us much to work with. She said the guy had short hair. Blond. Maybe brown. About the same height as her dad, which is five-ten. The girl had been at the vending machine, and she saw them when she went back to her room."

"Well, like you said, she's ten, so, I won't hold my breath," Calloway said.

"Don't discredit a ten-year-old," Knox was quick to respond, and his words made her think of Emily and Liam's nine-year-old daughter. "He could be our shooter, which means he made a soft approach last night. Maybe made himself known to her."

"Then made his move today," Mendez said.

Knox nodded. "What can I do to help?"

"How about you work the threats with Calloway and Foster?" Mendez suggested.

Of course.

Knox glanced at Calloway and then at Adriana. "Sure."

Mendez motioned for them to leave the office and step into a room two doors down.

She removed her blazer and tossed it onto the couch alongside the round eight-seater table.

"The first stack contains threats deemed the most critical. They were checked out by Bennett's team prior to the rally," Mendez explained. "The other stacks are the ones they deemed non-critical."

"That's a lot of threats," Calloway commented.

"Any handwritten correspondence? The Secret Service works with pen manufacturers to embed ink tags into pens to help ID—"

"We handed those off to Rodriguez when he came up before you arrived. He's got someone on that," Mendez answered.

"Okay. Good." She smiled.

"I'll go make us some coffee," Calloway said and followed Mendez out of the room.

Knox pressed both palms to his cheeks and slowly dragged them down his face. "This should be fun."

"You sure you want to do this?" It couldn't be easy reading anonymous comments from people who hated his family, even a dad he wasn't all that close to.

"We gotta find the gunman. Hopefully, Sarah's still alive."

"You don't believe that, do you? Why would he let Sarah live unless maybe he's keeping her as an insurance plan?" She hated saying it aloud, but it was the truth. The horrible truth.

He dropped into a seat at the table and clutched the chair arms. "No, you're right. I don't believe she's still alive." His lids lowered. "But it sucks. I don't want someone to die because of my dad's political ambitions."

"You can't look at it that way." She slid into the chair across the table from him. "But we'll find whoever did this. We'll get justice for Sarah." She pulled a stack closer and began reading over the papers. "Your dad always get threats like this?" she asked a few seconds later.

"When my dad first became a senator, not everyone was happy about it. We dealt with a lot of bullshit."

"Why didn't you ever tell me?" Was there even more he'd been keeping from her over the years?

"Why would I? It was an ugliness I didn't feel like sharing."

"But this is me—"

"Pity," Knox snapped out. "I didn't want it from you."

Was he kidding? Pity. She knew a thing or two about that being the kid of a mom who was shot and killed. She'd struggled to even touch candy for months because her mom had been buying it for her moments before she'd died. "I'm not—"

"You are." He softly sighed. "Besides, we met my senior year in high school. Dad got elected when I was thirteen. Threats had become so normal, at that point, I probably didn't even think about it anymore."

She'd been a sophomore when they'd met. He'd been this shining light—this popular basketball all-star.

She hadn't thought he'd noticed her, but one party changed everything.

Her fingers feathered lightly over the inside of her right wrist—to her one tattoo.

His brown eyes, flecked with gold, snatched her focus and held on tight. Sitting across the table, he held her captive at that moment.

Time encapsulated them, and they were no longer in the room, but back at the party the night they first met. To the night they shared their only kiss.

She took a steadying breath and blinked back to the

present. Knox still held her eyes, the same look on his face he'd given her that night when she was fifteen.

But that was the problem, wasn't it? Most days, he still saw her as that girl—someone he had to protect.

"I lied back then," she said as if he'd been walking down memory lane along with her and could follow her line of thought.

"Lied about what?"

"When I told you the night we met that I had experience." Heat touched her neck and worked north. "I hadn't even kissed a boy."

He arched a brow as if waiting for her to continue.

"You were my first kiss." The admission felt good after keeping it from him for going on twenty years. Guess she had a few secrets, too.

"I know." He smiled, and the tightness he'd been holding in his face dissolved.

"You could tell? Was it that bad?" The warmth of embarrassment heated her skin.

He leaned back in his seat and let go of the paper he'd been holding. "Of course not."

"So?"

"Remember when we went camping the summer after my sophomore year at Duke? We were fairly shit-faced, and you admitted it to me."

"I would've remembered that." She hadn't been that drunk, had she? She remembered wanting him that night, though.

"Well, you said it." His pupils absorbed some of the brown of his eyes, and it had her skin pebbling.

"I, uh, don't know why I brought up the kiss." *Or anything else tonight for that matter.* She closed her eyes, heat still in her face—hell, everywhere. A warmth in places there shouldn't have been, especially not now.

"Did you know I used to walk out of my way to get to my seventh-period class so I could catch a glimpse of you at your locker?"

Her palms slipped beneath the table to her lap. "What?"

"You'd transferred a week after school started—the designated new girl—and there was something about you. I was drawn to you. I tried to stay away from you, but then at the party after seeing you drop that idiot to the ground who came on to you, I couldn't help myself."

Maybe Knox was wrong earlier, and there was indeed a full moon tonight. "Yeah, I was a kid on scholarship." *Attending a school for the richer-than-rich.* "I didn't fit in."

Calloway strolled into the room, balancing three cups of coffee between his hands, killing the moment. "Ready to get started?"

Story of her life when it came to Knox. Fate had done everything in its power to prevent her from crossing the friendship line every time an opportunity arose.

Knox took the coffee Calloway extended and tipped his head in thanks. Things were less awkward between them than she'd anticipated, which was good. Knox didn't see Calloway as a threat to her safety, which meant he probably didn't really see Calloway at all.

Knox shifted his focus back to the threats in front of him. He'd hit the reset button. She needed to as well.

"What's your father's story, anyway?" Calloway asked thirty minutes later.

"You don't know my background? What kind of agent are you?" Knox asked in a light, semi-playful voice. Another surprise. Had Calloway spiked his coffee?

Calloway knew Knox's background. It was their job to

know. So, he was either making small talk or fishing for the kind of info an agent wouldn't find in a file.

"Well." Knox shifted a few papers off to the side into the elimination pile. "My dad served in the military, met my mom in D.C. while she was working for the State Department, and then after he got out of the service, he inherited some money." He scratched at his neck. "He invested in a few early dot com start-ups. The nineties and the Internet . . . got lucky. He later decided to serve his country again, but this time in politics."

"How'd your mom feel about him first running for senator?" Calloway asked.

"My dad was going to run for office when I was younger. Nine, maybe? My mom was against it." He gripped the chair arms, clearly not comfortable about digging into his past. "Couple of years later he ran for senator, anyway. I guess she decided to support him."

"And you never liked the life, I take it? Is that why you quit med school and joined the Navy?" Calloway asked.

Knox straightened in his seat. "I needed to do something different, and I'm not a fan of politicians."

"Including your dad?" Calloway probed.

"Are you trying to assess whether I'm a threat? Because I have a pretty solid alibi for the time of the shooting."

"Just curious. Maybe I'm on the fence as to who to vote for. I like the VP Leslie Renaldo on the other ticket. Not so sure about the guy running, though. Kind of douche-y." Calloway lifted his shoulders in a half shrug. "But your dad's pretty moderate. It's hard to figure out what side he's truly on."

"Let's hope he's on the *people's* side."

Was Knox now defending his dad? She wasn't sure if she'd ever witnessed that before. What changed?

He dropped his focus back to the threats and Calloway followed suit.

"Man," Calloway said with a shake of his head a few minutes later. "So many of these threats are—"

"Racist?" Knox's lips rolled inward, and his face tightened. His dimples exposed and not from a smile. A slight twitch to his jaw.

"What was it like growing up? A Black dad and white mom?" Calloway asked.

She shot Calloway a look out of the corner of her eye.

He didn't give Knox a chance to answer. "My mom's family is Japanese, and my dad's about as Irish as they come. It wasn't always easy growing up. Kids would—"

"Look at you differently?" Knox found his eyes.

Calloway nodded and flattened his forearms to the table and let go of the papers he'd been holding. "And did you hate those standardized tests as much as I did growing up—when you had to choose one of those boxes? It felt like I had to pick a side. If I chose white, was I offending my mom? Choose Asian, and how would my dad feel?"

"They've been adding an 'other' box to some forms," Knox said. "I don't know what the hell that's supposed to mean, though."

"Right?" Calloway shoved back in his seat.

And . . . were Knox and Calloway getting along? Knox visibly relaxed, and he and Calloway continued their conversation, making her wonder if she'd stepped into a parallel universe.

But when he glanced her way a few seconds later, he tensed up again. What was that about?

"I, uh, need some air, if you don't mind." Knox stood and left the room without another word.

"Shit, did I piss him off?" Calloway looked genuinely

concerned. "I was actually trying to be nice even though he blew my chances with you this year."

"He didn't . . ." Okay, so maybe he did, but Knox had been right. Dating a coworker was a horrible idea. "He's fine, but I'll be right back."

Knox was standing in the hall, facing the elevator when she found him. "I'm okay, really," he said, spotting her in the reflection of the steel doors. "It's been a crazy day, but I'm solid."

"I know, but since I'm here, maybe talk to me?" She reached for his bicep, not caring who saw her.

He glanced over his shoulder. "I still need that, uh, air, I was talking about."

She retracted her hand when the doors parted, and they stepped inside. "Why don't you go back to the hotel and be with your family?"

"I can't relax with what happened today." He propped a palm on the interior elevator wall off to his right. "And with you here, I'm a little wired. And your ex is in the room, and I was suddenly getting along with him, which is crazy."

Yeah, he wasn't acting normal, that was for sure. But she wasn't her typical self, either.

"He's not my ex. We went on a few dates. He didn't make it past second base." *Because of you.*

"I don't know what that means, and I don't want to know."

"You're handling today way better than most." She needed to get this conversation going in the right direction. "Not only were your parents shot at, but you've had to come back to a life you did your best to leave behind."

"And was I a dick to do that?" A slight grunt touched her ears. "Was I an ass to walk away from them for so long?" His arm fell hard to his side. "The way my mom and dad have been looking at me. And—"

"They're happy to see you, but you don't owe them anything. You made your choice. And they made theirs when they chose not to support you."

She wasn't opposed to his change of heart, but it was surprising. The last time he forced her to go to dinner with his parents, he'd said he'd rather have her hit him in the face with a two-by-four and swim with the sharks after. And the guy was terrified of sharks, even the ones in the aquarium in Atlanta.

"I'm not making things any easier for you by being here," she spoke her thoughts in case he needed to hear them, too. She reached out and fixed the collar of his button-down shirt. "But you're my hero, you know that?"

He brought his hand beneath her chin, and he held her eyes. The overhead lights bounced off his pupils, making them gleam.

"You know how they say, *Be the change you want the world to see*, or something along those lines?" she asked. "That's how you make me feel. You inspire me. Make me strive to be better." She ignored the ding of the elevator doors opening. "I didn't just join the agency because my mom had wanted to be an agent, I joined because I wanted to do something with my life—watching you go for it made me believe I could do it, too."

"I'm one of the reasons why you chose this dangerous job?" His voice was low. Dark. Haunted. Guilt clung to every syllable of every word.

"Why is your focus always on protecting me?"

He stepped forward, and her back hit the panel of buttons at his movement, and the doors closed. His palm went to the wall over her shoulder, and his eyes jumped to her face, a fierce intensity there.

"Because you're the kind of person a man risks everything for." He brushed his thumb over her bottom lip, tugging it down. His eyes moved to her lips.

Kiss me. It'd be crazy. Totally insane. But also perfect.

"Sorry," he whispered, a knife to the heart. His brows slanted as he stepped away as if realizing he had her in a caged position.

"I, uh, need that air. Maybe alone, too."

Her throat squeezed as emotion trekked up. "Yeah, okay." She turned and pressed the *open* button so the doors would part again.

"Are you sure you want me to leave?"

"I think that'd be best."

CHAPTER SEVEN

"BROUGHT YOU SOME DONUTS AND COFFEE." KNOX SNAPPED his gaze up from the paper he'd been holding to see A.J. in the doorway.

"Thanks, man." He let the paper fall from his hand, and he reached out, grateful for the liquid fuel.

He and Adriana had stayed in the FBI conference room working all night, but he'd forced her to sleep on the couch off to the side of the table, since she'd refused to leave when Calloway had at three in the morning.

"Jessica learn anything from viewing the CCTV footage around the hotel after the shooting?"

A.J. glimpsed Adriana asleep off to his left and lowered his voice when he replied, "Nothing new on our end, and you know that's pissing off mama bear."

"Mama bear?" He smirked.

"Jess is gonna be a parent soon. You know how protective she is of us now—I guarantee she sharpens her claws even more once she's a mom."

"I feel bad that Jessica is working this case while pregnant."

"Nothing will stop her from working. She'll probably wear the baby on her back after the kid is born," he said in all seriousness.

"Not if Asher can help it. He'll build a nuclear bunker and keep his kid inside."

"Yeah, that man as a dad—gonna be interesting."

A.J. set the box of donuts on the table. "This whole working with the Feds thing makes me nervous, though." He munched on a glazed donut. "We're in their house, brother. I don't like it."

Yeah, well, they'd had some rough patches in the past with agencies, so he didn't blame him. But they didn't exactly have a choice but to play ball. This was the Feds' operation, and they were merely guests.

He took his first sip of coffee and grimaced. "You dump a gallon of sugar in here?"

"I know you like it sweet."

"Not *that* sweet." He tossed the cup in the nearest trash bin and snatched a donut, opting for something that was supposed to be ridiculously sugary. "Anyway, we know our gunman met Sarah the night before since he walked her to her room. We got her leaving the bar with a guy, but he must've known where the cameras were because we couldn't pull any clear image of him."

"Why not go into her room that night?"

"And risk leaving DNA behind?" He kept his voice soft to avoid waking Adriana.

A.J. nodded. "Right."

"So, he probably invited her to breakfast or something the next day, and after, he went to her room and subdued her."

"Then the shooter leaves her room, and ten minutes later, we have him on camera coming back down the hall with his bag this time. Then it's cameras out and gunshots fired.

Tricky bastard," A.J. said. "Well, Jessica, Asher, and Luke should arrive around four today. I'll feel better once they're here, and the Feds don't outnumber us so much."

"Any word from Owen?" He hated being without Bravo Two, but the man was about to have a baby.

"Liam talked to Emily on our way here. She said Sam's having contractions, so they'll be heading to the hospital soon."

"Good. And when does the rest of the team get to New York?"

"They should land within the hour." A.J. glanced at Adriana. "Wonder Woman," he said with a wink.

"Don't start, brother." He was already messed up in the head about her as it was, and he didn't need Echo Two adding fuel to the rapidly burning fire.

"How do you guys look like you do and eat that garbage?" Adriana spoke in a sleepy, slightly raspy voice as she sat up.

A.J. carried the donut box to where she sat. "Does that mean you don't want one?" He playfully opened and closed the box a few times.

She held out her palm. "Yes, please."

"Why don't you let me take over so you can get cleaned up," A.J. suggested as Adriana finished her patriotic donut covered in red, white, and blue sprinkles.

Knox lifted his arm and took a whiff. "What, do I smell?"

"I could smell you from outside." A.J. set the donut box back down.

"You bring me any clothes?"

"Of course, Sunshine," A.J. joked. "Wyatt and Liam stopped to talk to Mendez. They have your stuff. My hands were full with breakfast."

"A shower's not such a bad idea." Adriana stood. "There

99

are lockers here. I brought some stuff. I might go freshen up. You want to join me?"

Knox looked at A.J. "Don't say a word."

A.J. help up a palm. "I wouldn't dream of it. Now, you two enjoy that shower of yours."

"Is he always like this?" she asked after they left the room.

"Pretty much," he said while catching Wyatt's eyes as they'd walked toward him and Liam, who were already on approach.

"You look like shit." Wyatt tossed Knox the duffel bag.

"Yeah, well, you would, too. We're gonna hit the showers. We'll meet you back in the conference room. A.J.'s about to saddle up and start working."

"And how are you?" Liam asked, his eyes on Adriana off to Knox's right.

"As good as I can be," she answered, her voice still sleepy. Entirely too sexy.

"We'll be right back," Knox said, and they headed for the elevators so they could use the gym showers in the basement.

"Addy?" He clutched the bag handle tightly with one hand once they were alone in the elevator, and he kept his eyes on her face. There was something he had to ask her— it'd been on his mind since her arrival last night. "If my father becomes president, is there a chance you could get assigned to his detail?"

"Probably not anytime soon. Need more years on the job."

"Well, I don't know the protocol, but I'm assuming Secret Service can't hang out with the son of the president."

"I didn't think about that," she whispered, her eyes casting to the floor.

Yeah, well, he had.

The idea had rolled around in his mind nonstop.

If his dad was elected, he might be able to save Bravo and Echo, but by saving the teams, would he risk losing his best friend?

* * *

Post shower and an hour later, Mendez entered the conference room where he, Adriana, and the guys had been working and snapped out, "We may have found our guy. I'm assembling a team to pick him up for questioning."

"What?" Knox stood, his knuckles falling to the table in front of him for support.

"One of the threats we handed to your team this morning?" Adriana asked, swiveling in her chair to face the director, and he nodded. "You track an IP address?"

Most of the emails had been anonymous, so they'd had the Feds trace the source of the emails Knox and Adriana had deemed the most critical.

"Yeah. One email stood out. It came from Aaron Todd. He's a former sniper for the SEALs." Mendez's eyes left Adriana and crossed the length of the table to where Liam, Wyatt, and A.J. sat, before falling upon Knox. "He lives in Matthews, a suburb outside the city. That email you gave us was sent yesterday morning while Bennett was already en route to the rally. Probably why it got overlooked."

Knox turned toward the window behind him and placed a palm on the glass, his stomach dropping to the first floor.

Mendez cleared his throat. "Do one of you know him?"

"We were at BUD/S together." A.J.'s words were low and heavy like the man had lost a best friend. Knox whirled around to find him tearing his fingers through his brownish-blond hair. "He'd never do this."

"He matches the description of our mystery guy, too. Same height and build," Mendez noted.

"Sounds like a lot of guys I know," Wyatt said, a defensive edge to his tone.

Aaron Todd was one of them. A Teamguy. This couldn't be happening.

Liam stood next to Knox. "Doesn't mean it's Aaron."

"Which email was it?" They'd given Mendez's team ten earlier.

Mendez handed him the printed-off email, and he read it before giving it to A.J.

"I don't believe this," A.J. insisted. "Aaron wouldn't write this. He wouldn't put down our military like this."

"He thinks Bennett will put more boots on the ground in the Middle East." Mendez took the paper back. "And he claims he'll do anything to stop that from happening."

No damn way. "He's being framed."

"Just because he's a Teamguy doesn't make him innocent," Mendez pointed out.

"Or guilty," Liam bit back, coming around the table at a quick pace to stand before the director.

"If Aaron was the shooter, he wouldn't miss," A.J. said, grit to his voice. "He's a damn fine sniper."

"And you all said it was an impossible shot," Mendez reminded them.

"Yeah, for someone without Special Forces training and from the tenth floor," Liam returned. "Don't mistake my words."

Knox glanced at Adriana, checking her reaction to all of this. She was the only one still seated at the table. Her eyes were positioned on the window as if she couldn't handle making eye contact with him.

Did that mean she thought Aaron was guilty?

His parents had been shot at. Adriana was assigned to his father's detail. He'd nearly told her every ounce of truth he'd been keeping from her in that damn parking lot last night, too. And then he'd almost kissed her in the elevator.

He was losing his mind.

And now this?

There was only so much a person could take before the ground swallowed a man whole.

But Knox was a Teamguy. He didn't fucking surrender.

But like hell did Aaron try and shoot his parents. He was with A.J. on this.

"Well, we'll see what he has to say for himself." Mendez snapped his fingers in Adriana's direction, a request for her to stand and get a move on it.

"Let me come." A.J. stepped forward alongside Liam. "He knows me. You all might scare him off."

"Innocent people don't run, right?" Mendez countered.

"Won't NCIS join the investigation with Aaron in the mix?" Adriana finally stood, and he wanted to go to her. To be at her side. But he didn't move. He couldn't seem to get his body to do a damn thing right now.

"They'll send someone, yeah," Mendez replied. "Well, you coming, Foster, or what?"

"No." His feet were sure as hell working now. Knox moved to her side, prepared to block her path to the door if needed. "Rodriguez doesn't want her on the front lines. He promised my father."

She grabbed hold of his wrist and leaned in toward him. "Let me go. I'll make sure he's brought in unharmed," she whispered.

"If you think he's dangerous—"

"Aaron's not the guy," A.J. cut off Mendez when Knox's words died in his throat.

"I've got this." Adriana's eyes pulled him in, and he had to swallow as she observed him from over her shoulder. "Trust me."

"You got your vest with you?" Mendez asked, his words like a fist to the face.

A vest meant his best friend might possibly be in the line of fire. He knew Aaron wouldn't be dangerous, but the idea of Adriana putting herself out there had his stomach twisting into so many knots, not even the best sailor on the planet could untie them.

"Please." The word rolled out hard. Not a desperate plea but a command.

"This is her job," Wyatt reminded him from behind, and he resisted the sudden urge to turn around and go head to head with Echo One. But Wyatt didn't have a woman he was willing to die for, so he didn't understand the pain Knox was feeling right now.

"I'll be fine." Adriana pivoted to face Knox and squeezed his arm before darting off with Mendez, leaving him with his teammates and his anger.

"I shouldn't have let her go." He dropped his head into his hands and turned so he didn't go after her and make a scene in front of the entire agency. And she'd kill him for that. This was a job she was proud of, one she'd worked hard for, one chosen specifically to honor the memory of her mom. He respected the hell out of her for all those reasons. Anything he did to stop her from doing her job would only hurt her.

"You have to take a step back and let her do her thing," A.J. said, agreeing with Wyatt.

Knox lowered his hands and looked at Liam, the only one of them attached. He'd understand.

Liam lifted his palms in the air. "Emily is stubborn, too.

I've had to make peace with that. Let her be who she is instead of standing in the way of that."

"For the record," Knox grumbled, "I hate you guys." He moved back to the window, but he couldn't get a good view of the parking lot. And seeing her leave would probably only make him lose his mind, even if he knew Liam was right.

He'd always stood by Adriana's decisions even when they'd scared the hell out of him. But damn it, this assignment was personal. Boundaries were tangled the fuck up.

"None of us thinks Aaron is the shooter, right?" A.J. asked, bringing Knox's focus to the other pressing issue. "I've spoken to Aaron a few times since he got out of the Navy," A.J. added, and Knox turned to give him his attention. "He's been having a hard time. The VA has him taking all kinds of meds. He asked me if he could work at Scott and Scott, but I told him he needed to get his head on straight."

Guilt clung to A.J.'s eyes. He didn't believe Aaron was the shooter, but at the same time, Knox knew he was already blaming himself for the possibility that it was true.

"What kind of meds?" Wyatt cocked his head.

"I don't know. He said he's been having nightmares. But that doesn't make him a killer."

"Of course not," Liam quickly responded, "but it's not going to help his case if someone is trying to pin this on him. People will see a vet with PTSD, and we know what they'll think."

"We have a hard enough time with people looking at us like we might snap someday." A.J. huffed. "We have to clear his name. He called me a few weeks ago and said he met someone and he didn't want to mess it up."

"We need to talk to her. Aaron give a name?" Wyatt asked, and thank God his teammates still had the presence of mind to engage in intelligent conversation because Knox's signals were jammed.

"Chelsea, maybe?" A.J. answered. "But what are the chances the Feds will find Aaron alive?"

"Why do you say that?" Knox finally found his voice. And apparently, a few brain cells when he grabbed his phone to call Jessica . . . the first smart thing he'd done all morning.

"Because how many times does the guy who gets framed for an assassination live to share his side of the story?" A.J.'s brows rose.

Frame job? Was it possible?

"Well, my dad didn't die, so if Aaron is being framed, let's hope he's still alive, too." He phoned Jessica, needing her help right the hell now. "Hey, we've got a problem," he said as soon as she answered.

"Does it have anything to do with the fact Aaron Todd's face is on the news as a potential suspect?" she asked in a soft tone.

"What? How could the media possibly know? We only found out." He looked at his brothers, trying to wrap his head around the news.

"Not sure, but I saw the alert on my phone before you called," she said.

"Shit," he hissed. "That can only mean one thing . . . there's a leak."

CHAPTER EIGHT

A DOZEN WHAT-IF SCENARIOS RACED THROUGH HER MIND AS Adriana strapped on her vest and secured the Sig P229 in her shoulder holster.

Part of her job was to assess and analyze every possible outcome and prepare solutions to all given situations.

But were Knox's buddies right? Was Aaron innocent? Possibly being set up?

The look on Knox's face when she left . . . she'd wanted to whisper *sorry* a hundred times and maybe a hundred more.

She had to focus, though. She couldn't let her personal feelings cloud her judgment or distract her.

Her team was about to infil Aaron Todd's home if he didn't peacefully surrender. She didn't want anyone getting shot because her head wasn't in the game.

The late August sun was beating down. Birds were freaking chirping. And from a nearby home, someone was playing a violin.

It was too cheery outside for a possible exchange of gunfire.

But it wasn't like God could lasso in the clouds and shoot

a thunderbolt or two overhead to set the scene. This wasn't a book or a movie. This was real life. And shit-tastic things happened on beautiful days and at beautiful moments. Like when her mom died.

"You think he'll be inside?" Calloway asked, and she averted her attention to her partner.

"If he's innocent, yes." *If.* Knox would hate her for that word, but what choice did she have? Aaron had sent the email, and unless she found out otherwise, she had a job to do.

She prepped with the multiagency team around the corner and out of sight from Aaron's home. SWAT was also there for an assist if the house needed to be breached.

"I still can't figure out who leaked his name to the media," Calloway said as he strapped on his own vest. "Not one of our guys, which means it may be FBI or DHS."

It was hard to believe anyone from the FBI or Homeland would offer up Aaron's name, though.

"Or the more obvious answer," Mendez joined the conversation while holstering his sidearm at his hip. "Knox or one of his buddies."

"No way." She bit down on her back teeth. "They'd never do that." She positioned her earpiece and tucked the coiled wire in place, the mic hidden beneath the vest.

"Unless they wanted to give Aaron a chance to make a run for it before we knocked on his door," Mendez suggested.

"How would they have time to do that? The media shared the news seconds before we left the office."

"That's enough time," Calloway said, and she wished he'd be in agreement with her on this. But in Calloway's eyes, Knox was the guy who'd ruined his chances of getting laid.

"Knox's parents were shot at," she reminded them. "He'd

never put his family in danger by letting the shooter get away."

Maybe he hadn't always been on the best of terms with his folks, but he wouldn't sacrifice their safety simply because Aaron Todd had been a SEAL.

"Teamguys are his family, too." It was as if Mendez had taken a disturbing dip inside her mind. "Until I know who leaked the name, you're not authorized to share any details of this investigation with Knox or his people. I don't care what the president wants." He stabbed a finger in the air. "Understood?"

"We got the warrant," Special Agent Quinn announced before Adriana could answer Mendez.

"Good." Mendez peered at Adriana as if he needed to check off the dominant box. They weren't in the same department, but she had to show him proper respect, even if it irritated her to be so looked down upon. It seemed the higher up people rose in their positions, the more dick-like they became. "I need to hear you say it before I let you come with us."

Calloway held a gloved palm in the air between where Mendez and Adriana stood. "She's good," he surprised her by coming in for the defense. "Foster would never risk her career, not even for a friend."

He really didn't know Knox. Or her.

Because she'd absolutely risk anything for Knox, including her life.

"Say it," Mendez demanded, refusing to back down from his ridiculous power play.

"Yes," she said, her teeth nearly clamping down on the word.

He gave her a long, hard look. Distrust in his eyes. Then

he flicked his gloved hand in the air. "Let's do this then. Get into your positions."

The different teams maneuvered down the street and into their assigned locations.

Calloway wrapped his hand over her shoulder from behind, giving her the all-clear signal to move.

With her Sig clutched, she shifted to the fat oak tree off to the side of Aaron's property and waited as Mendez and three other agents moved in for the front door.

It was a small two-story white shingled home. A bit rundown. The grass overgrown. Weeds reclaimed the flower beds along the front of the house.

There was a chance Aaron was still home and with a rifle pointed at them right now, and so they had to be on guard. And if part of Knox didn't believe that chance existed—he wouldn't have been so scared to let her go.

Mendez gave the signal, and then he rapped at the front door with a heavy fist. "FBI! Open up!" He shifted off to the side of the door and out of the line of sight of the window a foot away. "FBI!" he hollered again and pounded. "Move in," he gave the command a few seconds later, and SWAT approached.

"Preparing to breach," Mendez announced over comms.

This wasn't her first time out in the field. She'd been assigned to hunt down possible threats in the past. But this was the first time her heart nearly exploded from her chest because so much was on the line.

"All clear!" someone said over comms a few minutes later. No sign of Aaron.

She resisted the urge to reach for her phone and text Knox.

"Calloway. Foster. See if the neighbors are home. Find

out what you can," Rodriguez ordered over comms, and she'd happily take a command from him over Mendez any day.

"Roger that." She stowed her weapon and slid on her Ray-Bans with the far-too-cheerful sun in her face.

"Look at you," Calloway said with a smile.

"We're outdoors, and it's sunny." Her glasses hid her eye roll, but she shot him one anyway.

She pointed to the house across the street, which offered the best vantage point to Aaron's home.

The yellow home was well-maintained, unlike Aaron's house. It had character. It was loved. It belonged in the sunshine with violins and chirping birds.

A woman, maybe in her late seventies, sat on the front porch, which stretched the length of her home. One rocking chair, so she was probably the only one who lived there. Well, aside from the Yorkie she had on her lap.

"He's not home," the woman announced as they climbed the three steps of her front porch. "As you can see." Her Southern accent was more Alabama than North Carolina. "And who do you work for?"

Adriana showed the woman her commission book, which held her Secret Service badge, photo ID, and credentials.

The woman leaned forward and read the Secret Service motto inscribed there. "'*Worthy of trust and confidence.*'" She scooted back in her seat. "Are you trustworthy?"

"Yes, ma'am." But was this woman?

"Do you know when Aaron left?" Calloway asked.

"Yes, about twenty minutes ago." She arched a brow, her forehead creasing even more. "I was on my porch when I saw him leave."

"Car?" Adriana asked. "Motorcycle? On foot?"

"Bike. Not a Harley like my husband had. Sportier."

Adriana exchanged a quick look with Calloway. "He have anything with him?"

"Not that I saw."

"Let Mendez know," she said to Calloway, and he hurried back to Aaron's house. "Did you happen to notice if he was home on Monday or yesterday?"

"I was spending time with my son in South Carolina. I got home early this morning."

Too bad. It would've been nice to find out if Aaron had been away from home at the time of the shooting, or the night before when the gunman had been trying to get close to Sarah. Maybe another neighbor saw something. "Anything else you can tell me?"

"I have him over for dinner every Friday evening. He's never stood me up, either, even when he started dating that new girl." She set her dog down, and the Yorkie scurried off the steps and began barking up a storm at all the uniforms across the street. "Aaron's a nice boy. He'd never hurt anyone." She smiled. A genuine smile, too. "Well, aside from bad guys. He's a military hero like my honey was." She stood, her long pink cotton PJ gown skirting the wood planks beneath her feet. "If you find Aaron, be sure to tell him I'm still expecting him for dinner Friday. Making pork chops. His favorite."

Yeah, she was pretty sure Friday dinners were off the table for now. "Do you know his girlfriend? Her name? Where we might find her?"

Her attention dropped to her feet. "If I tell you, you're going to think he's guilty."

Oh, shit. "Please, ma'am."

"His girlfriend works at the hotel. You know, the one where the gunman shot at Mr. Bennett."

CHAPTER NINE

"THIS IS YOUR SHOT, FOSTER." MENDEZ CROSSED HIS ARMS and eyed Adriana. "If you want to listen in to this interview, you have to give me your word that what you hear stays here."

They were back at the FBI field office but on the fifth level instead of the third. She'd discreetly texted Knox she was safe as soon as she'd had the chance, and he'd replied with a *Thank God*.

She'd hoped to see him when they'd returned to the office fifteen minutes ago, but she hadn't seen Knox's Suburban in the parking lot.

"Didn't we already go through this earlier?" she asked, irritation shooting an arrow to her heart for the second time in the last minute.

The first arrow hit when Mendez ordered her to hand over her personal and work cell phones. He was worried she'd call Knox while observing the interview of Aaron Todd's girlfriend.

She'd nearly snapped out an *Are you out of your damn*

mind? back at the FBI director, but Rodriguez shot her a please-God-don't look. So, she'd turned her phones over.

"Knox can't think clearly. He's already decided Aaron Todd's innocent." Mendez was still riding the trying-to-convince-her train, which she supposed meant he cared about her opinion, or he wouldn't give a damn what she thought.

He could've kicked her out of the room, or even off the investigation, because of her friendship with Knox, so she'd take her presence as a win and ignore the anger at having her phones taken away like a punished teen.

"A.J. knows Aaron. Maybe he can offer us better insight into the man. We shouldn't keep them in the dark." She had to try one more time.

"Sorry, Foster." He faced the glass as Chelsea Baker was brought into the room on the other side. "If we're not on the same page, you need to leave."

They weren't even in the same book.

He was reading a twisty political thriller, and she was maybe in a romantic suspense.

"Yes, sir. Understood." She buried the snark from her tone the best she could. "You didn't need to take my phones, though."

Rodriguez stood by the door waiting for Mendez, and he shook his head at her words. He was a guy who always played by the rules. Nothing wrong with that. But she'd learned at a young age from her mother that sometimes you had to color outside of the lines.

"Don't make me regret allowing you to stay in this room to observe," Mendez said before striding out, Rodriguez quietly following.

She took a few deep breaths and faced the window.

When the Feds had picked up Aaron's girlfriend at her

apartment thirty minutes ago, she'd answered the door with two black eyes and a swollen lip.

Not a good sign for Aaron.

Mendez slid into the metal chair on the other side of the small table.

The interview room was more like an interrogation room. No windows. Twelve by twelve in size. The black painted cinder block walls and concrete floor made it feel small and claustrophobic.

The only decor was the mirror on the wall, which was actually the one-way window allowing Adriana to view and hear the proceedings.

"Thank you for speaking with me," Mendez began, his voice much softer than when he'd spoken to Adriana. "This interview will be recorded." He pointed to the camera in the upper right-hand corner of the room.

Adriana glimpsed the screens over her head and reset her focus on the glass.

"As you're aware, you're here due to your relationship with Aaron Todd." Mendez waited for her to acknowledge with a nod before continuing. "When was the last time you saw or spoke to him?"

Even from where Adriana stood, she noticed the tremble in the woman's hand on the table. Chelsea slipped it to her lap. She looked like she'd been the underdog in an MMA fight.

Did Aaron do that to her?

"I saw Aaron yesterday morning. We got into an argument," she whispered, tears cutting lines down her cheeks long before the first question.

"Is that how you got the bruises? Did he hit you?" He lifted his pen and pressed the point to the legal notepad but didn't write.

"Yes." It was a small sound. A "woman afraid of admitting her boyfriend beat her" kind of sound.

"And what time did you leave Aaron's house on Tuesday?" Mendez needed to see if Aaron had an alibi for the time of the shooting without influencing her answers.

"I think I left around eight."

Adriana grimaced at the news. The shooting took place around ten, which gave Aaron time to get to the hotel.

"So, to confirm," Mendez said while writing something down, "when did you first arrive?"

"I spent the night on Monday."

"And what time did you get to his house on Monday?"

Adriana inhaled at Chelsea's words, waiting for an answer.

The shooter had been with Sarah Reardon the night before, and if the time frames didn't match up, Aaron might have an alibi.

She wanted to catch the killer, but she really wanted to deliver Knox some good news, to let him know a veteran hadn't tried to assassinate his father.

"I." Chelsea closed her eyes, showing more of the purplish-black marks over her lids. "I'm sorry. I can't remember. It's been a strange few days."

"I need to know Aaron's whereabouts Monday evening, and can anyone confirm your location?" Mendez asked.

Rodriguez remained quiet, hands in his pockets, his back to Adriana, his eyes, no doubt, on Chelsea.

"We were alone at his house." Chelsea shook her head, more tears falling when her eyes opened.

Did she think Aaron would kill her if she talked?

Aaron's alibi was slowly flying out the door with every falling tear.

"I went to his house pretty late. He said he had plans and

to wait for him at his house until he got there. That's all I can remember. I'm sorry." She chewed on her bottom lip.

"What was the fight about? Why'd he hit you?"

"I accused him of cheating on me. I thought maybe he was seeing someone else. It upset him."

Oh, shit. Adriana braced a palm on the glass for support.

"You ever fight before?" Mendez continued to jot down notes.

"No, but he's got a lot of issues. I haven't known him for very long, but he's been struggling. Nightmares. PTSD," she said around a sob.

"Any reason for you to believe Aaron would want Isaiah Bennett dead?" he asked.

"Is it true then? What the media has said about him?"

"I need you to answer the question, please."

They'd found an arsenal of weapons at Aaron's place earlier, none of which was the so-called smoking gun that took the shot yesterday. Not even any boxes of ammo to match the ballistics report.

"Aaron and I met at a coffee shop a few blocks from my work about four weeks ago. I was new to the area, and he was so friendly. We bonded over the fact we grew up only a town apart in Texas, and yet we'd never crossed paths until Charlotte. He, uh, asked me to dinner." She sniffled. "So, no, after four weeks, he never mentioned some crazy plan to kill a presidential candidate. I would have alerted the authorities and broken up with him."

"Have you heard from Aaron since your fight?"

"No."

And yet, Adriana could practically hear the *yes* float from her lips.

She was lying, wasn't she?

"Is this my fault? Did I upset him, and he snapped?"

"You're not to blame." Mendez reached across the table and pressed a hand over her forearm. The first sign of compassion she'd witnessed since meeting him. "But we need to know absolutely everything you can tell us about him. Places he frequents. A list of friends."

"I never met his friends. And we mostly only spent time at his house in Matthews. He doesn't have much money. He worked construction jobs for his cousin every once in a while, which was why he'd moved to Charlotte—there wasn't any work back home when he got out of the military."

Mendez didn't press the topic of Aaron's cousin. A team had already been dispatched to bring him in for questioning. Aaron hadn't been hiding out at his place, which had been the hope, but that didn't mean the cousin didn't know where he might have run off to.

"You ever see this woman before?" Mendez placed a photo in front of her. Probably Sarah Reardon.

"Only on the news as the missing woman. My friend told me she was a guest at the hotel the day of the . . . you know."

"I need to know if you're familiar with her aside from that."

She took the picture and lifted it. "We have a lot of guests coming and going. Aside from the news, I don't recognize her." She set the photo down.

"Did you ever provide Aaron with a service keycard so he could utilize the back entrance and—"

"Oh, God." She covered her mouth with both hands. The tears didn't feel as real this time when they streamed. Adriana's mom would've called them crocodile tears. Why the change now?

"It's okay," he said in a soothing tone. "Please tell me what you can."

And why was Mendez buying the act?

Chelsea took a few deep breaths and lowered her palms to her lap. "I didn't give it to him, but last week when I got to work, it wasn't in my purse like always. I thought I'd lost it. The card was terminated when I got a new one, though, so it shouldn't have been able to work unless . . . unless he used my laptop to reprogram it."

"And did he have access to your laptop?"

"I don't know. Maybe. He's been in my office at the hotel before."

"Has he been there since you lost the card?"

Chelsea nodded.

He glanced at Rodriguez. "Call the hotel. We need her laptop."

"This is my fault. He used me to shoot that man, didn't he? He probably bumped into me on purpose that day at the coffee shop." More tears fell. More fake tears. So different than earlier. "Was he even from Robert Lee?"

Robert Lee was a small town north of San Angelo, Texas, and it'd been where Aaron had gone to school. She'd read up on his background on her way back to the field office.

After the Navy, Aaron moved in with his parents, but he couldn't find work, so he moved to Charlotte with a promise from his cousin for some construction gigs.

His parents insisted he'd never shoot an innocent man, but wouldn't all parents say that?

"Did Aaron ever talk about Isaiah Bennett to you?" Mendez asked as Rodriguez rejoined Adriana.

"You believe her?" Adriana looked at Rodriguez as he lifted a phone to his ear, starting for the exit.

"I don't know," he said, then left the room to make his call.

"You already asked me that," Chelsea said, bringing Adriana's focus back to the interview.

"And I'm asking again."

"No." Her brows drew together. "Do you think Aaron will come after me? Will he know we talked? Am I going to be safe?" Real fear ebbed and flowed through her words this time, and if this was an act, it was one even Adriana was buying.

"We'll be posting two cars outside your building. One in the back and one out front in case he shows up. Anything else you can tell us that might help?"

"I'm sorry, but if I think of something I can reach out."

Mendez left the room a few minutes later and joined Adriana. Two other agents entered the interview room and escorted Chelsea out.

"Is it possible she knows more?" Adriana asked him. "Something is off. I can feel it."

"You heard her. She practically convicted him with her statement." He tapped the legal pad against the side of his thigh.

"Not exactly. She sounded conflicted."

"Her boyfriend tried to kill a presidential candidate after he beat the shit out of her . . . how do you expect her to feel?"

Her mouth tightened as she fought for the right words. "I'd still like to look into her a bit more." But would he let her? And would he give her phones back, already?

"Fine," he snapped, his approval almost surprising. "But as far as I'm concerned, Aaron's our shooter, and the sooner you get on board with that idea, the better."

CHAPTER TEN

"WHAT DO WE KNOW ABOUT OUR MAN?" KNOX ASKED Harper over speakerphone as they drove to the hotel to meet up with the rest of the team. Jessica, Asher, and Luke were setting up the temporary command center since they didn't have any safe houses to operate out of in Charlotte.

"Model student in school. Joined the Navy at nineteen. Became a SEAL at twenty. Served for twelve years. Left for medical reasons a year ago," Harper quickly stated. "He lived with his parents in Texas after he got out, then he moved to Charlotte and rented a home on the outskirts of the city. He's been working freelance jobs for his cousin's construction company."

"Anything else that could be relevant?" A.J. asked. "Aaron said he'd been seeing a therapist. Can we get his doctor's name? Should we look into his records?"

Harper was quiet for a moment. "You really want me to look into his personal VA files?"

"No," everyone in the car said in unison, including A.J.

There were some things they couldn't do, even for a mission.

"But if Aaron suffered from PTSD, the media will use that against him," Knox commented.

"Which is ridiculous," A.J. said from the back seat.

"What about the girlfriend? Anything on her?" Knox leaned forward, eying the mounted cell phone on the dashboard as Wyatt drove.

"Chelsea Baker," Harper said. "Moved from Colorado to Texas five months ago after losing a job. She also moved in with her parents before uprooting to Charlotte for a job at the hotel about eight weeks ago."

"Where in Texas? Any way we can see if contact was made between Aaron and her prior to Charlotte?" Liam asked.

"Her family lived in the suburbs of San Angelo, not far from Robert Lee, where Aaron was from. But she moved back to Texas after Aaron left—unless they knew each other when they were younger maybe," Harper answered. "You think she's an accomplice?"

"That would imply I think Aaron's guilty." He needed some positive news right now, and he'd take Aaron's innocence as a win.

"And if he tried to kill your dad?" Wyatt glanced at Knox as he pulled into the hotel parking lot.

"Aaron wouldn't have missed," he repeated what A.J. had said earlier.

"We're at the hotel now," Wyatt told Harper and turned off the engine. "We'll touch base after we meet up with Jessica and the others."

"Copy that. Stay safe, guys," she replied.

"Always," Knox said and ended the call. They made their way to the suite on the seventh floor, three floors below his father's room. "Glad to see you all here," he said straight away at the sight of Jessica.

She reached for him and pulled him in for a hug, and Knox shot Asher a surprised look from over her shoulder. Asher smirked and pointed to his abdomen and mouthed, "It's the hormones."

Knox fought a smile before stepping back.

"How are your parents?" she asked, her eyes filled with concern.

"This can't be easy for them." Luke came up alongside his sister.

"I haven't seen much of them since yesterday. My dad's got a fundraiser thing in Atlanta Saturday that he doesn't want to miss, so I know the Feds would like to get the shooter arrested before he leaves town."

Of course, that happening would be easier said than done. There were still too many questions.

His shoulders slouched as he thought about Adriana. She'd texted she was safe that morning after going to Aaron's, but it'd been radio silence since then. No returned calls or texts. He was going to lose his mind.

"Let's hope the Feds don't rush to any conclusions to get this wrapped up quickly." A.J. sat on the sofa alongside the wall and kicked his cowboy boots up on the coffee table. "This place is more my speed. That office has way too many cooks in the kitchen for my taste."

The hotel suite had two bedrooms, one on each side of the living area, and a kitchenette near the main door. Two three-person couches faced each other with a coffee table between them, and a desk was in front of the expansive window. This setup was more familiar to the guys than the federal building. They'd worked a number of cases over the years out of suitcases and hotel rooms. This was nothing new.

What *was* new was working alongside Adriana and hunting down an assassin who'd tried to take out his father.

And, oh yeah, his dad happened to want the gig as commander in chief.

"DHS. FBI. Secret Service." Wyatt popped open a suitcase stand next to the silvery gray couch on the right side, then swung a bag up on top of it. "Now NCIS. Yeah, it's a bit crowded."

"What are your thoughts on sharing intel with the Feds?" Luke strode farther into the room and walked to the desk. "This is your dad we're talking about, so I'll follow your lead."

And it was their teams on the line . . .

Knox sat on the couch against the wall next to A.J. He dropped his elbows to his legs and allowed his hands to hang loose between his thighs.

"I have a feeling Mendez isn't going to share any more intel with us." And honestly, if he had Mendez's job, maybe he'd do the same. Knox was too close to the case. He had way too much to lose, too. They'd probably have to operate on the sidelines and in the shadows. "I'm sure the Feds brought Aaron's girlfriend and cousin in for questioning, and since we haven't heard jack shit from them since they went to Aaron's house this morning, it's safe to assume Mendez thinks we leaked Aaron's name to the press to buy him time to escape."

Adriana would never believe that. He had no doubt. He hoped she didn't get herself into trouble by defending him, though. As much as he wanted her kept out of harm's way, he knew how much her job meant to her. To serve and protect was in her blood.

Asher retrieved a laptop from one of the bags and sat across from Knox. "We need to know what the cousin and Chelsea said to the Feds."

"We might have to play by the rules on this one, though,"

Luke said, admitting what no one wanted to hear. "There are too many eyes on us, and we can't go perusing the FBI servers looking for intel they're keeping from us."

"Rydell stuck his neck out for us," Jessica added, pulling a chair up to the desk where her computer was already set up. She'd barely been there for five minutes, and she was jumping straight to work. "And none of you think there's a chance Aaron's guilty, right?"

"I get that he's on the run, which makes him look guilty," A.J. began, looking at Wyatt across from him, "but he could be scared or trying to clear his name."

"You know as well as I do that I don't want any Teamguy wrapped up in this bloody mess," Wyatt added, "but we also can't write him off as a suspect *because* he served."

Before A.J. could object, Jessica said, "The email. The girlfriend who works at *that* hotel. A gun license for the rifle used in the shooting. PTSD. Running from the cops. None of that bodes well for his defense."

"I wouldn't be surprised if the Feds found recon photos at Aaron's place earlier," Liam said with a grimace as he helped Wyatt unpack. "And I'm not saying that because I think he's guilty, but—"

"Because all the evidence is pretty much packaged with a neat little bow," Jessica finished for him.

"Sometimes, the simplest explanations are the truth." Luke, the voice of reason. He was Bravo One, though, and he had to remain objective.

"But how many times has that been the case for us? Shit is never what it looks like." There'd been times when people they'd trusted had turned on them, too. More times than he could count. That didn't mean Aaron was guilty, but they couldn't rule him out yet, either. "Shit, you okay?" Knox asked Jessica, noticing her leaning back in her chair, her skin growing pale.

"The morning sickness started hitting me on the drive here." Her hand went to her abdomen.

"Why the hell didn't you say anything?" Asher set aside his laptop and hurried to the desk as if she'd fallen even though she was seated.

"I didn't want to worry you." Of course that'd be the answer. This was Jessica. Stubborn like Adriana.

He wasn't much different, though. He never shared his life as Bravo Five with Adriana. He didn't want to lie or have her worry. He wanted to . . . protect her. He was tired of hiding so much of himself from his best friend, though. Tired of pretending omissions weren't lies.

Asher helped Jessica stand and guided her to the couch as if she were six months and not six weeks pregnant.

"It'd be nice to talk to the cousin and girlfriend ourselves," Luke said once it appeared Jessica wasn't going to lose her lunch, "but I have the distinct feeling Mendez will boot us. We need to find this woman, Sarah, from the eleventh floor."

Damn, he needed to fix this. Fix everything.

He had to figure out who the hell wanted his father dead before anyone else got hurt.

Did he truly believe Sarah Reardon was still alive? Mostly no.

After the shit he'd seen in his life, sometimes it could be hard to cling to hope.

But he'd also seen miracles performed by the teams. So, if anyone could make hope a reality, it was them.

CHAPTER ELEVEN

"THANK YOU FOR TAKING THE TIME TO SPEAK WITH ME." Isaiah Bennett poured a glass of Scotch and offered the tumbler. It was beyond late, and they were inside the living room of his suite. She should've been at the FBI office, but when the guy you've been assigned to protect beckons, you go.

"I'm working," she said with a gracious smile, "but thank you."

He tipped his head to say okay then took a sip from his glass. "So, I know you're very busy, but there was something I wanted to ask you."

Busy was an understatement.

After questioning Chelsea, they'd interviewed absolutely everyone Aaron knew, and no one had any information that could help the case. The Feds assigned detail to Chelsea and the cousin in case they were lying or if Aaron decided to pay them a visit.

"Of course, sir," she finally answered, and he waved her to the couch along the wall as he sat on the one across from her.

"Kathleen okay?" She'd meant to say Mrs. Bennett, but she'd known the family for forever, and she'd slipped.

Another reason business and personal shouldn't be mixed. She'd have to learn to call him Mr. President if he was elected. Of course, maybe she would never have any interactions with him.

She thought of what Knox had said to her early that morning and took a deep breath, hoping the influx of extra oxygen would calm her down. The idea of losing her best friend because of her job made her feel as if she'd been the one punched in the face instead of Chelsea.

"Kathleen's going over some talking points with my campaign manager in the suite next door." He turned toward Chen, one of the Secret Service agents quietly standing against the wall. "Can we have the room?"

Chen nodded at Isaiah before leaving.

"How's the case going? I obviously saw the news today. The media's saying a SEAL sniper is responsible." He leaned back and crossed his ankle over his knee, showing a polished shoe. "Does my boy know him?"

"Not personally, no."

And I can't even talk about any of this with Knox or you, but she couldn't lead with that, could she?

"I imagine Knox isn't taking the news well. He hasn't returned any of my calls." He finished the rest of his drink and set the glass on the end table next to him.

She checked the time on her watch. 11 p.m. "I haven't spoken with him since this morning," she admitted.

Mendez had only given Adriana her two cell phones back after he'd personally escorted her to Isaiah Bennett's door, as if he didn't trust she wouldn't make a beeline for Knox's room unless he played watchdog.

She'd had to chew on her lip to bite back the string of

curses she wanted to shoot his way at the sight of so many missed calls and texts from Knox.

"I believe Knox and his colleagues are probably going to be running their own investigation," Bennett said. "Is that going to be a problem? I don't want him to get into any kind of trouble." He clutched his ankle. "You know we haven't had the best relationship since I screwed up by not supporting his choice to join the Navy, but I really hope that changes."

For the sake of your campaign?

"He'll come around if he believes you're sincere," she answered as honestly as possible.

He angled his head to the side. "You and my boy, you go way back. You haven't had an easy life, and I'm glad my son never abandoned you when he—"

"He didn't abandon you," she interrupted without thinking. "Er, sir." She scooted forward on the couch as she sought the right wording to redeem herself. "He abandoned the political spotlight to follow his dreams."

"He says he wants me to be president now, and given our history, I guess that surprises me."

Me too. "Do you not want his support?"

"I want him to be happy. However that looks. Whatever that means. And I also want what's best for this country."

Was this the answer of a politician or a father?

"But I've gotten sidetracked. I asked you here for a reason, and I'm hoping you'll say *yes*. I've already spoken with the agent in charge, Rodriguez, and I put in the request before you got here."

Was he going to put her on his protection detail? At least she'd be out from under Mendez's thumb, but she also wasn't prepared to leave the investigation. Plus, there was Knox to consider. He'd lose his mind to know she'd be standing on guard for his dad.

"I'll be hosting a fundraiser ball in Atlanta on Saturday. Going back to where I first got my start in politics," he said after a moment. "And I'd like you to attend the event."

"Oh." Her hand went to her chest. "I'm honored. I won't let you down, sir."

He held out a hand. "I think I misspoke. I want you to attend as my guest. I'll be honoring men and women who have served abroad and at home, particularly those who've lost their lives."

She lifted her eyes to the ceiling, hoping to keep her emotions at bay. "My mom." Her voice remained soft, so it didn't crack.

"She'll be one of the honorees, yes, and I'd like you to say a few words on her behalf, as well. Her old partner will be speaking. Your dad's also invited to attend."

"I don't know what to say." She wasn't afraid of public speaking. She used to lecture to a hundred students at GW. But talk about the greatest loss of her life in front of a crowd?

"I know it's a last-minute request, and I wasn't planning on putting you on the spot like this, but since you're here, it'd mean a lot."

She forced herself to stand. "I really should focus on the case."

"From what I hear, there are too many people crowding the FBI office as it is."

"Will Knox be there?" she asked.

"If he'd ever answer my calls, I planned on requesting his presence in a non-working capacity as well."

"I don't know if he'll take the night off."

"He would for you." He smiled, and now she couldn't help but wonder if she got the politician-pull-over. AKA . . . played.

CHAPTER TWELVE

"Before you say anything, hear me out." Adriana sat on her bed and kicked off her shoes. Heels had been a dumb idea given all the running around she'd done that day.

Mendez had instructed her not to head back to the office after she met with Isaiah Bennett. It'd actually been an order, not a request. He'd said something about her needing sleep as if that was possible.

But when she returned to her room after visiting Isaiah's suite, she hadn't expected to find Knox sitting outside her door.

She'd been about to call him, but here he was instead. His eyes had drawn her in the second he'd looked up, and her spine had bowed ever so slightly with regret for being forced to keep him at a distance today.

"Well?" He leaned against the wall alongside her bed, arms crossed and lips in a hard line that'd probably intimidate any other person. "Who gave the order to withhold information from me? Mendez? Your boss?" He shoved off the wall and strode around the bed to stand before her. "You know I didn't leak Aaron's name. None of my guys did."

She stood so she wouldn't have to peer up at him. Of course, she was still several inches shorter without heels, so, up was the only direction to go if she wanted to make eye contact.

The normal warmth in his eyes was gone, hidden behind enemy lines. But they weren't enemies. They were on the same team. Yet, their jobs were hammering an uncomfortable wedge between them already. Partially Mendez's fault.

"I went to bat for you, I promise." She wet her lips, searching for a sign he believed her. "But both my phones were taken from me this morning. I just got them back."

"What?" His brows shot up. "Mendez?"

She was almost afraid to nod, worried he'd lose his head and go after the director. "There were concerns I'd provide you updates."

"The president authorized my team access to this case." There wasn't much fight in his tone, though. He must've anticipated the FBI would keep his people in the dark, but he probably hadn't expected Mendez's dick move of taking her phones.

"The Feds don't know you like I do. They're trying to protect the integrity of the case even if I disagree with their methods," she answered on a frustrated sigh.

He remained quietly observing her, and she shook her hands out at her sides, waiting for him to ask her the question she could feel coming.

It may have been small, but the step he took backward was the same as one step forward and a smack in the face. "You think he's guilty, don't you?"

This wasn't what she wanted. A fight with her best friend. And she still had to find a way to bring up his father's request.

How could she answer his question without divulging classified details she'd been sworn to withhold from him?

"The evidence points to Aaron," he said while offering his back.

He'd changed his clothes from earlier. Black jeans. Dark running shoes. And a gray tee.

"The girlfriend works at the hotel. The email. Rifle registered in his name. He ran. I get it." He braced the back of his head with both palms and tipped his chin to the ceiling. "The real shooter went through a lot of trouble to not only buy himself time to get away with multiple diversion tactics but to ensure he *was* seen on camera. I think he wanted us to connect the dots about the girlfriend and the hotel—well, once he'd gotten far enough away first. We'd find a guy with the same build as Aaron on camera. Stacked evidence."

It was apparent he'd figured out quite a lot on his own, and she didn't want to know how.

"You think Aaron's being framed?" She tossed her black blazer and was in the middle of popping open a few buttons on her white starched blouse when he faced her.

Dark brown eyes moved over her chest, and her skin heated beneath his stare.

His eyes were on her hand, at the touch of exposed cleavage beneath her fingers.

"Knox?"

He blinked not once but twice. What was that all about? The moment in the elevator when she thought he was about to kiss her . . . had she *not* dreamed that up?

He was one more throat clear away from her asking what was really on his mind, but then he spoke. "If Aaron was going to kill a guy, why send an email that morning, which implicated him, but then go to all the trouble to escape unnoticed?"

She yanked at the tie in her hair and let the locks fall over her shoulders. "He missed. He wants a second chance." She had to play devil's advocate, even if she may have agreed with him.

"Someone, not Aaron, wanted us to find that email." He spoke with authority. From a place of experience.

Was this the kind of work he did for Scott & Scott? She'd never known exactly how he helped people, but she hadn't imagined it'd be so investigative in nature.

"The email was traced to Aaron's IP address," she reminded him.

"Come on, Addy," he drawled. "Anyone with access to the Internet could've learned how to hack his account remotely. That's not hard at all, and you know that."

True. Ugh, how had he roped her into a conversation she wasn't supposed to have?

"Your people figure out yet that Chelsea's and Aaron's parents live within thirty minutes of each other? Maybe their paths crossed before Charlotte."

"I'm sorry I can't tell you anything. I wish I could, but I have orders. And, if anyone should understand that, it's you with all your secretiveness about your job."

His jaw tightened beneath his five-o'clock shadow. His eyes contemplative. Shoulders going back with an extra oomph of tension. "I can talk to Chelsea myself," he said after expelling a deep breath. "I guess I'll head there now." He started for the door.

"Please, don't," she whispered, struggling to find her voice. "Showing up at her place at night might not be the best idea. Plus, there are two patrol cars parked outside her apartment in case Aaron decides to make an appearance."

"Do they have orders to stop me?" His brows rose in question.

"I don't know." And that was the truth. But her gut screamed *yes!* Mendez would probably throw him in jail for felony obstruction.

The man who faced her wasn't the same guy who'd chosen a star for her mom, or eaten peanut butter out of the jar with her while watching her favorite flicks. And he wasn't the same guy who willingly—okay, he complained, but still—binged the entire first and second seasons of *Buffy the Vampire Slayer* with her over the holidays. In her defense, he'd bought her the DVD boxed sets. Limited editions with exclusive bonus scenes. Also autographed. He'd said he knew a guy who knew a girl. Probably Luke's famous wife.

But no, the man in front of her right now, wasn't that guy.

This man was the SEAL, the person he tried so desperately to keep her from as if to . . . what else was new? —protect her.

"I know you're frustrated. I get it." *Believe me, I do.* "But don't be upset with me."

He was quiet for a moment before saying, "I know it's your job on the line. I'm not mad at you." His eyes dropped to the ground. "I hate being left out of the loop."

She turned and glimpsed the minibar beneath the flat-screen TV on the other side of the room. She needed a drink, and since Mendez wouldn't let her return to the office until tomorrow, why not? "You're hell-bent on clearing Aaron's name because he was a Teamguy. It may influence your perspective." She hated herself for basically offering Mendez's words to him. A sour taste remained in her mouth as she crossed the room to the bar.

"You know something is off, too." His voice remained even and steady, owning his convictions.

She opened the little fridge and snatched two beers and

faced him. "Are your people working the case right now?" she deflected.

"Of course," he said. "Are yours?"

"Yes, but I'm being forced to take the night off." She extended the beer, and he ate up the space between them in three strides, but he didn't take the beer. "Take the night off with me."

He shook his head. "How can I relax with all that's going on?"

"You're angry and rightfully so. But you haven't slept, and you're running on adrenaline. It's not a good combination. You need to rest so you can think clearly in the morning. Let your friends handle things tonight."

"And get drunk with you?" He palmed the stubble on his cheek.

"I didn't say drunk." She set his beer down and popped open her can. She took a long swig of the beer, allowing it to hit the back of her throat, cooling her off. "I need my best friend right now, and I think you need me, too." She lowered the can and rested it against her thigh. "You have your teammates, but—"

"I need you." The words rushed out, catching her off guard. Not his admission, but the way he'd delivered it. Gruff. Gritty. Sexy.

"You do?" Of course he needed her. She had no idea why those words popped out. She supposed she was trying to buy herself some time.

"I do." His tone had changed. Less iceberg and more honey. But the touch of sexy remained.

And then, he stepped back, kicked off his sneakers, and snatched his beer.

He was staying. Thank God.

He moved across the room and sank onto the floor at the

foot of the bed, pressing his back to it for support. He stretched out his long legs and rested the unopened can atop his thigh.

Her attention moved to her beer, and she willed away the swarm of activity in her stomach. The clash of jet planes. The fluttery sensation of anxiousness. The . . . desire.

Knox Bennett was all kinds of sexy, but he wasn't all kinds of sexy with her. He probably saved that for other women. So, whatever she thought she'd witnessed or heard from him lately, stemmed from an overactive and sleep-deprived imagination.

He hadn't nearly fled her apartment last weekend because he was worried he'd slip a hand under the covers and between her thighs.

He hadn't almost kissed her in the elevator last night.

And he certainly hadn't checked out her breasts or used his sexy voice on her right now.

He was tired. Stressed. Maybe even scared.

What he wasn't was a man finally stepping out of the friend zone.

. . . Right?

"We, uh, we'll find whoever is after your family." She needed to switch back to the reason they were both in Charlotte.

Facing him, she sat on the floor and matched his position by extending her legs. She supported herself by propping one palm on the floor off to her side.

He popped open his beer can. "I should probably let my people know I'm not coming back."

"So, you're spending the night?" Her heart shouldn't have beaten so quickly.

"I thought you wanted me to stay." He frowned.

"I do."

"The couch," he said, tipping his chin toward the small seating area by the window, "is fine."

"You're sleeping with me. Period." She purposefully huffed, and he actually smiled.

"Oh, am I?" He let his brows rise and fall twice. And *her* Knox was back. "You don't let other guy friends sleep next to you, do you?" He took a drink. "Because I'll be needing their names and numbers."

He knew the answer, but if he wanted to play this game— "What, you can't get tactical and find their numbers on your own?"

"Oh, I can, but for expediency's sake, I'd appreciate the—"

"You know I don't sleep with anyone but you." She lifted her palm from the carpet and smacked his leg.

His smile stretched, damn him.

"You know what I mean." She dropped down, so her back was flush with the carpet. She kept a hold on her beer off to her side.

"You going to reschedule that blind date?"

Why in the hell are you asking me that now of all times? "Why are we talking about this?" she asked, echoing her thoughts.

"Because you won't talk about the case."

She let go of the beer but remained flat on the floor. "Well, I don't have time to get to know some stranger. Play the twenty questions game. Most men only want to screw, anyway."

He muttered something then asked, "Are all guys assholes?"

"No, not all of them." She closed her eyes at the feel of his hand on her leg. He began massaging her calf muscle, and she resisted a moan. "How'd you know I was sore?"

"Because you've been in heels all day running around with the FBI chasing leads. I'm betting you didn't stretch this morning."

"It wasn't high on my to-do list."

"You gotta take care of your health," he said as he worked at the muscle. He knew exactly how she liked to be touched. This man really did know everything about her, didn't he? Everything except for the fact that she wished he'd be the one to get into her pants. But it was a dream she needed to let sail away and live in the land of it-will-never-happen.

He reached for her other leg next, but this time, he shifted her pant leg up and moved his hand over her skin.

"Yes," she said in a soft cry. "Right there."

"How are your quads?"

"They're tense, too," she admitted, but if he touched her legs that high up, he'd discover the truth. He'd know she'd been lying to him for years. Well, *omitting* how she felt about him. But that was the same as a lie, right?

He removed his hand from beneath her pant leg, and he must've repositioned himself because both hands worked above her left knee atop her pants.

She shifted up on her elbows to view him. "I'm supposed to be comforting you."

"This is comforting me. Seeing you at ease makes me feel better. Makes me forget all the dark shit." He was on his knees, resting back on his heels, as his hands moved over the top of her leg. "You have so many knots."

"Uh-huh." She shifted to her back again, unable to look him in the eyes as he massaged her, worried her cheeks were candy apple red. "This is better than sex." She swallowed a moan, worried it'd come out like she was indeed having sex.

"Sounds like you're doing it wrong then." He mumbled something indiscernible under his breath. "And, Addy?"

"Yeah?"

"Don't actually talk about your sex life with me." That gritty voice wrapped in sex had returned.

"You'll need more names and numbers?"

"I'll be needing my gun," he replied in an even tone.

"How long are you going to be protective of me?" she asked when he moved to her other leg. "What happens when I finally meet *the one*? Do you need to approve of him first?"

He grew quiet, and then he let go of her. The next thing she knew, he was on his feet and cupping the back of his head with both hands. "I don't think anyone will ever be good enough for you."

"You know, you don't need to step in for my dad anymore." She stood, willing away the flutter of nerves in her stomach. "He got his two-year chip last month."

His arms fell to his sides as he observed her. Zero response. No eye contact either.

"What is it?" She moved to him.

His brows drew together, but he'd yet to show her his eyes. "I'm off with everything that's happened. Been a long two days."

Of course. And maybe his father winning the primary a few weeks ago was another explanation for his odd behavior that month. Why hadn't she realized that sooner? "That's understandable." She reached for his arm and slid her hand up to his bicep and squeezed. "What can I do for you? How can I help?"

He lifted his free arm and pinched the bridge of his nose, shutting his eyes. "Maybe I should sleep. I think you're right." He shook his head, and his dark lashes lifted. "I can't think clearly."

"Okay." She forced a smile. "I'm gonna get out of these

clothes then." *Force away my insane thoughts. Get a clear head.*

She snatched her pajamas from her suitcase and went into the connecting bathroom.

After removing her pants and blouse, she turned toward the mirror over the sink. Her eyes wandered over her reflection and to the tattoo on the inside of her wrist, a reminder of what Isaiah Bennett had asked of her.

Could she really stand in front of a room full of people and talk about her mother?

"Addy? The hotel have a spare toothbrush?"

"Yeah. Come in, it's unlocked." She grabbed the camisole off the counter as he opened the door, and she remained facing the vanity, eyes on the mirror.

"You should've warned me you weren't dressed."

"It's not a big deal." But maybe it was given his peculiar behavior lately because there was no way she could explain away the heat in his eyes as his gaze fell to her back and continued downward.

She could come back from this, though. Find their version of normal again. Even if she didn't want that, they needed it right now with everything going on with Knox's family.

"A bra and panties is basically a bikini." She'd tried to keep her voice from breaking. To prevent the dip, but she'd been too late. It'd happened too fast. Her desire for him was too great.

"For some reason, I never pictured you wearing pink panties now that you're Secret Service." His voice was three octaves south of normal.

"Since when do you ever picture me at all?" she asked, unable to move. To act. To get freaking dressed to save her life.

BRITTNEY SAHIN

All she could do was observe the caress of his eyes on her body as if it were his hands instead.

He never looked at her like this, even when she paraded around in swimwear or that one drunken Ace-of-Base-singing-night.

Well, she didn't think he had, at least. But was it possible all this time she'd been as clueless as him?

He stepped closer, his body nearly touching hers, and she stilled, not sure what he was about to do.

"I'm your best friend." He held the sides of her arms and brought his mouth to her ear. "But I'm still a man. And it's been a long damn time for me." He looked up and found her eyes in the mirror. "So, I'm going to go back into the bedroom and do my best to forget what you look like right now."

Oh my God. Her lips parted, but then he turned and left as promised. After he pulled the door closed, she dropped her palms on the vanity and hung her head.

What just happened?

He'd barely said a thing, but her panties were soaked. Had he stayed in the bathroom any longer, he would've witnessed the pool of her desire at the crotch of her pink underwear.

She wanted to take time to wrap her head around what happened, but she was terrified he wouldn't be in the room when she returned.

She hurriedly pushed her thoughts away and put on her PJs and went back into the bedroom.

He was on the bed. Shoes back on.

A what-did-I-do? look in his eyes.

Regret.

Shit.

"You're not staying, are you?" she asked, hoping to hide the disappointment in her voice.

She'd scared him off. A man who could drop into war-torn countries without a second thought was afraid of her pink underwear.

"Like I said, I'm not really in the right state of mind." He slowly rose, a slouch in his posture she wasn't used to seeing unless he was so drunk he'd allowed his body to actually relax.

"Adriana." The rough texture of his tone had the same effect as if he'd reached out and placed his palm between her thighs and found her panties drenched with desire for him.

She took two small steps his way. "Sometimes I wonder what would've happened if we'd met at a different time," she admitted. "But I know I wouldn't have survived that night if I hadn't met you. There are not a lot of teenagers who would take on someone's problems the way you did. You'd known me for maybe two hours, but you stayed by my side."

"And I'll stay by your side until the day I die," he said, his voice level.

"And I'm also not fifteen anymore," she whispered when cutting off the space between them.

He reached for her arm and surprised her by kissing the inside of her wrist where the tattoo of her mother's badge number lay like a memorial script for all of time. "I know. Trust me," he said in a husky voice, "I know you're not a kid anymore."

And maybe he did know, but he held back. He looked at her with guilt in his eyes. He still looked at her like she might break and it'd be his fault.

He let go of her arm only to brush the back of his hand over her cheek, catching a stray tear.

"It was my mom's idea to go to that party. New school. No friends. She even dropped me off down the corner, so no one saw me getting out of a squad car." She smiled at the memory even though her insides hurt thinking about it. "Not many moms, who are also cops, would encourage their daughter to go to a party."

"I never met her, but if she was anything like you, I would've loved her." He lowered his hand from her face, his brows scrunched together as if fighting the urge to unleash a storm of words.

"Sometimes, I think my mom knew something was going to happen to her." She sniffled. "It's crazy, but I think she knew I'd meet you, and you'd be the hero I needed to get through what happened."

"I'm not—"

"You are."

"And maybe you have to stop looking at me like that." He paused. "You pulled yourself together, put on a brave face, and grew into the woman you are today. I had nothing to do with that. You found the way back, and you would've done it with or without me."

She drew in a shaky breath. "Your dad is honoring my mother Saturday night in Atlanta." She allowed her words to sink in for a moment. "He wants me to take the night off work and talk about her."

"What?" He stepped back and looked heavenward.

"I think your dad wants you there Saturday, and he may or may not be using me to try and make that happen." She stiffened when his eyes flew to her face. "I'm going for my mom. Not for him."

"I should've known he hadn't changed. Always a politician." He pressed both hands to the top of his head. "I'm sorry." Shame floated through his words. "I'll handle this."

"No."

He slowly lowered his arms to his sides.

"Don't say anything to him." She set her palm atop his forearm. "I don't want to cause friction between you two."

"He's the problem. Not you."

"And he was shot at yesterday. Let's—"

"No one uses you. Not now. Not ever." He moved out of her grasp and started for the door.

"Wait, please." She wanted to do this. Her mom deserved it. "I plan on going, but I think it's best if you don't."

He let go of the door handle and faced her.

"That way, he doesn't win, but at least my mom is still honored."

He remained quiet for a moment, indecision crossing his face before his shoulders slouched. "So, I can't hit him?"

She almost laughed. "No, you can't."

He cursed under his breath.

"Redirect your frustration toward the case. And pick me up close to eight tomorrow. I'll take you to Chelsea's apartment if you still want to question her."

"What?"

"I'm not allowed to tell you anything, which means you'll have to talk to her yourself."

His chest fell as if a weight had been lifted. "Thank you."

"And, Charlie?" *Charlie*, not Knox, because at the moment, she was fifteen again, and he had yet to become the SEAL. "Maybe don't stop protecting me."

His mouth tightened briefly as he stared at her. "I never planned on it."

CHAPTER THIRTEEN

"I THOUGHT YOU WERE GOING TO TRY AND GET SOME RACK time." Luke checked his watch. "Let us handle things for a bit."

After what almost happened with Adriana, how the hell could he sleep?

He'd nearly taken her into his arms and let her know how he really felt about her.

His dick was growing hard thinking about it. Sitting on a couch in front of his team leader no less. *Damn it.*

He grabbed a pillow and brought it to his lap.

"I can't sleep. I'm doing everything I can to refrain from banging down my dad's door and telling him to fuck off." And to keep from banging down Adriana's door and tackling her onto the bed where he'd rip off those tiny pajama shorts of hers.

But he'd been good for almost twenty very long years.

He'd done his best not to cross the line. Even when she tiptoed along like she was on a tightrope, he carefully kept her from falling.

Maybe if she didn't skirt that line only after she'd been

hitting the hard stuff, he'd give in and tell her how much he wanted to be not just her eighth date, but her final one.

She knew he cared. Didn't she? He didn't know too many straight guys willing or able to recite the lines of every Patrick Swayze movie, and yeah, that was all for her. And he had no regrets.

Well, except for his greatest regret of all, the fact he'd kept his true feelings hidden from her.

He'd thought after Adriana had healed from the loss of her mother—maybe when she was eighteen, he'd tell her how he felt.

Then college and the Navy became barriers.

And in his current line of work, how could he start something "more" with her when the lies about his job felt thicker than the phonebook?

How many times had he wanted to say, *I'm still a SEAL, but the world doesn't know it?*

When Bravo Three, Marcus, had died and Asher replaced him . . . *God*, he'd wanted to break down and tell her, but instead, he'd shown up shit-faced at her door with zero explanation.

When Jessica had a bomb strapped to her chest in Berlin last year, he'd been a nervous wreck. Adriana had never met Jessica, which was a good thing because she might have recognized her on the news. And how would he have answered those questions?

And then there was the time when Liam was in a coma, on the verge of death. Knox kept it together for the sake of Emily, Liam's wife. He'd been her rock when in reality he felt like he was dying on the inside, so desperate to hear Adriana's voice to get through it.

The list went on and on. All the times, good as well as bad, that he'd wanted to confide in her, tell her everything.

But he hadn't.

He'd kept the world of cartel leaders, terrorists, and murdering thugs to within the teams.

"What happened?" Luke's voice startled him. *Shit*, he'd forgotten where the hell he was.

What had they been talking about?

He regrouped. Remembered. Then whispered, "Political bullshit."

"You want to talk about it?" Luke set aside his black-rimmed glasses and leaned back in the swivel chair at the desk.

"Not really." He glanced around the empty suite. "Where's everyone?"

"Getting rack time like you should."

"But Bravo One doesn't need sleep, huh?" He rested his head on the back of the couch and stared at the ceiling. "You ever regret bringing me onto the team? You were worried about my dad before we started." He shifted upright at his words. "Scratch that. Dumb question. But damn."

"You know the man I was up until a few years ago isn't the man I am now."

True. Luke had been different. Colder. Harder. A no-marriage rule for the guys.

"But Eva changed everything. And Sam for Owen. Emily for Liam." *Am I the last single guy on Bravo?* "And well, *Asher* changed things for Jessica, I suppose." The guys on Echo would probably be next. "I'm gonna die single and alone."

"You won't be alone. You have Adriana, a woman you've apparently been holding out on us."

"Yeah, sorry. I thought if I brought her around, it'd make lying to her more difficult." The truth flew quickly from his lips because he knew if anyone would understand it'd be Luke.

"It would've never worked out with Eva if I'd kept a lie between us."

"And luckily you didn't have to—"

"I broke the rules." His jaw tightened beneath his beard as his brows lowered. "You know that."

"And you had your reasons. Things were different." Was Luke giving him unspoken permission to tell Adriana the truth?

Knox rose from the couch and locked his arms across his chest, attempting to decipher his team leader's message.

"Yeah, Eva got caught up in the middle of a shit show, and the woman is crazy inquisitive, but rules are rules, man."

And you broke them. But Luke hadn't lied to Eva for seven years. Would Adriana forgive him? She said she wanted to be included in his so-called other life, but she didn't really understand what that meant. Even if the teams were done after the election, he knew himself and the guys, they'd never stop helping people, as long as they were able to, which would always put a target on them.

"Anyway." He couldn't think about this right now. He'd been off since his dad won the primary and shit had gotten real for the teams. Couple that with spending the last few weeks in D.C. with the woman he wanted but couldn't have . . . well, yeah, wires had been crossed, and he was on the verge of short-circuiting. "I don't know if we can trust my dad to do the right thing if elected."

"Your father may be the only chance we've got, but so we're clear, if you leave Bravo because of him . . . we all leave. But before we worry about the election, let's—"

"Find the real shooter." Knox nodded. "Anything new?"

"No." Luke reached for his glasses and pulled his laptop

closer. "Harper's coming up empty in New York. No visuals on Aaron or Sarah since the shooting. And whoever it was that actually took Sarah out of that hotel yesterday must've known where every camera was located because he pulled a Harry Fucking Houdini."

"I gotta figure out who hated my dad enough to try and kill him, and who'd have the means to nearly pull it off."

"Not to be a dick, but based on what I heard, there are a lot of people who've threatened your family. That's a lot of names to go through, and I honestly don't think our shooter, or whoever hired him, is dumb enough to send a threat."

"Right." He placed his hand beneath his chin and cracked his neck. "We need to clear Aaron's name so we can get the full weight of the government behind us. Aaron must be in the woods somewhere. He's trained to blend in. Maybe he hunts."

"No, the guy hates killing animals." A.J. was in the doorway of the connecting bedroom.

"Thanks for not coming out here in your boxers." A smile landed on Knox's face.

"Yeah, well, the damn Brit threatened to cut off my nut sack if I slept in my skivvies in the same room as him." The man bled Alabama with almost every word he spoke when he was tired.

"So," Luke began, "you don't think Aaron would ever hunt? People can change."

"Nah." He strode farther into the room. "Terrorists were like cockroaches to him, though. He made a distinction. But maybe his cousin or a friend has a hunting spot he knew about."

"I'm sure the Feds have checked all that out, but we'll take a look in case," Luke said.

"And how'd it go with Wonder Woman?" A.J. plopped onto the couch and yawned.

It hadn't gone how he'd expected, that was for sure. He hadn't intended to see her in her pink panties with her ass cheeks peeking out like a please-bite-me surprise. "She didn't tell me anything," he said with a cough to try and keep his dick from leaping to attention again at the thought of her. He just got that sucker back down. "But, um, she's going to take me to Aaron's girlfriend's apartment in the morning so I can question her."

"Mind if I come with?" A.J. asked. "There's something I don't trust about this Chelsea woman."

"You haven't even met her," Luke commented.

"I don't need to, to know something ain't right about her," A.J. said. "She applied to every single job that hotel had available. From reservations to room service."

"She was new to Charlotte and needed a job," Knox replied.

"Did she apply anywhere else?" A.J. asked.

"I don't think we checked," Luke responded. "We've been focused on—"

"Everyone but Chelsea," A.J. cut him off. "I think she's another tenth-floor distraction."

Knox's spine straightened. "You think she targeted Aaron, not the other way around?"

"Maybe you're right." Luke flipped his computer around. "She *only* applied to that hotel, which seems odd for someone who might be desperate for a job in a new city."

"I don't think I want to wait until tomorrow to talk to her. I want answers now." He moved to their heavy-duty weapons case at the far side of the room, pressed his palm to the scanner, and waited for it to unlock to grab his 45.

"You can't go knocking on her door at night," Luke reminded him.

"And shit, she has detail parked outside her apartment, too," Knox grumbled.

"Let's stick to the plan of heading to her place in the morning," Luke said. "I'll have Harper run Chelsea's face through our program and find out what she's been up to lately."

"If she's framing Aaron, she could've easily typed up that email from his computer, too. Someone, maybe Chelsea, planted the threat to lead the Feds to Aaron. A last-minute email that wasn't supposed to be found until after the shooter killed my dad."

"But since the shooter missed, the real gunman couldn't let Aaron get picked up by the police yet," Luke added.

"They need him on the run so they can come after my dad again and make it look like it's Aaron."

"Still don't get why they let Aaron live in the first place. But then again they picked a guy without two names to frame. They clearly don't know their political assassination history," A.J. said. "Lucky for Aaron."

"But does this mean what I think it means?" Luke looked at Knox. "That whoever leaked Aaron's name to the press could be the real shooter, or at least connected somehow?"

CHAPTER FOURTEEN

ADRIANA PLACED HER SIG INTO HER SHOULDER HOLSTER AND hid her weapon beneath the blazer. She was hiding so much more than a gun beneath the bulk of her clothes. Her toned body, for one. And maybe more pink lingerie?

Now was not the time to get hard, he reminded himself at the feel of his cock getting a bit jumpy.

"You sleep okay?" he asked.

"I tossed and turned all night. You?"

He'd barely slept even an hour. Another stupid idea since he couldn't seem to think straight. "Same."

"Does that mean you honored my request not to punch your father?" She closed one eye as if afraid he'd admit to knocking the shit out of his old man.

"I was good." He smiled. "Promise."

"Show me your hands," she commanded.

He held both palms out to show her he hadn't crossed his fingers.

"Good." She grabbed her commission book off the dresser. "By the way, I had to tell Mendez I was heading to Chelsea's to talk to her again."

Work. Yeah, they should talk about that. "Does he know I'm coming with you?"

"I may have forgotten to mention that detail." She adjusted the collar of her shirt beneath her blazer. All her buttons fastened. Not much skin. Probably a good thing.

"And if he finds out?" he asked.

"I'll deal with it. I don't answer to him, anyway."

He didn't want to get her into trouble, but he also needed her help. "There's something we have to tell you once we're in the car," he said when they reached the stairwell.

"We?"

"A.J.'s coming with us." He opened the door leading to the rear side parking lot.

"No, he's too close to this. Closer than you since he's friends with Aaron."

He slipped on his Ray-Bans and turned to face her once outside. "I trust him. And if you trust me, you won't question me on this."

"Fine." She'd dropped the word so effortlessly it took him a second to realize it.

She went to the parked Suburban waiting alongside the curb and hopped into the front passenger seat.

"Hey, gorgeous." A.J. probably waited for Knox to get in the back before flirting to push Knox's buttons. But hell, Knox had done the same to Liam, hadn't he? He'd pushed Liam's *Emily* buttons, so the man would fess up to his feelings for her. Of course, it'd taken a drunken night in Vegas for Liam to figure shit out.

But, wait . . . did that mean . . .

Great. Even his thoughts were stammering.

Yeah, sleep was needed for sure.

"Don't you smell good," A.J. went on. Damn him.

"Maybe I shouldn't have brought your Alabama ass along," he complained.

A.J. jerked a thumb toward Knox in the back but kept his eyes on Adriana. "He's grumpy. Forgive him. When he doesn't get his beauty sleep, he gets testy."

"Don't I know that," she returned.

"So, what is it that you boys need to tell me?" she asked as they pulled onto the main road heading for Chelsea's loft in the Noda district of town.

"I think you know where we stand," A.J. said. "Aaron's being framed. But what you don't know is we think the real gunman had help from a petite blonde."

"Chelsea?" She shifted in her seat to look between Knox and A.J. "Someone beat her up, though, and she said it was him."

This was news to Knox. Intel she probably hadn't been authorized to share.

Judging by the flutter of her lashes and the deep inhale of breath, she'd forgotten that fact and was now kicking herself for it.

Knox edged forward on the leather, remaining unbuckled. "Well, we did some digging earlier. Before Chelsea moved here, she worked as an admin at a trucking company in San Angelo. She made sixty K a year."

"Then she up and quit and moved to Charlotte without a job. She applied to every single vacant position at that hotel. And only that hotel," A.J. added. "Her new job only pays thirty thousand."

"People move all the time. I need more." She remained twisted in her seat and focused on Knox.

"That doesn't sound suspicious to you?" Knox asked. "Come on."

"Maybe she got out of a bad relationship and needed a fresh start," she proposed.

"Okay, I'll bite. Why only apply to the hotel? There were plenty of other places she could've tried. And for more money, might I add," Knox countered.

"No, she only wanted to work at that hotel. And then *she* pursued Aaron. He was her target, not the other way around." A.J. spun his worn-out black ball cap backward as he drove. The only part somehow untouched from age was the American flag on his hat. The colors remained as vibrant as ever.

"Someone's pulling her strings? But who?" Adriana straightened in her seat and peered out the front window.

"We both know there has to be someone higher up calling the shots. This isn't some crazed lone shooter. This was a coordinated effort by more than one person," Knox returned.

"Why choose Aaron?" she asked.

"Why not? A former sniper with the SEALs. Financial issues. Struggling with PTSD." A.J. glanced over at her.

"And what, these people got lucky that Chelsea and Aaron used to live near each other and used that to rope him into dating her?" She shook her head. "I don't buy it. But I'm willing to go along with the theory Chelsea and Aaron were in on this together."

"He moved to Charlotte long before Chelsea, and months before Bennett was a sure thing for the party nomination," A.J. said. "No way was this planned that far back. Besides, she wouldn't have waited until the last minute to try and get a gig at the hotel if the plans started a lot sooner. Too risky."

Adriana shifted in her seat again. "There still has to be something connecting them, a reason she'd target Aaron if that were the case. Whoever bankrolled the attempted assassination could've picked a different city or event, but they chose Charlotte for a reason."

"For Aaron," Knox said.

She flipped her ponytail off her shoulder to her back.

"All I know is the real shooter's mission isn't complete. My dad's still alive. And they'll make sure Aaron's not been caught until after they assassinate my dad."

"We need to see if the reporter who first broke the story about Aaron can provide us with her source," A.J. said.

"It was an anonymous tip from a burner phone," she said.

"Have the Feds checked Chelsea's phone records?" A.J. asked. "Her bank statements?"

She looked down at her lap.

No one was looking at Chelsea at all. No one except them.

"Whether Aaron took the shot or not, he had no idea he was going to go down for it," she said.

"What makes you say that?" Knox asked.

"Because he took off from his house right after his name was flashed all over the news. His neighbor saw him. If you're guilty, you don't wait until the last second to run."

More intel. More regret in her eyes.

"Well, I'm a bit of a conspiracy buff," A.J. began, "and if someone is setting up Aaron, they would've had a plan for his death around the time of the shooting. You don't let the guy you're framing live to talk."

"So, now you're saying Aaron must be guilty because he's alive?" Adriana raised a valid point, and Knox waited for how A.J. would pull himself out of this one.

"Hell no. I'm saying that not only did the shooter miss the shot, he must also be an amateur to let Aaron go before he finished the job." A.J. looked back at Knox. "For the record, I'm glad he sucks at frame jobs."

"I don't know about conspiracies," she said, "but if Aaron's innocent and on the run, it's clearly for a reason."

"The Feds didn't find the rifle at his house, right? The one that would've been used in the shooting?" Knox asked.

"He had a lot of weapons there, but not the kind used at the hotel." She paused. "I'm sorry I kept this from you. I—"

"It's your job," he cut her off. "And I'm sorry we're coercing you into telling us."

She faced the front again and remained quiet. Knox knew exactly what was going on in her mind—the conflict between an oath to her job and the one she made to Knox as his best friend. He knew how that felt, and he hated putting her in that position.

"If he's being set up, someone went to great lengths to ensure all the evidence led back to him, which means they used Aaron's rifle that day at the hotel." A.J. parked the car a block down the street from the apartment complex. "And as long as Aaron is still alive and not in police custody, the *real* shooter can use the weapon to make another attempt to kill Knox's dad."

"I still don't know what to think, but it's gonna be a hard sell to Mendez," Adriana said. "But I guess we're lucky to have you working the case. I had no idea you were investigators as well."

A.J. slapped a hand to his chest. "What? You think we just blow down doors?"

"I honestly don't know what to think right now." She turned back to view Knox, a dozen questions probably hovering in her mind.

Over seven years of withholding the truth and all it was going to take was working a case together for her to figure it all out.

"Well," she said while reaching for the door handle, "you all seem to know more than my team."

Knox stepped out of the Suburban and circled the vehicle to get to Adriana's side.

"Let me talk to her detail first and—shit." She tipped her head toward the redhead stepping out of the car parked up ahead. "It's Quinn. I'll handle this."

"Mendez said you were coming, and he suggested an assist." Quinn shielded the sun from her eyes. "He didn't mention Butch and the Sundance Kid would be here."

"Okay, are you Butch or am I?" A.J. looked over at Knox. "And don't they both die?"

Adriana and Quinn ignored A.J.'s attempt to forestall what was about to go down.

"They have some unique insight into the case, and I made the decision to—"

"From where I stand, you were given orders not to share intel with these men without authorization," Quinn interrupted Adriana. "Foster, a word?" She flicked her finger off to the side, and Adriana followed after shooting an apologetic glance Knox's way.

"You think Quinn's asking about me?" A.J. folded his arms and observed the two women as they spoke. "She's got the hots for me, I can tell."

"Maybe it's indigestion," he returned with a low laugh.

A few seconds later, Adriana turned toward them and motioned for their approach.

"For the record, I don't agree with you all being here," Quinn began, "but since we seem to be on the same page about the girlfriend, I'll—"

"Wait, what?" Knox looked back and forth between Adriana and the Fed.

"Something has been bothering me about Chelsea,"

Quinn explained, "so, my team looked into her last night, and we drew the same conclusion as you guys did. I don't know her angle, but she's got to be involved somehow."

"What'd Mendez say?" Relief hit Knox knowing they had at least one FBI agent on their side.

"He didn't want to hear it. Mendez is a good guy, but he's been in D.C. too long. He wants this wrapped up and quick," Quinn said.

"I like this one." A.J. jerked a thumb toward her.

"You happen to check her phone records or bank statements?" Knox asked.

"There are rules to follow. I need more evidence before I can subpoena her records," Quinn said.

And shit, he'd forgotten about the red tape.

Plus, they were operating on American soil, which meant not even his team could violate certain civil liberties for the sake of a mission.

They'd have to go old school and find information out the hard way until they had enough evidence to prove Chelsea's involvement.

"We'll see what she says and go from there," Quinn said.

"Let's roll then." Knox followed Adriana and Quinn toward the two-story brick apartment building. There were a hell of a lot of trees in the area, which made him uneasy.

"The unit posted out front said Chelsea hasn't left her apartment since they escorted her home last night." Quinn pressed the buzzer outside the main door of Chelsea's apartment building. And then three more times when there was no answer.

"Deep sleeper?" A.J. joked.

"Something isn't right," Adriana said while looking at Quinn. "We need to get—"

"Someone's leaving." Quinn grabbed hold of the door

after a teenager left the building, and they followed her lead inside.

"You think she took off?" Adriana asked as they moved down the hall to Chelsea's apartment.

"That'd be the best-case scenario." Knox retrieved his 45 and kept it low as Quinn pounded on Chelsea's door.

"Ms. Baker. FBI! Open up!" Quinn withdrew her 9mm, and now, all four of them were standing armed outside the door.

If Chelsea was inside with a weapon, the idea of Adriana anywhere near a gun had his pulse racing like a jockey on speed.

She's trained, he tried to remind himself, but hell, it wasn't calming his concerns.

"What's protocol here? Can we bust this door down or what?" Knox asked, because hell, he honestly had no clue about standard procedure since he didn't operate within the realm of typical laws.

Quinn shook the door handle once more, nodded, then stepped back. "Now," Quinn ordered, and he used the weight of his body to kick down the door.

It only took two tries before he breached the place. Thankfully the building was old, and the hinges were shit.

"Let us go in first." He motioned for A.J. to enter, not giving a damn whether Quinn would be okay with his decision. He wouldn't risk Adriana or the Fed's safety.

Knox rounded the first corner, and A.J. came up behind him.

The living room and kitchen appeared normal.

But the place was also dead silent.

With two fingers, Knox pointed toward the closed door off to their right, and A.J. nodded.

Knox shifted to the side of the bedroom door and placed

his back to the hall wall. He waited for A.J. to get into position on the opposite wall then gave a nod.

Knox slowly pushed open the door with one hand, holding his 45 with the other.

The bedroom was a mess, and when he rounded the bed, he found Chelsea facedown in a pool of blood.

"We've got a runner!" A.J. pointed toward the open sliding door and carefully sidestepped Chelsea's body. "I'm gonna pursue." He took off as Knox crouched over the body.

Chelsea's shirt was covered in blood and the carpet beneath her soaked in it. He checked for a pulse but got nothing. A lamp beside the body had blood on it, but he doubted it was the murder weapon. She appeared to have been stabbed, not that there was a knife in view.

"Adriana! Quinn!"

"Oh, shit," Quinn said from behind.

"Call it in." He stood. "Someone just left, and A.J.'s chasing him down." He moved out to the small patio area, trying to get a glimpse of A.J. through a bank of trees obstructing his line of sight.

He shielded his eyes from the sun, spotting a flash of movement.

It was a Thursday morning. Schools had gone back into session this week. And a school was up the block.

"Inform the area we have a situation. Get the local schools locked down!" he yelled before taking off in the direction A.J. had run.

Once he'd cut through the wooded area, he had a better view of A.J. and the guy he was chasing.

A.J. was one of their fastest runners, but Knox was faster. He shouldn't have stopped to check the body.

Knox hid his gun at the back of his pants beneath his shirt as he tore through the freshly cut grass.

No comms. No time to pull out his phone and contact A.J. or Adriana.

The bastard had taken a right, and he was heading for a busy street, but at least he was going away from the school.

Knox's lungs were burning by the time he halted at Tryon Street, anxiously waiting for a chance to dodge the heavy flow of traffic without causing an accident. But a patrol car with the lights and siren going swerved in front of him.

It was Adriana. "Get in!"

He quickly climbed into the passenger seat and pointed in the direction A.J. had gone.

He took a few quick breaths and swiped at the sweat on his brow as she jerked the car to the other lane and made a sharp turn to cross the road.

"How'd you—"

"Borrowed it from the detail parked out front."

"I've lost sight of them," Knox said. "If he shoots someone else . . ."

"There!" She shifted the car to the other lane and made a left.

They were closing in on A.J., who had gained some ground on the killer. *Thank God.* But seconds later the patrol car was sideswiped by a pickup truck. Adriana kept going, but when the truck came back for more, they knew it hadn't been an accident. Someone was gunning for them.

"What the hell!" Adriana floored the gas, then yanked the wheel to the right, and their car veered away from the Ford F-150.

He looked back. The truck was still following them. "The killer must not have acted alone."

The truck spun to the side in the middle of the road. "Gun!" Knox yelled at the sight of a muzzle peeking out of the driver side window.

Bullets punched the frame of their car as Knox retrieved his 45. "We gotta draw him away from here. Too many people."

More bullets popped, tapping the sides of the squad car. The back window caught two slugs. The first punched through the glass creating a wicked hole, the bullet hitting the floorboard of the vehicle. The second ripped clean and more precise, but the glass surrounding the entry point, while remaining in place, shattered.

Neither shot hit them, though, but they needed to get the hell out of there in case their luck ran out.

"I don't have a clear shot," Knox yelled. "Step on the gas." There were too many civilians who might get caught in the crossfire. "Take a right!" he said when spotting a side street without houses.

She grabbed the cruiser radio and rattled off the license plate and called for backup without ever losing control of the vehicle.

And if they weren't in the middle of a high-speed chase, he'd take a moment to be proud.

"He's gaining on us again," Knox warned, wondering what the hell happened to A.J. and the runner. "Dead end ahead." *Shit.* They'd be trapped.

"Hang on." Adriana threw the car into reverse without turning her head, clutched the wheel, and watched her mirrors as they flew backward, then slid into the other lane within inches of hitting the truck, but . . . she did it.

She let up on the gas, cranked the wheel, and the weight of the vehicle shifted to the rear tires. She was breaking traction and inducing a controlled spin.

After pulling a complete 180, they were now in forward motion without losing speed.

The truck slammed on its brakes, and the guy jumped out in a hurry.

"He's running! Let me out." Knox grabbed the handle as the man ran toward a park on their left. "Stay in the car and wait for backup," he ordered.

"The driver's on foot. Armed and dangerous," Adriana said into the radio as he took off.

Clutching his 45, Knox sprinted toward the entrance of the park but came to an abrupt stop when he got a view of what awaited him a hundred yards away.

The shooter was facing him with two guns drawn—but the weapons weren't aimed at Knox.

Knox's stomach dropped at the sight of one gun pointed at two kids playing about fifty feet off to his right with their mom. The other gun pointed at an elderly couple slowly walking a hundred paces on his left.

The bastard began walking backward, his firearms still positioned on his targets as a threat to Knox not to follow.

Knox could attempt a head shot and end this, but not without guaranteeing the gunman didn't have time to get a shot off, too.

"He's getting away," Adriana cried from behind. She was supposed to stay in the car, damn it. He couldn't protect her and everyone else out there.

A shriek hit his ears. The mother had spotted the weapons, and she forced her kids to the ground and threw herself on top of them.

More screams pierced the air, and Adriana shouted for everyone to get down.

"He's almost to the tree line. He'll turn and run once he hits the woods, and I can follow then." He blocked Adriana with his body and kept his arm locked straight in front of him, his gun on the man in case he changed his plans. "Now," he announced when the gunman turned for the trees.

"No." Adriana clutched his bicep. "He has the advantage. Wait for backup."

"I can't let him get away." As soon as the man ducked behind a thick oak, Knox took off.

The shooter had two football fields on him. And now he was deep in a wooded area, and Adriana was right. If the man decided to wait for Knox, he'd have the element of surprise. But what choice did he have? He couldn't let him get away.

Knox neared the trees and slowed his approach, then used the first oak for cover.

A twig on the ground snapped, maybe thirty paces out. He slowly stepped from behind the tree and moved ten feet before relocating behind another oak.

His heartbeat kicked up at the sound of a sob from somewhere in the woods.

A young girl, maybe.

He ditched his protection of the trees without thinking and followed the sounds. If the son of a bitch had a kid as a hostage . . .

A girl, maybe twelve, hugged her knees at the base of a tree, rocking herself as tears tore lines down her face. She didn't appear hurt, thank God.

"Are you okay?" He checked left and right for the shooter then crouched in front of her. "You see someone?"

"I-I skipped school. I was cutting through the woods." He helped the girl stand. "A man ran past me with a gun. He-he put a finger over his lips and told me to be quiet. I was so scared."

"You're okay now." He pulled her to his side. "Which direction did he go?"

"I don't know," she cried. "I fell to the ground and couldn't move."

"It's okay." He kept her close and reached for his phone. "Gunman is still on the run. He got away," he told Adriana. "I have a kid with me. I'm coming back to you."

"Police are here," Adriana replied. "They'll find him."

"Any word from A.J.?" he asked as another call came over the line. "That's A.J. calling me now. Hang on." He switched lines. "You okay?" he asked him.

"I lost him. I'm sorry."

Damn it.

"I had the shot, but I couldn't take it." A.J.'s breathing was labored. "I'm so sorry."

"We'll find him. Where are you?"

The line was quiet for a moment. "I was wrong," A.J. said in a low voice, guilt cutting through his tone with heavy strokes.

"What are you talking about?" Knox stopped walking when they neared the open area of the park.

"It was Aaron, man. The guy I was chasing . . . it was him."

CHAPTER FIFTEEN

Knox had his head bowed, his palms on the side of his Suburban, which was still parked outside Chelsea's building. It was as if guilt was raking over his skin with sharpened claws, and it had her cringing. But what happened wasn't his fault. Not even A.J.'s, even though A.J. blamed himself, too.

Uniformed officers and Feds swarmed the area outside the apartment complex. NCIS was there, too. The city was once again on high alert.

Two people had been at Chelsea's apartment. And one of them had been Aaron Todd.

She and Knox had lost sight of A.J. when they'd unexpectedly had to deal with the truck driver, and A.J. had cornered Aaron in a Target parking lot. In hindsight, not the best idea, but he'd been out of options.

Too many moms and their kids attached to their hips. Too many employees pushing those red carts. The risk too great for a potential shoot-out.

And when Aaron had shoved a twenty-year-old off his motorcycle, the guy's newly bought condoms falling to the ground . . . it was then that A.J. tackled him to the ground.

They'd fought. The knife had fallen. The bike owner had fled out of fear.

And eventually, Aaron got away on that motorcycle, because A.J. couldn't take the shot.

Maybe it was all those moms and employees, or maybe it'd been because Aaron was a friend. She couldn't imagine being in A.J.'s shoes, though, staring at a friend on the other side of her muzzle.

"This is my fault," Knox said, defeat in his tone.

"You were in an impossible situation. There were innocent people. Protect first. Shoot second. You know that." She wrapped a hand over one of his extended arms and urged him to face her.

"No, this is on me. I was so convinced Aaron was innocent." He dropped his arms and turned into her. Warm hands on her cheeks. Foreheads touching. He whispered, "I'm so damn sorry."

"Please, don't blame yourself." She clutched his forearms but didn't budge from their united position. "We wouldn't have even been here had you not pushed to talk to Chelsea," she reminded him. "We know more than we did yesterday. Aaron dropped the knife when A.J. tackled him, so we have the murder weapon now."

He lifted his head and found her eyes, keeping his hands on her cheeks. His dark eyebrows knitted as he stared at her. "A.J. couldn't shoot him, though. Too many people."

"I know." She let go of him and stepped back, reminding herself she was on the job. "I'm sure he blames himself like you do. And you both need to stop." She glimpsed A.J. talking to an agent off in the distance. "But we'll find both these guys. Don't worry. And I'm sure one of the traffic cams snapped a photo of the truck driver, so we'll get his name soon."

Knox was quiet for a moment, staring at her with narrowed eyes. "You were incredible out there," he said in a low voice. "The way you held yourself. The way you drove. I was impressed."

"It's the training," she said with a small smile.

No one but Secret Service drove the president, which meant agents had to handle a car like a driver from *Fast and Furious.*

"It makes me think maybe I've been a bit too overprotective."

"You think?" Her smile stretched.

"You can handle yourself," he said, sounding almost remorseful. Guilty for being too protective. Or was he sad because he didn't think she needed him anymore?

But she'd always need him. She could handle herself on the job, but that didn't mean she wanted her best friend to stop caring so deeply. She'd even told him as much last night before he left her room. But she didn't want him being brotherly or fatherly with his protection. *God no.*

"Does this mean you're a changed man?" she asked, part serious, part teasing.

His lips curved briefly at the edges, his eyes flicking to hers. "I'll still stand in front of a gun for you," he said gruffly. "Every day. All day."

"Like you did at the park?"

He gripped her bicep. "I guess I feel better knowing if I'm ever not around, you'll be okay."

"Ever not around? Like as in not in the same city? Or as in . . ." She pointed to the sky, knowing he'd get the reference to her mom.

"I—"

"There you are." Special Agent Quinn's presence had Knox shifting away from Adriana. She had her FBI vest over her white dress shirt now. Probably more so to signal to others what department she was with and less to do with a concern the shooter would return to the crime scene. "Come with me."

Adriana exchanged a quick look with Knox, wishing they could finish the conversation that'd twisted her nerves into a heap of scrap metal.

Was he worried he'd die on the job? And if so, it had to mean his position at Scott & Scott was riskier than he ever let on. He was protecting her from the truth, too, so it seemed.

"We should go." He pointed to where Quinn now stood fifty feet away.

"Yeah," she said under her breath as she matched his steps and followed him.

"I want answers," Quinn said to the two officers in front of her. "Two squad cars were supposed to be here. One parked at each side of Chelsea's building." She shifted her sunglasses to her head. "Where was the second vehicle?"

Shit, that was right. How could she have forgotten?

"We were between shift changes," one officer explained. "The other car was due any minute."

"How'd Aaron and the truck driver know that?" Quinn asked.

"You suggesting someone from our department leaked that information?" The tall, muscular officer had at least a hundred pounds on Quinn's lean frame. And when he took a defensive step forward, she did, too, not a speck of intimidation.

"All I know is someone is dead, and we have two suspects on the run." Quinn held her palms in the air as if she wanted to shove the guys out of her line of sight.

"There was no sign of forced entry, so either Aaron had a key to her place, or she let him in," Adriana pointed out.

BRITTNEY SAHIN

"If Aaron was tying up loose ends by killing her, why send that email from his home computer, which placed the guilt on his shoulders?" Knox chimed in.

"I don't know what their story is," Quinn began. "But Aaron stabbed her in the back. Literally. The lamp on the floor with blood—maybe she swung it at him. The bedroom was a mess. They clearly fought."

"An Ontario MK3. A *SEAL* knife." Knox put on his shades as if he wanted to hide any signs of emotion in his eyes.

"Maybe Chelsea double-crossed him. He found out about the email and that she used him in a scheme to not only kill Bennett but to stack the evidence against him as the killer," Quinn suggested, turning away from the uniformed officers and facing Adriana and Knox.

"And the truck, why'd that guy come after us?" Knox asked. "If he was Aaron's ride, why risk getting caught by hunting us down?"

"He wanted to make sure Aaron got away because he's still the fall guy," Adriana said. "Whether or not Aaron was the one who actually took the shot at your father, someone still wants to make sure we think he did."

"Aaron killed his girlfriend. If he was innocent of anything, he wouldn't have done that," Quinn remarked. "And based on how he killed Chelsea, it's looking to me like Aaron felt betrayed, which means he didn't know he was going to be thrown to the wolves following the assassination."

Adriana spotted Mendez and Rodriguez stepping out of an unmarked vehicle down the street. Mendez was the last person she wanted to deal with right now. He'd flip a lid when he saw Knox and A.J. at the crime scene.

"This is a mess. How the hell did this happen?"

Rodriguez snapped, pushing his dark blazer back as his hands secured a grip on his hips above his black belt. "And what in God's name was the son of the presidential candidate doing in a vehicle chase . . . which involved bullets flying? Our job is to protect the Bennetts, not get one killed."

"This isn't her fault," Knox came to her defense. "I made her bring me here. This is on me." He stood his ground, eying Rodriguez.

"And Aaron should never have gotten into Chelsea's building unnoticed," Quinn reminded everyone.

"Are you at least ready to accept the fact Aaron's the gunman?" Mendez directed his question to Quinn. He'd yet to make eye contact with Adriana, and maybe he was too angry to do it. Afraid he'd blow a fuse.

"Aaron was clearly involved somehow, but now we know there are others connected to the shooting as well," Quinn answered him. "This isn't a case about a pissed-off guy shooting a presidential candidate."

"Really?" Mendez cocked his head. "I doubt that. The truck belonged to a friend of Aaron's who works at his cousin's construction company. We have men going to his house now."

"What?" Quinn's brows shot up in surprise.

"Aaron and his friend planned this whole thing together. Sarah Reardon's probably in a ditch somewhere. And Aaron killed Chelsea because he blamed her for talking to us. End of story." Mendez huffed and set his sights on Knox. "You and your men are too involved. I called the president on the way here to tell him I'm revoking your privileges. You're officially off the case, Bennett."

"But, sir—" Adriana began.

"That goes for you, too," Rodriguez interrupted her, his voice low. Guilt-laden. "You violated orders by bringing

Bennett here. Pack your bags. You're going back to D.C. today." The word *sorry* hung on the tip of his tongue, but she knew he couldn't say it in front of Mendez.

"Wait." Knox removed his sunglasses. "Don't take this out on her."

"I can't make you leave the city since you're Bennett's son, but if I so much as hear you're looking into this case, I'll arrest you for obstruction." Mendez got in his face. "I assume that won't look too good for your father's campaign, am I right?"

Knox's jaw clenched. His fists tightened at his sides.

Adriana wrapped a hand around his arm, a plea to back down.

"Gentlemen, enough of the pissing match." Quinn worked her way between where Knox and Mendez stood. "We have eyes on us." She tipped her head toward the media. This was going to be all over the news today, and Knox's dad would lose his mind.

"We got a problem?" A.J. asked while striding toward them, removing his hat in the process as if he had no problem throwing down with everyone.

"No problem at all, right?" Mendez sidestepped Quinn to get a direct line of sight on Knox.

Adriana looped her arm around Knox's and tugged. "Let's go. Please."

"Yeah, I think we're done here," Knox bit out.

* * *

"You're sure this is what you want?" Knox asked Adriana as they stood in her hotel room a few hours later. "I don't want you getting fired when you go back to D.C."

"Your dad bought me some time with Rodriguez. I don't

have to be back until Monday." She had the ball to attend in Atlanta, which had been her saving grace. Her mother was somehow still looking out for her.

"But if anyone finds out you're still working the case, and with me, no less, it won't be good for your career." His Southern accent, which seemed to come and go like the wind depending on his mood, thickened with his regret-laced words.

"Some things are more important," she answered honestly. "And I want to help." *Need to help.*

"Addy," he said, his voice softening, "I don't want anything happening to you."

"I seem to recall a few hours ago you were pretty impressed with my ability to handle myself."

"Don't go to Atlanta. Maybe heading back to D.C. is for the best." He'd ignored her comment, focusing on her safety. Typical.

Before she could muster a defense, her work phone began ringing. "It's Calloway. Should I answer?"

"Yeah." He sat on her bed.

"This is Foster," she answered.

"You okay?" Calloway asked, concern in his tone.

"Yeah, I'm good. I'm, uh, resting at the hotel."

"Liar," he said, but she could detect a smile in his tone. "I know you, and you're not going to back down."

"What's up, Calloway?" she asked, not in the mood to get reamed out by her coworker right now if that was his plan.

"I thought you'd want to know agents arrested Aaron's friend. He was at his home watching *The Price is Right* when the police broke down his door."

Yeah, okay, that doesn't make sense. Shoot at agents then go watch daytime TV. She placed him on speakerphone so Knox could hear, although she had no idea why Calloway was risking his neck for her. "They find any weapons? He say anything?"

"He had a Glock registered in his name, but the casings left behind and ammo pulled from the squad car aren't a match," he answered. "He reported his truck stolen last night, but he doesn't have an alibi for today, so—"

"The FBI thinks he's lying, right?" For some reason, she believed Mr. Price is Right.

"The photos from the traffic cams were too fuzzy to ID the driver." A soft whistle came through the phone. "Preliminary autopsy findings suggest Chelsea died of manual strangulation first, then she was stabbed in the back with the knife. We're still sweeping her place and processing all the DNA evidence found on scene."

"Calloway, why are you telling me this?" It didn't make any sense. He was up next for a presidential detail position. She may have butted heads with him after their dating failure, but she didn't want him losing his job because of her.

He was quiet for a moment. "Because regardless of what you think of me, I'm not a dick. And I know Knox is your friend and you'll do whatever it takes to help him. I don't want you getting hurt because of that, so I'd rather you know everything before you jump blindly."

"I don't know what to say." She looked at Knox, and his eyes were on the floor.

"See you around, Foster."

She ended the call and tossed her phone onto the bed. "That was unexpected."

"He clearly has a soft spot for you." Knox's mouth tightened briefly. "We need to talk to my team and let them know what we found out."

"Yeah, I just need a second." She pressed a hand to her

stomach, wrestling with her emotions with everything that'd happened since Tuesday.

"Say the word, and I'll take you back to D.C. myself. If you don't feel right about this, I'll—"

"I'd never leave your side," she said while peering at him, a near wobble to her chin. "Don't you know that by now?"

CHAPTER SIXTEEN

"THE DARK SIDE SUITS YOU. I LIKE IT." A.J. FLASHED Adriana a smile as he sat across from her on the couch in Jessica's suite. "I'm still sorry we got you tossed from your assignment."

She also knew he was sorry he lost Aaron that morning, and like Knox, he wouldn't let that go. "I'll be fine." She glanced at Knox standing behind where Luke worked at the desk.

Luke had given her a warm introduction when she met him, and he'd invited her to dinner with his family when this was over. The man appeared a bit hard around the edges but with a good heart. In fact, all of Knox's friends seemed amazing.

Even though it hurt he'd kept them from her, at least he had friends like them when she wasn't around.

"Where's Jessica and Asher?" She pulled a pillow on her lap and played with the silver-and-black-colored tassel. "I was hoping to say *hi*."

"Jessica's morning sickness has kicked into gear," A.J.

said. "She's been throwing up, and papa bear acts like this ain't the norm."

"He's forcing her to rest in the suite across the hall," Luke translated with a smile. "Asher won't leave her side, so . . ."

"Should she even be here?" she asked.

"I'd like to send her home, but the woman's stubborn," Luke answered.

At his words, Knox peered her way, and she could pretty much read his thoughts. *Like you*, he'd probably been thinking.

But she wasn't nearly as stubborn as Knox, and he had to know that.

"Harper's been doing a lot of the leg work for us since she's at our home office in New York," Knox explained, returning his focus to Luke's laptop. "She's an intelligence genius like Jessica."

Home office? Knox had mentioned he worked out of New York City a lot, but how many offices did they have? And why so many? *What the hell do you really do?*

"We should hear from Harper soon," Luke added.

"You think she can ID the photo your people pulled from the traffic cams of the driver in that truck?" The FBI couldn't, but Knox had said Jessica's software was better, so maybe there was hope.

"I'm sure she will," Luke said with enough confidence that she believed him.

Knox turned toward the window behind the desk and palmed the glass. He'd changed since the morning into khakis and a white tee.

"What are you thinking?" she blurted, forgetting they weren't alone.

Knox faced the room, his eyes connecting with hers. "About how Chelsea died." He brought his hand around his throat, his bicep flexing in the process. "Takes about thirty-three pounds per square inch to close the trachea. Four to five minutes for brain death if strangulation persists." He lowered his hand. "Strangulation is usually personal."

"Unless he was trying to keep her quiet," A.J. suggested.

"But the knife to the back after she was already dead was either a statement or—"

"Another form of misdirection?" A.J. cut Knox off. "Shit. But Aaron was there. He had the bloody knife. He fought me when I wrestled him to the ground."

"You said he looked surprised to see you, and he was fighting to get away, not to hurt you." Knox's eyes lifted to A.J.'s face. "Then he stole the bike and took off."

"But it had to be him, right? What else could've happened?" A.J. placed a hand over his heart.

Knox closed his eyes as if placing himself back at the scene of the crime that morning. "The suitcase by her bathroom door. Clothes on her bed. She was packing."

"She was on her way out of Charlotte." Adriana set the pillow aside and stood.

"It's also possible Aaron found her dead, realized it was his knife in her body, then grabbed it and took off when we breached the place," Knox added.

"But why was Aaron there in the first place?" It was still the unanswered question of the freaking day.

Luke folded his arms. "Not sure, but it'd be nice to get a chance to talk to Aaron and find out."

"I guess because Aaron looks guilty doesn't mean he is," she said.

A.J. slapped his palms together in prayer. "Are we thinking there's still a chance he's innocent?"

"We need to identify the son of a bitch who shot at us this

morning," Knox said. "And we need to figure out how Chelsea is connected to this."

"Guys," Luke hollered loud enough for Wyatt and Liam to hear. "We got a hit. Harper emailed me."

The door to the bedroom opened, and Wyatt and Liam entered the room. "What's up?" Wyatt glanced at A.J. "And why do you look so bloody happy?"

"Because Aaron might still be innocent." A.J. smiled.

"Or maybe not," Luke said, and everyone's attention winged his way.

"Don't go raining on my parade, brother." A.J. circled the desk to look at Luke's screen.

"Recognize him?" Luke asked.

"Son of a bitch." A.J. dropped a few more expletives.

"What is it?" Adriana looked back and forth between the guys, her heart racing.

"Ike Jeramy, he's the SOB who shot at us this morning?" Knox grimaced.

"Who's Ike?" Now she was the one feeling out of the loop, and it was irritating as hell.

"He was in BUD/S with me. With Aaron." A.J. scrubbed a hand over his closely trimmed beard. "He got kicked out, though. He had a problem with authority and running his mouth."

"So, Aaron's friend wasn't lying. His truck was stolen." She sat again, worried her legs would betray her nerves.

"And guess where he's from," A.J. said. "Robert Lee, Texas."

"He still lives there, so it looks like he's just visiting," Luke said as his cell rang. "Putting you on speaker, Harper. We, uh, have a guest present. Adriana Foster."

Was Luke letting Harper know to tread lightly with Adriana in the room? Probably.

And the apologetic look Knox shot her meant she was right.

"I found our connection to Chelsea," Harper said quickly. "Ike works at the trucking company in San Angelo where Chelsea worked before she quit and moved to Charlotte. He's one of their rig drivers. And guess where his rig is currently located? A truck station off route seventy-seven in Charlotte. I pulled up satellite footage of the area. As of this morning, his truck was there. I'm texting you the address now."

"Good work," Luke replied.

Wow. They *were* good.

"I'll do some more digging and see what I come up with," Harper said. "You gonna let the Feds know or handle this without them?"

The guys looked at each other and then pivoted to Adriana, the question written on their faces.

"If Mendez finds out, he'll arrest you," she said, worry darting up her spine. "And shouldn't we get this guy's face all over the news?"

Would they be making the right decision in leaving the Feds out of this?

Of course, her people had unceremoniously kicked her to the curb.

"All that will do is scare Ike underground. As far as he's concerned, his diversionary tactic worked when Aaron's friend was arrested," Luke said.

"Ike and Aaron are from the same town. They probably all know each other and Chelsea lied about that. And now we know Aaron and Ike were in BUD/S together. They're all connected, which means—"

"We're back to thinking Aaron may be involved," Knox finished for Adriana.

"Or it could be why Aaron was chosen as a fall guy," A.J. suggested.

"You really think Ike would set up a friend? A guy he knew in the SEALs? And for what? Why?" Her eyes met Knox's as her mind raced with possible theories.

"Because someone else is still calling the shots," Luke said. "And we need to figure out why . . . because the *why* usually leads us to the who."

Usually? How often do you do this?

She looked at Luke, and then at Wyatt and Liam. A.J. next. And finally Knox. "Who the hell are you guys? And for real." She could no longer hold back. After seven years, she needed answers.

CHAPTER SEVENTEEN

"I KNEW THIS WOULD HAPPEN." KNOX LET GO OF A SIGH AS he sat shotgun in the SUV while Wyatt drove to the truck station off route 77. "I knew if she got too close to me she'd figure out I've been lying to her."

He'd been rotating between two worlds. Hell, if he counted the world of politics that would make three. He was like one of those guys you read about in the tabloids who had separate families . . . wives, kids, houses, and neither one knew about the other.

But could he live in all of them at once? Was it possible? Could he merge his worlds without the entire house of cards falling? Without losing the person he cared for more than anything?

Adriana would forgive him. He was certain of that because he knew her. Her heart was too big not to, but did he deserve it?

Yes, he'd taken an oath, and when she'd pushed back the other day about not sharing details because of her job—he'd understood more than she probably realized.

But everything he'd ever done, everything he did, was to keep her safe, wasn't it?

Even if it wasn't necessary to live such a secretive life, wouldn't it be better for her not to know the details? Easier for her? She'd worry with every mission. And he'd worry about her worrying . . . then he'd lose focus.

Last year, he'd had to parachute into Argentina, and he'd jumped stiff. Had to use his reserve, and things could've very easily ended without his feet hitting the ground first. He'd told his buddies he was out of practice, but that wasn't why he'd messed up.

How could he tell them he'd been thinking about Adriana, a woman he'd kept hidden from them for years?

"Is that why you kept her away from us? The real reason?" Wyatt's question pulled him out of Argentina and back into the car.

"One of a few," he said under his breath.

"I think she bought the story," Liam said from the third row. "And you weren't lying. We do side gigs at Scott and Scott."

"I just left out all the other stuff we do." Omissions were lies. He couldn't pretend they weren't anymore.

And Liam was wrong. Adriana hadn't bought it for one second.

He saw the way she looked at him after the team recited their rehearsed lines about Scott & Scott and what they did for a living.

She'd only let the team think she believed them.

Adriana had put her neck out for his people by taking him to Chelsea's earlier, and she was still risking her job for them now. She deserved the truth.

"She'll be fine. She's a tough cookie," A.J. said as Knox

reached for the radio to change the song. "Don't even touch that dial. That's Kenny Chesney."

"Kenny who?" Knox glanced at Wyatt, and he shrugged.

"I'm gonna have a heart attack if you don't know *the* Kenny Chesney." A.J. mumbled something under his breath. "But hey, on a more serious note, when are you and Adriana gonna tie the knot?"

What? Knox shifted in his seat to face A.J., who was next to Asher in the second row. He lifted his sunglasses to catch the cowboy's eyes. "You're such an ass," he said at the sight of the grin on his face.

"Who wouldn't want to marry their best friend?" A.J. asked, zero hint of a joke in his tone.

"Don't get any bloody ideas," Wyatt said with a laugh. "You're not my type."

"Ah, you think we're best friends?" A.J. teased. Wyatt lifted one hand from the wheel and reached back to try and smack him. "Sorry, brother, I got a thing for redheads. Maybe one in particular, too."

"For being in our line of work, you guys should pay better attention to details," Liam said. "Quinn has a white line around her wedding finger. She either doesn't wear her ring to work, or she's recently separated. So, I think you'll strike out. But that doesn't mean I wouldn't like to see you try." His phone began ringing. "It's Emily," he said, interrupting whatever response A.J. would've managed. "She must have news." He placed the call on speakerphone.

Knox dropped his shades back in place and kept his eyes on Liam. He was in need of a distraction to temporarily remove his guilt.

"He's seven pounds and six ounces. He has Sam's dark hair. He's so stinking cute," Emily made the announcement as soon as Liam answered. "Owen wanted to call, but he's busy making the nurses crazy to ensure Sam and the baby are okay."

They should've been there for Bravo Two. It killed him they weren't, and he couldn't help but feel to blame. Then again, unless they solved this case, they might not even have a team.

"What's his name?" Liam asked.

"Oh, right!" Emily exclaimed. "Matthew Jason York."

Jason was Owen's brother's name, a SEAL who'd died on a covert operation over ten years ago.

Another loss. There'd been too many over the years.

"Tell them congrats," Wyatt called out.

"Send us some photos," Liam requested. "And let them know we'll be there to see them when we can."

"And how are things going?" Emily asked in a soft voice as if nervous to hear the answer.

"We're good." Liam coughed into a closed fist, clearly not comfortable with the lie. It was contagious.

"Liam James Evans, don't you lie to me," Emily said, her Southern accent about on point with Adriana's.

"Shit, she three-named you, bro. You're in trouble." A.J. laughed.

Adriana loved to throw Knox's middle name at him, too. Emily and Adriana would probably get along well. Maybe if he'd brought her into the group sooner . . . hell, he didn't know where to go with that thought.

The past was the past.

He had to move forward and figure out how to deal with everything now.

"I'll call you later," Liam said. "Give Elaina a kiss. Love you."

"Shit, man. You're going soft," Wyatt said, looking at Liam in the rearview mirror.

"Yeah, well, wait until you meet the one, and then we can talk," Liam grumbled.

"Hell no," Wyatt shot back as he pulled into the truck station. "I already tried the marriage thing, and I'm gonna die alone. Happily so."

Wyatt's ex-wife.

It was something the man never talked about.

It'd been how he got his citizenship. But that's all anyone knew.

"You feel like talking?" Asher slapped a palm on the back of Wyatt's seat. "We're here for you, man."

"Shut the bloody hell up." Wyatt flicked a dismissive hand.

"By the way," Liam said, "Asher's officially the softest of us all. Has anyone seen the way this guy acts around Jessica?"

"Do you blame him?" Wyatt turned off the car and hooked his sunglasses at the front of his tee. "The woman can scare the balls off a man."

"Yeah, I kind of love that about her," Asher said with a smile.

"Brother, you got stars in your eyes." Knox faced forward and sought out Ike's rig. "I think that's his truck. It's still here." He pointed to the rear of the parking lot. They had to put their game faces back on. No more kidding around. And no more thoughts about Adriana for now. "I'll text Luke and let him know."

He sent Luke a message then retrieved his 45 and tucked it beneath the back of his tee, hiding it from sight.

"Let's take a look at the truck first. We'll flank the sides, and one of us can come up from behind," Wyatt said. "If Ike's inside, assume he's armed." He reached into the console of the car and retrieved comms.

"Good idea. I hated being off comms this morning when we got split up," A.J. said.

Knox dialed the frequency to the correct setting and positioned the next-gen wireless tech Jessica had designed into his ear. No extra hardware needed. The comm could pick up his speech, and he'd be able to hear his teammates. One tap of the earpiece turned it on. Two taps muted his speech. Jessica had unveiled the design not too long ago, and the comms had worked beautifully on their last op in Panama.

"Rules of engagement?" A.J. asked.

"We're Stateside," Wyatt replied, "no firing unless fired upon."

"But let's try and not get into a shooting match out here in broad daylight if we can help it," Liam said with a wink then slipped on his shades.

"That'd be ideal." But assholes weren't always predictable, and after the shit Ike pulled in the park earlier by positioning his firearms on innocent people, he expected the worst to happen if the prick was there.

Liam pointed to a rig four parking spots away from Ike's. "I'm gonna see if that red truck is empty and climb on top for a better vantage point."

"I'll do the same from the left side," Wyatt said, which meant Asher, A.J., and Knox would take the truck directly.

"Roger that." Knox adjusted his shirt, ensuring his gun was hidden as the team split up and moved into positions. He nodded at a trucker pulling his rig past him as he approached Ike's eighteen-wheeler, hoping to hell he blended in.

"This is Echo One," Wyatt said three minutes later. "I'm in position. Bravo Four?"

"This is Four. The trucker was asleep inside. I'm looking for an alternative. Copy?"

"Copy that," Echo One replied.

Knox flanked the side of Ike's truck, skirting along the edge and out of notice of the extra-large mirrors on the driver side window.

"Bravo Five. Come in?" Asher came over the line. "I'm in position."

"This is Five. I'm ready."

"Echo Two?" Wyatt came on the line.

"Ready to roll," A.J. answered.

"This is Four. No movement in the parking lot on my side. From my vantage point, you're clear to approach," Liam said.

Knox kept his hand at his back with the gun clutched if needed as he headed toward the front side of the rig, hoping he didn't have to use his 45.

There was a truck directly opposite of him, hiding him from the view of the convenience store a hundred-plus feet away. And thankfully the owner of the truck was either sleeping or not inside.

"This is Echo Two. The back's locked. No sounds from inside that I can hear."

"One second," Asher said. "Shit, I think I see something in the back cab. Hold your positions, Two and Five."

"I've got eyes on you. Approach with caution," Bravo Four told Three.

A second later, "This is One. I've got a visual on the target. He's not the one in that rig. He's between two trucks off to your left. I don't have a clear shot yet."

"We need him alive." Knox dropped to a plank, trying to identify Ike's position.

Ike was crouched beneath the rig two over, and his eyes were locked onto Knox.

Damn it. "This is Five." He went for his 45. "He's got his gun on me."

The bastard kept his gaze pinned on Knox.

Was Ike playing chicken—see who'd blink first?

Sweat trickled down the sides of Knox's face. "I'm going to try and draw his fire." Knox went flat to his stomach and rolled to his right side in one fast move as he stretched his arms out in front of him with the gun in hand, hoping Ike would take the bait and shoot.

Knox shifted to his back in a split second, assuming Ike would fire, which he did. The bullet clipped Knox's forearm. He ignored the sting as he listened for what he knew would come next.

One quick pop. A thud of a body dropping after.

"Target is down," Wyatt announced as someone screamed. Their presence was no longer a secret.

Knox tucked his gun away, ignoring the blood on his arm, and rounded the backside of the rig to maintain cover to get to Ike's body.

"Bravo Three, have you confirmed if someone is in the back of that rig?" Liam asked.

"Yeah," Asher snapped out over the line. "And I think it's Sarah Reardon. If we want to keep her alive, we gotta get her out of this heat."

Sarah?

"I'm calling an ambulance," A.J. announced. "And I'm getting Bravo One on the phone for an extract."

An extract? How?

They were going to be screwed. Possibly arrested.

This wasn't normally how their operations went down. Not so publicly, especially on American soil.

The president would be hesitant to stick his neck out for them again. It'd be too risky. But . . . "Tell Bravo One to get ahold of Deputy Secretary Glenn Sterling from Homeland. He's in town for the investigation and a friend of the family." Maybe he could finally take advantage of his political past.

"Roger that," A.J. responded.

"Ike's unconscious, but he's got a strong pulse. He'll live," Wyatt said as Knox approached the body facedown on the ground.

Knox knelt next to Ike and rolled his body face up. "We need to get that rig unlocked." He patted him down for the truck keys and tossed them to Wyatt as sirens began to wail in the distance.

"Shit, you get shot?"

"It's a graze." Knox peeled his shirt over his head and wrapped it around his arm and Wyatt assisted in tightening it over the wound to stop the bleeding. "But go." He tipped his chin, reminding him Asher needed the keys. "I'll stay with Ike."

"I'll remain on overwatch until the police arrive," Liam said over comms a second later. "We've got a bunch of scared people hiding out in the store. And some truckers who might be armed and think we shot one of their own. Someone has to watch your backs."

"Judging by those sirens, we're less than two mikes out from that happening. And two mikes from possibly getting our asses thrown in the slammer," A.J. said glibly.

"Right, well, here's how we're going to play it," Knox began, his mind racing. "I need someone to go calm down those people inside the store and let them know the guy we shot had a kidnapped woman in his truck, and he's wanted for the attempted assassination of my dad. Tell them we have a license to carry and we were fired at first."

"I'll do it," A.J. volunteered.

"Don't get shot," Wyatt bit out.

"I wouldn't dream of it," A.J. remarked over comms.

"Sarah's okay," Asher announced, and Knox looked toward the sky in relief. At least one good thing had come from the day.

"We need to try and talk to Sarah before the police get here," Knox reminded him.

"Looks like Ike's been keeping her drugged," Asher replied. "But Sarah confirmed he's the one who took her, which means he's our shooter, Knox."

But it wasn't over, was it?

Aaron was still out there, and he had to be connected somehow.

And someone still wanted his dad dead.

No, this was far from done.

CHAPTER EIGHTEEN

"You shouldn't be here." Knox sat on a gurney inside an ambulance as a medic tended to his arm, and Adriana remained outside the vehicle observing them.

He couldn't face her right now, not like this.

He didn't know what the hell to say.

Yeah, I got shot. Nothing new. Nope, that wouldn't work.

Or how about, *Hey, pretty much every time I say I'm going out of town it involves shooting someone.*

"You were shot." Her eyes lingered on his forearm before wandering to his naked chest.

"It's barely a scratch." He wanted to act casual. Needed to. Because it really wasn't anything. But her mom died from a gunshot wound, so her mind was going to head straight to worst-case *what-ifs*.

"Looking at all the blood on that T-shirt of yours, it was more than a scratch." Her eyes sealed tight, her lower lip quivering as she struggled with her emotions.

Damn it. "I'm all set here. Thanks." He stood, even though the medic wasn't finished.

"Be sure to see a doctor. You may need sutures," the woman instructed. "You don't want an infection."

"Sure. Thanks." He hopped out of the ambulance to get to Adriana.

"Addy, babe. I'm okay." He braced her arms, hoping she'd open her eyes and look at him.

But he still had no clue what to say to make her feel better right now.

"This is your life, isn't it?" she whispered, her eyes remaining closed.

"I, um." *Yes. It is. And now you know why I've never kissed you like I've wanted to.* "Sort of," was all he could manage, especially with the parking lot crowded with so many uniforms.

"Charlie." His name was a soft plea from her lips.

Oh fuck. She was using his given name. He was screwed.

"We need to talk to Ike when he's out of surgery to find out who hired him," A.J. said on approach, and he was actually grateful for the interruption.

"A.J." She blinked back her tears and shielded her eyes with her hand from the direct sunlight. "You guys are lucky Mendez didn't cart you all to jail for coming here."

The deputy secretary had put in a word, but Knox was pretty sure the crowd of people at the truck station saved them.

A witness had reported to the police Knox's team had acted in self-defense. Although, no way did the man actually see what went down since Knox had the cover of the trucks. But the man was apparently a vet, and he must've spotted A.J.'s military tatt and decided to go to bat for them when the police rolled up.

"I wish we could've questioned Sarah more," A.J. said. "She may have overheard something."

Knox glanced at Mendez and Sarah in the back of another ambulance fifty feet away. "I'm surprised Ike kept her alive." He'd hoped for it, but he hadn't truly expected it.

"Maybe he thought he might need her down the road for negotiations," she said, and when he peered at her, her gaze had settled onto his arm once again.

"I swear I'm fine," he said, hoping she'd believe him.

"Well." Jessica strode toward them. "You need to head to the FBI office and make an official statement, but you're not being charged with anything."

"And Ike? Any word on his condition?" Knox asked.

"He's in the OR, but Wyatt took a clean shot. He'll be fine." Jessica looked at Adriana. "You think you can get Calloway to let us know what Sarah tells the FBI?"

Adriana tipped her head, signaling to Jessica not to say more. Mendez was on approach alongside Rodriguez.

"It was POTUS first. Now the deputy secretary. Who else do you have in your pocket you can pull out when you need a favor?" Mendez removed his sunglasses. "You're damn lucky you found Sarah Reardon alive or—"

"Or what?" Knox stepped closer, in no mood for his bullshit power play.

"Now that you know Aaron's not the shooter, what happens to him?" Adriana asked, reaching for Knox's arm as if cueing him to back down.

Was it really the second time that day he was butting heads with Mendez?

"I assume you'll let his friend go, too," Adriana added in a soft voice. "Ike stole his truck and set him up. And it's pretty obvious he set up Aaron."

"You're off the case, Foster. You forget that?" Mendez switched his focus to her, and so help him, if the man yelled at her, Knox would lose his shit.

"And maybe that was a bad idea." Rodriguez's words drew Knox's attention. "*They* found our shooter, didn't they? *They* rescued Sarah. Maybe we ought to be listening to them." He stepped to the side to face Mendez. "Ike could've been in the apartment that morning, too, and he killed her and used Aaron's knife to do it."

"And yet, we found Aaron with the knife running from the scene," Mendez shot back.

"No." Rodriguez pointed to Knox. "*They* found him."

Knox's focus veered back and forth between the two men, and for once, he was happy to be a bystander as he watched two other people go at it.

"Sarah said she overheard Ike talking to someone named Todd." Mendez looked Knox's way.

"She heard the name Todd, but she didn't know if he was talking *about* Todd or talking to *a* Todd," Rodriguez pointed out.

"Maybe Aaron didn't take the shot, but he's in on this. My gut is never wrong," Mendez said.

"It sure as hell hasn't been on point," Rodriguez snapped. "Which is why the president called. He's placing Homeland in charge of the operation. I'll be running point and reporting to Deputy Secretary Sterling."

Mendez's jaw clenched, and his hands tensed at his sides, but the media had eyes on them, and so, he left without another word.

"You know, I don't remember him being that big of an ass when we worked with him last year," Jessica said to Knox. "Then again, we never dealt with him face-to-face, so maybe that was why."

"True." Knox glanced at Adriana before Rodriguez pulled her off to the side to talk out of earshot. "You think he's gonna bring her back on?"

He wanted that for her, although he couldn't help but cling to his normal overprotective ways. It was all he'd known for almost two decades when it came to her.

"Maybe, but it looks like we're back in the good graces of the government again, which wasn't what I expected to happen after you all opened fire in the middle of Charlotte." Jessica averted her attention to the Big Guy heading their way.

"You should get out of this heat," Asher said to her, worry in his eyes. "It may not be good for the baby."

"It's eighty degrees. It's not that bad."

"It's almost September. I can't handle it being eighty this time of year," Asher responded and pulled her against his side, protectively holding her in place.

"You're such a New Yorker," she said with a laugh as Luke approached with Liam.

"You guys good?" Luke asked. "What happened with Mendez?"

"Looks like Rydell is doing us another solid. He kicked Mendez off the case," Jessica told him.

"What does this mean for us?" Luke asked as Wyatt joined the group.

"Hopefully it means—" Knox dropped his words at the sight of Adriana.

"I'm back on the case," she announced.

"And us?" he asked.

"Freelance private contractors." She tucked her hands in her back pockets. "*Unpaid* private contractors."

"Not even insurance? A PPO? HMO?" A.J. held both palms face up. "How about petty cash? Lunches for free?"

Adriana chuckled, but when her eyes went to Knox's arm, a frown replaced her laughter. "You need to see a doctor."

"Ah, Knox is basically our doc." A.J. waved a hand in the

air. "You should've seen what happened to Liam last year. He—"

"I'm fine," Knox interrupted. He was already in enough trouble with her. He had a lot to fix between them, and it'd have to start with the uncomfortable truth.

"Since you all have to go give your statements, Luke and I will head back to the hotel and see what else we can find out about Ike," Jessica said. "Maybe get a few hours of rest before you come over." Her gaze wandered to Adriana before traveling to Knox. "Take all the time you need. We've got your back."

Take time? Why?

He looked back at Adriana again, to how her green eyes tracked the length of his body from head to toe, once again settling on his naked chest.

And when she pulled her gaze up to his face, her cheeks pinked, and she swallowed.

Was she checking him out?

No.

But *was* she?

His stomach knotted at the idea. His heart pounded.

"Can I talk to you for a second in the car?" He pointed to his Suburban.

He placed his hand on the small of her back and didn't say a word until they were inside the back seat of the SUV.

"What's going on?" she asked.

His eyes lingered on the V-neck of her white tee.

"I have a crazy-ass question to ask you." He cupped his jaw, feeling insane right now, but after the last few days . . .

"Are you turned on right now?" His forehead tightened. "I mean"—he stumbled his way through his words—"does the action and stuff make you hot? Is this something I don't know about you?" And why would he? They didn't talk about

199

each other's sex lives aside from him offering friendly dating tips—like guys are jerks and avoid them.

"You're right. It's a crazy question. You getting hurt would never turn me on, but I . . . I don't know."

"I'm getting a vibe of some kind, and I feel like I'm losing my mind. Did you think I was going to die today?"

"No, I, um." She looked out her side window. "I can't talk about this. Not here." She reached for the door and pushed it open. "Later, okay? But not in here."

"Addy."

"Sorry," she whispered and hurried out of the car, leaving him so damn confused.

CHAPTER NINETEEN

THREE HOURS LATER, KNOX STOOD IN THE HALL OUTSIDE HER hotel room, and she observed him with her heart in her throat.

The crisp white button-up shirt stretched over broad shoulders and wrapped around hard biceps like a fitted glove. Long legs were covered in dark slacks that matched the color of the bluish-black tie.

The man before her looked more like a billion-dollar businessman, or heck, a politician, than a Navy SEAL.

"Why the tie?" she asked, untangling the words caught on her tongue as the bite of desire clipped down her body, consuming her inch by inch until she had to press a palm to the doorframe for support.

"And why are you already in your pajamas?" His eyes journeyed the length of her, starting at her pink painted toenails up to her pale pink shorts and on to the matching camisole.

He checked his black wristwatch, a thick and heavy thing that was the only giveaway this man didn't normally wear a suit. But the luxurious material fitted him to absolute perfection.

"It's barely eight."

What were they talking about? Right. The time. Her clothes.

They weren't talking about how sexy he looked right now. Or his brown eyes ringed in mahogany. The confident clench of his jaw.

She stepped to the side to allow him entrance. "I'm tired. It's been a day."

He remained in the hall. Maintaining a firm position. Regarding her with curious eyes.

And then he lifted his hands and worked at the knot of his tie, allowing it to drape loosely around his neck. He popped the top two buttons of his shirt next.

Despite undoing his tie and shirt buttons, he still appeared to be standing at attention, uncertainty in his eyes.

"*Should* I come in?"

For the last several hours, her mind had been racing, thinking about the bomb he'd dropped on her earlier and what she was going to say to him when he showed up and wanted answers.

There was an angel on one shoulder and a devil on the other, and they were in the midst of a scorching-hot tug-of-war.

Had she been turned on? Not by him getting hurt—of course not.

But what if she'd lost him without him ever knowing how much *more* she wished there was between them? And after last night, for a fraction of a second, she'd thought he wanted more, too.

She had so much to say. So many questions. But she managed out a "yes."

Still no movement from him on the other side, though.

That clenched jaw could pulverize titanium with one look.

His eyes moved to her camisole, and she followed his gaze to her nipples pressing against the thin fabric.

No bra. Because who wore a bra with PJs?

"Please, come in." She struggled to keep her voice even.

When he finally stepped inside, she shut the door behind him and turned to find him right there. "I, um, why the tie?" she asked, flustered.

His brows slanted. "Were you the only person who didn't tune in to the news today?"

"My entire team, apparently. We've been a bit preoccupied. Why?"

When they returned to the FBI field office, she and Knox had parted ways, and she wasn't sure what Knox had been up to. She assumed he'd gone back to his friends' suite after giving his statement. So, the shirt and tie? No, she was clueless.

"I had to give an interview. My mom insisted on the tie." He flipped his brown eyes to the ceiling, the movement in his throat noticeable. A clash of the Titans raged in those eyes when his gaze returned to her face.

He'd had the same look in the SUV earlier when he'd accused her of getting turned on.

"Word got out that I took down Ike, and my dad decided it'd be best if I fess up to it and give a press conference or whatever."

"You? On camera?" she asked in surprise. "Tell me there's a recorded version I can watch."

.His attention veered to her neck. He was still so close. Could he see her pulse hammering against her skin?

She breathed in his Nautica cologne, wishing they were on a beach somewhere as the touch of the ocean met her nose. The sand beneath her toes, his eyes on her—yes, that'd be much better than reality. But they'd experienced several beach trips in the last twenty years and none ended with her naked beneath him getting sand in inappropriate places.

"You're red," he said while looking into her eyes.

"I'm what?" She blinked.

He placed his palm to her cheek. "Your cheeks are red. Maybe that's not the right word. They're that shade of embarrassed you get sometimes. You know, when you're . . ."

Checking you out? She covered his hand with hers. She intended to remove it, but he'd already felt the truth of his statement in the heat radiating from her skin and onto his. So she left it there. "You were talking about the, uh, press conference."

"Yeah, I had to take the blame for shooting Ike so my guys didn't wind up on camera." He lowered his hand, the mention of his friends a punch back to reality.

She flipped through his words in her head as if turning the pages of a novel trying to find meaning. "Blame?"

He offered her his back, facing the window even though the curtains were drawn and the ruddy brown fabric the only view.

"You're a hero." Blame made no sense.

"We don't take credit for . . ." He dropped his words, his shoulders lowering with them. "It's not an easy thing for us to do." Quiet descended upon the room. The kind of quiet that offered her a moment to collect her thoughts and pin them back onto the it'll-never-happen-for-us board.

She thumbed back through the pages of her mind, slower this time so she could formulate a response that'd make sense given her jumbled mess of thoughts. Her body still aroused when it shouldn't be, especially given the events of the day. Given his words right now.

She strode closer and placed a tentative hand on his body.

His broad back expanded as he took a deep breath and let

it free. "What'd you find out after I left you at the field office?" he asked. His voice was gritty, the question forced as if he had no choice but to change the subject.

"Ike's out of surgery. Not awake yet." She removed her hand, and his shoulders relaxed. "There are uniforms parked outside his room waiting, though."

He turned, and her world narrowed down to Knox—his slow-motion progress toward her, the intense energy emanating from his powerful body, the heat in his eyes that never left hers as he grew closer.

"Ike came on to Sarah the night before the shooting. Invited her to breakfast the next day. He bound and gagged her after." She swallowed. "The FBI traced several unknown calls from Ike to a burner phone, which matched the one at Chelsea's place." The business-like talk of assassins and murder dialed her from slow and intense to just north of normal. She had to stay focused. Get through this moment. Even if this wasn't the conversation she wanted to have right now.

"What about Aaron? Did Ike ever call him?"

"Not on his regular cell, but Aaron may have a burner we don't know about."

He swiped a hand over his shaved head, and a touch of red appeared on the sleeve of his shirt.

She reached for him, trying to hide the panic in her eyes at the sight of blood, evidence he could've taken a bullet to the chest or abdomen instead—she could've lost him like her mom.

"I have bandages. Let me get you something."

"Why do you have—"

"Part of the job." She rifled through the bag atop the dresser. "Secret Service who work with POTUS even have to carry his blood around with them."

"Yeah, that's not a visual I want to picture, especially if the next POTUS is my old man."

She motioned for him to come into the bathroom. With his sleeve rolled to the elbow, she discarded the old bandage saturated in blood and tended to the wound.

"I'm not used to someone taking care of me like this," he murmured as she worked. "I'm usually the one fixing people up."

"Why do you have to fix . . ." She refrained from finishing her question because she knew why, didn't she? After this week, she understood. How could she not? His work was much more dangerous than he ever let on, and he'd been afraid to tell her. "You should get stitches," she said instead and wrapped his forearm.

"It's fine."

"And you're stubborn." She turned on the sink and caught his eyes in the mirror as she washed her hands. "You planning on meeting up with your team to try and figure this puzzle out?"

He perched a hip against the vanity and folded his arms. His gaze a slow caress of her body. And now her need for this man returned. Maybe it never left, but it'd been suffocated by the sight of his blood and talks of murderers.

"I stopped here first for a reason."

"To find out what I learned about the case?" Her voice was weak when she spoke. Guarded, even if she didn't want it to be.

"You know why." His proper posture returned when he pushed away from the vanity to stand tall before her.

The bathroom was too small for them now.

She slipped away, allowing fear of the *what-ifs* to strong-arm her.

His shirt was untucked from his pants when he entered

the living room. Another button undone. He wanted out of those stiff clothes as much as she wanted them off him.

Her fingertips dragged across her collarbone as he moved toward her. And she nearly drew blood from biting into her bottom lip.

He stopped a foot away, his body rigid once again. His jaw clenched beneath his sexy stubble, and his very kissable lips tightened. An impenetrable force field seemed to hum around him—one maybe only she could get through.

She almost lifted her hand to see if she could reach out and touch him.

"Do you want me?" His words were a deep rumble.

Four words. Four words that had her faltering. One step back to adjust her view of him as he continued to speak.

"You usually only flirt, or look at me like you did earlier —like you're looking at me now—when you've been drinking." The rough texture of his words should've hurt as they cut across her skin, but instead, they dampened her panties. "I've always chalked it up to the alcohol."

Tequila and their buddy Jack brought the words out— loosened her lips. But liquor only allowed the truth of her desires to skim the surface, offering a brief and quick view of what she wanted.

"So." He paused, his eyes thinning. "Do you?"

Heat rolled like soft waves over her skin as his words floated through the air.

"Yes," she whispered before biting back the truth as always.

"Okay." He gave a light nod, his eyebrows drawing together. "So, then, I'm gonna go ahead and kiss you now."

He enveloped her in one quick movement before she knew what to think or say. His hands on her. Bodies touching. The hardness between his thighs pressing against her.

A sweep of his tongue parting her lips.

Tender and soft.

Then hard.

Harder.

She matched his pace, but in truth, she was hanging on to the edge.

His rigid arousal so close to her was like an invitation to a party she'd longed to attend but had never been given the chance.

His kiss was everything. Years of want rolled into this one moment.

When his hand slid between them and skimmed the hem of her shorts, her knees buckled.

A low, guttural moan vibrated against her lips when his finger swept up, tracing a line over her clit, discovering her sans panties.

He stroked her while his other hand cupped her ass and squeezed, and his lips wandered to her cheek, to her neck, to the shell of her ear.

She was going to lose her mind. Was this actually happening? Right here. Right now. Was this a dream? If it was, she refused to wake up.

She buried her fingertips into his shoulders as he made love to her with his hand, with his mouth back at her neck, gently sucking.

And when she didn't think she could withstand any more sensations, he buried two fingers deep inside of her. "You're tight," he said into her ear. "So tight and wet." His tone was sex and strength. Love and passion. Total commitment to this moment.

She wanted more. More of him. More of everything.

But then he stepped back.

He ended her world in that one step.

Her chest lifted and fell with heavy breaths as she feared he was on the verge of changing his mind.

"I've fantasized about this moment for so long," he rasped. "I didn't know if it could ever happen."

She wanted to reach for him, wanted his touch again, but he needed to say something. She could see it in his eyes, and so she waited with hands clenched at her sides.

"I've been trying to protect you. I've been afraid I might leave you someday the way she did, and I didn't want to hurt you."

A world without her mom and Knox would be two levels below hell.

Her chin slightly wobbled as fear fast-tracked down her spine.

"But you're my best friend, and if something happened to me, it would hurt you no matter what." His chest lifted with a deep breath and sank on an exhale. "There are other reasons I've convinced myself to stay away. I've been waiting for the right time, but I don't think right times exist, do they?"

She brought her hands to his chest, unable to stop herself, worried she'd lose him to some invisible reason she could neither see nor touch.

He stared at her for a long minute. Indecision blanketing him once again.

"Please." She reached for the messy bun at the top of her head and unleashed her long locks.

Then his body went flush with hers, and he tore a hand up her back and to her hair, fisting it gently. Tugging so her chin tipped.

His hand raced down the column of her throat in the tight space between them before dipping into her top and palming her breast.

"How long have you wanted to do that?" Her tongue skirted the line of her lower lip.

"A long damn time," he growled and kissed her again. Much harder this time. Needier. And it was going to be her undoing.

"I told myself I wouldn't go past second base tonight," he whispered when their mouths parted, and his lips tilted into a smile. "I had to Google those bases on my way here, by the way."

She chuckled, even as she regretted the loss of his touch. "You and the baseball metaphors lately. You planning on pulling a Jordan and switching sports?" Her palm went to his chest.

His smile converted into a full-on grin.

"And what made you so confident you'd get anywhere?"

"Because I knew if you felt even a tenth of what I've been feeling—*suppressing*—I'd be good."

Her palm slid north, and she wrapped her hand around the back of his neck. "Please tell me you're not going to leave here without—"

"You do have an eight-dates-before-sex rule."

"At your insistence!"

"I had advised eight hundred to somewhere along the lines of never. You dropped the double zeros."

"And do you really want to wait until eight dates to make love to me? Or talk about the fact I had to date anyone other than you at all since you've been so damn stubborn?"

He grimaced. "Might I remind you that you've been stubborn, too?" He held a finger in the air between them and closed one eye.

"I've given you plenty of clues, and you never got the message."

"Like those shorts you're wearing?" He twirled a finger.

"I swear you must have them in fifty colors, and you always wear them when we hang out."

"What's wrong with the shorts?" She attempted to hide a smirk to no avail.

She gasped when he surprised her by sliding a hand up her cami and rolling her nipple between his thumb and forefinger.

"Tell me you don't wear them on purpose whenever we hang out." He guided her chin with his free hand so her eyes were on his, a silent demand. "Tell me you weren't trying to get me to break down. Probably had no underwear on, too."

"I don't know what you're talking about."

"Liar." He pinched her nipple. "You keep the peanut butter on the highest shelf in your kitchen, which makes absolutely no sense given your love of the stuff. And I have to watch you on your tippy-toes reaching for it, with your ass cheeks on display in those short shorts, and then I'm left with one of two choices."

"Wh—"

"Two choices." He held a hand between them. "Grab hold of you, spin you around, and kiss you . . . or get the peanut butter for you and immediately disappear for a good five minutes and think about anything and everything to get my cock to calm down."

Oh, shit. Last weekend after the barbecue when she'd reached for the peanut butter jar . . . the look he'd given her after. He *had* gone to the bathroom right after, and then he'd returned with all his crazy talk about why he shouldn't spend the night.

"You rarely ever looked at me like you wanted me," she said, trying to make sense of his words.

"There's a reason why I'm good at covert ops and poker."

He crossed his arms. He was standing his guard. Businessman gone. The SEAL had returned.

This man she couldn't win a battle with. He'd been conditioned for war. Trained by the best of the best, and he *was* the best of the best.

"You know how many times I had to hide an erection around you? Well, I lost count, so I've got no idea, but it was a lot."

"Why fight it? Why keep it such a well-hidden secret from me?" He said he'd been waiting for the right time, but still.

"After that night, we couldn't. And then . . . more timing issues, I guess."

That night. *The* night her mom had been dying while he'd kissed her.

She forced away the pain and found his eyes.

"I've accepted for a long time we'd remain friends. Only friends. It was safer."

Safer?

"But that doesn't mean I haven't contemplated various ways of killing every guy you've dated." A smile slipped to his lips. "Now, tell me the truth, since I'm being so honest. Did you, or did you not, want to bang me in the back of the Suburban earlier?"

A laugh bubbled up in her chest, and she let it free. "Knox, you'd been shot."

"Maybe the rush of emotions got you hot and bothered."

A fluttering sensation of goose bumps erupted over her skin.

"I'm right, aren't I?" Before she knew it, he had her back to the wall, his palms over her shoulders.

But he didn't kiss her. He didn't make a move.

He simply stared at her. A touch of fear coloring his eyes. A battle of restraint she didn't want him to win.

"What is it?" she whispered. "Are you serious about the date thing?"

His eyes dropped to her lips. "We have a lot to make up for. You gotta let me do this right, Addy. I owe you twenty years of right."

"You don't owe me anything except for maybe your cock inside of me right now."

"Fuck," he said as his mouth took hers.

Owned her yet again.

The sound of a palm hitting the wall had her eyes opening, and he pushed back. "Damn you," he said. "But I'll take my time if it kills me." Emotion cut across his face, deep and hard. "You're not just anyone. You're *the* one. The one I thought I couldn't have, and I plan on giving you the entire world."

Her heart may have exploded in her chest, but she couldn't resist—"The whole thing, huh?"

He lowered his hands to her face and held her there. "The whole fucking thing." Then he kissed her again. Kissed her so hard she was going to lose her mind.

"Okay," she murmured against his mouth. "We'll wait." She lifted her hand between their now parted bodies. "Two dates, though."

"Two?"

"And tonight counts as the first."

He angled his head, his brows pulling together.

"It's that or eight hundred and somewhere along the lines of never," she repeated his earlier words.

"You're a tough negotiator." But he'd give in because she could see that, like her, he was barely hanging on.

"Now let me get dressed while you go get changed and

then meet me in Jessica's suite," she rushed out before she changed her mind and dropped to her knees, bringing his pants with her.

She lowered her eyes to the tie on the floor and crouched to grab it. She hadn't noticed it fall. She pulled the material through the loose circle of her hand, maintaining eye contact with him.

"Give me twenty minutes before you join us," he said.

"Why?" Her gaze fell to his hard-on as he took the tie from her.

"Because I'm gonna go jerk off, so I don't snap the arms off the chair in Jessica's room, and so my balls don't die."

"That's all your fault."

He draped the tie around his neck. "I know." He inhaled sharply. "Make that five minutes. It's not gonna take me long at all."

Years of concealing her carnal thoughts now over, she leaned in and mouthed, "I'm really tight. Really, really tight."

Her back hit the wall again.

Her arms above her head this time.

"I hate you," he murmured against her mouth before kissing her roughly.

And when he tore his lips from hers, she added, "Go. If you're not going to change your mind, I have a date with my vibrator."

He angled his head and took a quick step back, releasing her from her boxed-in position. "Since when do you own a vibrator? I know everything about you and—"

"Apparently not everything." Her lips rolled inward to suppress a grin when his phone rang.

He grabbed his cell from his pocket. "It's Jessica."

"What does that mean?"

"It means no vibrator and my balls are gonna fall off."

CHAPTER TWENTY

He couldn't stop staring at Adriana from across the room. Jessica and Luke had been taking turns talking. Something about Ike refusing to speak. But he barely heard a thing.

His heart had been pumping too hard. Too fast.

Adriana was all he could think about.

That sexy mouth of hers. Those damn short shorts he'd finally been able to shift out of the way and touch the slickness between her thighs.

He was thirty-seven and had wasted too many years denying himself, denying Adriana, of what they'd both apparently wanted for a long time. But he had to believe everything happened for a reason, or he'd lose his mind thinking about it.

They didn't need to find their way back to the night they'd first kissed. Because the relationship they'd built over the years was bedrock, solid, indestructible.

In the SEALs, the plan was to track what you knew and could see to keep moving forward. And tonight, when he'd held her in his arms, what he saw was a future with her.

BRITTNEY SAHIN

And to know she felt the same had him on the edge of his control back in that room.

At the very least, though, why hadn't he stripped her naked and drank in the sight of her so he could get through the night?

The only time he'd seen her naked had been years ago. He'd walked out of his bedroom to find her dancing naked in his living room. A heart-shaped ass swaying from side to side atop a pair of long legs. No tan lines, and he remembered losing his mind wondering if she tanned naked, and if so, did any guys see her? Hell, women, too. He didn't want to share the sight of her with anyone.

And as he observed her shake and shimmy, holding his remote like a mic and singing—he'd remembered, she wasn't even his to look at.

"Addy," he'd said, finding his voice even though his cock strained against his navy blue shorts.

"Dancing and singing naked. It's so freeing. You want to try it?" She'd faced him, inviting him to view her tits. To let him see the evidence of the Brazilian bikini waxes she'd always mentioned getting as if forgetting he was a guy and not one of her girlfriends.

He'd wanted to charge the room, to steal her into his arms and deposit her onto his bed and make love to her that night. But he was about to deploy, and he couldn't do it. It wouldn't have been the right time to test if they could have more than friendship.

So instead, he'd insisted she sleep away her drunken state, and he'd scooped her into his arms and brought her to his bed, covered her up, and then left.

"You okay, mate?" Liam snapped his fingers in front of Knox's face, and he tucked the memory away where he'd kept it all those years. A giant don't-fucking-look-into-that-

216

box warning sign had been placed in front to prevent hard-ons and temptation.

But he didn't need that box or the warning anymore.

He could burn the sign. Torch the box.

New memories could be made every day.

"What are we talking about?" He cleared his throat.

Adriana shot him a shy look as she stood near Luke at the desk. She knew he was thinking dirty thoughts. But thank God, they were on the same page.

"We're discussing the Liberation Defense Force," Liam said, probably knowing where Knox's mind had gone. Everyone probably knew. Adriana's cheeks would no doubt give it away. They were beet red.

"Yeah, right." Knox stood. "And who are they?"

"You been daydreaming, buddy?" A.J. was on the couch across from him with a computer on his lap and a grin on his face. His ball cap was pulled low, so he tipped the brim to catch his eyes.

"Tired." Not a total lie.

A.J.'s lips stretched, and Knox resisted the urge to throw something at him.

"And what or who is the Liberation Defense Force?" He needed to focus. He and Adriana had time to figure everything out.

"A private militia based in Texas and not far from Robert Lee. They have about a hundred acres of land there. From what we've gathered, it's a small operation. Fifty or so men and women who've joined their so-called cause." Luke pushed his black frames higher on his nose and scooted closer to the desk. "They have a website that explains their mission, and you need an account and password to access it."

"I got on to the server and found a list of accounts," Jessica explained. "Chelsea and Ike are active members."

"Well, guess not Chelsea anymore," Wyatt noted as he took Knox's previous spot on the couch.

"Chelsea became a member four months ago, shortly after her move from Colorado to Texas. And we think that's how she met Ike, who then got her the job at the trucking company. He's one of the founding members going back to twenty eighteen."

"Any chance Aaron was a member?" Knox asked.

"An account was created for him in February, but it was deactivated two weeks later," Jessica answered.

Knox circled the desk and stood next to Adriana to share her view of the screen. His arm brushed against her body and that zap of electricity, the one she said only happened in books or romance movies—yeah, well, it was real, because he'd gotten a jolt right now. "And, uh, what's their mission?" He swallowed and did his best to remain focused.

"To form a private armed militia to protect themselves against tyrannical rule, but they're pretty anti-government in general, from what I can tell," Luke answered. "They believe the government can't be trusted. Spying. Secret operations."

"Only two of their people actually have military training, and one of those was Ike, who failed out of BUD/S, so . . ." Jessica pushed away from the desk and stood. "It doesn't feel too organized, and I'm honestly not sure how Ike even managed to hack the security cameras at the hotel. His background isn't very impressive. Someone had to have walked him through the steps."

"Regardless, from what I can tell, most of these guys in the compound are harmless. It's more like a club of guys hanging out and hunting," Luke said.

"So why the change? Why get into the business of assassinations?" Knox asked.

"Money is always a motivator," A.J. reminded him. "And

maybe the group saw Aaron's departure as betrayal, so they decided to use him as a fall guy."

"There's been no communication between Ike and Aaron since Aaron moved to Charlotte. Well, not on their personal cell phones or by way of email," Adriana announced, "but when we checked previous records, they talked on the phone regularly before he moved."

"He moved in February right after he quit the group, which can't be a coincidence," Asher said, sitting next to A.J.

Jessica began pacing the room, walking back and forth between the two couches. Her mind was working. Wheels spinning. "Someone hired the militia to kill Bennett. Ike had the most experience, but they recruited Chelsea in hopes she'd have the best luck getting hired at the hotel."

"They had their pick of cities to choose from, though— my dad has a lot of scheduled events—I guess they settled on Charlotte because Aaron lived here. And if Ike knew Aaron well, he'd know about his PTSD, his weapons collection. Hell, even the type of woman the man liked."

"But why choose a fall guy that could link back to your group?" Liam scratched at his jaw. "If they were smart enough to come up with the tenth-floor distraction and evade the FBI the way they did, wouldn't they realize the risk of setting up a man who had once been a member of their militia?"

"Something doesn't jive," Jessica said. "I agree."

"Unless the Liberation group was the intended fall guy and they didn't know it," Luke commented.

"Someone else is giving the orders, structuring the plan, and the militia are following along," A.J. remarked. "Most likely promised a big payout."

"Would Ike kill Chelsea because he was told to?" Adriana

asked. "Why would a militia turn on their own? Doesn't seem likely."

"Unless Chelsea had a change of heart and wanted to confess," Knox said to her, "and he killed her not to tie up loose ends but to cover his own ass."

"Anything is possible at this point," Luke noted. "We really need to focus on finding Aaron to see what the hell he knows. Whoever is truly behind all of this will be working on another plan to assassinate Bennett."

"Well," Adriana began, "my team didn't find any abnormal funds in Ike's or Chelsea's accounts. So, I'm betting whoever is funding this thing has yet to pay, or never planned on it."

"Because whoever hired them had every intention of killing them all after the job was done," Liam added.

"What do we know about the leader of the militia? If someone got to him, I'd like to know how. I get money is a motivator, but there's often more to it than that." Knox brought his focus Luke's way.

"His name is Darius Hilton. He's fifty-five. Has a wife. An eight-year-old daughter," Luke read from the screen. "He quit his job at an oil company when his wife inherited a ranch in late twenty seventeen. They converted the ranch to the compound a year later. ATF sent a few drones up to check them out last year to make sure they weren't trafficking arms, but they didn't find anything."

"Why would this guy up and start a militia in the first place? Something or someone had to have been the trigger, right?" Knox asked as Jessica took a seat next to Asher.

"Darius has been arrested a few times for participating in government protests that turned violent. He was very opposed to boots on the ground in Iraq and Afghanistan," Luke said. "Burned a few flags before. And, well . . ."

"What?" Knox crossed his arms.

"His dad was in the military, and he died during the Persian Gulf War leaving his mom to raise him," he responded.

"Could be why he didn't want more troops on the ground. He doesn't trust the government to run the military, so he created his own militia," A.J. proposed.

"We need to try and talk to Darius," Adriana said. "And get Ike to confess."

"If we approach Darius, we might spook him," A.J. grumbled.

"What if we send someone in as a possible recruit?" Knox suggested. "Get a look inside the compound. See what we can find out."

"That could work, and in the meantime, I can keep looking into things." Jessica nodded in agreement.

"It's too risky for any of you to go," Adriana said, worry coloring her tone. "We don't know if anyone else from the militia is in Charlotte who may have gotten a look at your faces."

"She's right," Jessica replied.

"Chris, Finn, and Roman can go with Harper," Luke suggested.

"I'd prefer to be with my team if they go," Wyatt said while standing.

"*Your* team?" Adriana's brow furrowed.

"We, uh, work in two teams. Like the old days," Luke was quick to reply.

The lie was still there. Hanging hard and heavy on a thin line, which was close to snapping. Damn it. He needed to tell her the truth.

"I should go as well," A.J. said. "But Wyatt and I can hang back and out of sight."

"Yeah, okay." Luke focused back on the screen. "Fly in to Dallas. Get what you need from our site in Fort Worth. It's a three- or four-hour drive to the compound from there."

"I'll call Harper." Jessica went into the connecting room, and Asher followed her.

"Maybe I should head back to the office and look over everything again." Adriana gripped the back of her neck. "Find out what else Sarah Reardon heard or may have seen."

"Didn't Rodriguez demand you take the night off?" Knox raised a brow.

"More like a firm request," she said with a smile.

"And when do you leave with my dad for Atlanta?" he asked.

"Wheels up at three tomorrow. Before you suggest you come with us, I think it's better if you stay. You need to find Aaron and try and get Ike to talk. Secret Service won't let anything happen to your parents."

She wrapped a hand over his injury-free arm. He'd forgotten about his wound and was surprised it hadn't started bleeding again during their make-out session. Then again, most of his blood had been running south.

"You can trust me," she said softly.

Trusting her had never been a problem. It was worrying about her that was going to do him in.

Maybe Secret Service could protect his dad, but then who'd be protecting her?

CHAPTER TWENTY-ONE

Adriana rapped at the door, her heart pounding in time with the two knocks.

When Knox swung the door open, she whispered a quick, "Hi." She'd been unable to find her voice with his eyes locked onto her mouth as if he wanted to kiss her.

She still couldn't believe what had happened between them last night. Apparently, it took working together and a bullet for them both to admit the truth that'd been dangling above their heads like mistletoe, taunting them for years.

His eyes moved north to hers, and he lightly shook his head as if scolding her for the bulge he was now sporting in his pants. And yeah, she noticed.

His smile converted to an I-want-to-spank-you kind of smirk. Okay, so she'd made that part up, but the thought, even if inappropriate, made her hot. Everything about this man drove her wild, though, and she could finally scream the truth from the rooftops if she wanted.

"How's Sarah?" he asked but didn't move out of the doorway yet, and it was probably because he was trying to "de-tent" his faded denim jeans.

She'd visited Sarah at the hospital, took a detour to Ike's room after—still no luck with him—then worked at the field office for a few hours before coming back to the hotel. She wanted a chance to see Knox before she flew to Atlanta.

"She's okay. The doctors gave her something yesterday to flush the drugs out of her system. She'll probably be leaving the hospital this afternoon. She doesn't like being there with Ike in the building."

"I don't blame her." He brushed her hair off her tense shoulders, studying her neck. And . . . he spotted the hickey he'd given her.

Yeah, they really had kissed like they were teens again in the room last night. So much time to make up for, though.

A smile met his eyes, and her cheeks heated as he repositioned her hair to hide the evidence.

"How are things with your people?"

"A.J. and Wyatt arrived in Dallas," he said and finally shifted to the side to allow her entrance, "so they'll be leaving for the compound soon."

"Oh, good." She sidestepped him, her body skimming the lines of his hard chest in the process. "I have to meet up with the rest of your father's protection detail at two to prep for the flight to Atlanta. It does help he has his own jet for traveling, though."

Knox checked his black wristwatch. "Rodriguez staying back to work the investigation, or is he going with you?"

"He's coming. He didn't want to risk having your dad go out of town without him. Quinn will report to him if she finds out anything new." She viewed the team at work in the room before looking back at Knox. "Quinn's smart, though. I don't think it'll be long before she makes the militia connection."

Jessica removed her glasses and focused on Adriana. "We can't afford to have the FBI showing up at the compound this weekend, not with our men there. We'll need to keep an eye on her and what she finds out."

"I'm still not sure who we can even trust on the inside. If anyone in the FBI field office is actually working with that militia, they'll give the compound a heads-up if the Liberation Defense Force's name is brought up," Adriana said. "I've asked Quinn to speak to me first before sharing new intel."

"You think she will, especially given your connection to me?" Knox raised a questioning brow.

"I think we can trust her," she said with a nod. "Even if there's not an insider, once the Feds discover the militia, they won't be in a rush to go after them. They'll get blowback from the higher-ups. DHS will be worried about another Waco incident, and they won't be eager to move in on the compound anytime soon unless Ike confirms he was sent to kill Bennett by Darius." She sat on the couch and glanced back and forth between Asher and Jessica working side by side at the desk.

"Are you feeling better?" she asked Jessica.

"At the moment." She smiled. "Lots of saltine crackers. Little sips of water. Thanks for asking, though."

Asher reached for Jessica's hand between their laptops. The guy was pretty built, but he reminded Adriana of a cuddly teddy bear with how he looked at Jessica. It was endearing.

"Adriana's right." Luke's words pulled her attention his way. He was sitting across from her, dressed in khakis, a white tee, and wore black-framed glasses. A military-grade laptop rested in the hard-shell case on his lap. "The FBI's hands will be tied without ironclad evidence."

"We'll get the evidence Quinn needs and hand it over when the time is right," Liam said.

"But if any evidence is obtained illegally it won't be useful," she reminded them, even though, surely, they'd know that. "The case would get thrown out of court, and Darius would walk."

"We'll figure this out." Knox sat next to her and clasped her hand, taking her off guard. "It's what we do."

Her heart stammered at the gesture. And when her gaze traveled across the room, there was a twitch to Liam's lips as if fighting a smile before his eyes returned to his screen.

"Any luck tracking the whereabouts of the rest of the militia members?" Knox's grip of her hand tightened.

How many times had he held her hand before?

And yet, this time was different. So. So. So. Different. Electric. Warm. Tingly. All the things. Touching her in all the places.

"Asher and I are working on that now," Jessica said. "None of the fifty members have taken flights out of Texas, but that doesn't mean they didn't leave another way."

"But we're hoping our guys can make some positive IDs on the members tonight," Asher added.

"You think everyone will be at the compound this weekend? Well, most everyone?" she asked in surprise.

"The group convenes the last weekend of every month. It's mandatory," Asher explained.

"We'll have to keep the situation fluid and see how it goes. I don't know if I want one of my guys there more than a night," Luke said.

She knew Luke and Jessica were the owners of Scott & Scott, but the guys still gave off an intense SEAL vibe.

The chain of command in the military was strong. Respect stitched into every line of their dress blues, both literally and figuratively.

And it was obvious the respect for leadership had

continued outside the Navy because she felt it in the room. They were a tight unit. There was a shared trust amongst them. But when she'd Googled Jessica out of curiosity the first time Knox had mentioned her name years ago as co-owner with Luke, she'd found an IT background only. Not a military one. Her presence had always been a bit of a question that tickled the back of her mind. There was more to Jessica's story, wasn't there?

More to all of their stories, but she couldn't quite put her finger on what it was.

They'd explained they were in the private security business, nothing Knox hadn't already told her, but something didn't add up.

And she was beginning to think that "something" was why Knox had held back so much of this part of his life from her.

"Did Sarah confirm if Ike had a laptop on him the day of the shooting? Something he used to take down security?" Liam asked, fixing his attention on her. "Or did he have outside help on that?"

"He didn't drug her until after he got her out of the hotel, because he needed her to be able to leave by foot, so she remembered a lot from that day," she began. "She said he was on the phone with someone before the shooting while on a laptop. Someone had walked him through how to cut into the security feeds."

"Any ideas who?" Liam asked.

"No. Quinn checked Chelsea's work laptop to see if she accessed the hotel's servers at that time, but she didn't find anything abnormal, and Chelsea wasn't logged in then. But Chelsea did have a background in IT, so she may have been able to assist," she explained.

"What are you thinking, Addy?" Knox's phone rang after

his question. "It's A.J." He placed the call on speaker and rose.

"Hey, call me back on a secure line. Call my burner," A.J. said abruptly and hung up.

Luke pulled out a cheap-looking flip phone from a bag by his foot and dialed up a number before placing the phone to his ear.

Knox tucked his cell back into his pocket, never losing hold of her hand.

"Can I put you on speaker?" Luke asked as soon as the line connected, and was that code for *Adriana is in the room, can you talk in front of her?*

Knox squeezed Adriana's hand briefly as if in apology, but then Luke placed the call on speaker.

"Our boy Aaron called me, and he wants to meet," A.J. announced.

"What?" Adriana let go of Knox's hand and stood in surprise. Her heart a hammer in her chest. Her breastbone the nail it was pounding. "Where?"

"He said he's innocent and has information, but he can't go to the FBI," A.J. answered. "He saw Knox on the news yesterday, and he figured Knox was working with me. He wants to meet at seven tonight. No address provided, though."

"So, how are we supposed to find him?" Jessica asked.

"Get this, he said the pretty Secret Service agent working with us would know where to find him on a Friday night."

Everyone in the room turned and looked at Adriana. *What the hell was he talking about?*

Luke shifted the computer off his lap and stood, clutching the phone with eyes on Adriana. "Does that make sense to you?"

She dragged her palms down her face when realization

dawned on her. "Yeah," she said. "I know where he'll be." Her stomach tucked in. "She's serving his favorite tonight. Pork chops."

"What?" Knox rose. "Who?"

"The woman who lives across the street from him. She told me that Aaron never misses a Friday dinner." How had she not realized Aaron could be hiding in plain sight all this time? But why would the woman hide a possible assassin?

"We'll handle this," Luke said to A.J. "Call us when you're at your next location."

"Roger that."

Adriana turned away from the room, her mind spinning.

Knox wrapped a hand over her shoulder, but she couldn't face him. If she looked into those beautiful brown eyes, she'd do anything he wanted, even if it meant jeopardizing her career.

How could she not tell Rodriguez Aaron's location, though?

He shifted her hair off her shoulder. "You do what you need to do," he said close to her ear, but not so low his people couldn't hear him. "I'll respect your decision."

"But if the FBI arrests Aaron, the militia might panic and know we're onto them, and then our guys could be in danger," Jessica said, and her words were like an icy whip of reality against her skin. "And we could also lose our best lead."

"This isn't an easy decision to make," Luke added. "I don't envy your position, but—"

"There's only one choice," she said, trying not to let fear swallow her words. "And that's whichever one keeps you safe."

CHAPTER TWENTY-TWO

Adriana was risking her career for them, and he hated his team was putting her in that position, but he wasn't sure if they had any other choice.

"I really like her," Jessica said over speakerphone as they drove.

Knox, Luke, Liam, and Asher were en route to Aaron's neighborhood to meet him as scheduled.

"I wish you'd brought her around sooner," Jessica added.

"And you would've scared her off," Knox replied. "You weren't always so lovey-dovey."

"That's fairly accurate," Luke said with a laugh.

"You're no one to talk," Jessica shot back.

"Any word from the boys yet?" Asher asked from the back seat.

Echo Team would be attempting to infil the militia compound in a not-so-covert way by knocking on the door. Or fence. Whatever the hell they had for an entry.

"They're thirteen mikes out," she said. "If this militia is as low-tech as they appear to be, this should be an easy in and out. But Roman's going to wear the new camera I designed. Harper will be able to see and hear everything, and there's no tech on the market that can detect it."

"Wait. We're sending Roman?" Liam asked. "Chris or Finn. Yeah. Roman? No. What kind of conversation will he have? The guy hates talking."

"Yeah, exactly. Chris and Finn aren't the best actors. You've seen them," Asher said, sitting alongside Liam.

"Roman has the whole quiet thing going for him. It'll work, I promise," Jessica added.

"If you say so," Liam responded on a sigh.

"Anyway, we're here. If Knox and I are still inside with Aaron, let Asher know when Roman enters the compound," Luke said as he parked on the street.

"Stay safe," she said, and Luke ended the call and handed out comms.

"Liam, stick to the front. Keep an eye on the squad car that's monitoring Aaron's house," Luke instructed and shifted his focus to Asher. "Stay in the car. Be on standby if we discover this is a trap."

Knox got out of the vehicle, and a few seconds later, he and Luke made their way to the property and climbed over the fence to get into the woman's backyard.

The back porch light was off, but one interior light was on. No movement from the inside from what they could see.

The back door swung open. "Come in," a female voice called out.

Luke approached first and announced, "We're good."

A whiff of fried meat met his nose once inside. The woman really was cooking, wasn't she?

They entered the kitchen and found her standing over the stove. "You staying for dinner?" she asked as her dog ran up to them and began excitedly spinning in circles.

Knox resisted the urge to reach down and pet the Yorkie, needing to keep his hands ready if he had to draw his weapon.

"No, ma'am," Luke responded. "Are you okay? Did he hurt you?"

"What?" She set her spatula down and faced him. "Of course not. He's a sweet boy. He's in my son's old bedroom. Second door down on the right."

Luke glimpsed Knox with a surprised, *Are we in the Twilight Zone?* kind of look.

"Someone has to stand up for vets. God knows people have turned their backs on them." She pointed to the hall. "If you change your mind, dinner will be ready in thirty minutes."

"Thank you, ma'am." Luke moved first, clearly hesitant as if worried the woman had a shotgun hidden under her apron and this was an extravagant mind fuck.

Knox tapped his ear. "We're on approach. Good so far."

"Roger that. Back is still clear," Asher replied.

"Good out front," Liam noted. "The officer did a perimeter sweep of Aaron's house, and he's in his car."

Luke peered at Knox from over his shoulder, his Sig in hand, and he called out Aaron's name. "Show me your hands," he said at the sight of Aaron peeking out from the bedroom, and Knox drew his 45.

Aaron raised his hands above his head. "Come in."

Luke checked the room and motioned the all clear to Knox. "I'm gonna take a look at the rest of the house. Stay with him."

"Roger that." Knox went into the bedroom with Aaron and motioned with his gun to sit on the bed.

"We're clear," Luke told Bravo Three and Four over comms when he rejoined the room. "So, you want to tell us what the hell is going on?"

The room had a twin bed, one nightstand, and a small desk. A few faded posters of Charlotte Hornets basketball players—from about thirty years ago—clung to the walls for dear life as the tape peeled at the edges.

"I had nothing to do with this, you can ask her." Aaron pointed to the door, even though the woman wasn't standing there.

"Then why not go to the police? Why'd your neighbor say she saw you take off on your bike after your face was all over the news?" Knox asked.

Aaron appeared young right now. Like the teen who once inhabited the room. Lonely and scared. Not one bit a SEAL. "Because I asked her to lie."

Luke shook his head. "Let's go over what we know. You were dating a girl who worked at the hotel from where shots were fired at Senator Bennett and his wife. When questioned by the FBI, she had bruises on her face, and she said you were responsible for that." He paused for a breath. "The same rifle that you own, and is missing from your home, was used to shoot at Bennett. Then there's the email."

"And Chelsea being dead and you dropping the knife—well, it clearly looks pretty shitty for you," Knox added and Aaron held his palms in the air. "But it's also why we think you're being set up. The problem with that theory is usually the guy being framed never lives to see the light of day so the truth can die, too."

"But the shooter missed, and so, they needed you alive until they went after Bennett again," Luke said. "But why would they let you run in the first place?"

Aaron tore his hands through his hair. "Monday night I went to bed with Chelsea, and the next morning, I woke up tied to my bed and both Ike and Chelsea were there. I hadn't

seen him since I lived in Texas, so to see him—and with her
—was a surprise."

Knox glanced at Luke then focused back on Aaron, not
sure if they could believe the guy.

"Ike had unlocked my safe with my key, grabbed my rifle
and ammo, then informed me I'd be doing my patriotic duty by
dying in the name of liberty. Then he kissed Chelsea and left."

"Are they a couple?" Luke asked.

"I guess so, but I don't think she loved him. Not anymore,
at least. She'd been trembling when she went on to my laptop
in my room, and tears started pouring down her face when
she returned from my bathroom with bottles of my meds."

"Make it look like a suicide?" Luke asked.

"Yeah. I tried to get her to explain to me what was going
on, but she could barely talk. Just kept crying." He took a
shaky breath. "She sat by the bed with a phone in her hand,
and then when the call came—"

"It wasn't the call Chelsea expected," Knox finished for
him. "Because Ike missed the shot. And since they sent the
threatening email and already set everything up to make it
look like you were the shooter, they couldn't risk you'd get
arrested before their second attempt to kill my dad."

"So, how'd you get away?" Luke asked, but he kept his
gun in the same position, pressed against his abdomen with
his free hand resting atop his other.

"She was supposed to force me at gunpoint to get into my
car, then drug me once I was in the back seat so she could go
meet up with Ike."

Knox's gaze dipped to the faint bruises on Aaron's
knuckles.

"I asked Chelsea to let me go. I said I'd take the fall for
the shooting if that's what she needed to happen, and I'd

never show my face again if she'd let me live. She told me to hit her a few times. She said it'd be the only way. She'd tell Ike I overpowered her, we struggled, and I got away—that was going to be the plan." His arms stretched, palms up, as shame slid across his face. "She kissed me goodbye with her lip still bleeding, then took off."

"All that planning, and she let you go?" Knox asked in disbelief.

He smoothed a palm over his bruised hand. "I guess she didn't plan on falling in love with me."

"Why not go to the police as soon as she let you go?" Luke asked.

"I was worried he'd kill her, and I made a promise."

"You didn't really plan on holding up that promise, did you? You'd let my dad die to save her?"

"I knew the police would never believe I was innocent, anyway, so I came over to Judy's house and asked a pretty big favor. And then I was going to come up with a plan to save Chelsea and take down Ike."

"So, you were here when the Feds went to your place on Wednesday?" Luke asked.

"Yeah."

"Why have your neighbor lie and say you took off from your home only after the news broke the story that you were a suspect?" Knox holstered his gun at the sight of Luke stowing his Sig.

"Because I was hoping that'd trigger some sort of alarm for the Feds, so they'd wonder why I waited to run until then."

Well, it worked. "You saw your neighbor talk to the Secret Service that day then?"

He nodded. "Then I saw the same agent on the news with

you guys at the truck station yesterday. I figured you guys were solid since you took down Ike."

"And who do you think leaked your name to the press?" He wasn't sure if he was prepared to buy the story yet.

"I don't know. Maybe Ike thought it'd help draw me out to find me quicker." He shrugged.

"So, how'd Chelsea die?" Knox asked. "If Ike killed her, why wait almost forty eight hours after she let you go to do it?"

"I killed her." His brows drew together.

Knox began to reach for his gun, but Aaron held up a palm.

"Not literally, but if I hadn't convinced her to let me go, Ike probably wouldn't have hurt her."

"So what the hell happened?" Knox's shoulders relaxed a touch.

"I'd been keeping an eye on her. I saw the FBI pick her up for questioning, then I stayed outside her place that night. I hoped Ike had bought her story about me, but I wanted to make certain she was okay."

"But when you saw one of the police cars leave that morning you couldn't resist talking to her, right?" Knox brought his hands into prayer position and tapped them at his lips as it all came together.

He closed his eyes. The true burden of guilt now showing. "Ike was probably worried Chelsea lied. He used her as bait to draw me out to test his theory. I was helping Chelsea pack her bags when he came through the back door. We fought, then he knocked me over the head with a lamp, and when I came to, she was already dead. My knife in her back." His eyes grew glossy.

"If Ike cared about Chelsea and saw her helping you as a

sign of betrayal—the strangulation and knife weren't only to frame you," Luke said. "A crime of passion, too."

"I know it's crazy that I'm sad over her death when she played a role in trying to kill your father, but I loved her. I'm sorry."

"Sometimes love can make you crazy," Knox admitted.

"He had the gun to my back, trying to get me to leave when I heard you guys hit the buzzer. I dropped to my knees, refusing to leave." He glanced at Knox. "He wanted to kill me right then, but he had orders to keep me alive."

"Until my dad was dead so he could frame you for his murder?"

"He said I was lucky they didn't have time to find someone else to pin the murder on, and that was the only reason he didn't double-tap me."

"What happened next?" Luke asked.

"Since you showed up, and I wouldn't leave with him, he had to take off." Aaron stood, and Luke stepped back to give him space. "I was going to stay, but she was dead, and it was his fault. And I wanted him to die for it."

"So, you grabbed your knife and ran. Why fight A.J.?" Knox asked.

"I had no idea whose side he was on. A.J. had been in BUD/S with us, and I wasn't sure if he was friends with Ike and part of it."

Luke lifted a hand to his ear. "You getting this?"

"Yeah," Asher replied. "Calling Jessica now."

"Do you have any idea who else Ike could be working with?" Knox asked. "Chelsea and Ike were part of the Liberation Defense Force. What can you tell me about them?"

His eyes stretched. "She was in the militia, too?" He slumped back onto the bed in surprise.

"You didn't know?" Knox cocked his head.

"No, she didn't tell me, but now I understand why I was chosen."

"Why is that?" Luke asked.

"The group was pissed I left. You don't exactly turn your back on them, and they said I'd pay eventually."

"Why'd you leave?" Knox asked.

"Ike pushed me to join. He'd said it'd be like being in the Navy again. The friendships and stuff, and I missed that. But they were a bunch of angry government-hating people. Wannabe killers. No bonfires and beers like Ike promised."

"You're saying the laid-back attitude is a sham?" Luke asked.

And shit, what would Roman be walking into tonight?

"I think it's an act to keep the ATF off their back," he replied. "But hell, their perimeter might look weak, but it's booby-trapped with land mines."

His words had Knox's spine bowing. Roman was minutes from making contact.

"Bravo Three," Luke said in a rush. "Tell Jessica to order Echo Team to stand down until further notice. Do you copy?"

"Copy that," Asher said abruptly.

"You've already been cleared of the assassination attempt," Knox told Aaron. "Sarah confirmed Ike took the shot. But the Feds aren't convinced you didn't play a part, especially given you all have a history together. And innocent people usually don't run."

"We can't turn him over to the Feds before we clear his name," Luke said. "Our best chance to take down the militia is to surprise them, and if they know Aaron's been taken in, they'll go underground, and we may lose the chance to find out who hired them."

"You think the militia even knows who hired them?" Knox couldn't help but ask.

"Maybe not directly, but I think they're our best shot at finding out." Luke averted his attention back to Aaron when he stood and crossed the room to the desk.

"They may have changed the compound since I was there, but I had to memorize every square inch of that property, so I didn't get blown to hell. I can draw you a map of sorts. I assume you're thinking to infil at some point. I'd go, but you probably won't be able to get me across state lines."

"Yeah, thank you," Luke replied.

But would they be able to get onto that property and without it turning into a blood bath? Operations in the U.S. were a logistical nightmare. Maybe if they used rubber ammo . . .

"Aaron, we're trusting you to stay put here, okay?" Luke kept his voice firm. "You're not planning on heading to the hospital and killing Ike out of revenge, are you?"

Shit, why hadn't Knox thought about that? If anyone ever so much as touched Adriana, he'd end them.

"I want you to find the pricks who are responsible for Chelsea's death."

"Doesn't mean you don't want Ike dead," Luke said. "Don't make me regret trusting you."

Aaron focused back on his notepad and Knox wasn't sure what to say, but he also didn't want to leave one of their people behind to babysit, and they couldn't exactly take Aaron with them.

"Bravo One, this is Three. You copy?" Asher came over the line.

"Copy, this is One," Luke replied.

"We have a situation. We didn't reach Echo Team in time. Echo Four has already made contact. He's gone inside."

Luke's eyes widened.

"Do we send the boys in after him?" Asher asked, and Luke pivoted his attention to Knox as if not sure what the hell to do right now.

"They'll be outnumbered," Luke replied. "Is Echo Four's cam working? Do we have eyes and ears inside?"

"One sec." Asher disappeared from the line for a minute.

"We could put up a drone if we have to," Knox said before Asher returned on the line.

"Roman's talking to someone," he began, "and I think they're buying it. But I don't think we're out of the woods yet. Not by a long shot."

* * *

KNOX GLIMPSED HIS PHONE AS HE HURRIED UP THE STAIRWELL to get to the hotel suite and meet up with Jessica.

Adriana: *Your father is secure. We're all set here. I'll call you when I can.*

She was on a government phone, and so he couldn't mention Aaron or anything he'd learned. He gave her a burner phone before she'd left so she could call him when she had a second alone. But seconds were turning into hours. Well, it felt like it, at least.

"My dad's at the hotel. Safe for now."

"Some good news, at least," Luke said, unlocking the door to the suite.

Asher blew past them and hurried to Jessica as if she was the one infiltrating the militia in Texas, not Roman. He practically crushed her against him as he pulled her into his arms.

"What do we know?" Liam asked once Asher released

her, and she pivoted the laptop around to showcase the screen.

"I'm sharing Harper's screen," she said. "Roman's okay. It looks like the militia bought his story. If they run a background check on him, the alias I created should hold up."

"Are we sure they're buying it and not just letting him think they bought it?" Unease burrowed in the pit of Knox's stomach. If anything happened to Roman . . .

"Let's hope so," she said, worry in her eyes.

"But we're not going to rely on hope," Luke said. "You get our tickets to Dallas?"

"Yeah." Jessica checked her watch. "You have an hour to get to the airport."

"I hate leaving you." Asher gripped both her shoulders.

"We can't exactly leave behind a case full of weapons in the hotel room. And the airline frowns upon rifles being brought on board." A small smile touched her lips. "I can stay here and work." She glanced at her brother. "If shit goes south for Roman, what will you do?"

"Private property. American soil. The guys at the compound would have every right to defend themselves if we go in, and we could end up on the wrong side of the jail bars for it," Luke began, slowly making eye contact with everyone in the room, probably remembering their fallen brother Marcus, who'd gone in alone on an op and died years ago. "But I don't give a damn as long as we bring our brother out alive."

CHAPTER TWENTY-THREE

"How are you holding up?" Adriana asked Knox over her cell phone. Knox had startled her awake with his call at three in the morning, but she'd hid her sleepy voice the best she could so he didn't feel bad about waking her.

"I hate not being with the team," he grumbled.

She dropped her eyes closed at the gritty texture of his tone—the pain there. "They needed you to stay back for a reason, right? Help with the case. Plus, it's good you're with Jessica. She's pregnant and shouldn't be alone."

A crackling came over the line from a deep breath. "This is my fight, too. I should be with them. We can't lose someone else."

"'Someone else'?" She sat upright with open eyes. "Who'd you lose? And why don't I know about it?"

These were the parts of his life he'd kept from her as if he needed to protect her from the truth. To prevent her from worrying even more than she already did when he was working.

Her insides hurt. Everything hurt.

And she wanted to weep for him. Weep about a loss that must've shredded him.

Her stomach dropped as she traveled back to the past—to the moment he may have been referring to.

He'd shown up at her doorstep. His eyes had been bloodshot. Booze on his breath. *"Can I crash at your place for a few days?"* He'd stumbled into her apartment in D.C., a brown bag in hand, and he'd barely made it to her couch before passing out.

And when he'd woken, he'd grabbed the bottle again.

She'd called out of work sick, afraid to leave his side.

He'd drunk himself into oblivion those few days—barely talking.

The only time she'd seen someone drink himself, practically to death, had been when her father lost her mom.

How had she not realized Knox had lost someone close to him? He'd been drunk before but not *that* kind of drunk. The kind that's meant to obliterate the deep, cutting pain of a monumental loss until you gather the strength to deal with it. If you ever do.

"I wasn't allowed to talk about it," he said after a few moments of silence. "Still not. But . . . a friend on my team, well, he died."

She let his words sink in, wondering how many other dark and painful stories he'd held back over the years. *Not allowed to talk about it? Whose orders?*

"I wish you'd told me so I could've helped." She moved off the bed and went to the window and peeked between the blinds and up at the sky. No stars in sight. Her mother's star wasn't visible, and she needed that star right now.

"Marcus died on an operation," he admitted slowly. "The, uh, details weren't made public."

"What kind of operation? I don't understand."

Knox had never even shared the names of everyone he'd worked with in the last seven years. A few had slipped into their conversation here and there. Jessica. Luke, of course. Wyatt. Liam. It wasn't until the barbecue she'd met the entire crew. Well, except for Luke and Eva, who'd been traveling at the time.

"We almost lost Liam last year, too," he said instead of answering her question, and there was a slight slur to his voice she hadn't picked up on before.

Lost Liam? Liam was a parent. A husband.

"Jessica, too."

His words had her stomach shriveling to nothing. Pain darting in crisscross patterns inside of her.

"A lot of close calls, but we can't lose anyone else." Emotion broke down his words into practically nothing, and —*oh, God*—was he crying? "You mind opening up? I probably shouldn't be drunk in the hall."

Her heart jumped at his words, and she whirled around and rushed to the door and swung it open.

He was sitting outside her room. A familiar brown bag in one hand and a burner—a cheap flip phone—in the other.

"I'm not your father," he said as she crouched before him. She held his face between her palms. "I don't have a drinking—"

"Shhh. I know." Tears hit her face as she leaned in and pressed her mouth to his. He returned her kiss with a lazy, whiskey-flavored one. "What are you doing here?" she asked when pulling back.

"Jessica decided we should stick close to my dad."

"Why didn't you tell me?"

"I-I don't know." His eyebrows pulled together, and she helped him stand. "I should be with Jessica and working, but Roman's okay right now. Asleep at the compound."

Once in the room, she took the bottle and phone from him and set the items on her dresser.

"But I have a bad feeling." His free hand converted to a fist, and he pressed it to his abdomen. "Right here, you know?" His eyes were barely open as he spoke, and she guided him to her bed. "I need to be with the team," he whispered as she unlaced his black sneakers and pulled them off. "I need to be with them," he said again.

"And they need you here to protect your dad. Find who is after him. You're helping from here," she tried to remind him. "Your dad needs you, too. Your mom." Still kneeling before him, she held both his hands between hers. Her lip quivered, her heart breaking for him.

He pulled his hands free from her grasp and tucked her hair behind her ears. "Are you mad at me?"

"Why would I ever be mad at you?" *Hurt for keeping things from me, but not mad.*

"I've been lying to you for so long." His hands fell onto the bed at his sides. "I'm so sorry. I was scared if you knew how dangerous my job was you'd be afraid to . . . I'm so damn sorry, Addy. There's so much I need to tell you and—"

"Stop," she begged. "If you want to tell me the truth, you're going to have to do it when you're sober. I won't let you do this now. You kept a secret from me for a reason." She palmed his cheek. "No liquid courage, okay?" It had to be that way.

"I need to get back to Jessica, but maybe I can close my eyes for a second." He started to shift to his back when he paused. "Damn those PJs of yours," he murmured before passing out.

The man had been running with barely any sleep since Tuesday. It was no wonder he was out of it right now.

Probably more tired than drunk. But, of course, he'd noticed her yellow cami and matching shorts.

She shifted him all the way onto the bed then searched his pants pockets for his room key.

After covering him, she changed and left the room for Jessica's suite.

"Is Knox with you?" Jessica asked the second she saw Adriana on the other side of the door. "I was in the bathroom changing, and when I came out, he was gone. I've been calling his phone, but it's off. Tried his burner—no answer."

"He's asleep on my bed. I wasn't sure if you knew where he was, so I thought I'd stop by."

Jessica's shoulders slumped with relief. "Thank you." She motioned her inside. "Is he okay?"

"He's been drinking. I don't even know where he got the bottle at this time of night, but he's finally sleeping, and I don't think he's slept since the shooting, so . . ."

"Thank you. I'm glad we came here." She sat at the desk, a similar setup to the hotel back in Charlotte. "I knew he'd feel better if we were near you. He's not used to being pulled from, um, *cases*."

"He's thinking about Marcus, too." She sat on the couch and kept her gaze steady on Jessica, noticing the slight twitch to Jessica's lips at the mention of the name. "He's worried about Roman."

Jessica pulled her focus from the screen to Adriana at her words but didn't speak.

"He didn't tell me anything, don't worry."

Jessica fidgeted with the knot of her ponytail as if not sure what to say.

"He's sad. It's been a hell of a week. Maybe you should be asleep, too?"

"I slept in the car on the way here, and right now, I'm

monitoring Roman's live camera feeds. Harper will take over soon when she wakes up."

"When do the guys meet up with the rest of the team?" Knox had filled her in on everything that'd gone down with Aaron before Luke and the others had flown to Texas. Only, Knox had left out the part about him heading to Atlanta.

"They picked up their gear at our location in Fort Worth around one, so they still have some driving ahead of them." Jessica brought her face closer to the screen and grabbed her glasses. "What the hell is he doing?"

"Roman?" Adriana stood and rounded the desk to view Jessica's laptop.

"I'm gonna kill him myself! He left his room, damn it." She reached for her phone and called someone. "It's me. Sorry to wake you, but Roman's on the move. He may be making a run for it."

"I don't think so." Adriana directed Jessica's focus to the screen. "He's hovering near that building."

"Get the guys ready in case things get hot, and Roman needs an extract." She was probably talking to Harper, but could four Navy SEALs go up against an entire armed militia and without it turning into a bloody mess?

"Should I get Knox?" Adriana asked her once Jessica ended the call.

"No, not unless things turn ugly. There's nothing he can do right now, anyway, and he'll lose his mind watching this." She dialed someone else next.

"Do you hear that?" Adriana crouched and pressed her ear closer to the computer. "Can you isolate the background noise? I think he's listening to someone talk, but it's pretty faint."

"Hang on, Luke." Jessica set her phone down, placed it on speaker, and began playing around with the sound.

"You getting this?" Roman's voice came through the screen. "Moving in to see who's talking."

"Roman," Jessica hissed as if he could hear her.

Could he hear her? What the hell kind of technology were they using? "He's looking through a window now." Adriana pointed. "Looks like a woman inside. Can we freeze the frame and get an ID?"

"What's happening?" Luke asked, alarm in his tone. "Tell me something."

"Roman's got eyes on someone talking," Adriana answered while Jessica worked at making the image clearer since they were looking through a window with partially open blinds.

Maybe she should get Knox? He'd be pissed to be kept out of this, but he'd also be useless to them without sleep.

"I have a visual. I recognize her. It's Darius's wife, Nina, on the phone," Jessica said after a moment. "I'm still working on making out the conversation."

"Roman's leaving now," Adriana said, her heart pounding wildly. "Looks like he's heading back to his cabin." Now he needed to get there without getting caught. Her hands fisted at her sides as she waited. "He made it!" She briefly hung her head.

"Thank God," Luke rasped over the line.

"I'm about to play back what I strung together from the recording. It's gonna be fragmented, but here we go." Jessica pressed play.

"Ike won't turn. I trust him," Nina said. "That wasn't the . . ." She paused. "If you change the . . . I can . . . you still want Bennett dead, right?" Another long pause. "Terms have changed. You forget that I came to . . . I . . . who you are."

Shit.

"Keep your hush money," Nina replied to the caller a few

seconds later. "This was never about . . . and if you think I don't . . ." Quiet filled the line after that.

"That's all I got," Jessica said. "I'll keep playing around with it to see if I can get more."

"I don't know what the hell to think," Luke replied. "Sounds to me like Darius's wife is the one in charge, not Darius."

Adriana replayed Nina's words in her head. "What the hell was she talking about?"

"Sounds like someone tried to buy her silence," Luke said. "And maybe he convinced her to kill Knox's dad."

"Yeah, well, lucky for us, the plan failed." Jessica stood. "And we're for damn sure gonna keep it like that."

CHAPTER TWENTY-FOUR

Adriana leaned against the wall alongside the bed in her hotel room, using it for support as she contemplated how to tell Knox what went down while he'd been asleep.

Sitting upright, he dropped his feet off to the side of the bed. He was still in his khakis and black tee from last night, but she'd brought clean clothes for him to change into.

His gaze swerved up to hers as he scratched at the stubble on his jaw. His eyes were still a bit bloodshot. A few hours of sleep wouldn't make up for all the hours he'd lost that week.

"I'm really sorry I showed up at your door in the middle of the night drunk." His voice was scratchy, and he smoothed a hand down his throat.

She pointed to the coffee she'd placed alongside his bed. A bottle of water and two ibuprofens, too. She'd had experience with her father over the years. Thankfully he was sober now, and she knew Knox wasn't her dad, but hangover slash lack-of-sleep headaches were known to be brutal.

"I'm glad you're here," she admitted. "The reason sucks, but I'm always happy to see you."

After he popped the pills and took a few sips of the

coffee, she pushed away from the wall to get a touch closer to his side of the bed.

On a scale of one to ten, how pissed would he be at her and Jessica for letting him sleep?

"So." Her tongue clicked to the roof of her mouth as she fought for how to unveil the truth.

"We should probably talk about what I said to you last night." He set the coffee aside and straightened his spine.

"As much as I want to hear what you have to say, there's something I need to share first," she said softly.

"What's wrong?" Worry inched through his tone.

"I went to your room when you fell asleep," she began. "I wanted to let Jessica know you were okay, but Roman—"

He rose immediately. "What happened?" His chest lifted and fell with deep inhalations.

"Roman left his room and wandered the compound. He was trying to find out information, I guess."

"He did what?" He tilted his face to the ceiling, closed his eyes, and cursed under his breath. "Tell me he didn't get caught."

"He's fine." She probably should've led with that, damn it. "After some digging, Jessica discovered Darius is really the muscle, and his wife, Nina, is the brains behind the militia. She's running the show."

"What?"

"Roman overheard Nina on the phone. Someone tried to pay her to keep quiet about something, as well as hire her to kill your father." She tipped her head to the door. "Jessica can fill you in on the rest. I'm sorry I didn't wake you. We, uh . . ."

"Don't apologize. It's about the last thing in the world you ever need to do." He reached for her hand and tugged her against him. "We'll get through this, I promise." His eyes lowered to her mouth, and then he kissed her with gentle lips.

She struggled to hide the moan building inside of her, but after years of staring at his mouth and dreaming of his kisses, she couldn't hide her feelings anymore.

"Addy." Her name vibrated against her lips, and he deepened the kiss. His hands went to her backside, and his fingertips buried into the denim fabric of her jeans. His mouth moved to her neck, and he lightly nipped her earlobe. "I wish you had those shorts on from last night."

"And we'd never leave this room if I did." Heat traveled through her body, and her silk panties dampened.

"True." He pulled back and lifted his palms to her face. "I wish we could stay in this room," he said gruffly, desire darkening his eyes.

But they couldn't.

There wasn't time for "date two."

"You should change. Jessica is waiting." Softness curled around her words as she did her best to be good and not fist his shirt and pull him back against her.

"Yeah," he said, his voice low. His hands still framing her face. "One more kiss, though." He leaned in and brought his mouth to hers, stealing her sanity. Her desire to be good.

For the first time in her life, she wanted to be bad. She wanted to be the little devil in red leather sitting on her shoulder, the vixen who'd whispered naughty thoughts about Knox over the years.

And when his hands dipped and slipped under her shirt once her back was to the wall, and he shoved her bra up to get to her nipples, she cried out a gasp, one that could probably be heard in the room next door—Calloway's damn room.

"Fuck, Addy." He palmed her breasts, breaking his mouth from hers so he could drop a few more curses.

He moved his hands to her thighs, guiding her to wrap her legs around his hips, and she followed his command, her body greedy for whatever moment they could steal before they had to get work-focused again.

"We." He kissed her, his hands wandering back up her shirt and to her breasts. "Should." Another quick kiss. "Go."

"Then." She kissed him back. "Stop." One more time. "Pinching my nipples."

She could feel his smile against her mouth, and she lowered her legs to the floor once he removed his hands from beneath her shirt.

"This sucks." He brushed her hair off her shoulders.

"You're the one who decided to make us wait the other night," she reminded him, then tucked her lip between her teeth.

His palm went to the wall over her shoulder, and he angled his head. "I should probably take a quick five-minute shower first. Care to join me?"

She laughed. "That shower would last a lot longer than five minutes. And you don't make a pregnant woman wait."

"You don't make Jessica wait. Period." He smiled. "We'll pick this up later. I promise."

But later was the ball, so . . .

Knox swapped his clothes for the clean ones. He'd changed in the bathroom, per her request. She'd been worried what seeing him naked would do to her. She also quickly traded her underwear for a new pair since she smelled like sex after their near hookup.

A few minutes later, they made their way to Jessica's room, but the heat between her thighs remained no matter how many times she'd tried to reset her focus.

"You okay?" Jessica asked the second they entered the room as she made her way to Knox.

They really were a tight unit, weren't they? There was a lot he had to tell her, but she'd be patient. She'd waited years. What were a few more hours or days?

"I'll be better when I know what's going on," he said while hugging Jessica.

She let go of Knox and went to her desk. "I found some photos of Nina and Darius together before they were married. Looks like they met during a government protest both were arrested that day. Married six months later."

"Why does she hate Uncle Sam? My parents?" he asked as Adriana settled onto the couch.

"Still working on a theory about your parents, but what I do know is her dad worked for the government. He was stationed at the American Embassy in Iran in the late seventies, and so the family lived there. Her father died in a car accident three weeks before the Iranian Hostage Crisis of seventy-nine. Nina found her mom OD'd on pills in the bedroom a few hours after learning of the father's death."

Knox stood off to the side of the desk. "Why does this sound like this is a bullshit cover-up?"

"Because it feels like one," Adriana responded.

"According to the reports, her mom couldn't handle the husband's death, and so she killed herself," Jessica said. "Nina had a younger sister. They were shipped back to the U.S. to live with an uncle, but he didn't want them. They were bounced around in the system. Nina was adopted but not her sister. And six years later her sister got ill and passed away."

"So, she blames our government for everyone close to her dying because her dad had been stationed in Iran," Knox said.

Jessica straightened in her seat. "I think Nina's background shaped who she became, but I don't think it's reason enough for her to suddenly want to kill your dad.

Something had to have set her off, and I'd assume more recently, or she would've gone after him before now."

"It sounds like this person specifically hired Nina to kill your dad," Adriana said. "Maybe even provided her with the motive—a motive aside from money. Although from the sounds of it, Nina went to the mystery caller first if she was being paid to keep quiet about something, right?"

Instead of answering, Jessica lightly rubbed her stomach, and her lips tucked inward as if there was something she wanted to say but resisted.

"What is it?" Knox asked, clearly noticing the look, too.

"Nina's dad worked for the State Department," Jessica began, "but everything about his work, his death . . . those files are redacted. Line by line almost all of them have been blacked out."

"So, his death *was* a cover-up?" His hands rested on his hips, and he appeared to be in military-mode again, all evidence of his desire replaced by his need for justice. Or maybe he hid his feelings better than her?

"Not only his death," Jessica said.

"You're thinking—"

"Nina's dad was CIA," Jessica said with a nod. "And I'm thinking her parents were murdered."

"But what does that have to do with my dad?" He shifted to the side and caught Adriana's eyes before focusing back on Jessica.

"Not your dad." Jessica was quiet as she stood. "Your mom ever tell you anything about her job at the State Department?"

"You're not actually suggesting my mom was a spook, are you?" he asked. His tone all hard edges and zero humor.

"I don't have an answer for you. But your mom was at the embassy in seventy-nine, and she may have known Nina's dad. Maybe someone told Nina your mom is responsible for the death of her parents," Jessica offered. "Things were a mess over there at the time, and if she blames your mom, maybe she wants to kill your dad as revenge. Nina might want to make your mom suffer the way she feels she has."

Shit. Adriana brought a hand to her mouth.

"There has to be another explanation." He cut his hands through the air and spun around to face Adriana, but his shoulders slumped with defeat. "My mom can't be a spy, and no way did she have anything to do with Nina's family dying."

"There's only one way to find out, right?" Adriana kept her voice soft.

Knox closed his eyes, his hands bunching at his sides. "Yeah," he said after taking a deep breath. "I'll, uh, be right back."

CHAPTER TWENTY-FIVE

"I NEED THE ROOM." KNOX FACED CALLOWAY AND THE other Secret Service agent in his father's hotel suite. "I need to speak to my parents privately." His entire body tensed. Muscles atop muscles locking tighter.

Echo Four was alone on a compound with a shit-ton of armed government haters, and it was very possible his mom was the reason for it.

"What's wrong?" Frowning, his mom removed her glasses and set aside the newspaper she'd been reading. Her questioning gaze held his, searching for answers. And then the frown dissolved and the delicate skin around her blue eyes relaxed a touch when realization hit her.

She knew why Knox was looking at her with barely restrained emotions. He saw it on her face, and in her rigid posture, which meant everything he thought about her had been a lie.

His knees buckled as a thought struck him. *He* was his mom. He lived the same lie. How the hell had this happened?

"Sir?" Rodriguez sought permission from Knox's dad whether or not to clear Secret Service from the room.

"Yes." His dad motioned for Knox to have a seat on the chair in front of him.

Knox waited for the room to empty, but he didn't sit. How could he when . . .?

"Does he know?" he asked, his voice straining.

The color drained from her face.

"Know what?" His dad semi-smiled as if he was missing out on a joke. "*Know* what?" he repeated, angrier this time.

"No." Her gaze moved to the window overlooking the buildings in the city.

Thirty-nine years of marriage. Thirty-nine years of lies.

"Somebody better fill me in before I lose my damn mind." His dad stood and looked back and forth between his wife and son.

But she still wasn't looking at them, damn it.

"How'd you find out?" she asked, her voice eerily calm. Maybe she was in shock? Her eyes dragged from the window to his father at an irritatingly slow pace.

"While trying to figure out the damn mess you seemed to have gotten us all into," he seethed through barely parted lips.

His dad stabbed a finger in the air. "Boy, don't you talk to your mother like that."

"Are you gonna tell him?" Knox's fingertips tucked inside his palms. "I don't want to do it for you. I *won't* do it for you."

"Dear." His dad lowered his voice this time. "What's going on?"

"I was planning on telling you," she said softly. "It never felt like the right time, but I was worried it may come out sooner or later if you ran for president." She clasped her hands together in her lap. "I should've told you sooner. I'm sorry." Her gaze moved to Knox, and her next words were spoken in the manner of a seasoned politician's wife, a role she played so well—calm, methodical, all about the facts. "Who broke the story? How can we get on top of this? I can make a speech, I guess. I've thought about this since they mentioned it might come out and . . ."

"The press don't know—only my people." *The press. The fucking press. Really? That's your focus?*

"I still don't know what in the hell you're talking about," his dad snapped, and for the first time in Knox's life, he felt sorry for him. "Now, damn it, if someone doesn't tell me what the hell is going on—"

"I was in the CIA, Isaiah," she interrupted. "This isn't about that, though. Your son is referring to the off-the-books team I was part of."

What? His stomach dropped at the news. *No. No. No.*

President Rydell's words from the Situation Room on Tuesday flew back to mind. *"Lyle also mentioned rumors of black ops groups existing under previous administrations during the Cold War days. Groups that'd gone sideways."*

She was more like him than he realized, wasn't she? He'd been doing his best not to be like his father, but he never stopped to consider the possibility he was like his mom. How could he have ever known, though?

"I don't understand." His dad fell back onto the couch as if he'd been pushed.

"I'd been recruited to the CIA during college. My cover story was that I worked for the State Department," she explained, her voice soft. "But in the mid-seventies, the government decided to put together a unique team of agents for specific black ops missions. We were a team of five—a small group, less chance of leaks. Not many in the government knew about us."

He knew a thing or two about that, but it was still too hard to believe the words *black ops* came from her mouth.

"What happened in Iran?" Knox asked, his question almost an accusation. "In seventy-nine. Three weeks before the hostage crisis."

Her lashes fluttered, and she looked up at him with sorrow in her eyes. "At first, my assignment was to identify American agents who were double-crossing us by handing intel to the Russians and Iranians. But we quickly realized it'd be more beneficial to keep those men and women in their positions without them knowing we were onto them, and then purposely feed them the wrong information."

Knox crossed his arms but shifted his attention to his father.

His dad's elbows were on his thighs, his head in his palms.

Broken.

Lied to by the woman he loved.

"Our plan had been working, but then—"

"Someone died, right?" *That's what always happens.*

"One of the men at the embassy who we believed to be selling intel . . . well, as it turns out, he wasn't. His wife had been stealing information from him, turning it over to the Russians. The Russians probably thought she was working with us since she'd provided them the wrong information so many times. We assumed they staged her death. Faked an overdose."

So Nina's dad wasn't CIA. "But not before murdering her husband as retaliation first, right?"

She nodded. "We were instructed to clean up the mess, hide what happened, and never talk about it again. And then the hostage crisis took place, and we were ordered back to the U.S."

"How could you lie to me all these years? Do I even

know who you are?" his father finally spoke up, bringing his eyes to her.

"You're the reason I quit, Isaiah. Please," she said as her eyes became glossy. "I met you, and I realized I'd never be able to be with you and lie about my job, and since I was sworn to secrecy, I quit." Genuine tears cut down her cheeks. "I chose you over the job."

Knox couldn't move. He could barely think straight as he witnessed the parallels between her life and his own.

"You still lied," his dad said bitterly.

"I did it to protect you, too. If anyone ever tried to get information out of you about me—"

"Don't. You were protecting yourself." He stood.

"I promise I was planning on telling you. I was afraid you'd look at me differently, and if the press found out, I didn't want it to hurt your chances in the election."

God, he had to tell Adriana the truth. He couldn't hide from reality anymore. Damn the consequences.

"Jefferson Lyle's people will have a field day with this if they find out you were part of some sort of black ops group gone wrong," his dad seethed in a bone-chilling voice.

His father's words were like a stab in the heart. No way would his dad accept Knox's true line of work after such a shocking discovery.

And he wasn't sure if he could blame his father, but that didn't reduce the pain in his chest.

"I need some air." He hurried past Knox, and his mom's shoulders flinched when the door slammed shut.

She stood, ready to go after him, but Knox blocked her. "Don't."

"I need him to understand. I didn't have a choice." More tears hit her cheeks. He hadn't remembered her crying like this since his grandfather died ten years ago.

"You need to give him time, but right now, I need names of everyone who would've known what happened in Iran in seventy-nine. One of them might be behind the attempted assassination."

"What? No." Her brows flew together, and she stumbled back a step. She cleared the tears from her face with the backs of her hands.

His heart hammered in his chest. Angry vibrations. "I —" His words died at the realization of something his mom had said, but he'd nearly missed it. "You said 'they' mentioned it'd come out—the truth, right? Who told you this? When?"

She blinked a few times. "My old team. We got together three months ago. Glenn said someone knew about us, and we needed to handle the situation."

"Glenn?" His stomach dropped, and he gathered a breath.

Her shoulders sagged. "Glenn Sterling."

"Your close friend, and now the man in charge of the investigation, was on your team in seventy-nine?" He kept his voice even despite the disbelief at what he was saying.

She nodded. "Paul. Charlie. Greg. All close family friends. The five of us. They'd never hurt your father, though."

He stepped back, his mind spinning. "What exactly did Glenn say to you? You need to tell me everything."

"Only that someone came to him with evidence that could expose us."

"And what'd you say?"

"I didn't believe someone would turn up with information after forty years, so I told him not to worry, but then—"

He reached for her arm, frantic. "What?"

"I said we should go ahead and tell Isaiah the truth. Maybe even the media. We could be in charge of how the story unfolded, and hopefully, Isaiah would walk away unscathed."

"And?"

She closed her eyes. "Everyone was adamant that I keep my mouth shut. They said we could lose the trust of the people. Paul's a governor. Glenn's with DHS." Her lids lifted, and her blue eyes shimmered. "Glenn said he'd handle it."

"And what'd you say?"

"That if the truth came out, then it was meant to be. I'd stand by my actions. I was protecting my country."

"And you didn't think it'd be relevant to tell me any of this when Glenn showed up in Charlotte the day of the shooting?" He let her go and turned his back.

"I never thought he'd try and kill your father. It'd been months since we talked, and I believed everything had been swept back under the rug."

"Mom," he hissed and faced her again. "Don't you get it?"

"What?"

"The shooter wasn't aiming at dad. The Bennett he wants dead is you."

* * *

"I can't believe it," Luke said over the phone.

"I'm still wrapping my head around it, too." Knox stood in the parking lot away from the hotel, ensuring no one was around so he could talk in private.

"Would the deputy secretary really rather your mother die than risk the truth going public?"

He squeezed his eyes closed. "It was the Cold War. They were protecting American secrets from getting into the wrong hands. They weren't ruthless killers."

"But they were operating without the knowledge of Congress and . . ." Luke let his words go even though they were on a secure line, but Knox got his point. It was the same reason why they stayed in the shadows now.

"Every name on the list has a lot to lose if they were ever connected to that team," he said when opening his eyes.

A governor. A senator. Congressman. And, of course, the deputy secretary now in charge of the investigation.

"You're thinking Glenn didn't act alone?" Luke asked.

"It's possible. The five of them got together not too long before Chelsea moved to Charlotte when the assassination plot began, so Jessica's trying to see if any of them were ever together after that but without my mom present."

"What about Nina?"

"Jessica's checking her whereabouts three months ago, too," he replied. "If she flew to D.C., we'll try and track her movements to confirm she confronted Glenn."

"Since he didn't kill her on sight to keep his past a secret, she must've been smart enough to have a plan to get out of there," Luke said.

"But he also managed to manipulate her into blaming my mom and no one else for her parents' death. A smart fucker," he said through gritted teeth. "He probably wrote out the plan for her, too. Told her to frame someone. Helped out with the cameras. Gave her the details of the event—he'd know more because he's friends with my mom and with DHS."

"Nina may have something on him, but Glenn had no intention of letting her live after the assassination. He'd make the militia the fall guy for everything."

"Which means he has a plan to get whatever evidence she has from her before then," Knox replied. "But why'd Nina wait so long to approach Glenn if she suspected someone murdered her parents?" He'd discussed theories with Jessica and Adriana before calling Luke after confronting his mother, but he wanted Bravo One's opinion on it, too.

"She couldn't have been sitting on that information all her life, which means she only recently found out, but as to how —damned if I know, but I'd stake my life on Jessica figuring it out."

He leaned against the Suburban, his eyes on the hotel. "I assume when Harper traced the call Nina made last night, it went to a burner?"

"Yeah, and it's been turned off so we couldn't ping a location, but if it gets flipped on, we'll try and get a signal." He was quiet for a moment. "You really think you can convince Quinn and Rodriguez to withhold intel from Glenn until we know more, especially without bringing your mom's past into it?"

"I'm sure as hell gonna try, but I hate to do it, even if we get all of this figured out and my dad wins the election, I don't know if he'll keep the teams going. He might compare me to my mom and—"

"You're not like her," he quickly responded. "What you do and what she once did are very different."

"This could be our last operation," Knox admitted, his voice grim. His entire body tensing.

"I know," Luke said. "But I'll be damned if we go out without a win." He paused. "Tell Adriana. Don't wait, okay? I know it's eating at you, and if you need to hear me say it, I'm doing that now. I'm giving you permission."

He cleared his throat, unable to answer without his voice breaking. "I, uh, what's the plan for you guys next?" he asked instead.

"So far, Roman's told us to stand by. He doesn't want to leave yet. He's trying to find out more, but we flew the drone over the compound to get a better visual from above."

Their drone was small and would be well-hidden from view with its camouflage panels, but it wasn't completely invisible. It was much better than what they had up until last year, though. Jessica and Harper had borrowed the latest tech the SEAL Teams used on aircraft, and they used it to upgrade their drones so they could be, for the most part, unseen.

It was nice to finally have a bird's-eye view of a location before they dropped in. As long as no one looked too closely in the sky, they'd be fine.

"Any place for the boys to get into position for overwatch?" Knox asked. They couldn't leave the drone up in the sky for more than thirty-seven minutes, which meant they'd need eyes on the militia.

"Not really any high ground, but it is heavily wooded. Before the Hiltons took over the property it'd been a hunting site, so the tree stands have come in handy. The boys have a decent look inside at the north side of the compound. Liam's working on trying to get a better view of the south side. He might need to use a tree saddle to get up high for the vantage point we need."

"Anyone tell Owen yet what's going on?"

"Honestly, I don't want him to know about Roman," Luke said. "He has a newborn, and I'm afraid he'll steal a plane to get to us if he has to."

"Damn straight he would, and I'd be with you, too, if—"

"Don't," he cut him off. "You're where you should be. End of story. Besides, someone needs to watch out for my stubborn sister, or we'll have to answer to Asher, and I swear her pregnancy hormones are rubbing off on him."

He also wasn't ready to leave Adriana, but if this was truly Bravo Team's last operation, how could he not be with his people?

CHAPTER TWENTY-SIX

Knox: *What are you wearing tonight?*

Adriana: *Oh, I thought clothing was optional.*

Knox: *Your humor is lost on me right now.*

Adriana: *Shouldn't you be working on the case with Jessica while I play dress-up?*

Knox: *Yes, but I'm thinking about you and what is under that dress.*

He was deflecting. He had to be. The man had learned his mother had once been part of some secret black ops group, and a close family friend may have been behind the assassination attempt to cover it all up.

So yeah, he had to be reeling. And he was dealing in the way he knew best by making jokes.

They still didn't even know if his dad would show up tonight.

Would he drop out of the race altogether?

Adriana: *Maybe I'm wearing a pantsuit.*

Knox: *No way. This is your first ball, and you love Disney films. You're in some fancy gown. Am I right?*

Adriana: *Maybe I'm in something pretty, but I did put panties on since you won't be the one taking me.*

She stood in front of the mirror and smoothed a hand over the layered black fabric, which had a slit going up one leg. A halter style for a top and a low-cut back.

She'd done her makeup, too, which was a rarity.

Dark eyeshadow, black liner, and mascara. A touch of blush on her cheeks and a semi-nude lipstick with gloss. She'd left her hair down in soft waves over her shoulders since her mother had always loved it that way.

Knox: . . .

Knox: . . .

Adriana: *What?*

Knox: *And I'm now imagining twenty different ways I'll be making you scream my name after we have that second date.*

Adriana: *One for each year, huh? And I see you've given in to my 2-date request.*

Knox: *Everything will be okay. You know that, right? You have my word.*

And he was protecting her again. Always.

Adriana: *I know.*

And there were so many other things she wanted to say to him, but not over text and not with so many lives on the line.

But could she go to a ball and give a speech in the meantime?

She looked at her phone, not sure what else to say, when there was a knock at the door. Her dad lived only twenty minutes away, so he'd be escorting her to the ball tonight.

Adriana: *My dad's here. I won't be long. I'll meet you back up in the suite soon.*

"Coming," she called out, tucking her phone in her black clutch.

When she swung the door open, she nearly tripped backward in her tall heels at the sight before her.

"You're not my dad."

She observed Knox in his tux. Black slacks, a crisp white shirt beneath the jacket. Broad shoulders. A bow tie to boot. He'd also shaved, and he was a man who looked hot with or without the scruff.

"Who are you, and what have you done with my best friend?" She looked left and right in the hall. He reached for her hips and pulled her tight to his body, and she surrendered to him in every possible way.

"I asked your father if I could take you instead," he said. The rich huskiness of his voice had her thighs squeezing. "I was hoping for a redo."

"A redo?" She slung her arms over his shoulders, hating how much she actually loved he'd shown up, even though he wasn't supposed to be there.

"Senior prom."

"But you brought me to prom."

"And you know I screwed that night up," he said as he moved his mouth near hers but didn't yet kiss her. "I wanted to be there as more than your friend, but you were only seventeen and too young for the things I wanted to do to you, and I also never thought—"

She kissed away his words. Apologies and remorse for the should've-could've-would've no longer needed.

"What was that for?" he asked with a smile after she pulled back.

"For being you. For always being you."

She could see the conflict in his eyes.

He thought there were two sides of him. The Teamguy and the man he was with her. And maybe he'd done his best to keep it that way, but he didn't need to do it anymore. No more barriers between them.

"You talk to Rodriguez?" he asked after letting go of a breath, and she turned from his grasp to retrieve her clutch from the room.

"Yeah, and he's not sure how he feels about keeping Glenn out of the loop, especially since I provided him with spotty details." She frowned when facing him where he stood inside the room. "I hate lying. He's the agent in charge and has your father's best interests at heart."

"I can't risk the truth coming out about my mom or tip Glenn off we're onto him." Stress cut lines across his forehead as he observed her.

"You do realize people may find out anyway, right? I mean, from the sounds of it, Glenn's willing to kill to keep it a secret, too." She tucked her clutch under her arm and stood before him. "And whatever Nina knows may be all we've got to prove Glenn's behind this."

"I know." His eyes dropped to his black shoes. "And we'll cross that bridge when we come to it." His broad shoulders shifted back as he found her eyes once again. "I'm not used to trusting people not on my team, though, so this is all a bit of an adjustment."

"No?" She stepped closer. "What are you used to?" She swallowed when his eyes seemed to gleam with the overhead light shining above.

"Not this. Not having you right here with me, that's for sure." The deep timbre of his voice cut through to her belly and produced the battery of wings to flap and flutter. "Not having you within my reach when I need you."

"So reach for me. I'm here." She let her clutch fall to the floor when he pulled her into his arms.

His lips were so close to hers, but he didn't kiss her this time.

He held on to her, staring into her eyes as if he were seeing her as a woman right now and not the teenager who'd lost her mom.

"You know how much I care about you?" His hand slid up her bare back while his other shifted to palm her cheek.

"I think I have a pretty good idea."

"When this is over, I'll tell you everything. I promise."

"I trust you," she whispered and brought her lips to his, needing to be his right now. And every moment after that.

CHAPTER TWENTY-SEVEN

"MR. FOSTER, IT'S GOOD TO SEE YOU." KNOX EXTENDED HIS hand, but Adriana's dad pulled him in for a hug. "I know the event is formal, but like hell are you gonna shake my hand."

Her dad kissed Adriana on the cheek after, then gathered her in his arms. "Hi, sweetie, and don't you look beautiful."

Knox took in the sight of the ballroom, hating to be in a crowd of elitists, the press, and politicians.

He didn't belong in that world anymore. Probably never belonged there even when he was growing up.

Where are you? His dad and mom had yet to show. He had no idea what to expect tonight. Would his dad forgive her? Would he drop out of the race out of fear she'd be exposed?

Knox brought his attention back to Adriana's father.

Her dad had light hair to her dark. His eyes were brown to her green. She'd taken after her mom. Her hair. Eyes. Full lips and cheekbones. Her heart, too. Her desire to serve.

He was certain that one of the reasons Adriana had originally chosen to teach criminal justice instead of joining the academy was because she'd been scared something would happen to her, and she'd leave her dad the way her mom had.

She'd let go of those fears, though. And looking at her now, even if it terrified him to think of her in danger, she'd made the right choice.

"How are things going?" Knox asked.

"I've started teaching at a local community college in Atlanta. Mostly night classes." He reached for Knox's shoulder and gave it a squeeze.

Her father had lost so many jobs over the years because of his drinking, and he really hoped this was it for him. Adriana deserved a father she could depend on.

"You took care of my girl when I couldn't," her father said, surprising him. "And I'll never be able to repay you."

"You don't owe me anything, sir."

"How many times have I told you to call me Bobby?"

That'd be like calling his father by his first name, and he wasn't sure if he could do it, so he tipped his head and smiled, then looped his arm with Adriana's without thinking.

If the press saw them together as a couple, it could paint a target on her head in so many ways. But he couldn't seem to let go of her.

Eva, Sam, Emily—they knew the risks that came with marrying their husbands, but Adriana had no idea how dangerous it could be to stand at his side.

"You're finally together," her father said, a gleam in his eyes. "About damn time."

"Dad," she said with a laugh.

"I hope the next event I go to is a wedding. Nothing would make me happier than to walk my baby girl down the aisle to you, son."

"Dad, we, um . . ."

"Thank you, sir. I appreciate that." Like hell would there

273

be any man other than him greeting her at the end of that aisle. He'd always known that, hadn't he? He'd never had the guts to admit it, even to himself, though. But the idea of her marrying another man . . . he would've been the one to stand up in the church and yell *object*, for sure. Thank God it hadn't come to that.

He felt Adriana's eyes on him, curiosity there, but he did his best not to look at her. He wouldn't be able to stop himself from kissing her.

"Your mom's old partner is here," her dad announced. "He'll be speaking before you go up there, honey. If you want to talk to him, I can bring you over." He pointed to a man in a decorated uniform off to the side of the stage talking to a few other officers.

Knox had met him at her mother's funeral when he'd spoken about Patricia Foster with tears in his eyes. He was a good man from what he remembered. "If you don't mind me asking, when did my father first approach you about honoring your wife?"

"About four months ago. He said whether he won the primary or not he wanted to have this event," he answered.

"So, this wasn't a last min—"

"Adriana was a late addition," he cut him off and added a nod. "When your father called me, he asked if Adriana would like to attend, but I'd been worried with her busy schedule she wouldn't be able to come. I'm sorry I made the assumption."

Relief struck him.

"I, uh, probably would've been busy. Guess I still am. But never too busy to honor Mom." She shifted her focus to Knox, and he could see what was in her eyes. An apology.

She'd also assumed Knox's dad had invited her to try and rope Knox into coming. He didn't blame her for thinking that since he sure as hell had jumped to the same conclusions.

"Speaking of your father, it looks like he's arrived." He pointed to Isaiah Bennett entering the room.

Knox's mom was at his side in a stunning navy gown, looking every bit a secret spy from an old Bond film in his eyes now.

"If you'll excuse me," Knox said, his nerves moving into his throat with the anticipation of the conversation to come.

Adriana pulled her arm free of his but then wrapped a hand over his uninjured forearm and lightly squeezed, offering him her support.

He strode across the room, dodging the guests who attempted to talk to him as he made his way to his parents.

His dad spotted him and cocked his head to the left, signaling to follow him out of the main room.

Secret Service paved the way for them to exit the ballroom and go to an area designated for hotel staff only. The double doors were promptly closed for privacy behind them.

"You came." His father's hands were hidden in the pockets of his double-breasted tuxedo jacket, his eyes on Knox.

"I came for Adriana," he admitted, almost forgetting the fact his dad hadn't used her to get him there. "But now I'm also here for you."

He tilted his head as if surprised by Knox's statement. There was a warmth in his dark eyes he'd never noticed before. Maybe he hadn't wanted to notice, because he'd spent so much of his life *wanting* to be angry at him.

"Are you okay?" He couldn't help but worry how things went down between his parents after he'd left their suite earlier.

A brief, closed-mouth smile met his dad's lips, his broad chest stretching with a deep inhale.

"I'm sure it can't be easy," Knox added, "but I hope you're not considering dropping out of the race."

"I'm no quitter, and you know that." His brows drew together. "Just like I've got a feeling you never really quit the Navy."

Knox opened his mouth to speak, but his father held up a palm as if to say *No need to explain.*

Knox's gaze fell to the tiled floor, his mind spinning. Did he know? How was it possible?

"Do you forgive her?" Knox kept his focus on the floor, his voice low. He wasn't ready to see the look in his father's eyes—to discover whether he'd forgive him, too.

"It'll take some time. When you've been with someone for thirty-nine years, it's tough to find out they didn't trust you. She couldn't come to me with intimate details about her life."

He cringed. Would his dad feel the same about him when he learned the truth?

"But we sat and talked after I cooled down, and now I understand that wasn't the case." Any other man and emotion would've choked his words and strained his voice, but his dad had experience in dealing with curveballs.

"So, you forgive her?" He seized a breath as he waited for a response, not ready to let go of it until he heard the words he needed to hear.

"Yes," he said, and Knox allowed himself to exhale.

"In all honesty, it sounds to me like she's a hero." His voice did break this time, and when he cleared his throat, Knox looked up. "She didn't do it for the credit. No recognition at all. She silently served but then left that life for me."

"What would you have done if she told you the truth before she quit?" His heartbeat picked up as he waited. As his father contemplated.

"I wouldn't have asked her to make a choice between me and the job." He grew quiet again. "But I don't think I would've been able to be with her if she was in such a dangerous job. The worry and stress. You saw how I got when you joined the Navy. I'm a different man now, though."

He swiped a hand up the back of his neck a few times as he grappled with his father's words.

"You really think Glenn Sterling tried to kill her?" His dad's voice grew grave, a rush of intensity hardening his tone.

"Unfortunately." Knox allowed the truth to stretch between them before adding, "Sorry."

"I can't imagine he'd betray us like this." He shook his head in disappointment. "But I guess you never really can know a person, can you?"

And that was the truth. The sad damn truth.

"I'm going to end this, though. I promise." He stepped closer to his father. "No one dies on my watch. I won't let anything happen to you or Mom."

"I don't want you risking your neck for me, Son." He kept his voice level, even though his eyes shone with tears on the verge of escaping.

"The country needs you. You're a better man than I ever gave you credit for, and for that, I'm sorry."

His dad pulled him in for a tight hug, and Knox buried his face in his dad's shoulder, fighting to keep it together.

His dad had been worried that his mom had nearly taken a bullet because of him, and as it turned out, he almost took a bullet because of her. His world had flipped and then flipped some more.

"I love you, Son," he said, his tone strained.

His father's words caught him by surprise. At that moment, Knox broke down and became a son rather than a sailor. Not a man who harbored hate and secrets. "I, uh, love you, too, Dad." He pulled back and caught his dad brushing away a tear.

"We should go back in there, I suppose."

"Dad?" he called after his father had turned toward the ballroom doors.

"Yeah?"

"Thank you for including Adriana's mom tonight. She died a long time ago, but the city still remembers her sacrifice. It means a lot to the both of us."

The two agents stepped back and opened the doors to the ballroom.

"I saw you two come together, and I'm hoping you've finally taken your head out of your ass and admitted to her how you feel." He paused in the middle of the doorway, ignoring the many voices calling out his name.

Knox approached, and he couldn't help but smile. "It's been firmly removed, sir."

His dad slapped a hand on his shoulder. "Thank God," he said when they entered the main room. "Your mom was worried you'd never give us grandchildren."

Before Knox could respond, the governor approached. He wasn't in the mood for small talk, so he made a quick exit in search of Adriana.

She stood off to the side of the main stage, which was draped in bright lights. Rodriguez and Calloway were talking to her, but she must've felt Knox's eyes on her because she pivoted to find him in the crowd.

He navigated the throng of people drinking and talking to get to her, once again dodging questions and comments on his way.

After arriving at her side, he took her elbow and whispered into her ear, "Did I tell you how incredible you look tonight?"

"I believe you got tongue-tied earlier and forgot."

"Bennett," Calloway said, redirecting his focus.

"Calloway," he returned in an equally firm voice then nodded hello to Rodriguez.

Rodriguez brought the mic tucked in his sleeve to his mouth. "Hawk and Hummingbird will be heading to the stage in three minutes."

Calloway and Rodriguez were in tuxedos, probably to blend in with the guests, but the coil wires spiraling up the sides of their necks to their earpieces gave them away.

"How's your dad doing?" she asked softly once the men had left, and her gaze traveled across the room to where his parents stood in conversation with the governor. "And your mom?"

Knox took them in for a moment. He could tell his dad was working hard to maintain a brave face. His mom, on the other hand, remained stoic.

A spy. It'd take a lot more than a day to absorb that bit of truth. A couple lifetimes maybe.

"They're good, I guess. He's going to forgive her." He found Adriana's eyes, wishing he could tell her the truth now, too. "You ready to go up there?"

"A bit shaky." She held out a hand between them, and damn, there was a tremble. "And I know when I go up there my heart will pound so fast it'll make talking difficult."

He leaned in. "You've got this. Picture everyone naked."

"Your dad? Calloway?" she teased.

"Scratch that." He smiled, flashing her his teeth. "Only me."

"Well." She brought her finger over her lips and tapped a short nail there. "I'll be rendered speechless then."

"Oh, trust me, when I have my way with you, you'll be a lot more than at a loss for words."

Her emerald green eyes greeted his, and all he could think about was how close he was to taking her that morning in her room. The way she'd responded to his kiss—the feel of her in his arms.

"And what will I be?" she rasped in a sensual voice.

"Mine," he responded without hesitation.

Her gaze wandered south of his belt buckle and to his crotch, and it was as if she'd known he was ready for her despite being surrounded by a crowd. "It's been twenty long, long years."

"You don't think I know that?" She arched a brow and pointed to the stage. "Your dad is about to make introductions."

He hooked an arm around her back, and they advanced toward the stage. He didn't bother hiding his erection since the place was so crowded. But at the sight of his father and mother on the stage—yeah, that was a boner-killer for sure.

His dad said a couple more words to the crowd, his eyes catching Knox in the audience for a brief moment. "This room is filled with many brave and special men and women," he continued. "Men and women who've helped this city in different ways. Whether you've served in combat abroad, or on the streets at home . . . or in the classrooms to educate our youth, so many of you have made great sacrifices for this city." He pivoted to face the man who'd been Adriana's mother's partner. "It's an honor to be here with you all. I know we've had problems in the country. This city, too. Division. But I truly believe we can all come together and be united as one. And I'd like to highlight some exceptional men and women here tonight who have fought to create a strong sense of community here."

His father continued to speak for a few more minutes and then turned the mic over to Mike, Adriana's mother's old partner. And now it was Adriana's cue to join the stage. Knox forcefully shoved his hands into his pockets, wishing he were at her side as she climbed the steps to get to the stage.

"Patricia Foster never wanted to be a detective. She wanted to remain on patrol," Mike began. "She said she didn't want to solve crimes, she wanted to prevent them." He smiled. "Patricia was optimistic. Compassionate. A woman who cared about her community. She believed in equality for all, and she fought tooth and nail to make sure everyone in the city was treated fair. She used to say that the badge is only as good as the trust people have in it. And trust was something she had from the people." He turned to view Adriana. "She'd be so proud of the woman you've become." His eyes met the crowd briefly. "I'd like to introduce you all to Adriana Foster."

Adriana took the mic, and when she stepped closer to the podium, the lights overhead basked her in soft tones, as if the lights were her mother embracing her.

"Thank you, Mike." Adriana hugged him and directed her attention toward the audience. "I'm humbled to be here. I'm grateful for all that you do." Her eyes connected with Knox. "Whenever I've thanked officers or veterans for their service, so often they say to me, '*don't thank me, just be the kind of person worth protecting.*' I believe my mom felt the same way, too."

Her words reached inside and touched his soul, and a tightness stretched across his chest.

"A little over seven years ago, I learned my mother had considered joining the Secret Service when she was younger.

She chose to stay with the precinct, and I'd thought that choice had been because she'd had me, but standing here now, I think I was wrong." She took a breath as if fighting to keep her voice from faltering.

She turned to Knox's dad off to the side of the stage.

"As important as it is to protect people in your position," she began, directing her words toward Isaiah Bennett, "I think my mom was where she belonged. Her home was Atlanta." She held her free hand open. "When she died, I was a heartbroken fifteen-year-old kid. I wanted to blame myself. Blame the world. The shooter. Absolutely everyone for her loss."

He couldn't see the tears in her eyes, but he knew they were there. He could hear the emotion in her voice.

"But she wouldn't have wanted that," she said, a tremble in her tone. "She'd want me to focus on something—more like *someone* else. You see, my mom died so another could live. Actually, so two people could live." She sniffled. A tear slipped. "The woman my mom saved was pregnant. She'd gone to the convenience store in the middle of the night because an ice cream craving had hit her." She forced a tiny smile on her face. "My mom was on her way to pick me up from a party, but she'd promised to pick up my favorite kind of candy bars on her way."

She took a shaky breath that reverberated over the speakers. Her eyes met Knox's as if searching for the strength to continue. He put a hand over his heart and tipped his head.

"My mom was there that night, so Naomi and her daughter could be here today." She motioned toward the two women next to Knox's dad on the stage. A woman in her late forties with her daughter. "Naomi's daughter was born because my mom jumped in front of a gunman who'd gone there not to rob the store, but merely to kill innocent people.

My mom shouldn't have died because of him, but a lot of things in life shouldn't happen."

His eyes remained locked with hers, never breaking the connection as she spoke. But his heart . . . damn, it hurt so much.

"But my mom didn't hesitate to save Naomi and her unborn child. She used her body as a shield, drew her weapon, and took down the man that night—but he also took her down, too."

More tears fell, but she didn't brush them away. She let them show. Wore them proudly.

And God, did he love her so much.

Naomi moved toward the stage and hugged Adriana, tears on her face as well.

Not a dry eye in the ballroom.

Knox blinked back his own tears and maneuvered through the crowd in preparation for her exit off stage.

Once she said a few parting words and headed his way, he didn't hesitate. He gathered her in his arms and held her against him, never wanting to let go.

"Addy," he whispered into her hair, ignoring the click of cameras off in the distance.

"I'm okay," she said, pulling back, her cheeks damp with tears. "I promise."

"Can we get out of here then?" he asked, nearly choking on his words. "There's something I need to tell you."

CHAPTER TWENTY-EIGHT

"You don't have to do this tonight."

"Actually I do." Knox's strong masculine hands dipped down the sides of her body, over the material of her gown, settling on her hips. He held on to her like he was afraid she'd run when he revealed whatever it was he needed to tell her.

She hadn't been all that nervous about learning the truth earlier, more so anxious, but maybe she should be considering his viselike grip.

"I, um." His chest lifted with a deep inhalation, and he let it go as he closed his eyes.

Her legs became as shaky as her quick breaths while she waited for him to continue.

"Learning the truth about my mom today," he finally spoke, eyes still sealed, "the secrets she kept from my dad for almost forty years . . . it was a shock. To be honest, I'm still reeling. Which makes it that much harder for me to tell you my truth, what I've been keeping from you." His eyes opened and found hers. "Because you see, I'm like her."

Like her? Her knees buckled as his brown eyes remained

on her as if searching for a reaction since she had yet to speak.

But she wasn't sure how she felt.

Her lips rolled inward.

Her eyes lowered to the ground between their close bodies.

"A spy, you mean?" she whispered.

"No." He let go of her, but she didn't think she could stand on her own.

A chill cupped the sides of her body in place of the warmth of his hands.

She stumbled back a step and stretched an arm out in front of her for balance before turning away from him.

"Sit." His voice was low and deep behind her, and she moved to the bed.

The soft mattress sank a little beneath her weight, and she shifted the fabric of the gown when the slit exposed nearly the entire length of her right leg.

"I'm not CIA." His hands disappeared into his pockets, and he remained several feet away.

Then what are you? "You said you're like your mom." She lifted her eyes, but the farthest she could go was to his dark bow tie. Nerves prevented her gaze from reaching his. She needed to hear more first.

"One of the main reasons you never met my friends is because I was terrified you'd put two and two together and realize I never really retired."

This time, she did look up. How could she not? "I don't understand," she said, hating the weakness in her tone.

"Black ops," he said, his throat moving with a swallow. "That's how I'm like my mom."

Another cold chill touched her skin, coaxing goose bumps to pop. "Navy SEALs run black ops missions already. I-I

285

don't follow." She tightened her hands into fists atop her lap, hoping to ground herself and channel her strength so she could get through this conversation.

"Yes," he said. "But the Navy still follows the chain of command. Operations can take weeks, even months, for approval. My people, well, we don't follow the same guidelines, because like my mom's team, we don't technically exist."

He took one step closer to the bed. Only one, though. He was worried she'd run, wasn't he?

"The night I told you that I was quitting the Navy . . . it was really to be on Bravo Team."

His words played in her head a few times before she asked, "Who do you work for?"

"Usually, President Rydell."

She swallowed back a lump in her throat.

Of all the outlandish theories she'd come up with over the years, why hadn't this been one of them?

"What kind of missions?" she asked, her voice less shaky this time. "What do you do?"

"Remember what happened to that communist guy in Panama last month?"

She pulled up the news story in her head. "That was you?"

His eyes went to the floor, but he murmured, "My team."

She had so many questions, but she didn't want to overwhelm him. Or herself, for that matter. Before she became Secret Service, she taught criminal justice. She believed in upholding the law. And . . . "What are the rules of engagement? Do you have some type of license to kill?"

"We still follow the same code as in the Navy," he answered in a low voice, his tone almost hollow, obviously worried about how she was interpreting his words. "If we're ever caught, we'll say we acted alone, though. It's why we have Scott and Scott."

He'd sacrifice himself, even go to jail, if it meant protecting his country. Would she expect anything less of this man?

She replayed his admission, and a thought struck her. Everything finally coming together piece by piece.

"With President Rydell's term coming to an end, you're worried you'll be exposed if Jefferson Lyle and his VP Leslie Renaldo win, right?" They'd never approve of such a group. But would Isaiah Bennett? "But if your dad . . ." She didn't even know where to go with this. It was all so much.

"We need my dad to win so we can remain active. Well, hopefully, he'll keep us around, but yes, the alternative to my father won't be good for us." Guilt glided through his tone with each word. With each step closer to the truth.

Her heartbeat had become a dull achy thud in her chest as she continued to absorb his secret.

He really had been living in two worlds, but she didn't want him to feel like it was necessary anymore. Not with her, at least.

She stood, fighting the tremble in her body. She needed to face him with strength and deliver her words with confidence. He needed to know how she really felt. How she'd always feel about him.

"Like my mom, I was sworn to an oath. And then there's the real possibility you could get hurt being connected to me if someone ever discovered the truth." He took another two steps back. "I couldn't handle if anything ever happened to you, Addy," he said, his voice breaking.

"Don't." Fear, the kind the devil whispered, tried to sneak up her spine, but she refused to give in. "Don't try and push me away. Don't let the truth do that to us. I just got you. The real you. I-I refuse to lose you."

He angled his head, but he didn't budge from his rigid stance. There was worry in his brown eyes. A fierce battle between his desire to love and protect her. Didn't he realize he could do both?

"I'd never let anything happen to you, but . . . that doesn't mean I can stop something from happening to me."

He could die.

She understood that.

Hated that.

And she'd fight like hell to prevent it.

"I know," she whispered, her eyesight blurred by unshed tears.

"What are you thinking?" He cupped his mouth briefly, his eyes capturing hers. "Tell me."

"I know the kind of man you are." One step closer to him. One tear hitting her cheek. "So that means this black ops group or not-so-retired SEAL life . . . whatever it's called . . . you're helping others. Making a difference. You wouldn't do it otherwise."

He sucked in a visible breath, and he held it until she reached him. She grabbed hold of his forearms and secured his hands to her hips where they belonged. "If I can trust you with my life, the American people can, too."

His eyes became liquid, and his mouth tightened as if struggling to contain his emotions. "I'm so sorry. I never wanted to hurt you."

"I love you, Charlie. I'm not going anywhere."

His lips crashed over hers. A nearly bruising kiss that conveyed both relief and apology.

Her body wilted, but he caught her. Held her in place as his tongue slipped between her lips.

When he pulled back, though, shame still filled his eyes, and his gaze fell to the floor between them. "This has been eating at me for seven years, and here you are being so amazing about it. I don't know if I deserve it, but damn it, Addy, I don't think I'm strong enough to refuse whatever you're offering me right now. Forgiveness. Love. I'll take it. All of it." A slight smile coaxed his dimples into making an appearance. "We don't have a lot of time, but I—"

"I need you, too," she cried. She needed him now more than ever before.

He untied the black lace halter of her dress, allowing it to drop. He sank to his knees, his firm hands dragging down the sides of her body, taking her dress with them in the process.

Within seconds, she was out of her dress, standing only in strappy shoes and a black silk thong.

He gingerly planted kisses over her hip bone, taking a moment to peek up at her with a devilish grin when she grabbed on to his shoulders. She hung on as he teased her with his mouth growing closer and closer to her center.

"You're incredible," he whispered as he slid her panties down her legs and helped her step out of them.

The command of his tongue, his lips—the gentle suction between her thighs—she wanted to cry out his name and come, and he'd only begun.

This moment was really happening. She wasn't that nineteen-year-old watching romance flicks and wishing for her happily-ever-orgasm anymore. It was finally here. Years later, but still, it was here.

Her body shuddered when he used his thumbs to separate her folds and sweep his tongue along her swollen flesh. Little pulses of hot need had her sealing her eyes tight and holding his head in place.

"Don't stop," she cried as he licked and sucked. Applied

extra pressure with his hand. "Knox!" She tossed her head back and bit down on her back teeth as she fought not to scream any louder as she came.

"That's my girl." He wrapped his arms around her thighs and lifted her into the air as he stood upright.

He deposited her on the bed as if she were made of glass and removed and tossed his tuxedo jacket. The bow tie came off next, and his heated stare combed the length of her body in the process.

She couldn't take her eyes off him. She lay on the bed, her knees bent, one hand draped over her navel, her heels digging into the comforter with the anticipation of what was to come.

She'd finally be able to see all of him. Every inch. Even the scars he'd refused to explain before. No secrets between them when they made love.

He was so damn fine. So handsome.

Her hero.

He slowly unbuttoned his white dress shirt, revealing his hard stomach. The abs he must've done a thousand sit-ups a day to maintain.

He peeled his shirt off and tossed it.

But when he lowered his pants, she couldn't help but allow her eyes to travel south.

She took the time to appreciate his muscular legs, and then his . . . "Wow," she said under her breath after he'd lowered his boxers to reveal he was fully erect.

A smile teased the corners of his mouth, and he gripped his shaft, the crown glistening with pre-cum.

Her hand slowly trailed a line down her abdomen to between her legs, her fingers feathering over her wet center. "Knox," she cried, needing him so much.

He knelt onto the bed and moved closer before positioning himself on top of her.

A desperate moan escaped her throat when he dipped his head down and took her nipple into his mouth.

Flicking. Nipping. Caressing it with his tongue.

Her hips lifted and rotated, needing to feel him skin to skin.

She reached between their bodies when his mouth reclaimed hers, and she raked her short fingernails down the hard planes of his stomach before grasping his shaft in her right hand.

He broke their kiss and lightly hissed as she gently squeezed and began fisting him, moving her hand up and down. He cursed under his breath and groaned her name softly as he screwed his eyes shut for a second.

When he wedged a hand between the bed and her back and squeezed her ass cheek hard, she yelped from the pleasure of his touch.

"I want that tight pussy fisting my cock."

She jolted at his words, at the heady desire in his tone. "Please," she nearly begged.

"I don't have any protection," he gritted out, as if angry at himself for not planning for this moment. Lines bracketed his mouth as he struggled with a decision, one he didn't need to make because nothing could stop this moment.

"I'm on the pill." She didn't want any barriers between them. Not ever.

"You're sure you're okay with this?" His brows knitted, but there was a look of relief in his eyes as he observed her.

"More than anything," she said with an anxious nod.

He squeezed his eyes closed for a brief moment, then pressed his tip to her center. And when his eyes opened, he filled her in one stroke and—*ohmygod!*

A cry tore from her lips, mingling with a guttural roar that came from deep within his chest.

He brought his face near hers, the scent of her arousal on his tongue, and he kissed her.

"Addy," he whispered against her lips almost as if he were in pain. "I'm so sorry," he murmured without stopping. "I'm so sorry I waited."

He picked up the pace. Moving harder and faster. And she matched every thrust with one of her own.

"It's okay," she whispered. "We're here now." She clutched the strong arms that held him over her. "And that's all that matters."

CHAPTER TWENTY-NINE

"HUMMINGBIRD AND HAWK ARE SECURE IN THEIR SUITE," Rodriguez informed Adriana when they entered Jessica's room at 11:00 p.m. that night, an hour after Knox had shared his secret and made love to her.

She was still digesting what he'd told her, but she didn't have any doubts in her mind about her feelings for him. Best friend. Now lover. No more secrets.

Knox wanted another four years on the job, which meant he needed his dad to win the White House, and then after, he'd have to level his father with the news about the teams.

She didn't envy his position, but she'd fight like hell to support it.

"Thanks for keeping my parents safe tonight," Knox said to Rodriguez before approaching the desk where Jessica sat working.

He'd changed into jeans and a gray tee before they'd come to the suite, and Adriana had traded her dress for khaki pants and a yellow T-shirt.

Rodriguez fiddled with the collar of his tuxedo jacket, a touch red in the face, as if exasperated by the fact he was taking part in some clandestine meeting. "I don't know how you've all managed to talk me into being here, but—"

"Your job is to protect my family," Knox cut off Rodriguez, "which is what you're doing."

Rodriguez reached for Adriana's elbow when she walked past him, and he surprised her by whispering, "Your speech tonight, I was at a loss for words."

She nodded, forcing the emotion to remain put for now. Her body was still Jell-O after her multiple orgasms from Knox. And her mind was mush after discovering the truth.

"Well." He let go of her and held his palms open. "You ready to tell me your plans to find the real assassin and why I'm withholding information from the deputy secretary?"

"Our main suspect is Glenn Sterling, but we're not sure if he's working alone." Knox picked up a notepad off the corner of the desk and handed it to Rodriguez. "That's our list of suspects." He left out the part about the suspects having once been part of a black ops group with his mom, though. She supposed that'd remain classified intel for now. "I'm going to take a wild guess and say it's not a coincidence Sterling got himself assigned to this investigation."

Rodriguez lifted his eyes from the notepad. "He hasn't done anything to interfere with the case, though. Not that I'm aware of, at least."

"He's probably not here to obstruct but to learn. To make sure he doesn't get pulled into the limelight by Nina Hilton," Jessica chimed in.

"The wife of the Liberation Defense Force?" Rodriguez handed the notepad to Knox and tossed his jacket.

"You know of her?" Adriana asked.

"My people made the connection an hour before the ball started tonight," he replied while rolling his sleeves to the elbows. "Both Ike and Chelsea have connections to that militia. Aaron, too."

Adriana's stomach dropped. "Please tell me no one informed Glenn of this." Jessica had said Special Agent Quinn had promised not to share intel, but Adriana hadn't anticipated the Secret Service might discover the truth on their own.

She should have known better . . . they weren't the Secret Service for nothing.

"They've been ordered to keep all intel privileged," Rodriguez explained. "No one outside Secret Service."

She touched her chest and breathed a sigh of relief.

Chen. Calloway. The rest of the guys. She trusted them.

"But you now have my full attention," Rodriguez said.

"We believe Nina's really calling the shots at the compound. She flew to D.C. thirteen weeks ago and checked in to a hotel there," Jessica shared what they'd learned. "I'm working on getting eyes on where she went and who she met up with, but my money is on Glenn. And then, after she left D.C., a plan to kill Knox's mother—not his father—was put into place."

Rodriguez held a palm in the air. "Say that again."

"We think Glenn orchestrated it to look like someone was gunning for my dad, but it would, in fact, be my mom who got *accidentally* killed in the crossfire," Knox explained.

"And why would Glenn want her dead?" Rodriquez jerked his head back in surprise. "Aren't they friends? Hell, they've known each other for forever from what I read."

"When Nina's uncle passed away, she inherited his ranch as his only living heir. At the time of her mother's death years prior, her brother, Nina's uncle, was the only living relative, so he received her belongings." She paused. "It's possible Nina recently stumbled upon something that'd give her a reason to have a grudge against Kathleen Bennett, Glenn Sterling, and the other names on that list," Jessica said, keeping her voice even. "We believe Glenn didn't want the truth to come out, though, and he was willing to do anything to prevent it from happening."

"This is insane," Rodriguez snapped out.

"That's all we can tell you for now," Jessica responded. "The rest is classified."

"You're really going to pull the classified card with me?" Rodriguez's arms fell lax at his sides. "You're civilians."

"Nina made multiple calls to the same phone number after she made contact with Glenn. To an untraceable burner," Knox went on, ignoring Rodriguez's words. "Her last call indicates she's gonna go off-script, and she has evidence of some kind that could prove damning for the deputy secretary."

"And how the hell do you know this?" he asked.

"Because we have a man inside her compound," Jessica spoke up. "We're civilians, we can do things you can't."

Since the world thought they were civilians, they could get away with things that wouldn't fly with the U.S. flag on their arms. But the flag was still there—an invisible one.

"You mean *illegal* activities," Rodriguez said with a shake of the head, and Adriana could feel his eyes on her. He was trying to figure out why she'd gone along with such tactics.

She couldn't look him in the eyes, though. She wasn't in the room as Secret Service right now, she was there as Knox's best friend.

"Quinn's calling," Jessica announced, offering Adriana an escape from Rodriguez's heated stare. "Maybe she has news."

"I've got teams on their way to Abilene and San Angelo,

and they'll be on standby awaiting orders," Quinn said once Jessica answered.

"You planning on going after Nina?" Rodriguez asked. "We can't arrest her without more to go on."

"We're working on a plan for Nina," Knox interrupted. "But like you said, we're civilians. We don't have to play by the same rules."

"Like hell." Rodriguez closed in on the desk to face Knox as he stood alongside where Jessica worked. "I'm not losing my job over this."

"You mean to tell me you'll take a bullet for my dad, but you won't ensure the bullet is never fired in the first place?" Knox shifted his focus to the computer a moment later. "What are you looking at?"

"I'm still trying to see who else Glenn's been meeting with since Nina's first approach," Jessica said.

"Can you pause there and zoom in?" Knox leaned forward. "She looks familiar."

"What do you see?" Adriana circled the desk to get a look.

Knox's brow scrunched. "Is that who I think it is?"

"What's going on?" Quinn asked, and Adriana had nearly forgotten she was still on the phone.

"We're looking at footage we caught on a bank camera across the street from a hotel where the VP pick Leslie Renaldo was staying in D.C. three months ago," Jessica said. "She's getting into the back of a town car."

Oh, God. Is Lyle's VP candidate part of this?

"And why is that relevant?" Quinn asked.

"Because I've been tracing Glenn's whereabouts, and the town car she's getting into is his," she answered.

Knox pointed to the screen. "Look at the time and date."

"A day after Nina showed up in D.C., Leslie met with Glenn," Adriana whispered. "What the hell is going on?"

Jessica worked quickly at the keys and popped up flight information a few minutes later. "I'm thinking their meeting can't be a coincidence."

"Does that mean Nina went to Glenn or did Nina go to Leslie Renaldo first?" Adriana asked, not sure what to think.

Knox peered her way. "I don't know." Confusion touched his words, an echo of how she felt.

"Keep me posted," Quinn said after a few seconds had passed, allowing everyone to digest the intel. "I've got agents I trust watching Glenn and the other names on that list you provided me. If they make any suspicious moves, I'll know about it. Do I need to assign someone to Leslie Renaldo as well?"

Rodriguez hung his head.

"If possible, yes," Knox answered.

"Thank you," Jessica replied. "We appreciate you trusting us on this. I know it can't be easy, but—"

"I'm after justice," Quinn interrupted. "I'll take all the help I can get to do that. Let me know when you're ready for my agents to roll." And then she ended the call.

"I don't know if I can do this." Rodriguez turned his back to the room.

Adriana rounded the desk to stand before him. "You trust me, right?" She reached for his arm, and she could feel Knox's eyes on her back as she spoke to her boss.

"Of course I do. But you're also friends with the Bennetts, which means your judgment has been compromised."

Before she had a chance to refuse Rodriguez's statement, she overheard Knox talking to Jessica in a low voice.

"I need to get to Texas," he said.

Adriana whipped around to face him. "I thought you were going to stay here."

Knox leaving wasn't part of the plan, and like hell she'd let him go without her.

His knuckles bore down on the edge of the desk. "We still need to find a way to get my man out of that compound and take Nina into custody." He peered Rodriguez's way. "Can I count on Secret Service to watch over my parents while I'm gone?"

"You should know the answer to that," Rodriguez said in a near whisper.

"Could you keep an eye on Jessica and Adriana as well?"

Her stomach twisted at Knox's words. "No," she sputtered, her cheeks heating. "No more protecting me. You're not going to run off to Texas and leave me here. If you go, I go."

She blew out a frustrated breath. She was ready to go head-to-head with him, but maybe not in front of Jessica and her boss.

"No damn way." Knox looked at Jessica next. "And before you say you're coming—"

"I'm not." Jessica's hand settled over her abdomen, and Knox's jaw locked tight as he nodded.

There'd be no stopping him from going, and Adriana knew it. Once he made up his mind, it was set.

If there were even the slightest chance his team needed him, he wouldn't back down, because that was the kind of man he was. She'd witnessed his grief last night. Heard his words earlier.

"How fast can my dad's private jet get me there?"

CHAPTER THIRTY

SO HELP HER, IF HE TOOK OFF BEFORE SHE MADE IT, SHE'D . .
.

At the sight of Isaiah Bennett's jet still on the tarmac with the stairs open, Adriana halted in place and bent forward.

She had friends in high places with the Atlanta Police Department, and she'd secured an escort straight to the airport.

She flicked her hand over her shoulder in thanks to her mother's old partner who'd driven her, then she started for the steps with her one small bag in hand.

At the sound of movement above, she flinched on the third step and dragged her gaze north.

"What in God's name do you think you're doing here?" Knox fumed from the doorway of his dad's jet. "I asked you to stay with Jessica. Hell, I begged." His tone bordered the fine line between angry and hurt. "You made me beg, Addy."

Yeah, and she'd begged, too. They were even. And she never actually agreed to stay behind.

"And then you kissed me in front of everyone like it'd be

the last time I ever saw you alive, and you left before I could give you a firm *I'm coming!*" She finished her climb and stood on the small platform near the entrance, but his frame filled the tight space, blocking her.

"I can't get the job done if I'm worried something will happen to you." He cocked his head to the side.

"And you need to stop worrying about me." She poked his muscular chest.

"I'll never stop worrying," he barked out.

"Then I call *ditto!*" she snapped back.

His tone softened when he replied, "Don't you pull *Ghost* on me."

Ghost had been one of her favorite Patrick Swayze movies, right up there with *Dirty Dancing*. She used to make him watch it with her. They ate ice cream, popcorn, peanut butter from a jar—and they watched it. And she'd sob each time. And she used to claim if she ever died like in the movie, she'd haunt him forever.

But no one was dying. Not today or anytime soon.

"You don't get to tell me it's okay for you to put your life on the line, but I can't put mine!"

"It's not the same," he said, his voice part groan, probably out of frustration.

She dropped her bag, and her hands went to her hips. "You have two women on your team. You're okay with them sacrificing themselves but not me?"

"No one is sacrificing anything!"

"Then it's agreed. I can come." She tried to shove past him, but nope. He was a wall of steel.

"Please." There was that plea again in his voice. He knew how to use it on her, but she wouldn't give in.

"You told me the truth, and I accepted it. I accepted you

for you. You have to do the same, it's only fair." The corners of her mouth flipped as she contemplated flashing him a smile to try and win him over because they were short on time.

His shoulders sagged. "Your dad has been grieving your mom for twenty years." He braced her biceps and held her eyes with his. "But I'm not him, because if something happened to you, I'd never survive that."

"But you're asking me to?" Tears filled her eyes. Their conversation from earlier wasn't done. It'd been delayed by orgasms and then work. "My mom wore the badge, not my dad."

"And she died," he said, his voice straining. "Fuck," he hissed and turned toward the inside of the plane.

She braced a palm to the exterior of the plane and took a minute to gather herself, then she grabbed her bag and followed him inside.

"What about Rodriguez?" he asked in a low voice, gripping the top of a chair in the cabin, his back to her. "How'd you convince him to let you come?"

She let go of her bag as someone from the flight crew closed the door. There'd be no turning back now.

"I handed over my commission book," she admitted once the woman brushed past her down the aisle, heading for the cockpit, giving them space to talk.

He spun around and faced her, his brows lifting in surprise. "You did what?"

"And does your dad know you've hijacked his jet?" She crossed her arms, trying to deflect.

"Yeah, I told him I was going to end this thing once and for all." He closed the space between them but didn't reach out for her.

"And he handed over the keys, huh?"

"More like his pilot." A smile she hadn't expected tugged at his mouth, and he lowered his head and cursed under his breath for it. "Damn you, woman."

"Sir, if you want to make the time, we need to go." It was the captain this time. "You need to buckle up." He glanced at Adriana. "Good to see you again, Ms. Foster." His eyes briefly roamed over her body, to her tight-fitting khakis before his gaze lingered at her cleavage in the pale yellow tee she was wearing.

"Thank you," Knox said in a clipped tone, clearly noticing the captain's focus.

"I'm staying." She sat in one of the seats off to her left.

"Why in the hell would you quit your job?" He shook his head.

"Because a Secret Service agent can't go into a compound with a nonexistent black ops group." Her hands settled in her lap as she looked up at him, fearful of the hard line his lips would become at her words.

"You think you're going inside?" He faked a laugh and held both palms in the air between them.

Maybe this was the wrong time to bring that up. But with Knox, would there ever be a right time? "You said I'm capable of handling myself, remember? After the car chase with the truck driver."

"I didn't mean you should drop into a compound with fifty armed guys." His hand came down like a hammer onto the top of the seat off to his left. "You can't do this to me, Addy. Please. You're going to give me a heart attack."

She stood and faced him, ready to throw down, but her palms landed on his chest for support when the plane started to roll forward.

He caught her hips and held her upright, and his throat

moved with a hard swallow. "You drive me nuts," he said as the captain came over the intercom.

"Prepare for take-off."

"You have to let go of me now," she murmured.

"Don't ask me to do the impossible," he said in a gritty voice and brought his mouth to hers.

* * *

HIS HAND TRACKED DOWN HER BACK, WANDERING OVER THE slopes of her ass cheeks as she lay flat on her stomach on the bed in the bedroom of the jet. She did her best to relish the moment, knowing they'd be facing a shit storm of problems when the wheels touched the ground.

She turned on her side to face him, her nipples grazing his pecs in the process.

His rigid arousal pressed against her—he was ready again, and so was she.

It'd be four in the morning when they arrived, and they had maybe thirty minutes before they needed to buckle up for landing, so the timing sucked, but she couldn't seem to care.

She was still pissed at him for his reaction to her presence, but this was Knox . . . he'd always been the man who eliminated threats to her safety, so she knew it'd be hard for him to willingly put her in danger.

"I can't believe we had sex in my parents' bed. I feel like a teenager again."

"I don't want to know about your wild sexual years as a teen when you could've been with me instead," she teased.

"I can promise you I've never had sex in my parents' bed before. You have my word. And I gotta be honest, it'll probably be my last." He covered his face with his palms and fell to his back, his length remaining hard, resting against his right thigh.

"You sure?" She dropped her legs off to the side of the bed and stood. She purposefully wriggled her hips, and he reached out and slapped his palm around her hip and pulled her back down.

"Danger does turn you on, huh?" he asked once she straddled him.

"Life does," she said in all honesty. "Taking advantage of the moment we have because—"

"Nope," he cut her off. "Don't tell me it could all end in a blink of an eye. You're living forever. You hear me? And we're going to have a lifetime of making love to look forward to. I've waited twenty years to be with you." He leveled her with a heated look. "You're trying to use sex to distract me so I won't turn this plane around and send your cute little ass home, aren't you?" He shifted up a touch, resting on his elbows, but she remained on his lap.

Okay, so maybe he was partially right. But only partly. Sex was way more than a distraction.

They were best friends who finally stepped out of the friend zone and connected on another level.

He palmed her breast and cupped the swell of her flesh, causing her sex to tighten at the jump of his cock, the head almost touching her center. "De-flec-tion. I know a thing or two about it, babe."

"Does that mean you want me to get off you?" she murmured.

Knox slipped his hands to her waist and held her firmly in place. "I do want you off me." He flipped her to the side and on her back before climbing over her in one swift holy-shit movement. "But only so I can spread your legs and bury my face between your thighs."

His strong hands traced lines down the sides of her body, and he buried his fingertips into her hips, holding her to his mouth. The pad of his thumb moved in tandem with his tongue.

She slipped to the edge of tomorrow, her head rolling back, as he sucked and kissed. "Knox, that mouth of yours is going to be my undoing." She bucked against him and came hard, not even a full minute later. She was putty in his hands —well, more like she became a puddle from his tongue.

Her whimpers were silenced with his mouth the moment he shifted atop her and buried himself deep, while she rode the crest of her orgasm.

Their lips disconnected as he pounded into her hard at first, as if unable to hold back, losing control. A frenzied need to be one, and it turned her on even more.

High in the air over the country—a hot and heavy scream of pure bliss tore from her lungs, and she didn't give a damn if the pilot with wandering eyes heard her.

No shame. Never. Not with this man.

When he brought his mouth back to hers, she wrapped her legs around his hips and held on tight as he slowed their rhythm.

He made love to her. And she came again. And she nearly forgot the dangers of the world while their bodies collided.

But a phone call from Luke when the plane touched down reminded her once again life was short. Life was anything but safe.

"Roman's in trouble," Luke reported over speakerphone as she unbuckled to stand. "His cams and mic are offline now."

The color drained from Knox's face, and he bowed his head, a clear indication of the dread delivered by Luke's news.

"We think Roman was trying to tell us something, but there was an issue—we couldn't hear him clearly," Luke said in a rush. "Next thing we knew, he was on his knees and lifting his hands in the air, and the men were shining lights on him outside. Pointing guns as he knelt before them. Then our feed died."

"How the hell did this happen?" Knox asked, fear in his eyes.

"I think he surrendered on purpose." Pain touched each of Luke's words.

"Why would he do that?" she asked.

Knox closed his eyes. "Because he knew we needed a valid reason to go in there, one that wouldn't get us arrested."

"He's sacrificing himself so our entrance can be legally justified," Luke explained, and the oh-shit moment hit her. These guys were willing to do anything and everything for the country.

"He's giving us an in," Knox added in a somber tone, which had her heart breaking for him.

"Why now, though? Why not wait and see how things play out? Jessica's working on evidence and—" She stopped talking when Knox opened his eyes and peered at her.

"He's letting us know we can't wait. Whatever he discovered, he needs us to go in there right now," Knox told her.

"One sec, I have Bravo Four coming in over comms." A moment later, Luke asked Knox, "How far are you from us?"

"Thirty minutes," Knox answered, already starting for the exit.

"Get here in twenty," Luke rushed out. "We can't wait. We've gotta head into the compound. We're mapping out a revised infil plan."

"What's going on?" Knox asked as they exited the plane.

"Liam has eyes on Roman from his position," Luke began, his voice slightly shaky. "He's been placed in the stables, but the fuckers are pouring gasoline on the structure." He paused for a second. "Looks like they're getting ready to light the place up."

CHAPTER THIRTY-ONE

Knox tightened his hand on the wheel, doing his best not to turn the car around and take Adriana back to the airport.

He'd told her the truth, but it wasn't an invitation to join him on his next operation, damn it.

Roman's life was on the line right now. They didn't even know if he was alive. And the rage on the inside, the desperate need to get to Roman in case there was a chance he was still alive—it was the only reason he didn't turn the car around and bring Adriana somewhere far away and safe.

But . . . was she right?

Was it unfair of him to ask her to sit out because he loved her? Cared about her? Because she was a woman?

Adriana was a trained agent, but was she equipped to go up against a militia? He'd seen her shoot. They'd hit the range in D.C. during his past visits, but had she ever been shot at? She'd never mentioned it, but that didn't mean it hadn't happened. She'd keep that shit from him for the same reason he kept all the crazy-ass stunts he'd pulled in his line of work over the years from her . . . to keep from worrying.

He glimpsed her as he drove. She'd traded in her khakis and yellow shirt for something that would blend with the setting. Dark pants and a black long-sleeved shirt. Her hair was pulled back in a tight ponytail, and her hands rested in her lap.

No slope to her shoulders, though. No sign of fear.

But he was scared. He was fucking terrified. When his phone rang, it was him who startled.

"Where are we at on connecting the dots between Leslie and Glenn?" he asked Jessica after placing her call on speaker. "My mom didn't mention Leslie's name, so she couldn't have been connected to her team back in the seventies."

"Maybe she didn't know Leslie back then, but Leslie was in Iran," Jessica announced. "While you were flying, I discovered her husband worked at the American Embassy in Tehran."

"What'd Leslie's husband do at the embassy?" Adriana reached for Knox's free hand and laced their fingers together.

They were working an op.

Together.

What planet was he on?

"The records are shit, but from what I can tell, he worked on the same floor as Nina's dad," Jessica answered.

"So maybe the connection isn't between my mom and Leslie—"

"But between Leslie and Nina's dad," Jessica finished for him. "Or hell, Nina's mom. It was her mom who was actually the spy."

"Are you suggesting Leslie was also selling secrets to the Russians? Using her husband for intel?" Adriana asked.

"Does that mean Glenn covered for Leslie?" Jessica

asked. "It'd explain why he wouldn't want the truth to come out."

"He could be trying to hide the fact he conspired with the Russians, and our potential VP may have as well." How the hell had this happened? "I honestly don't know what to think, but we need to talk to Nina and see what she knows."

"Right. We're spinning theories now," Jessica reminded them. "I could come up with a half a dozen other reasons to explain everything. We'll have to see how it shakes out."

"And what's the status on the compound?" He needed good news. So help him, if Roman was dead, he'd have no mercy.

"Liam and Wyatt are still in position. Harper flew the drone over five minutes ago. No change."

No change meant no fire, and they needed to keep it that way.

"Won't they see a drone?" Adriana's spine bowed as worry slipped to the surface.

"We have special technology," was all Jessica said, even though she could've talked for hours about luminance and angles.

Adriana relaxed her back against the seat. "Do you think the people at the compound know we're going to infil?"

God, he loved it when she talked infil and extractions to him. But shit, wrong time, wrong place for such thoughts. "Probably."

"I still can't believe he'd risk his life to give you guys some sort of legal grounds to go in there. I hope this will hold up in court when this is over, but——"

"We usually avoid courtrooms, in general. Doesn't mesh well with covert ops," he cut her off and refocused on the back road, which had shit for lighting. "But Roman did what any of us would've done."

"Quinn has the Feds in position," Jessica said.

"Hopefully, we won't need them for backup." They had to get Nina talking. They needed answers before the FBI took over and Glenn Sterling found out they were onto him. "Has Mendez picked any of this up on his radar yet?"

"Not that we know of, which is why Quinn only has small teams in Abilene and San Angelo. People she personally vouched for," Jessica replied.

Knox briefly dropped his eyes to their clasped palms, and his heart stuttered.

The woman was stubborn, and maybe he even loved that about her.

But he didn't want her to be stubborn right now.

No, he wanted her to be safe.

* * *

"THIS COULD VERY WELL BE OUR LAST OPERATION together," Luke said, his voice eerily low as if trying not to let emotion choke his words. "Let's make it count. Let's bring our man home."

They were standing in front of Luke with their helmet headlights at the dimmest setting so they could see each other without drawing attention to their presence. But with Adriana at his side, his stomach had that horrible sinking feeling.

"We'll get this done," Asher said with confidence.

Luke nodded. "What's the status, Echo One?" he asked over comms.

"It looks like there are some internal problems," Wyatt replied. "I guess not everyone at the militia is on board with burning the place to the ground. We've got five guys arguing about a half a klick from the shooting range."

"That may work in our favor if they're not a united front," Knox noted.

"Everyone's armed, though. We may not be able to stick to rubber bullets on this one," Wyatt added.

"We'll carry both, but let's do our best not to kill anyone tonight, not unless it comes down to either you or them," Luke instructed.

"Where is Echo One?" Adriana faced Knox.

"Wyatt's positioned on a tree stand used for hunting. He's outside the compound," he explained. "Liam had to improvise."

"And that means?" she asked.

"It means our boy is hanging off the side of a tree," A.J. joined their conversation. "He's in a type of sling." He pointed to his hips. "The tree saddle gives him three-hundred-and-sixty-degree shooting mobility, and he's up high enough to see what's going on inside."

"Oh." She looked at Knox. "Sounds dangerous."

"He's done this before. He'll be fine." He wasn't worried about Liam right now because Liam wasn't going inside the compound—Adriana was.

"Prepare for infil," Luke announced, and Knox's pulse jumped. "Five minutes."

"I think they're about to set the place on fire. They just moved the horses from the stable to another part of the grounds," Liam said a few seconds later.

"Well, at least they care about animals." A.J. shook his head. "I have zero tolerance for a man who'd hurt a horse."

"Or a Teamguy, right?" Chris, Echo Three, stood off to A.J.'s left. "Roman sure as hell better be okay and make it out alive or so help me God."

"He will," Harper said, but Knox detected a hint of fear in her tone.

"We'll get him out." Knox nodded at Harper, doing his best to appear calm, even if he was anything but.

"Got a chest plate on under there?" Adriana asked him while he packed his vest with ammo.

"Of course." He peered at the bulletproof vest she had on, then his gaze dipped to the pistol strapped to her leg. Another weapon at her hip. A rifle slung across her body. Combat paint on her face.

Was this really happening?

"Please stay here." His voice broke, and he didn't give a damn if his brothers witnessed the emotion.

She may have looked like G.I. Jane, but she was still Adriana, the woman he'd known and loved for twenty years. *His* Addy.

"You go, I go," she repeated what she'd said at the hotel before they'd jetted off to Texas.

He'd give anything to be back on the bed inside the jet, even if it was his parents' bed if it meant keeping her away from danger.

"They've got me covered." He jerked a thumb behind him toward the guys.

"We need all the help we can get," Luke said, and his words had Knox turning toward him. "We're heading inside an unknown situation with fifty armed men inside."

"Harper will have eyes on us with the drone up there. We'll be fine," Knox countered.

"And she won't be able to communicate their locations when our comms go out," Luke reminded him.

The last thing Knox needed was for Luke to defend Adriana's decision to join the operation.

"I should go," Harper said. "Roman needs us, and . . ." She looked between Knox and Luke, her concern for Echo Four obvious. "Let me go instead. Adriana can stay back."

"We need you to jam the frequencies, control the drone, and maintain contact with Quinn—"

"Harper can tell Adriana what to do," Knox interrupted Luke, and Asher reached for his arm as if saying, *She'll be okay.*

But if this was Jessica about to walk into a gunfight no way would he be cool with that.

"We don't have time for a lesson," Finn, Echo Five, said. "Roman's inside."

"It's Adriana's call, but she does have training," Luke pointed out. "And if she says she's got our six, then, brother, she's got our six."

Harper reached for Luke. "Let me go."

A battle between the women as to who should put their lives on the line. Great.

How about neither?

But he knew that wouldn't fly. They were both strong and independent, and so . . .

Before Luke could say anything, Finn stepped closer to Harper. "You shouldn't—"

"Roman is in there," Harper said, her voice breaking. "I'll go."

"While I respect you want to get your guy out," Adriana interjected herself into whatever was going on between Finn and Harper right now, "Luke and Finn are right. There's no time for you to teach me everything. I've got this. I promise."

"Luke, if this was Eva, you'd never let her go in there." Knox had to try one more time.

"And Eva's not Secret Service," Luke shot back the reminder.

"Neither is Adriana. She quit," he said, regret continuing to fill every inch of him that he ever let her get on that plane.

This was on him. If something happened to her, he'd be

done. No turning to booze like her father had when he'd lost his wife. He meant what he'd said to her earlier.

His brothers would have to bury him six feet under because life wouldn't be worth living without Adriana.

"You have to trust me." Adriana rested a hand over his bicep.

"Please," he begged, contemplating whether he could cuff her inside the van. "If you care about me, you'll stay here."

"I won't let you lose anyone tonight. Not Roman. Not me. No one." A grit of confidence blew through her words, and he wanted so much to believe her. To see her in this moment as only a badass agent. But the woman he was in love with would always come first.

"You can't see the future," he said, his chest throbbing.

"I can, and I'm looking at it."

"Damn it, Addy." He removed his helmet and angled his head so he could reach her lips with her helmet still on. He ignored the taste of face paint touching his lips in the process. Ignored the awkward coughs from his teammates around them.

"Let's go get your guy back," she murmured after their kiss.

"You kiss and make up? Can we roll now?" A.J. asked as Knox placed his helmet back on.

"If anything happens to her," Knox gritted out but was cut off when a shotgun popped in the distance. A 12-gauge.

"This is Echo One. Darius Hilton shot one of the five guys gunning for the exit. What do you want me to do? I can't let these men die."

Luke dropped his head for a second. "You have Darius in your line of sight?"

"Yeah," Wyatt returned.

"Take him down," Luke ordered.

A few seconds later, Wyatt said, "Target is down, but these people will be wondering what the fuck happened. Better get a move on it."

"Roger that. We're going dark in less than two minutes. Prepare to engage," Luke responded.

No comms. No way to communicate with each other when Harper killed all radio and cell frequencies for three minutes. But it was also their best chance to get in undetected.

The power would be cut, too. Meaning, the guys in the compound had no way to communicate with each other, either, or have eyes on them with their security cams disabled.

"Are we ready to go in there and get our brother back before Nina lights everything on fire?" Chris asked.

"Yeah," Luke said. "We're ready."

Knox faced Adriana, and she pulled him in for a hug, his gear clanking against her vest, getting in the way of any real contact between them.

"Now," Asher rasped, motioning for them to get a move on.

Knox turned off his headlight and positioned his NVGs in place, the familiar green hue filling his line of sight, then he followed Bravo Three with Adriana at his side to their assigned position.

The compound was surrounded by a metal fence that could easily be climbed once the security feeds were disabled.

But they had to rely on Aaron's rudimentary drawing of where the land mines were located—*if* they were even still in the same spots. There always the possibility that new ones had been added. Or hell, the land mines might have only been a scare tactic to keep people off the property.

They rushed about three hundred meters along the river to one of the weaker spots at the perimeter—not too far from the stables . . . where Roman was hopefully still being held. And hopefully still alive.

"Damn it," Liam said over the line. "Nina's rushing toward the stables now."

"Which one?"

"First," he said. "Shit, I don't know. They're side by side. There could be openings between them, which means she may not stay in the first one."

"You in position, Bravo Five?" Luke asked.

"This is Five," Knox said while looking at Adriana. "In position."

"Prepare for infil," Luke ordered. "Going dark for exactly three minutes in three, two, one."

The comms died. The entire compound went black. And Knox's stomach dropped knowing what he was about to do— put Adriana in danger.

He placed one hand on top of the other, and Adriana positioned her booted foot in his palm for a boost over the fence. He and Asher quickly followed.

"Land mines," he mouthed to Adriana, not that she'd needed the reminder, but he couldn't help himself.

Gunfire, from somewhere on the compound, rang in his ears. His teammates had already been forced to engage.

And like hell were those rubber bullets the militia fired.

"No targets in sight," Asher whispered, standing off to Knox's left, as they made their approach to the stables.

"We still sticking with rubber?" he asked, moving with caution, avoiding the landmarks Aaron had pointed out on the map where the explosives were buried.

"Do what you have to do." Asher held a fist in the air, signaling for them to stop.

The three side-by-side stables loomed twenty feet out. They'd each take one, which meant he'd have to leave Adriana's side.

"Smoke," Adriana whispered, remaining crouched with her Sig in hand.

"It's coming from the first building," Asher said. "I'll take that one." He looked at Knox. "You get two."

"I'll take the third then," Adriana said.

Farther away on the grounds, more gunshots rang like fireworks popping in the air.

"Be safe," Knox bit out, willing his voice not to break. Then he took off for the middle stable before he changed his mind, doing his best not to look back and check on her. He had to stay mission-focused even if it killed him.

Please let her be okay, he said a silent prayer once his back was flat up against the exterior wall of the middle stable.

He started to go for his weapon that fired rubber bullets, but if Nina was inside the stable with Roman, he wanted her to know he'd kill her if necessary. He needed answers, but he wouldn't sacrifice Roman's life for them.

Flames licked the sides of the first stable, and smoke filled the sky. His night vision goggles auto-corrected with the presence of the fire, cutting off his lights.

He opted for his rifle and moved inside. With the flames out of sight, the green hue of his goggles returned, allowing him to see in the dark.

He pivoted fast, turning to the side at the sight of movement. His boots tracked slowly across the dirt floor as he cleared each stall left and right.

As he neared the last two stalls, he halted at the familiar sound of a round being chambered.

The exit, which led to building three, was only ten feet away. Adriana could enter the stable any second. Asher would soon approach from the other side, too. He had to end this before anyone got hurt.

He shifted his NVGs up and wielded the stock of his rifle firmly to his cheek, his trigger arm winged to the side and his support arm against his chest. With his back to the wall, he maneuvered around the stall to his right, identifying two subjects.

"I know you can see me through your scope, which means you can see the shotgun pointed at this man's head. And my eyes have already adjusted to the dark, so I can see you."

A woman's voice. Nina.

Roman was in a seated position with his back to the wall, his body slumped. Head hanging forward. Hands hidden behind his back. If he was tied up that meant they'd been worried Roman could escape—he had to be alive.

But he couldn't help but ask, "How do I know he's okay?" He held his rifle steady on Nina, and she kept the barrel of her shotgun on Roman.

She kicked his leg with her boot and Roman stirred. His chest lightly lifted, the signs of life evident. *Thank God.*

"Comms are back up." Harper's voice popped into his ear a moment later. "Based on what I'm seeing, the compound appears to be secure."

Almost secure. He had to get Roman out of there. "You don't need to do this, Nina," Knox said in a clear voice so Harper could hear him. "You kill him, and you die, too. You know that."

"He's alive?" Harper's voice cut out, static interrupting, or maybe they were tears.

"You think I'm alone?" Nina asked, pulling his focus to her.

"In this moment, yes. You ran here to kill him when you discovered we were here. You were probably planning on hopping the fence and escaping. Leaving your people behind."

"Bravo Five needs an assist," Harper rushed out. "Echo Four is alive, but . . ."

Harper's voice faded in the background as Knox focused on Nina.

"Who are you?" Nina asked, a rough bite of distrust in her tone. "Y'all can't be Feds. They wouldn't dare step onto our property. This man a Marine?" She kicked Roman's leg again. "Army boy?" Her words dragged out slowly.

"Bravo Five, I'm two stalls back from you," Asher announced in his ear. "The fire isn't far behind me, though."

"I've got eyes on you, too." His heartbeat jumped at the sound of Adriana's voice in his ear, but he didn't dare turn to get a visual on her because he needed to keep his rifle on Nina.

"This only ends one way," he informed Nina. "Let us help you take down Glenn Sterling."

"I made a mistake in trusting him. He's as bad as her. They all are."

"Who?" *My mom?*

Shit, he needed answers, but smoke was filling the stable.

Knox maintained his position, trying to figure out a way around this without Roman getting shot.

"We're ready to move in when you need us," Adriana said, keeping her voice steady. She was his damn rock right now.

"This is Bravo One. Approaching now," Luke said over the line.

Adriana was okay.

The rest of his teammates were good.

And he had to keep it that way.

"A bunch of Polaroids are gonna bring down the

government," Nina said. "At least my parents' deaths can serve a purpose."

Roman's breathing was evening out. He was coming to. A slight twitch to his leg he hoped Nina didn't notice.

"Is that what you found in your uncle's things? Polaroids. Of what? Of Glenn? Kathleen Bennett?"

"Can you believe Polaroids last forty years? They were tucked inside a book, barely faded. They slipped out when I was going through the box a few months ago. The timing must've been fate, what with Bennett and Renaldo running in the election."

Keep talking. "I can help you if you'll let me."

"I don't know who you are," she drawled, "but I sure as hell am done trusting people."

"Let's step outside before this fire kills us both, and I'll show you who I am," he said in a level voice, even though smoke was gathering above him, and the stable was heating up at an alarming rate.

"I always knew my parents were murdered." She started coughing. "And I'd suspected it was by our government, and like hell will I let any traitors take over the White House."

"Bennett didn't kill your parents." Knox had trained in these types of conditions before. He could handle himself, but Nina wouldn't last much longer with the smoke breathing down her neck, which meant she might make a move soon. "Glenn's lying to you. I don't know if it was the Russians or Glenn who murdered your parents, but my . . . *Kathleen* Bennett's not responsible."

"Maybe Bennett staged my parents' deaths. Maybe not. But she was involved somehow, and they'll all pay. Bennett, Sterling, Renaldo—everyone. My parents weren't traitors like he said. And I should've known Leslie would run to her lover for help when I went to her demanding answers."

Lover? Glenn?

He had to make a move. With her talking, the best time would be now while she was distracted.

Roman must've sensed the same because he mouthed, "Now." Roman threw the weight of his body off to his right side, and in one fast movement, Knox rushed the stall. He let go of his weapon as he moved, allowing the rifle sling to catch its weight.

Knox pushed Nina's forearms up, and she fired off a round. The bullet pierced the ceiling, but he quickly wrestled the gun away before she could shoot again.

He tossed the shotgun behind him. "All clear," he announced, so Asher and Adriana knew it was safe to approach.

He spun Nina around and pinned her arms to her back. "I could've killed you, you know. But we're not the bad guys," he told her.

Asher stepped into the stall, and Knox shoved Nina his way, then he swiveled around and twisted on his headlamp so he could better view Roman.

"Fuck, man. You okay?" He grabbed his blade and cut Roman's hands free and helped him up.

"I'm fine," Roman said on a cough, the smoke enveloping the stall.

"She could have shot you," he said while slinging Roman's arm over his shoulder for an assist when he noticed the limp in his leg.

"I trusted you," he said as they moved.

"Knox? Are you okay?" Adriana wheezed, the smoke affecting her as well.

"We're good, but get the hell out of here." He didn't need her destroying her lungs.

"Is he okay?" It was Harper's voice in his ear, worry

strangling her words.

"He's fine," Knox told her as they walked. "I think you gave Harper a heart attack."

Even with his headlamp, he could barely see. The heavy pulls of smoke smothered them as they maneuvered toward the side exit.

"Roman," Chris called out at the sight of them exiting the stable. "You okay?"

"Yeah," Roman rasped.

"Let me," Chris offered, and he took over for Knox in helping him.

He sucked in a breath of air as he searched for Adriana. A swell of relief struck him at the sight of her darting toward him.

She was okay, and he was so damn grateful.

He threw his arms around her.

"I was worried about you." She tightened her grip, and he never wanted to let go.

"I was never in danger. Only Roman," he said, but . . . *what the hell?* He stepped back and studied her. "Where's your vest?"

"Nina's daughter was hiding in that third stable. I had to beg her to come out. I couldn't take her with me, and with all the gunfire out there, well, I put my vest on her."

He cupped her face, but she squinted with his headlamp in her eyes, and he turned it off. "You're something else, aren't you?" *Just like your mom.*

"Following your lead."

"The Feds are on their way," Luke said on approach, walking with Nina at his side.

"How many casualties?" Nina asked, but like she gave a damn about her people. The woman couldn't even protect her own daughter.

"Three wounded," Luke told her even though she didn't deserve an answer. "They'll survive. But the one guy your husband shot in the back is probably critical. That's on you, not us."

"Rubber bullets?" Nina asked.

"We may have a problem." Harper's voice popped in their ears. "The drone is picking up movement outside the compound on the east side. I'm zooming in. One second."

"Maybe you aren't the—" Nina's right shoulder jerked back, and Luke lost his grip of her.

"It's a sniper!" Harper exclaimed.

"What the hell!" Knox yelled as another shot snapped out. Then another one followed almost immediately. "Adriana!" He flew to his right and tackled her to the ground to protect her as Harper rattled off the coordinates to the sniper.

"I've got eyes on him," Liam yelled over comms, surprise in his tone. "Target is down. I repeat, target is down."

"Any more?" Knox asked, too worried to move off Adriana until he knew they were in the clear.

"Doing another sweep," Harper said, "but I don't see anything."

"I think one of the bullets nicked my arm," Adriana whispered beneath him, and he shifted off her in a hurry.

He stood and reached down to help her up, but she stayed down, unmoving. His heart took panicky climbs.

Her hand clutched her stomach. "I don't feel so . . ." His entire world came to a halt as he flipped on his headlamp. "I, uh, think I'm hurt."

He fell to the ground. His heart ripped from his chest. His life on the edge of over.

"I need a fucking ambulance!" he screamed at the top of his lungs and shifted her hand away from her abdomen.

Blood seeped from the wound, and she moaned as he pressed both palms over the area.

"She got hit? Fuck, I'm so . . . sorry," Luke said, but Knox barely heard him.

"Addy." Tears blurred his eyesight. "Babe, you're okay. You'll be okay." He maintained pressure on the wound to try and minimize blood loss.

"Adriana's down," Luke said over comms. "Repeat, Adriana's down."

"I'm sorry." Adriana brought her palm to his face, sliding it over the paint on his skin. "Don't be mad at me, okay?"

"I could never be mad at you," he said, fighting back a sob.

He swallowed, anger and fear raking across his skin like claws drawing blood.

He pressed his mouth to the inside of her hand and kissed her palm.

"You're going to be fine," he promised, but on the inside, he was begging and shouting, fear taking over.

Please, God, don't take her from me. Please.

He held on to her hand and lightly rocked in place as tears burned trails down his cheeks.

He tipped his chin toward the heavens, unable to stop rocking, and he begged. He begged for his life to be traded with hers.

"I love you," he whispered.

"Ditto," she said with a half smile. "Am I Demi Moore in this situation, or Patrick Swayze?" she murmured.

"You're not dying. No coming back as a ghost because you're gonna be fine. And damn it, babe, stop joking."

"De . . . flec . . . ting. Your MO," she said and winced. "Knox?"

"Yeah?" His body shook. His chest cavity rattled as if a bomb had been dropped nearby.

"I think I can see her."

"What do you mean?" He nearly choked on his words.

She lifted her hand toward the sky. "I see Mom."

CHAPTER THIRTY-TWO

Knox stared out the window in the hospital waiting room then bowed his head to the glass. The chopper had flown Adriana to Abilene to better care for a gunshot wound.

GSW. GSW. G-Fucking-S-W. He slammed his fist against the wall off to his right, and he gulped in a fat breath of air.

"She's okay, man. She's going to be okay." Luke wrapped a hand over Knox's shoulder, but he was rooted in place.

Her mom had died from a GSW. How the hell had he let this happen?

"So stubborn." The bright sunlight streamed through the window and burned his eyes, causing them to water. Or maybe he was crying. At this point, he didn't know, and he didn't care.

"You heard the doctor. They're waiting for her to wake up and then you can see her," Luke said, giving his shoulder a tight squeeze. "I'm so sorry, though. This was all my fault. You were right. I shouldn't have let her go in there."

Knox bit down on his back teeth and finally turned away from the window and focused on Luke's booted feet as they took a step back. *She's okay. She's okay.* As many times as he repeated the words to himself, the fear of her *not* being okay would remain until he saw her for himself.

"I'm sorry we didn't catch the shooter sooner," Liam said, and Knox glimpsed him leaning against the far side wall with his forehead against his palm. Guilt in the slouch of his shoulders.

Glenn Sterling must've sent the sniper to prevent Nina from talking.

The hired hitman was dead, but Knox wanted to bring him back to life so he could wrap his hands around his throat and end the man himself.

"This isn't on you," Knox admitted, eyes on Liam first before peering at Luke. "Or you," he said to Harper. "Any of you." He expelled a deep breath and looked at Roman. "And you should be in a hospital bed."

Roman was pretty banged up, but he'd be okay, thank God. He couldn't handle that, too.

"I'm where I need to be." Roman pressed two fingers to his right temple. There were bruises all over his body. The cocksuckers had beaten the shit out of him before they'd brought him to the stable with Nina's plan to burn him alive.

"We'll get Nina to talk. If she survives surgery we'll find out where the hell she hid those Polaroids, and we'll bring Glenn down." Luke's words brought his focus back his way. "I promise."

Knox shook his head, anger building up steam again. "Glenn's already underground." He turned back toward the window, unable to look at his teammates, who were crowded in the small room. They'd been taking turns pacing. Taking turns getting details from the Feds. And getting updates on Adriana's status every few minutes.

"Glenn knows he's fucked," A.J. said as if dragging his words over burning coals. Anger in each syllable.

"Glenn managed to slip the FBI agents Quinn had on him, which means he could be anywhere by now," Knox said bitterly.

Adriana was right, Knox hated killing. But that didn't mean he wouldn't do it. And in this case, when he found Glenn, he'd enjoy it.

"I can't believe Nina was going to try and blow up the stage at the debate in Cleveland on Tuesday," A.J. said, filling the silence that began to eat away at the room.

Roman had discovered Nina and her husband's scheme to have their men plant homemade explosives at the event in Ohio. Nina had planned to burn her compound to the ground once they dispatched their people.

Knox should've been shocked at the lengths people were willing to go in the name of revenge, but he wasn't. He'd seen his fair share of crazy shit in the past. But having Adriana in the mix . . .

"Mendez has a team en route to pick up Leslie Renaldo for questioning, so maybe she'll know something to help us find Glenn," Harper said, her voice small. "The Feds need to coax a confession out of her."

"Mendez say anything to Quinn?" A.J. asked. "Like maybe an apology for being so wrong about everything?"

Knox barely heard their exchange, his mind going back to Adriana on the ground with his hands soaked in her blood.

"I see Mom," Adriana had said to him before passing out.

He'd looked up at the sky and seen her, too. Well, the star he'd chosen for her.

Chills darted up his spine at the memory, but then Luke said, "The doctor's here."

He spun around in a hurry and moved through the waiting room to get to him.

"You ready to see her?" Doctor Frank asked. The man was officially his hero now.

"Yes, please." His voice cracked.

Knox reached the doorway but turned back to catch sight of his buddies. "Thank you," he mouthed and left the room.

He followed the doctor through two sets of doors, his heart kicking higher with each step closer to seeing her.

"She's a tough woman," the doctor said as they walked. "Sorry we made you wait to see her, but she was still under anesthesia. She should be waking up anytime now." He stopped walking and fisted a curtain. "You ready?"

He couldn't get the words out, so he nodded.

The doctor pulled the curtain to the side to reveal Adriana in bed. The steady electronic beats from the heart monitor and BP machine off to her side were reassuring. But the sight of them, and the IV . . . it was still too much. The breathing tube, which she would've had during surgery had been removed. That was a good sign.

He was on the verge of sinking to his knees, but he had to remain strong. He could get through this because she was okay. She got shot, but he didn't lose her the way her father had lost his wife.

He cupped his mouth, tears forming in his eyes as he approached the bed.

The face paint had been wiped off, although some traces were still at her hairline.

She looked like she was peacefully sleeping, not like a bullet had ripped through her that morning.

Her lashes fluttered a little.

Her right arm was wrapped in gauze where the first bullet had grazed her.

An hour ago, when Doctor Frank exited the OR with a smile, Knox had broken down with relief, his coffee splashing over the rim of the cup as he struggled to stand from his chair. He actually needed to lean against Liam for a moment.

"She's not going anywhere," Liam had whispered.

Knox's gaze floated to the doctor. "And she's going to be fine?" He'd asked the question about five thousand times since they'd first spoken.

"She was very lucky. We only had to repair part of her small bowel. We'll keep an eye out for infections, but other than that, no major damage."

It could've gone so much differently. He'd run through a checklist of all the major issues resulting from a gunshot wound to the abdomen while he'd been in the waiting room, and this was one of the best-case scenarios. Thank God.

"I'll give you some space." He left the room, and Knox moved to her side and reached for her hand, holding it between his palms.

"I got you," he said and closed his eyes. "Always."

"I know," she answered, her voice scratchy, but she was talking . . . and . . .

He brought his forehead to hers. "I'm so—"

"Don't apologize," she said softly. And after a few seconds, she added, "I'll withhold sex from you." Her voice was low and sleepy.

But how the hell was she joking after waking up from anesthesia? Only Adriana.

"Addy." He lifted his head to find her beautiful green eyes focused on him, but it was brief. The drugs pulled at her lids, and she closed them again.

"I promised you no one would die," she said. "See, I kept my word."

"What the hell am I going to do with you, woman?" He

smoothed the back of his hand over her forehead and gently kissed her lips.

Tears hit his cheeks again.

"I saw my mom," she whispered after a few minutes passed.

"I saw the star, too." He kept hold of her hand, sitting at her bedside.

"No. I saw her." She blinked until her gaze was focused on him, and she whispered, "She wanted me to find my way back to you."

CHAPTER THIRTY-THREE

It'd been twenty-eight hours since the love of his life had taken a bullet.

Twenty-one hours since she'd woken up from surgery.

And now an hour and a half since she'd forced him to go shower and change his clothes before he was allowed to come back.

He hadn't wanted to leave her side—prepared not to move a damn muscle. But she hadn't given him a choice. She even pulled her pouty lips and puppy dog eyes out on him. Morphine helped her pain, but it didn't dent her personality one bit.

He did feel better about showering and cleaning the filth of what happened off him, though.

"How are you feeling?" he asked once he was back at her side.

"Like I've been shot."

Of course. This woman. His *everything* would smile and joke.

"What do you have there?" Her eyes moved to his hand.

He held an iPad between them. "I downloaded some of your favorite movies for you to watch while you're here."

"Oh?" Her smile carried to her eyes, a sexiness to her tone when she'd dropped that little word, too.

He set the iPad on the rolling cart by the bed and reached for her hand. "Not *Ghost*, though. I'm thinking I won't be watching that movie anytime soon."

"But it's so good." Her speech was barely affected by all the pain meds he was sure the nurses were pumping into her. For the most part, you'd never think the woman had been shot if she weren't in a bed connected to IVs. "How about, *You had me at hello*?"

"*Jerry Maguire*?" He gently pushed a lock of hair behind her ear, noticing her ears bare. She almost always had her earrings on, the ones he'd given her. The nurses must've taken them off for surgery. "Yeah." He smiled and pulled his hand back. "Downloaded."

"*Ever After*?" She perked a brow.

"What's that?" He cocked his head to the side.

"It's a version of *Cinderella*. How could you not remember that's a favorite of mine?"

He reached for the tablet and swiped at the screen to unlock it. He pulled up the movies, and some of the color in her cheeks returned when she spotted *Ever After*.

"You."

"Of course I didn't forget. I know everything about you." He released the iPad and scooted closer to the bed, his heart still hurting at the sight of her in it.

It should've been him in that bed, but she had the heart of a saint, and she'd given her vest to a kid at the chance Nina's daughter could get hurt.

"Actually, I take that back, I didn't know about the

vibrator." His lips twitched into a teasing grin. "We still haven't talked about that."

She sucked her bottom lip inward. "About that."

"You were joking?" He leaned closer, his mouth hovering near hers.

"No, I was very serious." Her lips tipped into a smile. "But I didn't have you to satisfy me, so, what'd you expect?"

"Good point." He kissed her softly, not wanting to jostle her in the slightest and cause her pain. "My parents and your dad should be here soon."

Since Knox had jacked his dad's plane, Secret Service had to secure another private jet, so it was taking them longer to get there.

"Is it safe for your parents to travel with Glenn out there?"

She was lying in a hospital bed after having undergone surgery to repair a bullet wound, and yet, she was still worrying about others.

"Glenn only targeted my mom to protect his own secrets. He has no reason to risk going after her now that the truth is out there."

"But it's not. The truth isn't out there yet. Will your mom have to tell the press? And what does that mean for you? For Bravo?"

A question mark still hung over the fate of the teams, and he didn't want to think about that right now. "Don't stress about that, okay?"

"Easier said than done." Her eyes thinned. "If you're hurting, it hurts me, too."

"I—"

"Hey, sorry to interrupt."

Knox turned to see Luke standing in the doorway.

"I have news. Can I steal you for a moment?" Guilt still

shadowed Luke's eyes. He'd apologized a dozen times since the infil of the compound. Even Roman had said a million *sorrys* as if he was somehow responsible for what happened to Adriana.

But how could Knox be mad at anyone on his team? Ultimately, it'd been Adriana's decision, and he had to accept she was willing to do whatever necessary for her country. Same as him. It hurt like hell to think about her risking her life, but he loved her too much to stand in her way.

"I'd like to hear," Adriana said, trying to sit up a bit.

"You sure you're up for it?" Luke came closer to the bed. "So sorry again for what happened," he said. "Knox was right, and I—"

"No. I was where I should've been." Her brows stitched together. "You men love to take the blame for everything and hold the weight of the world on your shoulders."

Luke peered at Knox, and a smile skirted his lips as he pointed a finger Adriana's way. "Damn, if she's this tough while on morphine, I can't imagine what she's like without the meds."

"Tell me about it," he said, knowing full well she'd be swatting his arm if she hadn't been shot yesterday.

"So, good news or bad?" Knox redirected his focus to Luke, whose face was giving nothing away as he stood on the other side of the bed.

"We got word from Quinn. With the militia taken down, and Nina pulling through surgery without a problem—it must've scared Leslie. She confessed. I don't know if her story is bullshit or not until we can verify some of the details, but she said Nina came to her three months ago with a bunch of Polaroids."

"What'd the pictures show?" she asked.

"They were taken within a week of the death of Nina's

parents. Apparently, Nina recognized Leslie and your mom in the photos and accused Leslie of killing her parents to hide something."

"But Leslie wasn't part of my mom's team," Knox said, still not quite following.

"No, but she was having an affair with Glenn. They've been involved on and off for forty-two years. Since Nina's mom was following Glenn, she also caught their affair on camera."

"Is that what Leslie wanted to hide?" An affair was better than espionage, he supposed. "Was Nina right about anything?"

"Nina's mom had tried to blackmail Glenn back then with the photos. She knew the Americans were on to her as a traitor, so she spied on Glenn to find something to use against him."

"So, did Glenn kill Nina's parents?" Adriana asked, her voice soft.

"Leslie claims she has no idea if Glenn's to blame for that, and she said she didn't ask questions back then. The whole 'ignorance is bliss' thing. A day after Nina's mom attempted to blackmail Glenn, though, she and her husband died." Luke folded his arms. "Nina went to Leslie with the pictures, threatening to expose the affair and share her theory about her parents' death, so Leslie went to Glenn for help."

"And when my mom suggested she should go public about everything—disclose that she was CIA and a member of a covert group—Glenn realized both Nina and my mom could jeopardize his secrets." *Son of a bitch.* And all that time they'd been having him over to family dinners. He wanted to puke.

"So, Nina goes to Leslie, Leslie goes to Glenn, and Glenn pulls their former team together. When he realized Kathleen might reveal the skeletons in their closets, he scrambled to enact a plan," Adriana said.

"Manipulating Nina into thinking my mom staged her parents' deaths."

"Will people find out the truth about the covert group?" Adriana asked.

"Leslie knows Glenn was CIA, so it appears she made the assumption that everyone else in those photos was as well. She never mentioned to the Feds that Glenn or your mom were part of an off-the-books group, though. So, as far as I can tell, the only information that may leak to the press is that your mom was CIA," Luke explained. "I don't know if we can trust Leslie or not, but damned if I'm glad she's not going to be vice president of our country, regardless. She announced her withdrawal fifteen minutes ago outside the FBI office with Director Mendez alongside her."

Mendez had called Knox to personally apologize that morning, and Knox had a feeling it'd been at President Rydell's insistence. Maybe in a few years, Quinn would take over his job.

"The press must be going crazy over this." Knox stood and tucked his hands into the back of his jeans pockets.

Luke jerked a thumb over his shoulder and smiled at Knox and Adriana. "Sounds like your folks are here judging by all the commotion." He peeked out into the hall. "You ready to see them?"

"Yeah," Adriana said with a smile.

A few moments later, Secret Service escorted Knox's parents and Adriana's father into the room. Her dad pulled Knox in for a tight hug before quickly letting go to get to Adriana.

Knox's dad motioned for him to join him in the hall.

"You didn't . . . did you?" he overheard Adriana ask her

father, probably worried her near-death incident pushed him over the edge to drink.

"Still have my chip," he responded, but his voice broke in the process. Relief. Worry. Fear. Hell, all of the above, probably moved through him at the sight of his daughter in that bed.

"You holding up okay, Son?" His dad was dressed more casually than he'd seen him lately. Jeans and a navy button-down. Even the sleeves were rolled to the elbows.

Knox glanced at Rodriguez a few paces back before redirecting his focus on his father. "Yeah, she's okay, so I'm okay."

He braced a hand over Knox's shoulder. "That was a brave thing doing what you did. A little foolish since you could've ended up in jail for it, too, but brave, nevertheless. Not that I'd expect anything different from you."

Knox shifted his attention to the room, and to his mother standing alongside Adriana in one of her typical pantsuits. "You don't think Mom knew what Glenn did back then, do you?" A sinking feeling hit his stomach when he looked back at his dad.

His father's gaze lowered to the floor as if contemplating the question. He'd only learned the truth about his wife, and so, maybe he had concerns, too. But when his focus gathered to Knox's face, a look of confidence returned in his eyes. "No. She says she had no idea Glenn murdered those people and framed the Russians, and so, I believe her."

"I know, and I believe her, too." But . . . "People keep lying. People we trust. I feel like every time I turn around someone from the inside is betraying—"

"Don't let the one percent dictate how you look at the rest." He cocked his head. "Most people are good. Focus on that." He patted his shoulder twice.

"If the truth comes out about Mom, what will happen?" He leaned against the wall. The area was empty save for Secret Service. They must've cleared the hall for his father's visit.

"I guess we'll cross that bridge when we come to it."

"Dad, um, what are your thoughts about a group, like the one Mom was a part of?" *Like mine?* "Is it a risk, is it dangerous to even allow them to exist . . . operate off the books like that? People in power like Glenn, they—"

"Do you trust your buddies?" His forehead creased. A touch of concern dipped into his eyes, but it was brief. "Would they ever turn their backs on you? On this country?" His dad pinned him with a serious look, one he used to give him when he was a teen being lectured for doing something his dad had deemed irresponsible.

Knox straightened. "No, sir. They're nothing like Glenn," he said with conviction.

He extended a hand. "Then we're good."

We're good? He took hold of his hand and performed the handshake his father taught him at a young age. Firm grip, confident demeanor, eye contact. And then his dad pulled him in for a hug.

He stayed out in the hall and took a few seconds to gather his thoughts after his dad went into Adriana's room.

"I guess the president should've put your people in charge." Rodriguez approached. "You planning on telling me where Aaron Todd is now?" His lips crooked at the edges.

"What made you finally shave your mustache?" he commented instead.

"Don't deflect."

But shit, he'd almost forgotten about Aaron. "What makes you think we know his location?"

"Someone had to have given you insight into that compound. Hell, the place was rigged with IEDs."

So, it was true. "He's at his neighbor Judy's house. She lives across the street from him," he admitted. "He had nothing to do with this."

"My job is to protect Isaiah and Kathleen Bennett from all credible threats. Aaron's not one of them. But I still have no idea how you manage to color so far outside the lines without getting cuffs slapped on your wrists." He produced something from his pocket. "But I have a feeling I'll never find out." With that, he sidestepped Knox and entered the room.

Knox followed after him, curious what he was planning on saying to Adriana.

"I think you forgot something back in Atlanta." Rodriguez stood firm in his suit. His shoulders pinned back in a straight line. He extended Adriana her commission book. "What do you say? You want your job back?"

Knox walked farther into the room, and Adriana's eyes met his before lowering to the commission book.

"As long as I'm never assigned to protect the next POTUS." Her eyes winged to Knox's dad. "No offense, but I'm in love with your son, and that could pose some problems."

He loved her so damn much. Always had.

His dad looked back at Knox and smiled. Not a politician smile. A real one. "Can't have the son of a president jumping in front of a bullet for his detail, now can we?"

"You planning on getting shot at again, Dad?" Knox cocked a brow.

"Let's hope not, but I do plan on winning." His dad held his eyes for a beat. "And then after that, I'm thinking there might be something you and I have to talk about."

* * *

TWO DAYS LATER

"This isn't exactly what I had in mind when I said you should all fly under the radar for a while," President Rydell said over the phone in the conference room the guys had hijacked at the hospital. But when the commander in chief requests the room, even from a distance, you give him the damn room.

"Not how we normally roll, sir," A.J. responded.

"But nice work, gentlemen. I should've never doubted you for a second," Rydell added.

"At what point did you doubt us?" Finn scoffed, and Chris tossed a paper airplane he'd made at his face from across the table.

"With Lyle having to choose a new VP candidate, and your mom announcing to the world she was once a spy, I have no idea what will happen come November," Rydell said, ignoring Finn's words.

"From what I'm hearing, the American people have reacted favorably to Kathleen's announcement. They're calling her a Cold War hero." Harper thumbed through the updates on her phone. She'd been keeping up with the press's feedback since his mom had shocked the world with the news about her past.

If the public had reacted negatively, he didn't think his team would've had a chance at returning come 2021.

His mom had only spoken about herself, choosing to allow her fellow colleagues to come forward in their own time if they ever wanted to.

As for Glenn, his name had been tossed around by the media more times than Knox could count during the press

343

conference yesterday, but his mom had refused to talk about him.

And what could she say?

Nina's mom had been selling intel to the Russians, and she'd discovered the CIA was onto her—the Polaroids Nina finally handed over to the Feds had proven that. But Glenn appeared to have acted alone, killing them, assuming everyone would blame the Russians.

"Thank you for what you said about Aaron this morning, Mr. President," A.J. spoke up a moment later.

"He deserved the apology," Rydell responded in a deep voice. "He'd been victimized because he served, and no man should have his name dragged through the mud after protecting our nation like that. He won't be forgotten, I promise."

"Maybe Aaron will even work with us one of these days," Luke said, glancing A.J.'s way.

Rydell nodded and was quiet before saying, "I've decided to make veterans my main focus once I'm out of the Oval Office. I want to change how they're treated in our nation. More medical help, too. Better jobs. No vets should be sleeping on park benches, for God's sake."

"You tried to make a difference while in office, sir," Luke reminded him.

"I'll probably have a better shot once I'm not a politician, to be honest. I can start a foundation and—"

"I, uh, have a trust fund I've never touched," Knox said, nearly forgetting about the seventy-five million dollars that'd been sitting in his account since he'd turned twenty-five. He'd never cared about money, but that money could be used to help others. "I'll sign the trust over to the foundation."

Luke looked up at Knox. "I've got some money, too."

"I don't have much, but I'll do what I can to help our people," A.J. said.

The rest of the team nodded in agreement.

"No matter what happens come November, we stick together, okay?" Knox's gaze journeyed around the table to view his entire team. Jessica had flown in and was next to Asher. And Bravo Two had joined via Skype.

"No matter what," they repeated, and their words echoed throughout the room so loud they could probably be heard all the way in Washington.

CHAPTER THIRTY-FOUR

TWO DAYS LATER

"You didn't have to come to Texas to check on me, but it's nice of you." Adriana settled on her bed after she'd done her required exercise, which consisted of walking a few laps around the hospital floor to prevent blood clots in her legs.

"How could I not? We girls have to stick together." Agent Quinn glanced around the room filled with balloons and flowers, none of which were from Knox, because he knew her well enough to know she wasn't a balloons and flowers kind of girl.

He'd brought the peanut butter and the chocolates, which they'd both consumed while binge-watching her favorite movies on the tablet.

"How's Mendez handling what happened?" She pulled the covers up and resisted a slight groan at the pain in her side where she'd been shot. She'd been lucky the bullet had missed all her vital organs, or she may have not been there. "You know, how wrong he was about everything."

"I don't think any of us saw the whole Glenn Sterling

thing coming. Or Kathleen Bennett being a badass spy." She sat next to her bed. "We did a deep dive into Glenn's history. We couldn't find anything that would suggest he sold intel to the Russians, so I'm thinking he really did have Nina's parents killed to protect his team."

"And his affair."

Quinn rolled her tongue over her front teeth, her lips covered in a nude gloss. Her light auburn hair was pulled back in a sleek ponytail, but she was in jeans and a soft pink T-shirt, not her typical FBI look.

"But still no leads on his whereabouts?" She knew it was driving Knox and his teammates crazy not knowing where Glenn was, but she was nervous about what would happen once they found him.

Knox wasn't a vigilante. He wouldn't commit murder out of revenge.

But Glenn almost took her from him. He almost stole her life, and so, yeah, Knox was beyond pissed.

They'd talked a lot about the future since she'd been in bed, and as much as it pained him, he was on the same page as her. He'd support her job, and she'd support his. No matter what.

"We have every agent in the country looking for Glenn. I hope we find him before your buddies do," Quinn said before Knox and A.J. entered the room. "Just you two, huh? Where's the rest of ya?"

"Working like you should be." A.J. winked, which was probably a shit idea because Quinn didn't seem like a woman who'd go for that.

Knox moved straight for the bed and knelt next to her. "How are you?"

"Same as I was ten minutes ago when you were here." She leaned closer and whispered, "You hear anything?"

He pulled back and nodded.

There was a darkness in his eyes.

An almost angry gleam, but it wasn't pointed at her.

And that meant only one thing.

He knew Glenn's location.

"You ever gonna give me that first name of yours?" A.J. asked Quinn, but Adriana couldn't take her eyes off Knox, worry ratcheting higher inside of her.

"I thought it was your handsome friend with the British accent who'd asked for it," Quinn replied.

"I've never heard Wyatt described as handsome," he drawled, humor in his tone. "Stubborn. Bull-headed. Has that whole bad boy look going for him—sure. But handsome?"

"Oh, he's good-looking. And for the record, maybe I like a little bad every once in a while." She stood. "See you around, Foster." And wow, she winked back at A.J. before leaving.

A.J. fell to his knees once she was gone and gripped his chest. "Holy shit, I think I'm in love." He hung his head.

"Easy, cowboy." Knox stood upright.

"No way is she still married," A.J. said. "Divorced, maybe. But damn, that woman's got a fire in her belly."

"We don't have time for you to be drawing hearts with y'all's names inside of them right now," Knox said.

Adriana tried to sit up higher, but pain radiated in her side, and she cursed under her breath.

"Why won't you increase your pain meds?" Knox scowled at her.

"I will if you stay here and don't go after Glenn." She pressed her palms on both sides of the bed and held his eyes, hoping to God he'd stand down on this one and let the Feds handle it. There was too much on the line.

"He shot you, Addy," he said through barely parted lips.

"*No*, he hired someone to kill Nina," she corrected, hoping to get through to him.

"We won't shoot him." A.J.'s words pulled her focus to him. "We want a word or two before we toss his ass in the can."

"Sure." She shook her head.

"Can we have a sec?" Knox asked A.J.

"Don't leave me," she begged once they were alone.

Her words were the ammunition she needed to keep him in that room, even if she felt guilty for using them.

"I'm sorry," she rushed out. "I should never ask you to choose between staying with me and protecting the team." She sealed her eyes tight. "You should go."

He let go of her a minute later, and she couldn't open her eyes, because then he'd see that scared fifteen-year-old girl and not the woman she'd become. The tears would touch her cheeks. She couldn't risk it.

"A.J., get Quinn back in here." Knox's words had her eyes flashing open.

"What's up?" Quinn peeked into the room a moment later.

Knox stood alongside her bed, offering her his profile. "We know where Glenn is," he said in a low voice.

"And you're going to tell me?" Quinn asked in surprise.

Knox's hands went to his hips, and she knew it took all of his strength to say *yes*.

"I guess we are," A.J. said reluctantly, eying Knox with a what-in-the-Sam-hell look on his face.

"Get Luke on the phone," he told A.J. "He can fill her in."

"You're making the right call," Quinn said and glanced at A.J. "And the name is Anastasia, but I guess you can call me Ana." She left the room and A.J. dropped his head against the interior frame of the door and slapped a palm to the wall.

"You gonna go with her?" Knox asked.

He straightened and flashed a quick smile Adriana's way before disappearing into the hall.

"You didn't have to do that for me," she said when A.J. left.

He faced her, lowering his eyes to her mouth. "I did it because you were right. And I did it for us." He dropped onto the seat next to the bed and dipped in for a quick kiss. "I can't let the team go without me, and I can't leave you behind."

"What happens on the next op?"

"You mean if there is one?" His brows pulled together, a nervous look in his eyes.

She reached for his hand and clutched it. "This isn't the end for Bravo. For Echo. You'll have plenty of opportunities to go in for a hot extract. Fast-rope into a compound or do a HALO jump—"

"Now you're just talking dirty to me." He grinned, then leaned in and captured her lips again, kissing her hard before he said, "Say it again." He pulled back to capture her eyes. "'Hot extract.' 'HALO jump.'"

"Adrenaline and action turn you on, too?" She purposefully raked her tongue slowly over her bottom lip.

"It never did until you," he whispered on a kiss.

* * *

TWELVE HOURS LATER

"Why do I feel like my heart might jump from my chest while I wait for them to call?" Adriana's gaze traveled to Jessica and Asher sitting alongside her bed.

They seemed like an unlikely couple. A tall, jacked guy with tatts. A genius blonde in charge. He appeared overprotective, and yet, she was confident and strong and surely could hold her own.

They were adorable together. And it was nice to know that a love like theirs was possible in such an intense line of work. She didn't need for it to give her hope about her and Knox because she trusted in her relationship with him, but seeing them together still made her feel better. More at ease.

Knox gave her hand a gentle squeeze, and she turned her attention to him.

The rest of his team were somewhere, doing something . .
.

But since Knox, Asher, and Jessica were currently keeping her company, Adriana figured whatever that "something" was, it wasn't dangerous.

"It's never easy being on this side," Jessica said. "Most of the time I'm on the other side of the screen while these guys operate, holding my breath, waiting to see if everything goes okay."

She'd have to get used to it, though, because Knox didn't want to leave Bravo, and she wanted him to be happy. Safe, too.

Jessica placed a hand over her white tank top and massaged her flat stomach, still no signs of pregnancy. Asher placed his palm atop Jessica's hand. "Can you feel him? Her?"

"Way too early," she said with a chuckle. "This is nausea."

"You don't need to be in Texas. Go rest." Adriana tipped her head to the door.

"You took a bullet on an op with my guys." Jessica leaned back in her chair. "I'm where I need to be."

"She's as stubborn as you if you can believe it." Knox grinned.

"Now that can't be possible," Asher said, and Jessica smacked his arm.

"Hits like you, too, apparently." Knox laughed.

She started to comment, but Jessica's phone began ringing on her lap.

"It's Luke. He must know something." Jessica stood and placed the call on speaker.

"Glenn wanted to go out with a fight, but Quinn put his daughter on the phone and got him to surrender without anyone getting shot," Luke announced.

"Smart move." Relief blew over his face, and Knox let go of a breath. "He say anything?"

"He pretty much admitted everything we already knew," Luke answered. "Quinn asked him why he didn't put a hit on both your parents if he was trying to protect Leslie to make sure she made it to the White House."

"And?" Adriana asked.

"He still believes in the democratic electoral process and wouldn't want to influence the will of the American people by killing a candidate," Luke said, surprise in his tone. "His words exactly."

Jessica's eyes stretched, mirroring her brother's surprise.

"Crazy fucker," Luke said. "Anyway, we're wrapping up here in Tijuana. Heading your way soon."

"Thank you." Knox said a few more words then ended the call.

"Well, what the hell do we do now?" Asher folded his arms. "We have more than two months until the election before we find out what will happen to us."

Jessica bit her lip, and her eyes raked over the length of Asher.

Yup, pregnancy hormones were in effect. The woman was horny.

Asher cleared his throat. "We're gonna, you know . . ." He laced his hand with Jessica's. "See you later."

"I guess we're not the only crazy ones who get turned on when—"

"Babe, she's like a sister," Knox cut her off. "I don't want to talk about her having sex." He sat on the edge of the bed.

"And what do you want to talk about?" she murmured.

He grew quiet for a moment and gently cupped her chin. "Marry me." A statement, not a question.

"What?"

He lifted his eyes to the ceiling for a second as if getting choked up.

Before he managed to get out another response, or even look at her, she cried, "Yes."

His head dropped down, and his eyes touched upon hers. "I shouldn't have done it here and in a hospital bed. It's not romantic, but—"

"Didn't you hear me?" She smiled, tears forming in her eyes. "I'm saying *yes*." She reached out and placed her palm inside of his.

"But you have to promise me a few things." His voice wavered a touch as if fighting a pull of emotion gathering in his chest.

"No jumping in front of bullets for you?" She cocked her head and studied him, her lip quivering, emotion about to spill everywhere.

"Well, yeah, but I was going to say to always keep the peanut butter on the top shelf. Buy another twenty pairs of those sexy PJs you have because I'll probably destroy them daily when I rip them off you." He edged closer, his eyes glossy. "And then I want you to give me a daughter who looks like you, who has the same heart and spirit." His free hand braced the bed over her shoulder as he leaned in.

"Oh? Anything else?" she asked, their lips nearly touching.

"Of course." He smiled. "She'll be needing a brother for protection."

"Always with the protecting." Her body was tired, but she didn't care. She reached up and fisted the material of his shirt. "And maybe our daughter will be the one doing the protecting." Her brow arched.

"True. She'll be stubborn like her mother." He nipped her lip. "And strong like her, too." He slanted his mouth over hers and kissed her lightly before it turned into something so much more.

CHAPTER THIRTY-FIVE

"I DIDN'T EXPECT WE'D BE SO CLOTHED ON OUR honeymoon." He kissed her shoulder, the strap of her dress off to the side.

"Well, you're the one that invited over twenty people on our honeymoon, and we'll be late for dinner if we don't leave now."

His dad had basically reserved an entire island for them as their wedding gift. "And it was your idea to do so," he replied with a smile before bringing his mouth higher up her long, graceful neck.

"If you give me a hickey, I'll—"

"You'll what?" He pulled back to find her eyes in the mirror as she stood so beautifully in her flowy pink dress. She was all his, and he couldn't be prouder.

"I'll withhold sex from you tonight," she said but couldn't hide the quiver at the edges of her mouth, a mouth he wanted wrapped around his cock later.

"This dress, though." He held her tightly against him so

she could feel his arousal pressing into her, so she would know what she did to him.

He kept hold of her eyes in the mirror as his hand worked its way to the front slit of the dress and to her thigh.

"Panties or no panties?" The pad of his thumb found her sweet spot. "Mm. No panties. You're bad." He fingered her tight pussy, watching in the mirror as her eyes fell closed and her hands dropped forward and onto the counter. "And you'll be soaking wet for me all night now."

She moaned when he slid his fingers over her flesh in soft strokes, knowing what she liked.

"I'm going to be hard as a rock all night thinking about you like this," he whispered into her ear. "I'll be picturing you with your eyes screwed tight, your tits swelling out of the top of this dress . . . the want. The need. And we'll both lose our minds while we wait for the night to end all because you don't want to be a little late." He removed his hand in one fast movement and shifted away, offering her his back.

"Charlie Jackson Bennett, you better turn your ass around right now," she hissed, and he did as he was told, then brought his hand to his mouth, which smelled like sex. "We can be a few minutes late," she said on a sigh.

He smirked. "I was counting on that. So, how do you want me?"

"You know," she said, her eyes darkening.

He jerked at the belt on his pants, anxious to free himself. "Take off that dress."

She slipped the straps off her shoulders. Her hand went to the side zipper, and she allowed the dress to fall in time with his pants and boxers.

He pulled back far enough to take in her long legs and firm ass, and he couldn't resist lightly swatting her there. He knew she loved it, craved it, by the way she slowly caught her bottom lip between her teeth and moaned.

His hands smoothed up the backs of her legs and caressed her. When he guided her forward, she braced her forearms on the counter and tilted her ass in the air.

"There's wet, and then there's *wet*," he said as he spread the folds of her pussy to position the head of his cock there.

"You know what you do to me." Her eyes matched his heated intensity in the mirror.

"Ditto," he said with a smile and thrust inside of her, holding on to her to keep their bodies flush with each movement.

She groaned at the impact, and her fingertips curled into her palms, converting her hands to fists atop the counter.

Her breasts bounced as they moved as one, and her face pinched tight when he reached around between her legs with one hand and feathered his touch over her sensitive spot.

His eyes caught the wound on her abdomen, and he paused at the sight. It was still so damn hard for him to believe the love of his life had taken a bullet. And somehow, she came away from it with minimal damage. Maybe her mom really had been looking over her.

"You okay?" she whispered, and he brought his gaze to hers in the mirror.

"More than okay," he responded in a low voice.

He lowered his mouth to her shoulder and gently bit, pulling his focus back to the moment.

"No hickeys," she warned, her eyes lifting to the mirror, and he glimpsed her reflection, keeping his lips on her skin.

She didn't trust him to be good, and hell, he probably had no intention to, so she twisted her neck, offering her lips instead.

They had each other. She was his person. She'd always be

his person. And he'd always protect her whether she liked it or not. And maybe—just maybe, he'd consider letting her protect him, too. Never with her life, though. Only her heart.

She orgasmed, her sex clenching him hard. Her body quivering. Then he whispered into her ear as he came, "I love you, Mrs. Bennett."

EPILOGUE

ELECTION NIGHT

ELAINA, LIAM'S DAUGHTER, YANKED ON KNOX'S SLEEVE. "You have nothing to worry about." She tucked her dark hair behind her ears and shot him a toothy smile. Elaina was ten now. Her birthday had coincided with Knox's honeymoon, and since everyone had come along, they'd thrown her a huge party on the island.

He crouched to her side. "Actually, I think I do. Who is this Kenny kid you've been hanging out with for almost three months?"

Her cheeks softened into a rosy blush. "He's so smart. Funny. Totally amazing." She smirked. "He's a lot of fun."

"Exactly what kind of fun are we talking about?" Liam asked, overhearing their conversation, and his eyes nearly bulged as thoughts of his daughter and Kenny probably now plagued him.

"Dad," she said with an exaggerated eye roll. "Fun as in fun. Not fun as in what you do with Mom." She turned and sashayed away in her yellow dress, and Liam coughed into a closed fist.

"Did I hear her right?" Liam asked as Knox stood upright. He guzzled his beer and lowered it a moment later.

"Looks like she knows about sex," Knox said, fighting a laugh.

Liam braced a hand on Knox's shoulder and closed his eyes. "Never mention Elaina and that word in the same sentence again unless you want to die."

"You're in so much trouble when she's older." Knox smiled as he always did when his eyes landed on Adriana, his beautiful wife, across the crowded room as they waited for the official announcement.

The numbers were more than favorable for a Bennett win.

It was the conversation he was going to have with his dad afterward that had his heart in his throat.

If he said *no* . . . then what?

"Elaina said not to worry, remember." Liam straightened and dropped his hand from Knox's shoulder.

"She also said she's having fun with Kenny, so—"

"Thanks for that. Wait until you have kids. I swear you'll lose your bloody mind."

"Worth it, though, right?" Knox loosened the knot of his navy tie and rolled his sleeves to the elbows, the room much hotter than it was before.

Asher strode up to them, a whiskey in hand. "You're not nervous, are ya?" He wedged himself between Liam and Knox. "Your old man has this in the bag. Hell, I think your mother's spy days gave him a ten-point bump."

"Since when do you talk politics?" Knox side-eyed him.

"Since Bravo is on the line," Asher replied in a low voice.

"Speaking of Bravo. You're the last one of us on the team

not married. You planning on changing that any time soon? You do have twins on the way," Liam said.

Twins. Yeah, the Big Guy was going to lose his mind when they were born.

"Jessica wants to wait until after the girls are here like Eva and Luke did. But we're thinking Fiji or something. Nothing traditional."

"Yeah, I didn't exactly take you for a traditional guy." Knox looked at Adriana. She was laughing at something his dad was saying to her.

"We having a powwow here or something?" Owen clutched his son in his arm like he was carrying a football instead of a baby.

Asher handed Liam his whiskey and reached for Owen's son. "Give him to me, I need the experience."

"Don't drop him." Owen carefully handed him over. "You, uh, think Matthew and Lara will ever date?"

"You trying to give me a heart attack?" Luke shifted the fabric of the swaddle away from baby Matthew's face.

"Well, we all know how friendships turn out," Liam said with a laugh, eyes on Knox.

"Funny." Luke straightened. "I heard about Kenny. You got your hands full already."

Liam scowled and downed the rest of his beer then tossed back Asher's whiskey as well.

"Maybe you need to hit the range later," Owen said to Liam when Matthew began to cry, and Asher handed him back like he had a ticking time bomb in his hand.

"Damn. Bravo is turning into a real baby factory," A.J. said while striding up with Wyatt at his side.

Liam grinned. "So help me, Emily better be having a boy. Daughters are too stressful." He glanced at his wife across the room, who was chatting with Eva.

Emily was two months pregnant—a miracle by most doctors' standards. And the only one who'd seen it coming was Elaina.

"I hear you, man." Knox smiled, his nerves dying down a touch with all his buddies around.

"Maybe you'll be next," A.J. said to Knox. "Or hell, you." He looked at Wyatt. "Maybe you have a kid out there you don't even know about."

Wyatt nearly choked on his drink. "Hell no." He lowered the glass from his mouth. "No kids for me. You guys can have all the little ones you want. Pop them out left and bloody right for all I care, but I'm good." He shook his head for extra emphasis.

"They're about to announce the results!" Harper yelled, garnering the guys' attention.

"And?" Knox swallowed.

"What do you think?" Harper grinned, her eyes lighting up. "I, uh, think you're about to become the First Son."

"Is that a thing?" Asher looked around at the guys as if they'd have a clue.

"I don't know," Luke said. "Sounds like a thing."

"Come on." She waved them to the stage where Shonte, his dad's campaign manager, stood.

Shonte turned on the large flat screen on the wall behind her and stepped off to the side as the news announced, "And that's it, ladies and gentlemen, Isaiah Bennett has just become the next president of the United States."

Knox bowed his head at the news, his lungs letting go of a deep breath.

Maybe tonight wasn't the best night to spring the news on his father, but the guys couldn't wait. They needed to know their fate, too.

Adriana rushed across the room to get to him, and when she flew into his arms, he gathered her in for a tight hug. Their lips met in a searing kiss, tongues tangling, and hell, his heart was dancing.

"You still going to tell him tonight?" she asked a little later once the balloons and confetti raining down had settled.

His palm went to his shaky stomach. Nerves striking again. His dad was the next POTUS. *Is this real?* "We need to know. It's been killing us."

"I thought I did a good job keeping you distracted during the wait."

Yeah, she had kept him busy.

Their first home purchase, which was a block away from Emily and Liam's place. Adriana had discovered Emily shared her love of Patrick Swayze films, so they'd had a few movie marathon date nights together as well.

They'd also moved her dad closer. He even scored a job at GW and tonight marked date three with a colleague of his. Adriana had encouraged him to abide by an eight-date before "you know what" rule. Yeah, those were her words exactly.

Then there was their intimate wedding on Virginia Beach, and a honeymoon with friends on a secluded tropical island.

"You're not a distraction, babe. You're my wife." He brought his forehead to hers, resting it there, as he tried to slow his racing heart.

"Mm. I don't think I'll ever get tired of hearing you say that. And I have the notebooks from when I was a teenager to prove it."

"Notebooks?" He lifted his head. "Hearts with my name inside?"

"Hearts with *our* names inside," she repeated and bit into her lip. "Adriana and Charlie Bennett forever. I didn't know you'd become a badass SEAL and adopt a new name back in the day. Sorry." She pressed up on her toes and sealed her mouth to his, and he pulled her against him, holding on tight to his wife even though they were in the middle of a massive crowd in the heart of Atlanta.

They'd found their way back to where they always belonged, hadn't they?

"You ready?" It was Jessica.

He'd swear the Scott siblings had the worst timing.

Knox removed his tongue from his wife's mouth and resisted the urge to adjust his pants with his boss so close to him.

"You've got this." Adriana reached for his tie and tightened the knot, then gave him a nod, and he couldn't help but slip his hand over the curve of her ass in that tight-fitting gown and pull her back against him, even with Jessica there.

"Thanks for having my six," he whispered into her ear.

"Always."

He left her side and crossed the room with Jessica, heading toward his father.

His dad stopped talking to the governor of Georgia at his approach. "Everything okay?"

He swallowed, took a magnum-sized breath, and nodded. "Yeah, but there's something we need to talk about."

His dad smiled, his Denzel-grin, and reached for his son's arm. Bringing his mouth close to Knox's ear, he said, "The answer is *yes*, Son."

Knox lifted his brows in surprise. "You don't know what I'm gonna ask," he returned, glimpsing Jessica out of the corner of his eye, not sure what to make of his dad's words.

"I do, and the answer is *yes*."

Rydell must've talked to him. Taken the chance and told his father before election night, anticipating he'd win. And gambled that the president-elect wouldn't throw everyone under the bus at the discovery of the teams.

"Ninety-nine percent." His dad shifted his head to the side to catch Knox's eyes, then slapped a hand over his shoulder. His brows drew together, a touch of emotion on his face. "You handle the one percent for me so I can do my job and take care of the ninety-nine."

Knox closed his eyes and nodded in understanding at what his father was asking of him.

"Thank you," he said, forcing his vocal cords to work.

"No, Son, thank *you*."

Knox smiled, remembering what Adriana had said in her speech in this very hotel ballroom months ago, then he changed it up a bit and said, "Don't thank me, just be the kind of a man worth taking a bullet for."

He gave his dad a hug, then he strode away with Jessica at his side toward where Bravo and Echo were crowded off to the side of the room, along with Adriana.

"What happened?" Jessica asked as they approached the teams.

"We talking to him or what?" Chris spoke before Knox could answer Jessica.

"No need." A smile raced across his face with his teammates' attention fixed on him. "Looks like we're back for another four years."

"You jerking my chain?" A.J. stepped forward.

"No, man, I'm not." Knox grabbed at his chest as if his heart might explode.

A.J. turned toward the teams. "Brothers," he said with a nod and clapped his hands together. "We're back. And we need to celebrate." He looked at Wyatt. "Maybe I'll even buy you one of those girly mojitos you've been talking about."

"It's an open bar," Harper said with a laugh. "And what makes a mojito girly?"

A.J.'s palm flattened on his chest. "Anything alcoholic that requires a straw is girly. A real man drinks something that'll grow hair on his chest."

"I'm not a huge fan of chest hair," Harper said. "Except on Henry Cavill. Superman can rock the chest hair all day, all night."

"Henry who?" Chris asked. "I thought you liked Captain America, not Superman."

"I, uh." Harper turned to face Chris and stumbled, almost falling forward in her heels and into his arms, but Chris braced her forearms to keep her upright.

"You and that actor may have the same name," A.J. began, "the one who plays Mr. America—"

"Captain," Chris corrected him, still not letting go of Harper.

"Whatever." A.J. flicked a dismissive hand. "We both know . . ."

Their conversation faded into the background when Knox's eyes cruised over to his wife, and she shot him a massive congratulatory smile.

They did need to celebrate tonight, but right now there was something he needed to do first.

He cut a path straight to Adriana and held out a hand. "'*Nobody puts Baby in a corner,*'" he said, doing his best to maintain a straight face, hoping to hell he got the line right from one of her favorite Patrick Swayze movies. "Dance with me?"

She placed her palm atop his open hand, her gaze whipping up to his face. "You've watched *Dirty Dancing* with me a thousand times—"

"By force," he added in case his brothers heard.

"Right." A grin teased her lips. "But, babe, you never learned to dance."

"Because a movie can't teach me." He pulled her into his arms and surprised her by spinning her around. One of the guys whistled. And then another. He'd catch hell for this later, but he didn't care.

She gasped when he dipped her. And when he lifted her into the air by the hips, she braced his shoulders as he held on to her and moved in a three-sixty.

"Have you been faking the whole I-can't-dance thing all these years?" she asked when he lowered her heels to the ground. "Or you finally learn some moves?"

"I might have picked up a thing or two." He pressed his mouth to hers as the slow song ended.

Liam and Emily strode up next to them on the dance floor a minute later.

Then Jessica and Asher. Owen and Sam. Luke and Eva.

Roman remained off to the side of the dance floor while almost everyone else joined them.

"A.J. took over the DJ booth. He does realize this is a presidential event, right?" Chris shouted over Florida Georgia Line now blaring throughout the room.

"Maybe these people need a little excitement in their lives." Finn extended his hand to Harper for a dance.

But hell, Chris was on the other side of her with his palm extended, too.

Knox couldn't help but notice Roman's gaze on Harper while he brought his beer to his lips as if curious who Harper would choose.

"Who will she pick?" Adriana asked, bringing his attention back to her. "Apparently neither," she said before he could answer.

Harper flicked her finger, motioning for Elaina to join her instead.

Finn shrugged.

Chris held his palms open as if saying, *Well, I tried.*

And Jessica shot a scolding look at the both of them.

"Yup," Knox said even if no one could hear him. "We're back."

BONUS & DELETED SCENES

Did you get a chance to read Stealth Ops Bonus Scenes 4.0 or 4.5? These scenes were released after *Finding Her Chance.* They take place right before *Finding the Way Back,* featuring the barbecue & other events leading up to the Situation Room.

The new bonus scene - **Stealth Ops #5** is now live featuring Asher, A.J., Wyatt, and Jessica. The bonus scene takes place prior to the start of Wyatt's book, *Chasing the Knight.*

All scenes are listed and available on my website.

Be sure to subscribe to my newsletter so you don't miss out on the next Stealth Ops Bonus Scene and/or join Brittney's Book Babes to get updates!

Chasing the Knight - Stealth Ops #6 starring **Wyatt Pierson** is now live.

Continue for a few deleted scenes!

***

Deleted Scene 1: Flashback to Prom

She'd only been nervous like this twice in her life—the day she joined the agency and the night of senior prom.

She'd had every intention of going to the dance alone, but Knox had called that afternoon and announced he'd be at her door at seven.

Her fingers had trembled as she slid up the zipper at the side of her floor-length platinum-colored satin gown. Her dad would've had a heart attack at how low the back dipped if he hadn't already drunk himself to sleep that night.

She shouldn't have been nervous since it wasn't a real date—only her friend taking her to the dance. But as she'd walked toward that door, every hair on her body stood. Maybe he'd see her as a woman and not the broken-hearted girl he'd been kissing while her mother had jumped in front of a bullet.

She'd felt like *Cinderella* in the remake *Ever After* as she'd whispered the line from the movie, *"just breathe,"* before opening the door to greet him.

Knox had been standing casually on her porch, devastatingly handsome in a black tux, a pink corsage cradled in his hand, brown eyes dipping down, a slow journey back up.

A million butterflies had taken flight in her stomach when he'd said, *"Wow. The guys are going to go crazy when they see you. Thank God I'm here to protect you from them."* He'd stepped forward, a massive smile stretching his lips. Dimples deepening.

"You're here to protect me?" She'd done her best to hide

the slouch of her shoulders at his words. *"I should've known."*

Deleted Scene 2: Flashback to her date with Calloway

Calloway had copped a feel. Stolen a few kisses. But something had been missing with him. She'd figured it had to be the work thing standing in her way. It couldn't be Knox. But when he'd shown up at the bar on her fifth date with Calloway, she'd been relieved to hear her best friend's voice.

"What are you doing here?" She'd hopped off her stool and slung her arms around Knox, and he'd planted a warm kiss on her cheek.

A heavy throat clear nearby had reminded her of Calloway's presence.

"You use that friend finder app thingy?" She'd stepped back and pointed to Knox's pocket and smiled.

"I just got to town, and you weren't home."

It'd been Knox's idea to turn on the app whenever she was on a date in case she needed an emergency extract.

"Ever heard of a phone call?" Calloway had stood, directing his attention to Knox. *"Aren't you Isaiah Bennett's son?"*

"Yeah," Knox had said, his eyes still on her. *"It's been too long."*

It'd been three months since they'd seen each other, and she hadn't wanted to waste a minute of his surprise visit, which meant Calloway had to go.

"I'm sorry," she'd said, turning to face her date. *"I'll need to cut this night short."*

Knox had reached into his pocket. *"I'll cover the tab."*

Calloway's jaw had tightened, surprise in his eyes. *"Adriana."*

She'd walked him out to keep from feeling like a complete jerk, apologized a few times, then hurried back into the bar at full speed and had leaped into Knox's arms.

He'd guided her legs around his waist, and his hands had slid to her butt to hold her in place.

"*I really did miss you.*" She'd brought her forehead to his. "*How long are you in town for?*"

"*Only one night. I didn't mean to interrupt but—*"

"*You totally did!*" She'd rolled her eyes as she lowered her feet to the ground and motioned for him to sit.

"*What date number was this?*"

She'd held a palm up to display five fingers. "*But he'd never make it to eight, so the interruption was probably needed.*"

Eight dates before she agreed to have sex with a guy. Eight didn't guarantee sex, but it was another hard and fast rule of hers not to have it any sooner.

"*He Secret Service?*" He arched a brow and popped a peanut in his mouth.

"*Yes, and he'll be the last one I date.*"

"*You mentioned you were seeing someone, but you didn't say you worked together.*" His palms had moved to his lap, and his eyes held hers. Dark. Deep. Penetrating. Soul-seeing eyes.

"*Because I knew you'd give me a hard time.*" And maybe she should have so that he could've saved her from disappointing Calloway. "*So, where were you before here?*"

"*Eastern Asia.*" Generic. And typical. "*So, what's it gonna be tonight? A movie or tequila? Or our buddy Jack?*"

She'd laughed. "*How about all three?*"

"*Trying to get me drunk and take advantage of me, huh?*"

"*You wish.*" She'd picked up an unshelled peanut and thrown it at his muscular chest.

He hadn't responded. His lips had fallen flat for the briefest of moments.

Deleted Scene 3: Memory of their first kiss

"You're too young."

"I'm not that young."

He'd brushed a strand of her dark locks away from her face and palmed her cheek. *"Two years at our age is like an eternity."*

"I have experience," she'd lied and leaned into his touch. Unable to believe the moment she'd been dreaming about for six weeks—ever since she'd seen him walking through the halls at school—was actually happening.

Charlie Bennett had stood inches away with his hand on her face, a look of desire in his eyes. Desire for her and not the pack of cheerleaders always flanking his sides at school, begging for his attention.

His lips had split into a gorgeous, slightly mischievous smile. *"You're fifteen. I'm seventeen. And I'm just no good for you."*

"So kiss me anyway."

Deleted Scene 4: From chapter thirteen

He'd been seventeen again in that room with her tonight, transported back to a time when fewer obstacles stood between them. Sure, the night they met, he'd thought there were a million reasons why he shouldn't be with her, but the moment his tongue touched hers, every last one had disappeared. Well, until the call came that forever changed her life.

If it weren't for the physical distance that kept them

separated—first, it was college, then the Navy, and now traveling with the teams—he would have chased after more of her drugging kisses. Persisting until he'd made it to what Adriana referred to as "second base" and on to score a home run.

His lips crooked into a smile at the thought of her teasing him for using a baseball analogy. She'd bat her lashes and playfully swat him on the chest. He'd secure a loose grip around her wrist and fight like hell with himself to keep from going after what he'd wanted since the moment she'd walked onto their high school grounds.

**Continue for the music playlist!

PLAYLIST

Spotify Playlist

Old Town Road (feat. Billy Ray Cyrus) - Lil Nas X, Billy Ray Cyrus

Get Along - Kenny Chesney (Ch. 17)

Sugar - Maroon 5

Roar - Katy Perry

Dancing On My Own - Calum Scott

You are the Reason - Calum Scott (Epilogue)

One Kiss (with Dua Lipa) - Calvin Harris, Due Lipa

Meant to Be - Florida Georgia Line, Bebe Rexha (Epilogue)

I don't Care (with Justin Bieber) - Ed Sheeran, Justin Bieber

Whatever It Takes - Imagine Dragons

READING GUIDE

Find the latest news from my newsletter/website and/or Facebook: Brittney's Book Babes / the Stealth Ops Spoiler Room /Dublin Nights Spoiler Room.

Publication order for all books

Books by Series

Pinterest Muse/Inspiration Board

* * *

Falcon Falls Security

The Hunted One - book 1 - Griffin & Savanna

The Broken One - book 2 - Jesse & Ella

The Guarded One - book 3 - Sydney & Beckett (6/26/22)

Book 4 - Oliver & Mya

Stealth Ops Series: Bravo Team

Finding His Mark - Book 1 - Luke & Eva

Finding Justice - Book 2 - Owen & Samantha

Finding the Fight - Book 3 - Asher & Jessica

Finding Her Chance - Book 4 - Liam & Emily

Finding the Way Back - Book 5 -Knox & Adriana

Stealth Ops Series: Echo Team

Chasing the Knight - Book 6 -Wyatt & Natasha

Chasing Daylight - Book 7 - A.J. & Ana

Chasing Fortune - Book 8 - Chris & Rory

Chasing Shadows - Book 9 -Harper & Roman

Chasing the Storm - Book 10 - Finn & Julia

Becoming Us: *connection to the Stealth Ops Series (books take place between the prologue and chapter 1 of Finding His Mark)*

Someone Like You - A former Navy SEAL. A father. And off-limits. (Noah Dalton)

My Every Breath - A sizzling and suspenseful romance. Businessman Cade King has fallen for the wrong woman. She's the daughter of a hitman - and he's the target.

Dublin Nights

On the Edge - Travel to Dublin and get swept up in this romantic suspense starring an Irish businessman by day…and fighter by night.

On the Line - novella

The Real Deal - This mysterious billionaire businessman has finally met his match.

The Inside Man - Cole McGregor & Alessia Romano

The Final Hour - Sean and Emilia

Stand-alone (with a connection to *On the Edge*):

The Story of Us– Sports columnist Maggie Lane has 1 rule: never fall for a player. One mistaken kiss with Italian soccer star Marco Valenti changes everything…

Hidden Truths

The Safe Bet – Begin the series with the Man-of-Steel lookalike Michael Maddox.

Beyond the Chase - Fall for the sexy Irishman, Aiden O'Connor, in this romantic suspense.

The Hard Truth – Read Connor Matthews' story in this second-chance romantic suspense novel.

Surviving the Fall – Jake Summers loses the last 12 years of his life in this action-packed romantic thriller.

The Final Goodbye - Friends-to-lovers romantic mystery

Made in United States
North Haven, CT
24 August 2023

40704727R00243